The Winds

David J. Bunnell

Copyright © 2024 by David J. Bunnell

All Rights Reserved

ISBN:

Dedication

Wendell Lee Bunnell (1929 – 2010), my father, introduced me to the Wind River Mountains at a young age. It was with him that we identified over 50 kinds of wildflowers to distract me from feeling the pain and exhaustion while hiking with our heavy packs. It was with him, on one of the outings, that I caught a native Cutthroat Trout on every cast for nearly 45 minutes until my arm grew too tired to hold the rod (not a fish story. My dad always told the truth). It was with him I witnessed a helicopter land on the edge of a high mountain lake on his behalf, 1000 feet elevation over the maximum flight ceiling, to drop him off at a hospital 25 miles to the valley, to identify and treat a serious illness. When I witnessed that helicopter pilot position the craft to get the maximum speed possible to clear the cliffs above, I wondered, at 11 years old, if I'd ever see my father again. My dad made it an annual event to hike deep into the mountains with me until he could no longer do so. He was the one who inspired me to not only appreciate the backcountry but to continue the legacy of the "Bunnell Annual Hike" with my children!

Dad, I dedicate The Winds to you and your legacy.
Continue to Rest in Peace.

Acknowledgment

The youngest of my older sisters, **Marilyn Hansen**, was always supportive of my various adventures growing up. If we weren't playing "School" at the kitchen table, we were teaching our dog new tricks in the backyard. When approached about my desire to write, she was gracious enough to share with me all she had come to know about the English language, first through college, a Bachelor's Degree in English, and then many years behind a desk or in front of a chalkboard teaching High School students about dangling participles and run-on sentences. She was instrumental in me starting, fighting through occasional writer's block, and completing The Winds. Her unwavering support is much appreciated.

I met **Kerry Peterson** under unusual circumstances many years ago…one of those "friend of a friend" situations that turned into a two-decade-long friendship! She was one of the first to read my novel and well, she liked it, which gave me encouragement to continue to hone my craft. Both, her unwavering friendship and encouragement, are greatly appreciated.

Julia Bunnell, my brother's wife, is one of the most positive people I've gotten to know. She has an uncanny way of making one feel blessed, confident, and grateful in the most challenging of situations. Her initial critique of my work and ability to put into words what others couldn't was instrumental in me seeking to publish. I really don't think I'd taken the steps necessary without her influence.

My sweet wife, **Tonya**, was the very first person to hear of my desire to write a novel. She thought I was bat-nuts crazy at first and continued thinking I was completely out of my mind through the entire process until finished, but she gave me something that only she could give…time. Time to think, reason, contemplate, organize and finish! All this while I was secluded in a makeshift office in the small furnace room in the basement, and she was upstairs nurturing three wonderful but rowdy children. To her, I owe it all for enabling me to tell my story!

Table of Contents

Dedication iii

Acknowledgment iv

About the Author viii

Chapter 1 1

Chapter 2 13

Chapter 3 21

Chapter 4 34

Chapter 5 46

Chapter 6 61

Chapter 7 75

Chapter 8 81

Chapter 9 91

Chapter 10 108

Chapter 11 122

Chapter 12 143

Chapter 13 154

Chapter 14 167

Chapter 15 184

Chapter 16 192

Chapter 17 201

Chapter 18 217

Chapter 19 232

Chapter 20 249

Chapter 21 262
Chapter 22 279
Chapter 23 289
Chapter 24 304
Chapter 25 313
Chapter 26 327
Chapter 27 336
Chapter 28 348
Chapter 29 357
Chapter 30 366
Chapter 31 391
Chapter 32 405
Chapter 33 413
Chapter 34 428
Chapter 35 440
Chapter 36 451

About the Author

Over the course of his life, David Bunnell has lived with a sense of confidence and purpose, embracing every experience with enthusiasm and fearlessness. He's suffered two concussions while playing football, hit a home run in a major university ballpark located on the edge of the Wasatch Mountains, had his wallet stolen by a rogue monkey in Southeast Asia, and jumped from a 50-foot horse bridge while rafting the middle fork of the Salmon River. He has also found peace in the stillness of nature, fishing the high mountain lakes of the rugged Wind River Mountains.

David's life experiences have been the inspiration behind his writing, influencing not only what he writes but also how he captures vivid detail with a sense of confidence that leaves a lasting impression on his readers. He has spent countless hours in his makeshift den (the furnace room in the basement) waiting for that next adrenaline rush, where he finds himself fully immersed in a story, forming words faster than he can place the letters on the page. Of all the experiences he has had, those moments are the pinnacle!

Page Blank Intentionally

Chapter 1

The year is 1999… and counting

At over ten thousand feet, the air was unforgivably thin. Trees refused to take root on many of the barren granite slopes while lungs, unaccustomed to such high altitudes, burned with every breath and fingertips cracked from the dry, crisp air. However, this was not the case for the old Indian man. He had made this trip numerous times during the latter part of his life and considered this tiny portion of the world his home.

It was the last week of June. He sat on top of his faithful horse as the slow, distinct cadence of the hooves clapping against the rocky trail made his eyelids heavy. The worn leather reins hung loosely from his hands as his horse strolled in the direction of his camp nearly five miles to the northeast.

He was an old man. Deep dark wrinkles on his face and jagged scars on his calloused hands bore constant witness to his long, eventful life. The rich Indian blood flowed thick through his veins, evidence of the long heritage of brave warriors that had preceded him. His name was Running Bear, the Chief of the Shoshone Tribe who lived on the Indian Reservation nestled at the base of the mighty Wind River Mountains in Wyoming, part of the vast Rocky

Mountain chain that bully their way from upper Canada continuing down through most of the western states. Those who lived at the base of the foothills usually referred to this high mountain range as "the Winds."

In the late 1800s, the Shoshone Tribe found themselves being herded like cattle from one place to another by the unwelcome invaders. The white man who came from the east seeking rich dark soil, precious metals, and room to grow pushed the Native Americans off the western lands that they had hunted for centuries and placed them on reservations comprised mostly of land that was not suitable for much of anything. Nevertheless, the Shoshone fought hard for a small piece of the Winds to be included in the reservation. Many years of struggle, debate with the American government, and even loss of life resulted in a compromise to include the tiny portion of wilderness land. What the white man didn't realize was that the Great Spirit highly favored this seemingly insignificant plot of the Winds. It has blessed the Shoshone Tribe for centuries and continues to bless them to the present day.

Running Bear made an annual trip into this specific area of the Winds. This was a time he set aside for himself to converse with the Great Spirit, renew both his body and mind, and seek the rich blessing provided for the Shoshone Tribe in the form of pure gold. Not one white man knew of the thick, rich vein nestled secretly in a small cavern behind a well-hidden waterfall, and very few Indians presently knew, although many who grew up in the area, both white and Indian, knew bits and pieces of the legend.

He was into the third day of the first week of reaping such a blessing. He had spent all morning behind the waterfall with his bone-handled knife, diligently chipping and scraping until he filled his small leather pouch with fine shavings of pure Wind River gold. It was an exhausting venture for such an old man. Laboring each morning for six consecutive days, he would rest from his labors on the seventh to commune with the Great Spirit and thank Him for the bounteous blessing. This would be his lot sometime at the end of spring or the beginning of summer each year and would last three consecutive weeks. To avoid suspicion, he would vary the days from year to year, and the trip was never publicized. He made his camp in a different location, up to five miles from the sacred waterfall. If the white man knew of his journey, it could be dangerous and have an obvious negative financial impact on the Shoshone Tribe.

With a light tug on the reins, his horse stopped along the rugged, virtually unknown trail. The old man, his burning red eyes clearly showing the heinous struggles of his venture, carefully climbed down from his horse. His joints ached, and he winced as his foot touched the ground, stretching his tired muscles well past the point of comfort. Reaching into a saddlebag, he pulled out the small bulging leather pouch, the sinew string drawn tight. He stood motionless for a moment as he held the valuable small pouch in his hand and panned the broad expanse with his keen eyes. Other than an occasional snort from his horse's nostrils, it was eerily silent. The only movement he saw was a golden eagle soaring effortlessly in a circular path, riding the air currents hundreds of feet above him. However, Running Bear had the distinct feeling that something wasn't right. He could feel it. After hearing the piercing screech from the eagle overhead, he climbed back on his horse and quickly tugged on the rein, turning the horse around to head back up the trail.

Soon, the trot turned into a gallop. His long grayish-black braids and the large eagle feather that he wore around his neck fluttered violently behind him in the passing air. He was no longer tired and was now alert. His aching muscles turned into adrenaline-fed packets of energy as he lifted himself above the turbulent saddle. The horse lunged effortlessly over the jagged rocks and glacier-fed streams until he was within a stone's throw from his previous destination: the coveted rich vein of gold. Easing the horse to a slow gait, he approached the trees as it silently led him through a myriad of turns. He ducked several times to avoid being slapped in the face by the low-lying branches that protruded into the trail. Ahead was a small, inconspicuous clearing filled with crushed gray rock, the stubble of green grass, and the sound of water crashing against the rocks.

The Winds

Carefully, he climbed off his horse and laid the reins on a small bush. His horse became still as he crept silently toward the clearing until he was at the edge. Standing behind a large rock, he stared intently at the smooth glass-like waterfall. It was like no other.

The water from the stream flowed over a cliff into an intermediate pool and then over a large, smooth, almost perfectly flat rock, causing a thin, sheer sheet of water as it fell nearly another ten feet to a clear blue pool below. The contents of the pool were lost in the crushed granite rocks, giving the impression that it was being immediately swallowed by the very cliff it had come from. Several hundred feet down the mountain, the water emerged into a free-flowing stream again.

As Running Bear studied the thin sheet, the large bridge of his nose became wrinkled as he clenched his jaw, clearly portraying his sudden anger. Without so much as even a thought or hesitation, he removed the bow from around his neck, reached back, and picked an arrow from the leather quiver that hung from his shoulder. Placing the arrow on the string, he drew it back, taut, until his hand clipped the bottom edge of his ear. With both eyes open, he focused in on a dark portion of the flowing water and, with a snap, released the string. The arrow sliced through the scanty mountain air with accuracy and speed and penetrated the thin sheet.

Suddenly, there was a loud groan, and the smooth sheet of water became jagged as an arm, and then a body thrashed through it from behind. A large man emerged, yelling and grasping at the arrow deeply lodged in the side of his neck. Blood gushing from the gaping wound, the man violently pulled at the arrow, breaking it in half as he spun around on the slick, mossy bed of rocks and looked into the Indian's eyes.

"You bastard!" he yelled as his eyes rolled to the top of their sockets, leaving only the whites visible. His knees buckled, and his lifeless body plunged into the pool of water, turning it a crimson red.

You traitor, the old Indian thought to himself as he placed the bow back over his shoulder, approaching the edge of the water. Looking up to the sky and extending his hands into the air, he began to chant a prayer to the Great Spirit in his native Shoshone tongue. Overcome with emotion and with tears in his eyes, he beckoned the Great Spirit to forgive him, for this was the first man he had ever killed. However, he had successfully convinced himself long before he released the arrow that he'd had sufficient justification for doing so, keenly aware that some would attempt to follow him into the Winds and that one day, the age-old secret of the gold and the very way of life for him and his beloved people would be jeopardized.

The Winds

Suddenly, the old Indian discontinued his chant and lowered his hands. Hearing a horse that clearly wasn't his snorting behind him, he slowly turned his head.

"You stupid old man," the voice yelled from behind. "Did you really have to kill him?" The old Indian turned completely around to face his accuser. His black eyes locked on his.

"You tell me," he replied calmly. He started to approach the man but stopped when the man pulled a pistol from his holster.

"From what I've seen of it, you had no choice," the man replied. "You did me a favor by killing him. It saved me the trouble. He was starting to get a little greedy. Now I'm the only white man who knows this place exists, and I'd like to keep it that way."

The Indian looked at him with little expression as he contemplated his fate. After a short moment, he raised his head. "But I know of it," the Indian said.

The man coaxed the lever on the pistol into the firing position and started to laugh as he pointed the pistol at the Indian. "I've thought about that, and that's definitely a serious problem," the man replied.

"You've been following me. How long?" the Indian

asked.

"Three years now. You're good. Take a different route every time, camp in a different spot, ride your horse down the middle of a stream, you know, all that Indian shit you do, but this year we caught up to you. Stroke of genius or just sheer dumb luck—it doesn't matter. After I kill you, I'll be a very rich man." Bringing the pistol down, he rested it across the front of the saddle. "You can't tell me you didn't know about us."

"I knew, but killing me will only make it worse for you. There are others, others who know about the gold. If I don't return, they will come for me, that I am sure. I am their Chief."

"Let them look. They'll never find you. The reservation has what, six rangers? And the Sheriff, hell, I know he won't help. He's got better things to do than waste his time trying to find some dumb old Indian. After a few weeks, they'll call off the search. Everyone knows there are bears up here. Looks like you just became an entrée. I'll just lay low and use the bags you filled for me over the last few days." The old Indian glared at him. "That's right. I've been to your camp and found the other bags. We watched you leave this morning. Oh, and thanks for filling another one for me today. I'll be sure to put it to good use." The man started to laugh as he took aim at the Indian's chest. "Say hello to the Great

Spirit for me." He placed his finger on the trigger just as the Indian bowed his head and began to chant—softly at first.

His entire body moved up and down in a steady cadence as his head shifted from side to side, his movements becoming more and more animated as his chant increased in volume.

"Shut up!" the man yelled. The Indian continued to chant. "I told you to shut the hell up." But there was no stopping the old Indian Chief. The seemingly last breath he would take would be used to praise the Great Spirit above.

An Indian warrior was always prepared mentally and spiritually to meet the Great Spirit at any time in his life but would never accept death easily or without a fight, especially when it was at the hands of a white man. The Indian warrior inconspicuously reached behind his back as if it were an integral part of his ritual and grabbed his knife from the sheath. He expertly palmed the knife so the blade extended up his wrist, concealing it from the man's view. As a carefully orchestrated distraction, his arms flailed into the air, and his chant became louder with each long breath he took.

Climbing off his horse, the man continued pointing the pistol at the Indian. He took a step toward him, made a tight fist, and hit him across the face with the back of his hand. Blood immediately started to flow from the corner of

Running Bear's mouth, but the old Indian, unwaveringly, continued to chant.

"Shut up, you damn Indian, shut up! I'm warning you if you don't quit—"

Suddenly, Running Bear's chant turned into a high, piercing screech. His black eyes became slender slits. Thrusting forward, he flipped the knife blade around in his hand and gripped the polished bone handle. He slashed at the man with short, quick spurts. Retreating a step, the man grimaced in pain. Blood oozed between the gaps in his fingers as he pressed against the fresh, deep wound.

"Damn you!" he yelled, pointing the pistol at Running Bear's forehead.

Running Bear lunged again with the knife raised above his head. The man quickly took a step back and tripped over a small branch. Falling backward against the sharp rocks, he pulled the trigger. The canyon walls exploded as Chief Running Bear immediately dropped to his knees, falling face-first into the vivid mixture of blood and water.

Resting his head momentarily against a rock, the man stood up and looked around. He bent over and put his hands on his knees to try to catch his breath—not from exertion, but from pure shock. He'd underestimated the strength and determination behind the old Indian's tired eyes.

The Winds

There was an old Indian legend concerning the Winds. Her vast canyons and sheer rocky cliffs were believed to be the home of numerous spirits, those occupying the life beyond the grave. The legend speaks of a Great Spirit who poured out His blessings upon those who were faithful and true to their beliefs and honored and obeyed the land that was given to them for their subsistence. It was believed that the true reward for a Shoshone Indian warrior was to scale the steep cliffs of the Winds, thereby getting a fleeting glimpse into the spirit world, the pleasant, blissful life that he would undeniably ascend toward after bidding his final farewell to the good Earth. There would be vast fields of colorful wildflowers, lush grass, and an abundance of deer, elk, and moose awaiting him to provide warm meat to soothe his empty belly. He would never feel the pangs of hunger again, and beautiful virgin squaws would faithfully serve him throughout the eternities, and that Great Spirit above, the creator of all life on Earth, would smile upon him forever more.

Running Bear was now at peace. The problems he'd suffered throughout mortality were now gone, vanished, but not for the man left standing covered in his own blood; his problems had just begun. He looked at the bodies, face down, in the pool of endless red. Things didn't go exactly according to plan, but not many things of this magnitude do. At least he could see the big picture in his mind. The limited partnership between him and the other man had been quickly dissolved through a quick penetrating arrow. That was actually a good thing—sharing was never his strong suit. But he was now faced with the daunting task of disposing of two bodies instead of just one.

Chapter 2

Much later that night, Chicago

Cade sat up from his leather recliner, holding the crumpled piece of paper in both hands. Moving closer to the dim light from the small lamp on the table, he reread the words to himself. He was a middle-aged man, but the years had been very good to him. His hair and eyes were brown, and his complexion was dark, not from exposure to the sun or a tanning bed but from his mother's genes. He still managed to stay in good shape even though his profession didn't always allow him to spend time at the gym. A sudden movement near the door startled him.

"Daddy?" the little girl said. Walking up to him, she nudged close to his knee, holding her worn, faded blanket tightly to her chest. She held out her arms as Cade groaned, grabbing and pulling her onto his knee. She was small for her age and had dishwater blonde hair, usually worn straight that plunged past her shoulders.

"Brit, you're almost too big to sit on my knee anymore," he said. "What are you doing out of bed?"

"I couldn't sleep," she said.

"So, what are you doing down here?"

"I saw the light on, so I came down to see what you were doing," she said, nuzzling her head on his chest. "What are you reading?"

Cade started to fold the paper in half. "Nothing, just an invitation to go to something I don't really want to go to."

She looked at the paper closely. "Is it a birthday party?"

Cade smiled and gently stroked her soft hair. "I wish, but it's to my twentieth high school reunion."

"Wow, that's a long time. I just finished the third grade."

Cade nodded his head and straightened the flannel collar on her pajamas. "I've never been back there."

"Back where?"

"Lorenz, you know – where I grew up?"

"Is that another country?"

Cade placed both of his hands on the sides of her cheeks. "No, it's in the great state of Wyoming, but it's so far away from Chicago that it could be a different country."

Brit's eyes lit up. "Cowboys and Indians?"

"Wow, you're pretty smart. Where did you learn that?"

Brit, rolling her eyes, set her head back on his chest. "I'm going to be in the fourth grade, Dad."

"A lot has changed since way back then," Cade said. "The cowboys nowadays ride in rodeos, and the Indians live on reservations. They don't fight each other much anymore." Suddenly, the overhead light came on, illuminating the intricately trimmed hardwood den. Books neatly placed side by side lined the far wall, and various trinkets, mementos, and pictures of past family vacations filled the shelves on the adjacent wall. Cade was surrounded by many of the finer things in life and even people he loved, but he still felt very much alone.

"I thought I heard voices down here," Angie said as she walked into the room. Cade's wife was a striking woman with prominent features, with cascading blonde hair that fell gently over her shoulders. "You know Brit shouldn't be up this late."

"Hey, she found me. I was just sitting here minding my own business," he said, attempting to conceal the wrinkled piece of paper under Brit's blanket.

"What's that?" Angie asked.

"Oh, it's nothing… just doing some reading. I just can't

sleep tonight."

"Let me see it," she said, reaching out her hand.

Hesitantly, Cade handed it over.

"Let me guess, you're not going?" she said.

Brit turned and looked deeply into her father's eyes. "Why wouldn't you go, Daddy? Isn't there anybody you want to see?"

"Well, sure, there's a few old friends, maybe a couple of teachers, but–"

"Then why don't you go?"

He looked at her and softly caressed her cheek. "I think it's time for this little girl to go back to bed," he said. "It's late, Brit, and we all have a busy day tomorrow."

"Not me," she said. "Mom said I get to sleep in tomorrow – the piano teacher's sick."

"Then I need to get some sleep. A doctor doesn't get any time off for the summer." He grinned as he lifted her off his knee and rose from the chair.

"Race you up the stairs!" Brit shouted as she ran to the door.

The Winds

"Shhhh," Angie said with her finger up to her lips. "You'll wake your brother."

"Don't worry, Mom, he can sleep through a train wreck."

Helping his young daughter into bed, Cade tucked the soft covers under her neck, bent over, and kissed her on the forehead. "Good night, little one. I love you."

"I love you, too, Daddy." Brit's eyelids suddenly grew heavy as she clutched her blanket. "Tomorrow, will you tell me more about where you grew up?"

Answering with just a smile, Cade hoped that when morning came, she would have forgotten all about the question. Reaching over, he turned off the light and walked down the hall past his son's room and into the master suite, where Angie was lying on the bed comfortably on her side with the fluffy comforter over the top. Her arms were wrapped tightly under her feather pillow, and her eyes were closed. Confident she was asleep, he tiptoed carefully around the bed and crawled in effortlessly without as much as a ripple in the covers. Staring at the ceiling, he let out a small sigh.

Suddenly, Angie turned over and faced him, her eyes wide open. "Quit punishing yourself. Either you go, or you don't, but make up your mind. You can't just call in the day you catch the plane."

Cade responded with a glare, fully aware of what a doctor could and couldn't do. He was the head of the ER at Cook County Hospital, deep in the heart of Chicago. It was a great opportunity for him. He saw a variety of cases each day, ranging from small cuts and bruises to shooting and stabbing victims, but the stress was intense when he was there. Maybe a short vacation would do him good, even if it meant returning to a place he hadn't been to for twenty years or even cared to return. He continued staring at the ceiling as if he hadn't heard a word of what she had said. Angie reached over and forced him to look at her.

"Either you go, or you don't, Cade. Nobody's holding a gun to your head."

Cade immediately sat up. "It's not that simple. I don't even know if I'm welcome."

Angie lifted her head from her pillow. "It was an accident – twenty years ago! You're the only one that can't let it go."

"Because I'm the only one that was there when it happened. They didn't see the look on her face. They didn't feel her hand slip. They didn't hear her scream my name."

Angie sat up beside him and put her hand on his. "But it

wasn't your fault. Why torture yourself into thinking it was?"

"It shouldn't have happened."

"But it did, and you can't change that. Nothing you can do will bring her back. This same thing happened when you got your 10th and then your 15th. What'll happen when your 50th comes around?"

Cade threw the covers off him and shot out from the bed. "Don't patronize me, Angie. You don't understand because you weren't there."

"But I've lived and relived the nightmare over and over and over! I don't know how much more I can take. It's a problem, Cade, a serious problem. Either you figure out how to deal with it, or I'm giving Doctor Morrison a call."

"The shrink? Four hundred bucks an hour!"

"It's not about the money; it's about you," Angie said, wiping a small tear from her eye.

"It's about us."

Settling back into bed, she pulled the covers up around her neck, turning away from him.

As an immediate rebuttal, Cade slipped back into the

bed with his back toward her. *It'll be a cold day in hell before I see a shrink.*

Chapter 3

"Hello, um, I'm Cade Hobbs. I have an appointment to see Dr. Morrison today," Cade said, tapping his fingers on the top of the reception desk counter. "I generally don't see psychiatrists, uh… it was my wife's suggestion." There was a moment of awkward silence as the receptionist just sat there and flashed a fake smile. She'd heard it all before. "I just didn't want you to get the wrong impression of me, that's all. I'm a doctor myself. I head up the Emergency Medicine Department at Cook County Hospital on Harrison, just off Ogden Avenue."

"I've never been there, but I've heard it's nice," she replied, reflecting sincerity.

"Yeah, well, Chicago's a crazy place. Half the people admitted have either been stabbed or shot. It wouldn't be Chicago if we spent our time removing slivers or putting Band-Aids on paper cuts, now would it?" He flashed a joking smile, then turned and looked around the waiting room, evidently nervous.

"Dr. Morrison will be with you shortly," she said. "Feel free to look around or take a seat. We have several magazines you might find interesting."

At about the same time Cade was thumbing through the

magazines, the large, stained mahogany door opened, and an older but very refined gentleman with jet black hair, but grey at the temples, walked out and approached the front desk, handing the receptionist a few papers. He was one of the most prominent in his field – and dressed the part, too. From his white starched shirt and maroon silk tie all the way down to his dark-pressed slacks and polished leather shoes, he looked like a psychiatrist through and through. Looking up, he saw Cade sitting in a chair along the back wall next to the large ivy plant.

"Hello, Mr. Hobbs, I'm Dr. Morrison," he said. Cade got up and shook his hand. Dr. Morrison extended his arm in the direction of his office. "Please join me in my office," he said, putting his other hand on the small of Cade's back, nudging him gently toward his office.

Taking a moment to look around, Cade noted the stained mahogany trim with a large window overlooking the canal with various quaint shops and office buildings.

"Impressive, Dr. Morrison. This is a beautiful office," Cade said.

"Please, call me Robert."

"This view is incredible, Robert." Acknowledging Cade's comment, Doctor Morrison motioned him toward the high-back leather chairs.

The Winds

"Cade, could I have you sit over there in that chair?" Doctor Morrison walked over to his chair and waited for Cade to take his seat. Cade sat down and noticed a glass of water on the small table between them.

"For me, I assume," Cade said mid-reach.

"Indeed, have all you want."

Taking a few swallows, Cade leaned back in the chair.

"So Cade, your wife tells me you have been experiencing some anxiety lately."

Cade sat forward and started to rub his hands together. "That's correct," he said. "No big deal, but Angie seems to think so."

"Sometimes it helps to have someone to talk to. Now, I understand that you have some children."

"That's correct. I have a daughter, Brittney. We call her Brit."

"And how old is she?"

"She's seven."

"And a son as well?"

"Zac's 12."

"I'm sure they are wonderful children, and you're a fantastic father. I really believe that coming here is the right thing to do. Your wife's worried about you, and I'm sure your children are as well. Do they know about your anxieties?"

Cade thought for a moment. "They don't know everything. They just wonder why I never talk about where I grew up."

"Where did you grow up?"

Cade smiled a bit at the question. "Angie didn't tell you?"

Doctor Morrison smiled back at him.

"No, Cade, I had a very short conversation with your wife. So?"

Starting to feel a bit uncomfortable, Cade shifted in his chair as he looked around the room. "Really, Doctor Morrison, what has Angie told you?" The doctor just sat there, looking down at his notebook. Taking the obvious hint, Cade conceded and answered the question.

"I grew up in a small town in Wyoming called Lorenz."

Doctor Morrison looked up at him. "When's the last time you've been back?"

"Never, there's no reason to go back. Everyone that meant anything to me is not there anymore."

"You're talking about your parents, brothers, and sisters, right?"

"Just parents; I'm an only child." Gulping down the remainder of the water in the glass, Cade leaned back in his chair, bracing himself for the next question.

"I can't say I've ever been to Wyoming, but I would like to visit sometime. I hear it's beautiful."

Cade's eyes suddenly lit up. "Wyoming has a variety of beauty – high desert plateaus, rugged mountains, and streams that are as cold as the glaciers they came from."

The doctor nodded his head as he refocused on his notebook. "It's obvious that you still have a warm spot in your heart for the state." Cade nodded his head. "Why did you leave?"

"To become a doctor. I went to the University of Wyoming and got my undergraduate degree in biology and then continued on to Northwestern University here in Chicago."

"When did your wife come into the picture?"

"I met her on campus after my first year here – literally bumped into her at the student union building. She still has the silk shirt."

"Silk shirt?"

"Yeah, the one she was wearing when I spilled cranberry juice on her. It slid off my lunch tray. I tried to wipe it off, but I guess the rest is history. We've been together ever since."

"That's a good love story to tell the kids."

"That's why she's kept the shirt. Women have a way of blowing things out of proportion, you know. She's convinced it was fate."

"Well, was it?"

"I didn't know it was a silk shirt, and how could I have known it really belonged to her roommate?"

Dr. Morrison started to smile.

"You did it on purpose, didn't you?"

"I couldn't let her get away. Less than a year later, we were married, and now we have two crazy kids."

The Winds

Dr. Morrison sat back in his chair, crossed his legs, and put the pencil to his mouth.

"Ok, I think the ice has been officially broken. I'd like to return to the past, maybe your home life. Any special memories of your childhood?"

Stalling momentarily, Cade began clearing his throat.

"I had a great childhood. I had lots of friends, made tree forts, went tubing down Squaw Creek, and even shot a few birds with my BB gun, and no, I didn't shoot my eye out. Nothing you would call spectacular; I just grew up in an average home in a small town."

"And your parents?"

"They were good parents – always there for me. If I had a problem, I could always count on my Dad to be there for me. He would always know the right things to say." Cade hesitated for a moment. "God, I miss him."

"Oh, I'm sorry. I didn't realize that your father had since passed away."

"It's okay. He died the last part of my junior year in high school. I was in science class and heard an explosion – just a huge bang, shook the windows, you know. I had no idea at the time that it somehow involved my Dad. After class, they called me down to the office. I'll never forget their faces. I knew at that moment that my life was about to change. He owned a gas station, and something went terribly wrong."

"I'm sorry, Cade. I know that must have been devastating to you and your mother."

"Mom and I had to get through it together. After I graduated, she moved to Arizona to live with her sister. Her sister was a widow, too, so it worked out well. I didn't care much because I was heading to college anyway. That summer's really more of a blur to me than anything." Cade got up from his seat and ran his fingers through his hair. He walked across the room and stared out the window.

"Cade, I'm truly sorry. I can only imagine–"

"It was a long time ago," Cade said, not really meaning to be rude. "I've put it behind me. After Mom left, there wasn't any reason for me to return to Lorenz, so I never did."

"Angie told me about your reunion."

"Yeah, I figured she had. I paid my money and all, but going back would be like opening the floodgates."

Dr. Morrison shifted in his chair and crossed the other leg. Cade returned to his seat.

"I'm listening," he said, not taking his eyes off his

notepad. Cade shifted in his chair and suddenly felt like he was being interrogated. He felt as if a bright spotlight was focused directly in his eyes, and he could feel the intermittent drops of water thumping against his forehead. He chose not to reply. Dr. Morrison just sat there quietly, waiting.

It was the longest minute Cade had experienced in his entire life. The ticking from the clock hanging on the wall behind him seemed to get louder and louder and louder. Dr. Morrison was of absolutely no help either. He just sat there, motionless, relaxed, legs crossed, doodling on his notepad. He knew there was more to the story – another reason why Cade hadn't returned to the town of all his childhood memories. How did he know? Simple, *Angie must have told him.* Finally, Cade just couldn't take it anymore and immediately turned to putty.

"I didn't think I could experience a worse day than when my father died," Cade said, breaking the uncomfortable silence. "You can understand that, right? I mean, what could be worse than that?" Cade took a big swallow. "But it's one thing to hear about someone you loved dying and actually seeing it happen." His eyes glassed over, and tears started to tumble down his cheeks. "It happened just after graduation. My girlfriend… there was an accident."

Doctor Morrison looked up at him and nudged his

glasses slightly down the bridge of his nose.

"I've tried so hard to forget. It was terrible. I haven't told anyone about it."

"Except your wife, I suppose," Doctor Morrison interjected.

Taking a deep breath, Cade nodded. Doctor Morrison sat silently while Cade began by expressing how much he loved his high school sweetheart, and, at the time, he felt that he could never be happy without her. He intended to ask her to marry him that fateful day, but it didn't happen. The last thing he remembered was losing grasp of her hand and hearing his name on her lips as she fell to her death.

"Cade, the mind is a very complex machine, but it is a machine," the doctor said, summing up his understanding of the events portrayed to him. "It can be very strong at times, and then at others, it can be extremely delicate, vulnerable, but it's very resilient and forgiving. Sometimes, our minds are subjected to horrific things – things that we would rather entirely forget – but our minds do not forget. Our mind cleverly marks the event and stores it in a far distant place only to be retrieved at a much later time, suddenly triggered by something as simple as a word, a phrase, or an event."

"So what are you saying?"

The Winds

"It appears that you are suffering from post-traumatic stress similar to our boys who returned from Vietnam and the Gulf Wars. For twenty years, you've been able to, for the most part, suppress the vivid memory of this tragic event, but on occasion, it has surfaced, bringing back the horror, anguish, and helplessness you felt at the time it happened. It's like flipping a switch. Something happens in your life, and suddenly, you return to the past, causing you to experience severe anxiety."

"So what can I do about it? How can I make it stop?"

"That depends. Everyone's different, and every situation differs in complexity, but I'm committed to you. Together, we will put an end to your anxiety so you can get back to enjoying your wife and family, but it will take some time and effort on your part."

"What's the next step?"

"You need to be proactive, almost combative. The first thing I would recommend is to make a trip back in time. You need to make a trip down memory lane to face your fears. You need to return to Lorenz."

Cade leaned forward in his chair. He thought he could do anything but that. Ask him to walk across fiery coals in his bare feet. Ask him to run completely nude through Lincoln Park, downtown Chicago. Ask him to do anything but return to his birthplace. Cade became uneasy. His hands began to sweat, and he looked around the room as if looking for a secret trap door to duck into and escape. Robert sat patient but stern. He knew Cade would have to work it out for himself. Anything said by him at this point would be pointless. After a few quiet, tense moments, Cade finally spoke.

"Presuming I decide to go back, what do I do while I'm there?" A gentle smile came to Doctor Morrison's face as he reached across and put his hand on Cade's knee.

"Just visit your old stomping grounds, rekindle old friendships, and enjoy the kids."

"Kids?"

"Yes, I want you to take your children with you. You need to be fun and exciting to them. Just their very nature will force you to explore your childhood. As you start to reveal the past, they will continue to prod further and further into your experiences. Hopefully, before the trip comes to an end, you will have faced the demon, and then you will be ready to begin the healing process. You need to relive the traumatic events of your past and come to grips with them. It will undoubtedly be very painful at times, but I'm giving you these words of caution. You may be tempted to skip over or eliminate something that may be painful from your agenda. You will need to display courage and faith. If you do these things, maybe, just maybe, you'll find the peace you desperately desire." Doctor Morrison squeezed Cade's knee and then sat back in his chair.

"So, if I make this trip back to Lorenz – and I'm not yet saying I'm going to for sure – but if I do, it'll be over when I return, right?"

Doctor Morrison smiled but slowly shook his head.

"It's taken twenty years to get to this point," he said. "I wish there was some sort of pill you could take or magic potion you could drink, but I'm afraid it's not that simple. A trip back to Lorenz will begin the long healing process. Today's session is like, well, the tip of the iceberg. So much of this that lies deep under the water's surface has yet to be revealed. When you return, we will need to meet again. I look forward to talking with you after your trip, so keep my card in a handy place, like on the refrigerator door."

Smiling, Doctor Morrison rose from his chair, gesturing for Cade to do the same. "I think you've had enough for today."

Chapter 4

"May I have your attention, please? We are now ready for general boarding for Delta flight 1468, destination Salt Lake City, departing out of gate G10. All ticketed passengers seated in rows…" the intercom announced as Cade, Angie, and Zac sat forward in their chairs while Brit dug through her bag on the floor in front of them. Pulling the ticket from his pocket, Cade looked at his seating assignment. Before he could look up, Brit had zipped her bag and was heading toward the long line of people.

"Brit, not quite yet," Cade yelled across the rows of seats. Brit stopped, turned around, and let out a big breath.

"We're never going to get there," she said, a bit frustrated.

Zac quickly collected his small carry-on bag, placed the strap over his shoulder, and carried his iPod in the other hand. His brown wavy locks protruded from underneath his Bulls ball cap that he wore tilted and off-center, slightly to the left. This 12-year-old never went anywhere without his tunes, and his baggy jean pockets were stuffed full of various kinds of snacks.

"Now you're sure you have everything, right, Zac?" Angie asked, lifting one speaker away from his ear and repeating the question.

"Yep, got it," he replied. "Including a clean change of underwear in case I-"

"Get into a car accident," Angie said, completing the well-known phrase. "Hey, I have a right to be a little worried about you guys. Lorenz is a long way away." She gave Zac a hug and then approached Brit from behind.

Brit had her favorite cloth bag stuffed with colored pencils, paper, and other entertaining things to do on the trip to Wyoming, along with another larger bag with bright flowers on it. Her hair was pulled back into a ponytail, and she was wearing a ball cap, shorts, a colorful t-shirt, and leather sandals. Chomping on her glob of gum, she blew an occasional bubble as she watched the variety of people walk by. Suddenly, she turned and faced her mother.

"How do I look?" she asked. Angie's eyes started to moisten a bit, but she did her best to fight off the eventual tears.

"You look great. Did you remember your toothbrush? And don't forget to floss every night. The water, what about the water?" she said, quickly standing up and facing her husband. "Cade, is the water safe to drink? You'll be drinking bottled water, right?"

"Honey, we're going to Wyoming. It's part of the lower 48. The water's fine, and they even have indoor plumbing."

Angie glared at him.

"Hey, it's probably better than the recycled stuff we drink here. It's naturally purified through the constant interaction between polished rocks in all those high mountain streams."

"Please spare me the ecological lecture." Angie looked at her two children. "Now, no talking to strangers, especially the Indians."

"Mom, don't worry," Zac said. "Dad told us the reservation's mostly desert, and there's really nothing to do out there anyway."

"But I want to see a real Indian. Daddy promised me!" Brit said, looking up at Cade with her big blue eyes. "Didn't you, Daddy?"

"I'd rather you not go to the reservation, Cade," Angie said. "I have enough to worry about without adding 'wild' Indians to the list."

Grabbing Angie by the hand, Cade pulled her in close. "You worry too much. We'll be fine." He hugged her tightly and crossed his fingers behind her in easy view of his two children. "Ok, I promise I won't take them out to the reservation, but are you going to be alright? I can call it off right now and cash in the tickets for Jamaica. I really don't have to do this."

"Yes, you really do have to do this; Dr. Morrison said so. Either you go, or you sleep on the couch for the rest of your life. I can't take you tossing and turning and even screaming in the middle of the night anymore."

Cade put his lips to her ear. "Speaking of screaming, thank you for last night." Reaching down, he grabbed his bag. "I'm really going to miss ya, you know that," he said sincerely.

"I'll miss you too," she replied.

"Then come with us. It'll be fun."

"Cade, we've been through this. Someone has to stay here and feed the cat. Anyway, I'm not totally convinced Lorenz has indoor plumbing." She smiled and gave him another peck on the lips. "Remember, I love you. Don't ever forget that."

"I won't, and I love you, too. I'll see you in a few days," he said.

"Now boarding passengers in rows 10 through 22," was

announced over the intercom.

"Well, kids, I guess that's us." Both Brit and Zac hugged their mom and gave her a final kiss goodbye. Cade grabbed her again, hugged her tight, and softly whispered, "I love you," in her ear. Angie returned the same phrase, forming the words, but no audible sound escaped her lips as she waved goodbye.

The plane caught a jet stream at about 23,000 feet and landed 30 minutes earlier at the Salt Lake International Airport than scheduled. It gave the kids a little more time to look around and ride the long, flat escalator between the C and D terminals, where framed photographs of the various beautiful locations around the state were hung, evenly spaced, along the wall.

"Dad, is Wyoming as pretty as Utah?" Brit asked, stretching the gum out of her mouth and then nibbling it back in again.

"Every state has a certain beauty. Some are real flat and have fields of corn, cotton, or wheat; some have mountains, trees, and lakes, while others are deserts with cactus and rocks and sand, but all the states have something they're known for. Like South Dakota is known for Mt. Rushmore. Oregon is known for its beautiful coast, and Florida is known for its swamps."

The Winds

"So what's Wyoming known for, Dad?" she asked.

Cade stared blankly at one of the pictures of a southern Utah waterfall, not intentionally but ignoring his daughter's question. It was that trigger mechanism Doctor Morrison had talked about.

"Dad, you're doing it again," Brit said, tugging on his arm.

"Are you going to space out during the whole trip?" Zac asked. Cade blinked and then looked at them.

"What's that Zac?" he said. "I wasn't paying attention."

"Never mind, it wasn't important," Zac replied.

They continued to walk to their gate. The E terminal was very crowded. This terminal was for smaller city destinations like St. George, Utah, Elko, Nevada, and even Billings, Montana. Redding, Wyoming, was nearly twice the size of Lorenz, located about 25 miles away, and was the only city within a hundred miles with a commercial airport.

The two-prop, 22-seat airplane took off from the Salt Lake International Airport at about 2:30 that afternoon and was expected to arrive in Redding between an hour and a half and two hours later, depending on the weather. The weather in Redding was supposed to be just as hot temperature-wise, maybe hotter than in Chicago, but with very little humidity. The small plane immediately crossed the Wasatch Mountains and headed toward the Uintas, then soon passed directly to the south end of the Wind River Mountains of Wyoming. Cade pointed out the many features and places he had hiked and fished when he was a kid. Both Zac and Brit were amazed at the rugged mountain terrain. As far as they could see, there were jagged, glacier-covered peaks and dark blue scattered lakes. Zac even removed his earphones so he could hear his Dad tell the tales of his wilderness experiences.

"I never knew you did all that," Zac said. "How come you never told us about these mountains?"

"Yeah, Dad, how come?" Brit asked.

"I didn't know you guys would be interested. All I ever hear you talk about is malls, amusement parks, and the Bulls. Why all the sudden interest in the Wind Rivers?"

"Cause look at them, Dad, they're beautiful," Brit said. "They're the prettiest mountains I've ever seen."

"And those lakes. Look how many there are! Do you think anyone has fished every lake in the Wind Rivers?" Zac asked.

"There's probably a few die-hard fishermen in Lorenz

that would claim that, but you both need to realize something about true fishermen."

"What's that?" Zac said.

"They all lie."

"I'll be sure to remember that," Brit said. "So when are we going to land?"

"Soon," Cade said, pointing toward the window. "I can see Lorenz just over there at the base of the foothills and Redding's over there in the middle of nowhere, see it?"

After making a near-perfect landing at Redding Airport at exactly 4:14 pm, they noticed that there was only one other plane on the tarmac and basically had only one gate. A young man with earmuffs signaled the pilot to stop the plane within 200 feet of the terminal double door. Within minutes, the airplane door opened, and the stairs extended to the asphalt below. Both Brit and Zac walked past the flight attendant, grabbed a couple of mints from the wicker basket, and jumped the last three stairs to the ground.

"I can't believe this," Zac said, stopping to look around. "Where are all the other airplanes?"

"Where are all the people?" Brit said, continuing to walk to the double doors at the end of the terminal. Cade put his arms around both of them.

"I think we're going to have fun this week; what do you think?" Both kids nodded with a smile.

The rental car was adequate, but it wasn't the BMW 323 Ci convertible Cade was accustomed to driving. Throughout the 40-minute drive, Zac and Brit never stopped asking questions. They both had their windows rolled down and were pointing at everything they saw, from an antelope standing on a distant sagebrush-covered hill to an old farmhouse that desperately needed a fresh coat of red paint.

Zac coiled up the wires to his headphones and tucked them and his iPod in the back pocket behind the seat. He didn't want to miss a word of what his dad had to say. Both kids had only known the enormous city of Chicago. They had ventured into the smaller suburbs up north, but this was different. Everything was so wide open and spacious. The kids could see forever. Cade immediately slowed from 55 to 25 miles per hour just before entering a large clump of trees less than a mile ahead.

"What's up, Dad? Why so slow?" Brit said.

"Are we there?" Zac said.

"Once you've been caught, you never forget," he replied, scanning the road ahead. "The Sheriff's hiding around here somewhere. Hunter, Wyoming, population 392, at least that's what it was last time I was here twenty years ago, and from what I'm seeing, it probably hasn't changed." As they started into the curve entering the edge of town, they passed a sign that advertised, "Hunter, Wyoming, Population 391."

"I wonder who died?" Brit asked. Cade looked at her and smiled. Just off to the side of the road was a gas station with peeling paint.

"What did I tell you, kids? The old Sheriff's still there. It's called a speed trap. He just sits in his car all day long and waits."

"For what?" Brit asked.

"Tourists," Cade replied. "Most of the town's money comes from speeding tickets." They continued past the officer at just under 20 miles per hour. Cade couldn't help but look over at the officer and wave. The officer tipped his cowboy hat and smiled.

The main highway went right through the middle of town, past the post office and convenience store. Continuing on State Highway 138 for another 14 miles, the anticipation grew with each mile traveled. The road was elevated most of the way, with a river down below. Huge cottonwood trees lined both sides of the river as it wound its way west. The town itself was nestled in a valley at the edge of the foothills of the mighty Wind River Mountains.

The last mile or so took them to the very edge of the valley, where they could look out over the town. The trees were tall and mature. It was as though the valley basin was boiling with bodies of dark shades of green. There were only a few buildings and a tall communications tower that could be seen over the tops of the trees.

"It's beautiful, Dad," Brit said. "Is it as beautiful as you remember it?"

"You know, it's been so long I've forgotten just how breathtaking this valley is," he replied. Approaching the three-way intersection, Cade either had to turn right, which took him and the kids down into town, or he could go left, continuing into the desert of sagebrush – desert, because like most of the state of Wyoming, anything east of Lorenz was desert. It was nothing but slow-rolling hills and alkali-white dirt as far as the eye could see. Antelope were more common on the road than semi-trucks.

Lorenz had the best of all worlds as far as Cade was concerned. It was an outdoorsman's paradise. The view to the west of town was breathtaking. The hills were smooth and covered with various kinds of lush green grasses mixed in with both juniper trees and sagebrush. Broad canyons filled the horizons as they led the way upwards to the rugged mountains hidden behind them.

"Dad, the light's green," Zac said. Suddenly, looking into the rearview mirror, Cade noticed several cars waiting for him to proceed. He took a deep breath and turned right toward a town that he'd thought he'd never see again.

Chapter 5

They settled into the Dusty Saddle Inn on Main Street, about two blocks up from the high school. A large neon sign protruded into the street, consisting of a cowboy riding a horse with the name of the hotel underneath. In fact, most of the businesses touted a sign with a cowboy of some sort riding a horse or wrestling a steer. Cade pulled in through the entrance. It was similar to pulling into a garage; only once inside, it was open to the sky above. There was a large square corridor with two stories of rooms around the outside, with the doors to the rooms facing the inside.

"I wonder what's going on?" Cade said, pulling into one of the last available parking spaces. "I bet there's a baseball tournament." He looked around the complex a bit. "You kids, wait here while I go check in."

"I want to go with you, Dad," Brit said.

"Me, too," Zac said. "I want to get Mom a postcard. She'll never believe this place." Climbing out of the car, they took a quick look around, and then all three proceeded to the front office.

A loud, annoying cowbell clanked when they opened the glass door. An old white-haired man came in from the back room, separated by a brown curtain hanging in the

The Winds

doorway, and stood behind the large counter. The small lobby was scattered with penny candies, postcards, bolo ties with the ends tipped with sterling silver, tie tacks, earrings, and belt buckles. Most were made with a combination of silver, ivory elk teeth, and turquoise.

"Wow! This is neat stuff!" Brit said, turning to her dad and tugging on his pant leg. "Can I have one of these, please, Dad? I won't ask for anything else." She held up a small stuffed rabbit that appeared to have antelope antlers sticking out the top of its head just between the long ears.

"That's big-time fake," Zac said. "Rabbits don't have horns."

"Are you sure?" Cade said. "This one has them."

"Let me see that." Ripping the small animal from Brit's hands, Zac looked it over in detail and pulled on the small antlers. "Then how come we haven't seen one at the zoo?"

The old man behind the counter began to chuckle. "It's called a Jackalope – a cross between a jackrabbit and an antelope. You aren't from around these parts, are you, son?"

Zac looked over at his father without answering.

"Well, it's been a while," Cade replied.

***

The next morning, they were awoken early, about 8 am, not from sirens and street traffic, but from a bunch of kids splashing around in the swimming pool.

"Swimming this early?" Zac said as he rubbed his eyes and crawled out of bed.

"Hey, you're in Wyoming now. When I grew up, this place had the only swimming pool in town, and since you can only use the pool three months out of the year, you have to start early. Now, you two get up. We have a big day today."

"What are we going to do, Dad?" Brit asked.

"Well, I thought we'd run over to the Settler's Museum and see the two-headed sheep skull, then over to Rotary Park and show you where I-"

"A two-headed sheep skull? No way!" Zac said. "This isn't one of those jackalope things again, is it?"

"No, this one's for real," Cade said.

"That sounds gross, Dad," Brit said. "Why do we need to see that yucky thing?"

"Because it's something you don't see every day. There

are lots of other neat things to see, too. Lorenz has a lot of history. You know, the pioneers came real close to here on their way to Utah and Oregon. I'll tell you all about it when we get to the museum."

"So what else are we going to do?" Zac said.

"After the museum, maybe the old little league baseball park, and after that, we can eat at Dairy King."

"Dairy, who?" Brit asked.

"Dairy King! You know, fast food, like Dairy Queen."

"So what's the Tasty Craze?" Zac asked. "I saw that as we came into town last night."

"Same thing, fast food."

"But what's it supposed to be like?"

"You got me on that one, Zac. I just remember they had great shakes."

The kids really enjoyed the day with their dad. He was beaming the entire time as they asked him more and more questions and wanted to see more and more of what he did when he was a kid. He took them to where he used to go skinny-dipping with his friends down in Squaw Creek. They called it Twilight Hole, named after their subdivision. It was a much smaller creek now than he'd remembered; in fact, most of everything seemed much smaller than he remembered, including the home he grew up in.

Slowly, they drove past the small split-level home, painted two-tone colors like most of the houses in Twilight Division. Cade remembered it to be a nice neighborhood. The tree in his front yard never grew large enough to climb like he'd hoped in the 18 years he was there, but now, twenty years later, the branches stretched beyond the telephone wires and into the street.

"Let's stop and ask them if we can go in and look around," Zac said.

"Yeah, Dad, you can show us your bedroom in the basement you told us about," Brit said. "Remember, the one you were always scared of?"

"I never told you I was scared. I told you I had trouble getting to sleep with the spare freezer down there turning on and off during the night. Come to think of it, it did sound a lot like a monster," Cade said as he started poking Brit in the ribs. "I don't think we should bother them. It's not my house anymore." They continued to drive a few blocks until they reached Rodeo Park.

"Unbelievable!" Cade said. "This park never had any trees. It was as hot as a firecracker, and we'd play homerun derby all day long."

They continued past the park toward Granger Elementary School, where Cade went from kindergarten through the sixth grade, then turned left on Rivers Edge Road. They drove down the two-lane road past miles of pasturelands and large herds of cows and a few horses.

"Where're we going now, Dad?" Brit asked. She stuck her arm out the window to feel the cool breeze.

"Can't tell you. It's a surprise. You'll really like this."

Driving for another mile or so, Cade told them how he used to ride his bike all the way out there. They couldn't believe he didn't just call a taxi. Cade slowed down to barely a crawl and looked across the fields.

"I don't understand it," he mumbled to himself.

"What, are we lost or something?" Zac asked.

"No, I just can't see the bridge. I know I'm supposed to turn on a skinny dirt road right before this road makes a big turn."

"What's the name of the street? Maybe the sign just fell down," Brit said.

"It doesn't have a name. It's just a little dirt road, but it went across this big, rickety old bridge into the Indian reservation."

"We're going to the reservation?" Zac asked.

"Cool!" Brit said.

"No, kids, we're not going to the reservation. We're going to jump off the East Fork Bridge if I could just find it. It was right over there. Where'd it go?"

"Why don't we ask that guy?" Zac suggested as he pointed to a guy riding a horse on the side of the road.

"I guess it can't hurt." Cade approached him ever so slowly so as not to spook the horse. "Excuse me, sir, we're not from around here, but we're trying to find the East Fork Bridge."

"If you aren't from around these parts, how do you know about the bridge?" The guy tilted his cowboy hat up on his forehead and bent down to get a better look. "So where you from?" Brit stuck her head out the passenger side window.

"We're from Chicago."

"Back east, huh." He studied Cade's face intently. "You look awfully familiar, son. Do I know you?"

The Winds

"My name's Cade Hobbs. I used to live here a long time ago."

"It can't be," the man said. "Why, I haven't seen you since you were in high school."

Cade studied the old man's wrinkled, sunbaked face. "Mr. Burk? Is that really you? I thought you were, um….dead."

"That's ok, kid. I was pretty old even back when I taught you in chemistry your senior year. I don't blame you for thinking I'd be dead. It's this clean Wyoming air that keeps me kicking. Now, about that bridge, it's gone. They tore it down over ten years ago. Since there's barely a drop of water running down the East Fork anymore, I guess they didn't see a need for it. Sad, I used to love watching you guys jump off it. Kids, I think your father here did the best back flip off the top rail I'd ever seen." The kids hung on every word out of the old guy's crusty lips. "Your father here, they don't come any better than him. He was always a good kid, as far as I was concerned. If anybody else tells you anything different, they don't know shit." He started to laugh so hard he began to cough.

"The same ole Mr. Burk." Cade turned to the kids. "He was a sailor before he became a teacher."

"Now, don't be a stranger," Mr. Burk said. "You come out and visit me anytime. I'm still in the same house. I might even have a few chemistry experiments you haven't seen. I have a lab in the basement."

They said their goodbyes and continued down the country road until Cade decided to make another left, this time on Hillcrest Lane. It would eventually take them back into town. Suddenly, a big smile emerged on Cade's face as he started to accelerate.

"Are you ready for this, kids?"

"What if there's a sharp corner, Dad? You'll never be able to make the turn," Zac said. Both he and Brit made sure their seat belts were secured.

"No corners, guaranteed," Cade said, but suddenly thought of all the changes he'd seen since he'd been back. *Surely they wouldn't have put any turns*, he thought to himself.

Without warning, the car dropped immediately down a steep hill. Brit and Zac could feel their stomach tingle and flip.

"Dad, slow down!" Brit yelled.

"Wait 'til you feel this," Cade said as he gripped the steering wheel.

The Winds

The car suddenly reached the bottom of the hill and screeched up an even steeper hill. As soon as they reached the top, the road again dropped out of sight.

"We're going to die!" Zac screamed.

"You're crazy, Dad!" Brit said, but both of them were beaming with terrified delight as they gripped the dashboard in front of them.

"Hold on tight!" Cade further increased his speed to nearly 80 miles per hour. There were still very few houses, trees, or even cows, just a narrow, perfectly straight road full of steep rolling hills. After cresting the last hill, he slowed the car down to the posted speed limit, which was 40, and turned to see the kids' faces.

"That was great!" Brit said.

"Totally awesome!" Zac said.

"I thought you'd like it. Next time, we'll do it at night with the headlights off."

"No way, Dad, you didn't," Zac said.

"Yep, and I lived to tell you about it."

Later that day, they stopped at the Tasty Craze and each got a chocolate malt. Savoring every thick spoonful, they drove up to Deep Canyon State Park, just minutes from town. The canyon itself was created tens of thousands of years ago from the Popo Agie River. The river gained its strength from the countless winter meltdown tributaries that branched into the main river, starting up at the top of the highest peaks in the Wind River Mountain Range. The water was pure and cold.

It was easy to tell out-of-towners by the way they would pronounce the name of this life-giving river. They would pronounce it just how it was spelled, but those who were born in Lorenz knew that the correct pronunciation – according to the Indians – was "Po-po'-zsa."

Near the exit of the canyon, there was a place on the side of the mountain where the entire Popo Agie River was consumed at the base of a cliff. The water crashed and tumbled down the large, jagged rocks, twisting and turning as it made its steep descent into the unforgiving cave. About a quarter of a mile down on the other side of the two-lane paved road, the mountain gently expelled the once mighty river into a calm pool. The surface boiled with huge Rainbow Trout. This section of the river was protected by the state, so fishing was not allowed, but people who came to this beautiful spot in nature could stand on a large, wooden deck nearly 50 feet above and feed the fish. This was a favorite pastime of Cade's while growing up.

"One of my good friends used to fish here when we were kids," Cade said.

"No way," Zac said. "I thought you said it was against the law."

"It was, but that didn't stop him."

"So how'd he do it? I mean, didn't people see him?" Brit said.

"Simple, he did it at night. Let's just say you're guaranteed a fish every cast."

"So, did you ever actually see one of the fish, or did he just tell you about them?" Zac said.

"Well, I didn't actually see any of the fish, but–"

"Sounds like a fishing story to me," Brit said. "I'm pretty sure your friend was a big fat liar."

When they ran out of fish food, they continued driving up the narrow canyon. Cade decided to show them a few of the neat camping spots that he'd enjoyed when he was a kid. Pointing out the sheer cliffs on the north side of the canyon, he shared with them how he had climbed nearly every route. He once was an excellent rock climber but hadn't climbed since leaving Lorenz.

Cade slowly applied the brake as he neared the final bridge, bringing the car to a stop. Leaning forward over the steering wheel he looked through the far side of the windshield upwards to the canyon.

"Is something wrong, Dad?" Brit said.

Cade was silent for a moment as he let the dust settle, revealing a small sign positioned at the trailhead. Swallowing hard, his stomach began to knot up as he read the few simple words. "Nothing's wrong, kids. I just have a few memories of this place." He looked back to the road. "So what do you think? Have you guys seen enough for today? I need to get back to the motel and get ready for the dinner."

"I'd like to see more, but it's been awesome so far," Brit said.

"Totally," Zac said. "But where does this road go?" Cade slowly crossed the bridge and started to turn around. Stopping the car, he pointed up the side of the sparsely pine-covered hill.

"Kids, behind this hill is paradise. Those switchbacks take you up to the Winds. I love it up there. It's so peaceful, and the fish… there's no better fishing in the lower 48."

"How come you never take us fishing, Dad?" Brit said.

"Cause we live in Chicago."

"But lots of people go fishing in Chicago," Zac said.

Cade thought for a moment. "It just feels different in the

The Winds

Winds. You can fish on a stream all morning and not see even a hint of civilization."

"Can we go up there tomorrow?" Zac asked.

"Afraid not," Cade said abruptly. It's a long way up there, and we didn't bring any fishing poles."

"What about next year? Can we come back here next year and do it?" Brit said.

"Well, I can't make any promises, but wouldn't it be great next year, this time, the three of us in the middle of the Winds, catching fish, enjoying the sunsets, and running from bears?"

"I was going to ask if Mom could come, but there's no way she'd come if there's bears," Brit said.

Smiling, Cade took one last look before turning the car around and heading back across the bridge. As they crossed the bridge, he noticed a young couple walking toward them, just returning from the well-used trail that followed the river's edge up through the canyon. Walking hand in hand, smiling and laughing – no question, they were in love.

Suddenly, Cade was hit with extreme anxiety. His heart started to race, and his vision became blurred.

"Dad, look out!" Brit screamed from the back seat.

Cade quickly jerked the wheel. The young couple pressed themselves against the wood plank guardrail to avoid being hit by the front of the car. Quickly gathering himself, Cade applied the brake, stopping the car in a large cloud of dust. He jumped out of the car and ran toward the young couple.

"Are you OK?!" he said. The boy was helping the girl to her feet. She was visibly shaken and started to brush off her pants. "I am so sorry. I don't know what happened. Are you sure you're alright?" The young couple nodded their heads. Cade could tell they were shaken but saw no visible cuts or scrapes. Leaving his business card just in case they needed to get a hold of him, he returned to the car. He climbed in, shut the door, and took a deep breath.

"That was close," he said.

"What happened, Daddy?" Brit said. She put her hand on his shoulder and looked at him from between the front seats.

"Where were they coming from?" Zac said.

Quiet for a moment, Cade struggled within himself to say the two simple words. Taking a deep breath, he answered very simply, "The Falls, they were coming from Mirror Falls."

Chapter 6

Later that night, **the *Class of '79 Twentieth Reunion***

The Trapper's Lodge was the designated location for what was deemed the main event for Cade's 20th-year reunion activities. It was an opportunity for all the classmates and their spouses, if they came, to get together, drink, tell stories, laugh, and, similar to back in high school, drink some more.

The Lodge was located by the fifth hole of the nine-hole city golf course and surrounded by small trees and short stubble of grass. The parking lot had just been paved earlier in the week, and the paint around the outside doors was slightly tacky. The building had just been completed, and this was the first event to be held within its walls.

Everyone continued to wear their nametag from the night before to avoid confusion and embarrassment. Time has a way of changing people. Many of those who were skinny were now noticeably overweight, while many of those who had thick, beautiful hair were now nearly bald. Some were experiencing both extremes. Of course, there were a few who skipped metamorphous entirely and looked just as good as the day they left the school grounds.

Rock music from the late 70s and early 80s filled the main hall, where they all gathered to talk, laugh, and relive some of the crazy memories they'd experienced back in their younger years. The independent conversations escalated in volume as more and more people packed into the room.

Suddenly, there was a tapping on a glass. "Thank you all for coming this evening. From the sounds of it, I take you're all having a great time, right?" the announcer said. He was the strict but funny Math teacher – since retired – that most of the old students recognized and admired. Several glasses of wine and cans of beer were elevated above the sea of heads.

"Rock and roll, baby!" one person yelled from the back. He'd already prepped himself for the occasion by ducking into the Lorenz Bar earlier that evening.

"Yeah, yeah, Shane, always the life of the party. Now, all of you, if you can please take your seats, we can begin the dinner. Those seated at the back table, if you could come through the buffet line first, then the next table can come, and so on. And remember, take what you want, but eat what you take."

There were several empty chairs at various tables, but there was one that was particularly noticeable near the center table at the end. A stocky man, clearly of Indian decent, with long black hair, pulled back and in a single braid that hit the middle of his back, was sitting at one side of the empty chair. He didn't talk to many people; instead, he spent most of his time looking down at his watch and glancing toward the entrance doors.

After dinner, a young lady, very shapely, not jaw-dropping gorgeous, but considered cute by all standards – throw in the obvious fact that her breasts were probably the largest in the graduating class – approached the man while he was sitting by himself near the far back corner of the room.

"Shooter? Is that you?" She smiled at him as she motioned to give him a hug.

"Marybeth, right? What's your last name now?

"It's still Peterson. I took it back after the divorce."

"I'm sorry, I hadn't heard."

"Hey, no need… best decision I've ever made." She took a quick sip of her drink.

"God, I haven't seen you in ages," Shooter said.

"Probably not since the last reunion."

"Has it been that long? Man, you look great. Where do you live nowadays?"

"Here for the past four years."

"Really? Where do you work?"

"I'm a registered nurse at the new medical center, mainly the ER."

"The Emergency Room? I bet you get to see a lot a crazy stuff."

"Sometimes, but how crazy can it get here in good 'ol Lorenz? So what do you do?"

Shooter took a quick peak at the entrance door again. "Oh, me? I work, well, I live out on a ranch at the edge of the reservation near the Fort. I run a guide service, you know, in and out of the Winds. Just me and a couple of my horses. Keeps me pretty busy in the summer." He took a swig of his beer.

"Sounds exciting. What about winter?"

"Drink a lot of beer," he said with a smirk.

"Same 'ol Shooter. Do you still play basketball? I mean, they have a great city league."

"Not much." There was a brief moment of silence as they both looked around the room.

"It's really great seeing you, Shooter," Marybeth said.

He nodded his head and tapped the top of his beer can

The Winds

with his finger.

"It's great seeing you again, Marybeth. By the way, have you seen him?"

"Seen who?" She paused for a moment. "Cade, right?" Shooter acknowledged. "I haven't yet, but keep your fingers crossed. Word is he's coming, but who knows about that guy? He hasn't been to any of the reunions."

"You know, I just really want to see him. Best friends in high school, and I haven't seen him since graduation."

"Yeah, I know what you mean. I had a serious crush on the guy," Marybeth said with a flirting smile. Shooter laughed.

"Yeah, you and all the other females in this room." They both looked around in opposite directions, waiting for the other to start a new subject. Marybeth broke the momentary silence.

"So you've probably seen Denton, right?"

"I've seen him but haven't talked to him. Twenty years isn't enough time as far as I'm concerned. He's still a complete asshole." He looked over at the entrance door again and then at his watch, coming to the realization that his chances of seeing Cade were slim to none.

"I mean, look at the guy," Marybeth said, looking in the direction of the bar. "What a putz."

Shooter looked toward the bar and saw Denton, the center of attention, undoubtedly telling some childhood story using every limb and muscle as animation.

"Who's the girl next to him?"

"You haven't heard? Kimber's sister. Denton's been dating her for like the last year or so. "

"How come I never knew that?"

She looked at him like the answer to his question was obvious.

"Because you need to get out more, Shooter. Come to town Saturday nights and have a few drinks with me and the girls!"

"Drama, yeah, that's what I need more of in my life."

Marybeth slugged him on the shoulder and started to laugh. "Maybe, but wouldn't you rather ride a cowgirl?"

Shooter just shook his head.

"Kimber's sister? When we were seniors, wasn't she like in the seventh grade? Do you really think she actually likes him?"

"Beats me, but she's gorgeous. Denton's good-looking and has muscles on top of muscles, but he's still the same person inside – black as night. Nothing about him has changed – life is all about him."

"He's probably just *using* her."

"Yeah, like all the other girls in the class. I can't believe I ever liked that guy."

Shooter glanced over at her. "You mean you and Denton, uh… well, you know."

"Yeah, one time, not real proud of it either," Marybeth said, getting back on the subject. "She lived back East, like in New York, and had a few problems, bad enough to get her to move back here. I've just heard bits and pieces, but I really don't know for sure. She seems nice, but I haven't really talked to her." Leaning over, Marybeth whispered in Shooter's ear, "Some think that he's trying to use her to replace Kimber." She backed away and then continued to speak. "It was a shock to all of us when she died, but Denton really went over the deep end."

"Denton? What about Cade? He was planning on marrying her! I mean, that's the reason he hasn't shown up to any of the reunions."

"Kimber?" Marybeth said.

Shooter shook his head slowly.

"No, Denton." Shooter pointed discreetly across the room. Denton was still laughing and talking loudly with an old classmate. "It was probably a good thing that Cade moved away when he did."

"Why's that?" Marybeth asked.

"Cause Denton probably would have killed him." Shooter looked across the room again in Denton's direction. Kimber's sister caught his eye and smiled, then turned away. "Wow, that's amazing. She looks just like her," Shooter said.

Marybeth looked into the crowd of people. "I told you she was gorgeous."

Suddenly, Denton turned and caught Shooter's eye. Shooter quickly looked down to the floor. Denton immediately slapped his friend on the shoulder, nodded his head, and turned and walked toward where Shooter and Marybeth were sitting.

"Ah shit, he's coming over," Shooter said softly.

"Hey, Shooter," Denton said. "Long time, eh? What have you been up to?" Denton took a long swig from his can of beer. He was definitely built, obviously spending a lot of time in the gym. His black hair was shaved close to his scalp on each side and around the back left, slightly longer on top, very similar to a Marine's cut. At this late stage in the evening, he was clearly feeling the effects of the alcohol.

"Not much, Denton," Shooter replied. "Just hanging at the ranch."

"Ranch? Shooter, it's like 50 acres." Denton noticed Marybeth sitting beside him. "Marybeth, it's been awhile, like what, five days?"

Marybeth looked up at him and nodded. "So, how are the stitches?" she asked.

"Healing," Denton replied.

"Stitches?" Shooter asked.

"Yeah, fuckin' branch 'bout took me off my horse!"

"Went clear to the bone," Marybeth said.

"How do you know?" Shooter said.

"I treated him last week," Marybeth said, looking over at Denton. "How many stitches?"

"Twenty-six, and I felt every fucking one of them. You need to tell the Doc to be a little more gentle."

"Hey, he gave you your choice of lollipops, didn't he?" Marybeth said, grinning.

"Very funny," Denton replied. He turned partially around. "I don't believe you've met my girlfriend." Denton placed his arm behind the small of her back and pushed her to the forefront. "This is Tara Samuels." Tara smiled as she politely acknowledged Shooter and Marybeth.

"It's a pleasure to meet you, Tara. I've heard a lot about you," Marybeth said. "You look familiar to me. Have we met?"

Denton interrupted. "Ok, cut the shit," he said. "Marybeth, this is Tara, Kimber's little sister." Tara was slender and tall. She had deep green eyes that complimented her auburn hair.

"Weren't you in grade school when we graduated?" Shooter said.

"Nothing like robbing the cradle, eh Denton?" Marybeth said.

Denton quickly fired back. "Hell, she's like pushing 30, aren't ya Tara?"

"Actually, next month, 31," Tara said.

"Well, that explains the resemblance," Marybeth said. "I didn't want to say anything because, well– "

"Because she's dead?" Tara said matter-of-fact.

The Winds

"No, really, that's not what I meant."

"It's fine, Marybeth, really. It's been years since my sister died. I'll admit, it was tough being without her, especially the first few years, but time has a way of healing things. I can talk about her now, and all of you should, too. She left quite the legacy in your class."

"We all loved your sister," Marybeth said.

"She was a great friend," Shooter said.

"Ok, now that we're all aware I'm dating Kimber's younger sister, I hope we can still be friends," Denton said more as a joke than anything. "Isn't she great?" Denton grabbed Tara and hugged her, almost squeezing the breath out of her. "Babe, why don't you run and grab me another beer and I'll be right over." He patted her on the butt as she turned and left. Denton turned back toward Shooter and Marybeth.

"Hard to believe, eh – Tara and me, together?" They just looked at him. "I know what you're thinking; it's what everybody's thinking. I'm trying to live out some high school fantasy, blah, blah, blah. It's bullshit! I think she's attractive and smart, and we have great sex."

"Whatever you say, Denton," Marybeth said. Nothing that came out of Denton's vile mouth was ever a shock to her.

"It's none of our business anyway," Shooter said.

"Damn rights it's not," Denton said, now bored with the conversation and looking back toward the direction of the open bar where he saw Tara holding up a large glass of beer with his name on it.

"Gotta go." He turned and started to walk toward the bar and then stopped. "Any sign of Cade?"

"Haven't seen him yet," Shooter said as he glanced at the entrance again. Denton nodded slightly and then walked away. "Always a pleasure seeing you, Denton," Shooter said sarcastically under his breath, taking another quick peek at his watch. "I wonder what's up with Cade?"

"I really wanted to see him," Marybeth said.

"I think everybody was looking forward to seeing him."

"Yeah, well, everyone liked him," Shooter replied. "But damn it, I was his best friend. I think it sucks that he doesn't have the decency to show up! Twenty years! This is the big one." Shooter was visibly upset, disappointed, and drunk – not necessarily in that order.

"Maybe he had a good excuse," Marybeth said.

"Yeah, probably the same one he used the last two reunions; he just doesn't give a shit about us." Shooter looked at his watch again. It was a minute later than the last time he looked. He got up and straightened his shirt. "I'm blowing this joint; want to join me?"

Marybeth looked around and noticed all her old drunk classmates hanging around, talking and laughing about the good times that had long since passed.

"What about Cade?" she said.

"Fuck Cade!" Shooter said. Marybeth wished she could retract the question. "Look, if he walked through that door right now, I'm afraid I'd punch him in the mouth." He tipped his beer can and drank it to the last drop.

"In that case, let's get out of here," Marybeth said. "I think you could use a friend right now. Where to?" Reaching down, Shooter grabbed her hand to help her up.

"Any place but here." They walked out the double set of doors and into the parking lot to his car. Like a gentleman, he followed her to the passenger side and opened the door for her. Once they were both in, he slipped the key into the ignition and gave it a quick turn. The engine roared as he pumped the gas.

"Nothing like the sound of a Camaro," he said, grinding it into gear. Slamming the pedal to the floor, he laid a 30-foot trench in the newly paved parking lot as they headed down the long, narrow dirt road toward the highway.

From a dark, secluded parking spot in the far corner of the lot, Cade watched them leave. His hair was neatly combed, he smelled of his favorite cologne, and he was wearing the new shirt and blue jeans Angie had surprised him with earlier that week just for this special night. Glancing at his watch, he pushed the button to illuminate the face… nearly midnight. He chugged the rest of his beer, started the car, and drove back into town.

Chapter 7

Early the next morning, both kids took turns quizzing their father about the dinner the night before. They asked him if he had a good time, if his old friends recognized him, and if he recognized them. They also asked him if Mr. Burk showed up and if any other teachers came to see some of their old students. Cade had rehearsed the answers in his mind time and time again while sucking back his six-pack by himself in the parking lot the night before. Unfortunately, what he told his kids was quite entertaining, but all lies.

The truth of the matter was that he drove into the lodge parking lot the night before with anticipation and excitement, but when he attempted to open the car door, it was as if it had been welded shut from the outside. He couldn't get his fingers to lift up on the handle; his heart began to race, and his forehead began to sweat. He was suddenly overcome with anxiety. Resolved to the reality that going into the building and rehashing painful memories of his high school days was not an option, he reclined the driver's seat and, for several hours, observed the festivities from the privacy of his rental car.

After breakfast, Cade decided to let the kids hang around the motel and swim while he spent the rest of the morning on his own. Since there were a few baseball teams and their families in town for a tournament, there were plenty of other kids in the pool to keep them company. Brit had already met another girl her age and was taking her to the front office to see all the souvenirs, specifically the Jackalope.

Zac had something else on his mind, and it wasn't baseball. His interest in girls was starting to become obvious. Apparently, a young girl had given him a little attention the evening before at the pool, and he decided that it might be a good idea to hang out as well, even if it was with his little sister.

Cade hugged the kids and set off down memory lane, this time alone. Driving over to the north side of town, he went down every street in his subdivision. It was like he was in a trance, reliving his childhood. He hadn't kept in contact with any of his classmates. He had left so suddenly that summer after his senior year that he hadn't had a chance to say goodbye to even some of his closest friends. That's just the way it was, and until now, Cade really hadn't given it much serious thought.

Driving toward his old high school, he turned into the side parking lot, bringing the car to a sudden stop just inches from the brick wall. He turned off the radio, rolled down the window, and just listened. He could swear he could hear his old classmates.

He got out of his car and walked toward the front of the

building beside the long stone wall that ran the entire length of the school property along Main Street. The wall was about waist high and over two feet thick and flat on top. Everyone in the school, during lunch breaks or when they skipped class, would sit on top of it and wave at all their friends who were driving by.

He continued to walk along the length of the wall and around the corner of the school to the back, where the football stadium was located. He sat quietly on the bleachers about midway up, listening for the cheers he was so used to hearing when he put on the pads and helmet.

He exited out the opposite gate and walked across the parking lot to the back doors of the school. He tried opening them, but they were locked. It would have been fun to peek into the gym where he used to play basketball, but that wasn't going to be possible. There wasn't another car in the parking lot, and judging by the weeds growing up through the numerous cracks in the asphalt, there hadn't been a car back there for quite some time. Pounding on the door would be pointless and surely the broken lock on the window he used to sneak through late at night with his friends so many years ago had been replaced.

He continued past the entrance to the music room and into the small courtyard that had a couple of rusty benches and several aspen trees whose leaves were fluttering in the breeze. While sitting on one of the benches, he was flooded with memories of study hall, which wasn't used much for studying. He and Kimber would slip out together and sit on this very bench and talk. It was some of his fondest memories of her. He thought for a moment and then stood up and walked toward one of the trees in the far back by the gas meter. Approaching the tree, he peeked around to the backmost side. It was as plain as day.

Cade and Kimber dated steadily up until the time Cade's father was killed their junior year. The tragic event was devastating to him, and instead of leaning on Kimber for comfort and support, he completely shut her out of his life. The separation went on well into their senior year until one morning in English class, Cade's favorite English teacher, Ms. Bronson, said something while discussing the tragic love story *Romeo and Juliet* that would forever change his life and how he looked at Kimber. It appeared as though Ms. Bronson hadn't said it intentionally, but Cade felt that her comments were directed solely toward him, and in the last half of his senior year, he and Kimber managed to get together and stay together through graduation.

They went to prom together. It was a wonderful day that started early that afternoon when he, Kimber, and several other couples packed a picnic and went for a short hike in the hills. The wildflowers were in bloom, and the clouds were large and fluffy. They talked, ate fried chicken, and laughed all that afternoon. When it was time, just he and

Kimber went to dinner in Hunter. That was the place to go. Reservations were required and Cade thought to make them even before he asked Kimber to the dance nearly a month prior. She looked beautiful in her formal gown. His mother helped pick out the corsage, and it matched perfectly.

The dance was spectacular. Since the theme was "Sailing," the gym had a large sailboat in the center. Dry ice was used to set the mood by imitating the waves of the sea with a dim light glowing inside the cabin. Cade was assigned to build the boat and he did so out of a wood frame and painted cardboard. He hesitantly accepted the challenge, knowing it would be difficult without his father's help, and wasn't sure how the final project would turn out.

In the past, he and his father had been engaged in many school projects together; it was something his father loved to do. It was a bittersweet moment for Cade as he walked into the gym with Kimber on his arm and saw the sailboat sitting in the middle of the dance floor, its mast tilted slightly with its blue and silver metallic sail glistening under the bright spotlights heading for brighter horizons. It was a secret tribute to his father, and that night, he could feel him there.

After dropping Kimber off at her home in the early hours of the morning and giving her a tender kiss good night, Cade drove to the back of the high school to this very tree to capture a moment in history. Under the dim light of the moon, he pulled out a knife and began to carve. Thirty minutes later, and with a few minor cuts on his fingers, he was finished.

Cade suddenly surfaced from his memory and looked down at the tree. He pressed his fingers into the grooves he had carefully carved over twenty years ago – "C+K" surrounded by a near-symmetrical heart.

Chapter 8

Cade arrived back at the motel shortly after noon to find Zac and Brit still swimming in the motel pool. There were several other kids of similar ages splashing and yelling along with them. As he pulled the car into the parking space, Brit, dripping wet, saw him and started to run toward the car.

"Daddy, did you have fun? What did you do for so long? We were worried about you." He picked her up, held her at arm's length, and then gave her a big kiss on the forehead.

"I can see you two really missed me," he said, smiling. "You still have chocolate ice cream on your face. Here, let me lick it off for you." He started to lick her face.

"No, Daddy!" Brit struggled to get away. "Come over to the pool and meet some of our friends." Running over to the poolside, she motioned for him to follow. "Hey, you guys, this is my Dad." The kids gave him a quick courtesy glance and continued to swim. Zac swam over, stood up, and cleared the water from his face.

"Hey, Dad, you'll never believe it. There's a real Indian powwow out on the reservation tonight. I think we should go."

Cade thought for a moment, realizing the reunion family picnic was later that evening, but apparently, the kids had forgotten all about it. As far as he was concerned, a powwow would be a lot more fun than a picnic with a bunch of kids they didn't even know and would never see again. The truth was, since he sat out in the parking lot the night before, he was even more embarrassed to show up for the picnic.

"How'd you find out about it?" Cade asked.

"Just heard some guy talking about it. It sounds fun."

"So what do you say, Dad? Can we go, please?" Brit said. "I haven't seen a *real* Indian since we got here."

"What do you mean, Brit? What about that guy we sat next to at the Tasty Craze? He was a real Indian. And that lady we saw at the gas station–"

"But you don't understand… a real Indian has feathers and beads and stuff. You know, like in the movies."

"That's a great idea; let's just go to the movies," Cade said. Brit and Zac just stood there with a blank stare. Then, finally, Zac said something.

"Dad, the only movie playing here we saw over a year ago. It's already on DVD. My vote's for the powwow."

"Me, too!" Brit said. "Looks like you lost, Dad."

"I guess so. Well, go get dried off and get dressed. You'll both need to wear long pants and bring a sweatshirt just in case it gets a little chilly. Once the sun goes down, the temperature drops 20 degrees."

"You sound just like Mom," Brit said.

It took them less than 30 minutes to get to the reservation town of Fort Washita. The powwow was in a field covered in long grass on the other side of town, just outside the city limits. People parked along the edge of the fence and in the field near the various tents and flags. There were hundreds of people walking from every direction. Cade looked around as he and the kids walked in the same direction as everyone else, not unlike a herd of sheep, realizing they were the only white people there. The kids noticed the same thing. They continued to walk until they reached the main center ring. This was the area where all the traditional dancing was to take place later.

The kids marveled at the beautifully colored Native attire for both the men and the ladies. Long, colorful feathers and beads were fastened skillfully to leather skirts, blouses, and pants. The headdresses were incredibly fashioned into heads of animals and other spirit-like creatures. Even many of the younger children were dressed up in native costumes.

The three of them walked from booth to booth, admiring all of the trinkets and paraphernalia offered for sale. Nothing had a price tag. Cade began to dicker with one of the ladies for a colorful necklace. He felt it would make a wonderful gift for Angie.

Meanwhile, caught up in the excitement, the two kids ventured over to the other booths. Contrary to their father's instructions, Zac went one way, and Brit eventually went another.

Brit walked under the canvas cover and began admiring several of the items. She walked over to a rack where a colorful native costume hung by a hanger. It came with a fancy headdress, feathered fan, and matching beaded moccasins. As she stood there admiring, touching, and wishing, a tall Indian gentleman approached her from behind. Standing stationary momentarily he then spoke to her in a deep voice.

"Hello." Brit, quite startled, quickly turned around toward the origin of the voice. "I'm sorry. I didn't mean to startle you." Brit just stood there, frozen in place. "I couldn't help but notice you looking at this costume. It's very pretty, isn't it?" Brit continued to look into his deep black eyes without a blink. He had a long, narrow face with a rather large nose. His hair was jet black, long, and pulled back into a ponytail. He was a little taller than her father, only this man was slightly less stocky.

"It's very pretty," she said. She took a step back from the man.

The Winds

"Would you like to try it on?" the man said. Brit nodded her head. The man turned around and began to talk in a low voice to a lady standing next to him. Brit couldn't understand what they were saying. The lady stepped around the man and approached Brit.

"You want to see how it looks on you?" the lady said. Brit nodded. Reaching up, the lady took it off the hanger and motioned for Brit to follow her to the very back of the tent. Slightly hesitant, Brit glanced back at the man.

"Go with her, it'll be OK," he said, giving her a reassuring smile.

"Will you tell my Dad where I am?" Brit said. "He's at one of the booths over there. He's not an Indian, and his name's Cade."

"Sure, I'll tell him. Now you just follow the nice lady and don't worry about a thing."

Brit turned and followed the lady without hesitation. She really wanted to try on the outfit. Even if her dad wouldn't buy it for her, at least he could get a picture of her to take back to her friends in Chicago. The two of them disappeared out the back of the tent through a long slit in the canvas panel. The man looked around and then disappeared into the crowd.

"Forty-five dollars is my last offer," Cade said. "Hey, I'll just go to the next booth and get one just like it for half the price." He folded his arms and tightened his chin.

"Then go," the lady said, slightly angered at this point. "You go and buy it and then bring it back and show me. If it's the exact same, I'll give you this one for free." The lady sat back on the stool and folded her arms. She knew Cade was bluffing. This necklace was a *one-of-a-kind* piece of jewelry. She had made it with great care, pride, and originality. Its design had been handed down from generation to generation exclusively within her family genes.

Cade let out a sigh and reached for his wallet. "Ok, forty-five bucks, and you got a deal," he said, conceding the match.

"Fifty," the lady said. "Or forty-five bucks and a kiss." She jumped from the stool and smiled her near-toothless smile. Cade looked at her, and they both started to laugh. He pulled out three $20 bills.

"I don't suppose you have any change." The lady flashed her toothless smile again. "Didn't think so. Just keep

The Winds

the change." He smiled, grabbed the necklace, and turned to go to the next booth when Zac approached him from behind.

"Dad, you should see the cool stuff over here," he said. "They have pipes, whistles, and keychains that look like roach clips." Cade looked at him curiously. "We're from Chicago, Dad, remember? Even I know what a roach clip is."

"But have never used one," Cade replied. "So, where's your sister?"

"I don't know. She was just here a minute ago." Zac pointed over near the main circle. "She's probably in one of those booths over there."

"I told you two not to wander off."

"I know, Dad, but–"

"But nothing! Come on." The two of them began to walk toward the circle when, all of a sudden, the drum started to beat a slow, soft cadence. *Thump, thump, thump, thump...* They continued to walk and look, but still no sign of Brit. Cade quickened his step as he entered in and out of the various booths. Finally, without any other choice, he began to yell with his hands cupped to his mouth.

David J. Bunnell

"Brittney! Brittney!" he yelled over and over as he literally paced around the main circle, glancing at each of the booths. Crowds of people started congregating at the edge of the circle and sat down on the benches. The drum cadence became quicker, and the amplitude louder. Cade and Zac had to shove their way past and through the hordes of people.

Suddenly, an old man stepped up onto the podium and spoke into the microphone. He spoke in his Shoshone native tongue as the crowd listened intently. Nearly forty people, dressed in their colorful Indian attire, entered the ring. There was a long silence.

On cue, the dancers began to dance as the drum, accompanied by various instruments and vocals, continued to beat. The dancers jumped, spun, and swayed to the beat, jostling around the ring, amazingly keeping a few feet distance between themselves and the others. It was a wonderful display of Indian tradition, but Cade and his son couldn't enjoy it. They continued their frantic search for Brit.

The same Indian man who arranged for Brit to try on the Indian costume approached the old man at the microphone and whispered something in his ear. With a quick wave of

The Winds

the old man's hand, the drum cadence abruptly stopped, and the dancers became still. An eerie hush came over the crowd. The old man approached the microphone and said a few words again in his native Indian tongue. Everyone turned and looked at Cade and Zac. In turn, they stopped for a moment and looked around at all the people staring at them. The audience erupted in laughter as the crowd of dancers separated in the middle, allowing little Brittney to walk slowly into view. She jingled as she walked with the numerous bells attached to her beaded moccasins, and the feathers on her fancy headdress drooped over her eyes. The crowd started cheering as she ran into her father's open arms.

"I thought I'd lost you, Brit," Cade said as he hugged her close to his chest. "Don't you ever do that again? You scared me."

"I'm sorry, Daddy. I saw this costume, and there was a nice Indian man, and this lady helped me try it on in the back of the tent. I told him to go find you, and he said he would. Didn't he find you, Daddy?" Brit said. "Really, I told him to tell you." Cade shook his head.

"Nobody told me anything, Brit. How many times have I told you not to talk to strangers?" Suddenly, the Indian man approached Cade from behind.

"That's the man," Britney said, releasing her tight hold around her father's neck. Cade, lowering her down, stood up slowly. He turned around and began studying the man's face. Without warning, the man doubled his fist and hit Cade in the jaw, sending him tumbling to the ground. After a moment of clearing his head, Cade looked up at the unforgiving black eyes behind the solemn face.

"Shooter, is that you?" he said. Feeling a warm trickle down his chin, Cade brought his hand to his mouth, pressed gently, and looked at his open hand. Blood ran around his spread fingers and dripped onto the grass. "You son of a bitch! Why did you do that?" Cade said as he slowly lifted himself from the ground.

A slight smile came over the man's face as he stepped closer to Cade and embraced him. He slowly leaned into Cade's ear and whispered. "Twenty years—not even a postcard." He began to laugh as he offered his hand in friendship. The crowd that had gathered in hopes that the pale face would return a punch groaned with disappointment and dispersed back around the dancing ring. Suddenly, the drum began its slow, familiar cadence.

Chapter 9

Later that evening, the sun began to set behind the butte, turning the scattered clouds a bright orange, and the temperature became slightly cool. Cade and the kids decided to leave the powwow early and spend some time with Shooter at his place, a small portion of acreage at the edge of the foothills. Shooter shared the place with his father and eight horses. Cade and the kids followed closely behind as Shooter led the way down the narrow dirt road. Brit stuck her head up between Cade and Zac from the back seat.

"So, Shooter, he's a real Indian, right?" she said.

"He's as real as it gets," Cade replied. "Both his father and mother are pure Shoshone. He's lived out here on the reservation as long as I can remember."

"That's so cool, Dad. Your best friend's an Indian," Zac said. "Do you think he's ever shot a buffalo?"

"No, but I've seen him shoot six three-pointers in a row during a basketball game. The guy was incredible… never got tired."

"I hear Indians can run for a long, long time. It's probably from back when they used to chase buffalo," Brit said.

"What is it with you two and buffalo?" Cade said. "They did a lot more than just chase buffalo around."

"Yeah, they used to spend a lot of time dancing for rain," Brit said.

Cade followed Shooter up the long drive and stopped near the edge of the front yard. After getting out of their car, Zac and Brit immediately ran across the grass to the edge of the fence to see the horses. Cade sat down on the front porch while Shooter entered the house and returned with two chilled cans of beer. They enjoyed the evening's sunset while Brit and Zac explored the various corrals.

"This is a beautiful spread you got here, Shooter," Cade said. "You've really done well for yourself."

"Not bad, but not as well as you, I hear."

"What did you hear?"

"You're some kind of doctor making all kinds of money living back East somewhere in a big fancy house, driving a fast sports car and–"

"Hold on, Shooter. Where'd you hear all this?"

"People talk, you know, at the reunions and stuff." Shooter turned and looked at Cade. "You know all those reunions you haven't been to?" Cade could sense Shooter's disappointment and had to change the subject.

"Hey, Zac!" Cade yelled. "Be careful out there."

"I'm just feeding a horse!" Zac yelled back.

"Keep your hand flat. They can't taste the difference between hay and your fingers."

"Oh, Dad."

"Nice try, Cade," Shooter continued, "but you have some explaining to do. So, where were you last night?"

"I was there. Way to leave a patch in the parking lot."

"You were out there? Why didn't you come in?"

Cade looked down to the splintered porch. "I just couldn't face it. I tried, but when it came down to it, I couldn't go in."

"Same reason you came to the rez tonight instead of the picnic?"

"Well, that and my kids wanted to see a real Indian."

"I hope I didn't disappoint them. So you're leaving tomorrow, huh?"

"Yeah, need to get back to work. I've seen all I need to see."

"So if I hadn't kicked your ass, you'd got on that plane without looking me up?"

Cade grew tired of the conversation. It was apparent to him that Shooter really didn't comprehend the difficulty he was experiencing returning to Lorenz.

"Shooter, that's not a fair question," he said. "First of all, let me get something straight with you." Cade sat up and pointed his finger. "You didn't kick my ass, ok? You snuck in a quick sucker punch. I didn't go to the powwow tonight to get into a fight." He reached down, picked up his beer, and took another gulp in an attempt to calm himself. "You're probably right. I wouldn't have looked you up, but you need to understand, there are too many memories here. Just driving around town about does me in. One minute, I feel like I'm in heaven, and then the next, I feel like I'm a step past the gates of hell." Cade stopped rocking and bent over with his elbows on his knees. He stared steadily at a cat as it brushed against the inside of his leg. "I can't control it. It's too painful. I want to forget, but I can't, no matter how hard I try, I just can't forget."

"You're talking about Kimber, aren't you?" Shooter said. "That was a long time ago. A lot's happened since then. You got a wife and kids. You're a doctor. Let her go, dude;

it wasn't your fault."

There was momentary silence. This was the first time in twenty years that Cade had heard a voice from his past mention Kimber's name.

"So she's the reason you didn't come in last night?"

Cade slowly nodded his head.

"I don't sleep at night. This reunion thing triggers something inside my head. I thought maybe coming to one would help me find a way to deal with her death."

"So you been up there? Mirror Falls, man, you hiked up there yet?"

Suddenly, Cade's expression changed, and he looked straight ahead. "No. I thought about it, but I can't do it. When I get on the plane tomorrow, I'm leaving this place behind me for good. My kids have never seen where I've grown up; now they have an end to a chapter."

"So that's it? One quick trip back after twenty years, go through the motions, and make everything all better. Is that what you think? Did you think that facing your fears and coming to grips with your past was going to come without a price?" Shooter reached over, grabbed Cade's shoulder, and looked him straight in the eye. "You have to face it head-on, or this trip is in vain."

"Since when did you become the expert? You have no idea. The only reason I came back is because my shrink told me to."

"A shrink? Oh, that's right, I forgot. Big city hot shots, they all see a shrink."

"That's right. He said coming back to Lorenz is the only way I can stop the anxiety."

"So it's all about Kimber's death?"

"He didn't come right out and say it, but that's what I think. Something about the tip of the iceberg. I'll have a couple of follow-up sessions when I go back to Chicago."

"I'm not a shrink and don't claim to know anything about that shit, but when are you going to face yourself? You're not responsible. You didn't kill her. It was an accident. Nobody blames you. I think you took the first excuse to get away from here so you wouldn't have to face it ever again in your life."

"That's not true!" Cade leaped up from his chair and threw his can of beer in the middle of the grassy yard, spraying foam in every direction. "My mother moved away from here. She couldn't stay here alone. I had plans to go to college and there was nothing left for her here. Everything she had, she lost when my Dad died. Don't you understand? There was nothing for me to come back to, nothing." Cade paused to catch his breath. "My Dad died, Shooter, remember? We felt the windows shake?" Cade leaned over the handrail, and Shooter stood up and joined him.

"I do remember. How could I forget? Whether you're eight years old or thirty-eight, it still hurts. My mom died last summer. God, I miss her smile, and my father's never been the same since she passed away. She was his life."

"I'm sorry, Shooter. I didn't know. I'm sorry I haven't kept in touch." Shooter nodded and then looked out to the horizon to the foothills in the distance.

"My father's up there. Been two weeks tomorrow."

"He's up in the Winds? Why aren't you with him?"

"Once a year, he makes a trip for the Tribe. As the head of the Indian Counsel, he's required to do it."

"Head of the Counsel? Your Dad's the chief?"

"Been for nearly twenty years. He says he goes up there to cleanse his spirit and to renew his physical body, but this time, he had another, maybe even more important, reason to go."

"What's that?"

"To be closer to his wife." They were silent momentarily as they looked at the now darkened sky filled with countless sparkles of light hovering over the Winds. Zac and Brit were now starting to make their way out of the pasture to the house.

"So when's he due back?" Cade asked.

"Middle of next week."

Cade thought for a moment. "Maybe I could extend my trip by a few days; I'm sure the kids wouldn't mind. Look at them; who would have thought an old barn would be so much fun for a couple of big-city kids? I'd really like to see him again. I remember him coming to watch you play basketball. He was sure a proud Dad."

"Times were simple back then, weren't they? As long as I had a basketball and a date for Friday night, I was happy."

Cade put his arm around him. "Doesn't get any more simple than that. Tell you what, I really need to get back tomorrow, but maybe I and the kids can come back next summer."

"Let me get this straight. You hate this place and can't

wait to get back to Chicago, but now you're thinking of coming back next summer? Why the sudden change of heart?"

"Well, I kind of already promised the kids I'd take them into the Winds. You're a guide; you can take us?"

Just then, Zac and Brit sprinted across the front lawn and climbed onto the porch.

"This place is cool," Zac said.

"Yeah, I wish we could live here with Shooter," Brit said. She picked up the cat and started to rub it between the ears.

"Good luck with your mother on that one," Cade replied, smiling.

"Why don't you kids go in the house and get you something to drink," Shooter said. "The remote's on the table next to the recliner. You ought to see if there's anything good on TV." The kids turned and ran into the house. "And, Zac, stay away from my beer."

"They grow up so fast," Cade said. He grabbed Shooter by the shoulder. "You seem to know a little about me and what I've been doing for the last twenty years; how about you? What have you been doing with yourself?"

"Well, I didn't make it to the NBA, if that's what you're wondering. I played both years at Central Wyoming Community College and then joined the Army."

"Seriously? You served in the Army?"

"Four years. I got home, met someone, and got married. We had two kids, and then she left me."

"What happened?"

"I was a jerk. A while back, the reservation approved gambling. They said it would give a boost to the local economy. Well, it has, but it ruined my life. I lost nearly everything. It's a disease, you know. At least that's what the shrink said."

"And you've been giving me crap about seeing a shrink?"

"Hey, only a few sessions. And it wasn't by choice; it was part of my probation."

"So have you quit?"

"I haven't gambled or drank the hard stuff in nearly six years and don't desire to either. Gambling and drinking cost me everything."

"So, how often do you get to see your kids?"

"Almost never. They live in New Mexico. I've only seen them a few times since they left. The ex-wife trashes me behind my back. She's remarried. I guess their new Dad treats them pretty good. A lot better than I did."

"Don't be so hard on yourself. You just made some bad choices."

"You can say that again."

"So why probation? Gambling's legal on the reservation."

"Oh, on the way home from one of my binges, I got pulled over by Deputy Dickhead."

"Deputy Dickhead? Who's that?"

"Think back to high school. Who was the biggest dickhead you knew?"

Cade thought for a moment, and then the light went on in his head. "Son of a bitch, Denton, Denton Bauer, right? You're shitin' me. Denton Bauer's a cop?"

"He's one of the Deputy Sheriffs. Basically, he's an asshole with a badge. Anyway, I lied and told him I hadn't been drinking, but he didn't believe me. I barely failed the breath test, and he threw the book at me. He was ruthless. He waited until I was nearly home to pull me over. He had the flashing lights, siren, the works, anything to wake the wife up. She came down the lane and was all pissed and making a scene. It was embarrassing. Just like Dickhead wanted it to be."

"What an ass."

"She and the kids picked up and left while I was spending some time in jail. She wrote me last year after Mom died. She was really close to her, but she didn't come to the funeral. I've been here with my parents ever since that day. Pitiful, isn't it? Well, now you know a little too much about my life, but you asked. I often wonder how it would have turned out if she'd just given me a second chance."

Shooter stretched as he looked at the nighttime sky. "Well, no sense dwelling on the past. Let's go into the house; there's something I want to show you and the kids before you leave."

Shooter opened the front screen door and allowed Cade to enter before him. Both Zac and Brit were inside the family room looking at the various Indian crafts that decorated both the walls and the tables.

"Shooter has something he wants to show us," Cade said.

Brit put the small colorful blanket back on the recliner

armrest, and both she and Zac sat next to each other on the couch facing the rock fireplace. Cade sat next to them. Shooter grabbed the poker and stirred the red-hot coals. He placed a small log on the fire, and within moments, the orange flames began to shoot high above the logs, crackling and popping.

"I know what all of you are thinking: why have a fire in the middle of the summer, right?" Shooter said. "My father's in the Winds right now on a trip that he makes every year around this time. It's been a tradition in our family to keep a fire burning from the time he leaves until the time he returns home."

Brit was excited. She grabbed her father's hand. The bright flames flickered on their faces as they watched Shooter intently. He reached up to the mantle, grabbed a long earthen pot – fired with various bright colors – and sat down on the stone hearth in front of them. He removed the lid and started to pull something out. Brit's eyes widened as her anticipation grew.

"Do you know what this is?" he asked.

"It's a feather," Brit said.

"A feather, yes, but what kind of feather?"

"A turkey feather?" Zac said.

Shooter lowered his eyebrows and looked over at Cade. Cade, embarrassed, shrugged his shoulders.

"Close. It's an eagle feather. Golden Eagles fly over the Winds, protecting them with their strength and blessing them with their wisdom." Shooter stroked his finger down the length of the stiff spines. "As you wander the mountains, occasionally, you'll find an eagle feather. This means that the Great Spirit is watching you through their eyes."

"Whose eyes?" Brit asked.

"The eyes of an eagle. When you go into the Winds, you'll feel their presence. It's a strong feeling, a special feeling, and you don't want it to ever leave." Shooter paused for a moment. "Your Dad tells me you're going home tomorrow, and I understand. But I've told your father that he's welcome to come back here at any time; my teepee is always open to my friends. Next summer, I'd like to take all of you to the Winds so you can feel the power of the Great Spirit." Brit's eyes lit up. "So what do you think? Would you like to come with me to the Winds?"

"Yes, yes, we do!" Brit said.

"But what about Mom?" Zac said.

"If you can convince her to come, she's welcome," Shooter said. He pulled the feather the rest of the way out of the pot.

"Wow, that's beautiful," Brit said.

"What's that shiny gold stuff on the end?" Zac said.

"Legend has it that it's pure Wind River gold," Shooter said. "Purer than is found anywhere on Earth. It's a special gold that the Great Spirit has hidden to be used by men of faith." The children looked at him curiously.

"Men of faith?" Zac said. Shooter cleared his throat and took a deep swallow.

"It's Indian legend that the Great Spirit has hidden a deposit of gold in the Wind River Mountains. It's somewhere behind the great waterfall that is swallowed up by the mountain."

"We've seen that," Zac said. "We saw it yesterday. We fed the fish and everything."

"You were at Deep Canyon. The waterfall I'm talking about rises above the tree tops, and when the water hits the bottom, it disappears as if no water has fallen."

"Wow," Brit said. "Do you know where it is?"

"Yeah, can you take us to it next summer?" Zac said.

"Now, kids, don't get too excited," Cade said. "We still have to talk Mom out of going to Hawaii next summer."

"And miss the gold?" Zac said. Shooter held the feather straight up between his fingers and twirled it slowly in front of their eyes. The gold glistened in the light of the fire behind him.

"This feather has been dipped in the gold of that Great Spirit. My father gave it to me when I was a child. He told me it would bring me peace throughout my life." He reached over and set it on Brit's lap. She twirled it between her fingers.

"It's beautiful. Can I keep it?" Brit said. Cade looked at her sternly.

"No, you can't keep it, Brit. You heard him. His father gave it to him." Shooter sat back with a comforting smile.

"She can keep it, Cade. It's my gift to all of you. By coming here, you've blessed me and my house. These few short hours have meant a lot to me. I want you to take this feather and remember what it represents. I want you to display it proudly, not in some cold, worthless pot like I've done over the years. Display it for all to see. It will serve as a reminder that life is worth living and full of hope and meant to be happy."

The Winds

Moments later, they all stood up. Cade and Shooter shook hands and then hugged, knowing that they had rekindled a long-lost friendship. Shooter followed them out to their car.

As the two kids were fighting over the front seat, Shooter pulled Cade aside and whispered in his ear.

"I'm serious, Cade. To make this trip really count, you need to take the time to go," he said softly. "Tomorrow morning, get up before the rooster crows and face your fears head-on."

Chapter 10

The next morning couldn't have come soon enough for Cade. The neon motel sign buzzed softly and cast an orange glow through the thin curtains across the room. He couldn't sleep and even had trouble closing his eyes. He watched the second hand sweep across the dimly lit face of the cheap clock on his nightstand.

He was haunted by Shooter's last words and tried desperately to forget them, but Shooter was right, and Cade knew it. Was it a coincidence that he met up with Shooter the way he did, or was it something that had to be? These questions kept echoing through his mind repeatedly throughout the night. But there was one thing he could not deny: He had to face his fears. As difficult as it may be, it was something he was strongly compelled to do.

He rolled over and glanced at the clock. It was just after five. He figured he could slip on some clothes and be at the trailhead in less than twenty minutes and another quick hour to Mirror Falls. The kids wouldn't have any problem sleeping for another three hours, considering there weren't any police sirens, horns, or anything else associated with Chicago that would wake them in this small, sleepy town. He left them a short note but sensed he'd probably arrive back at the hotel before they even woke up.

The Winds

The streets were clear this time of morning. The few traffic lights down Main Street were still flashing yellow. Driving West down Main, he took a left on Ninth Street in the direction of Deep Canyon and eventually Mirror Falls. He drove past the Junior High and various small housing developments to the edge of town, passing the familiar sign stating that Deep Canyon was five miles ahead. Suddenly, he pulled his car to the side of the road and then stopped. Gripping the steering wheel tightly, he began to gasp for air. His hands and face began to sweat, and his heart started to race.

"I can't do this!" he shouted as he slammed his hands down on the top of the steering wheel. "Damn it, I just can't do it!"

Twenty years hadn't been nearly long enough to erase the tragic events that happened that day in early August. As he struggled to regain his breath, he turned the car around and retraced his course back to the motel. As he drove, his heart rate started to slow down, and his breathing became less intense, but he realized that he'd lost sight of what he was supposed to accomplish by returning to Lorenz. He'd been going through the motions, but because of the lack of courage, he had yet to tax his inner soul.

Doctor Morrison claimed that this trip was only the tip of the iceberg and if he didn't fully exploit and expose all of the painful past events of his life, his trip would be in vain, and that "tip" would sink into the dark depths of his memory patiently waiting for an opportunity to rise to the surface again. He couldn't allow that to happen. If revisiting Mirror Falls was an impossibility, he would have to resort to an alternative plan.

He continued East on Main Street, passing the entrance to the motel, past the old grain elevator, across the Popo Agie river bridge, and up the hill. The Catholic Church stood prominently on the horizon. It was located a little over a mile out of town, with hay fields and trees on one side and the town cemetery on the other. It was a beautiful church, and if his childhood memory was correct, it was just as pretty on the inside.

The road into the cemetery was just past the main road leading to the church. Cade turned left off the two-lane highway and onto the narrow paved road to the huge cluster of trees a quarter mile away. The cemetery was large and spacious, with plenty of room to grow. The history sealed up in the headstones could tell the story of a town that had its share of good times and bad.

Cade parked the car next to the edge of the trees and began searching for a few of the landmarks. The cemetery had changed so much he could scarcely remember them. He began to walk, and as he did so, his memory became clearer.

The Winds

He could visualize in his mind a large black polished stone ball on the top of a gravestone. It was a prominent marker, at least it used to be. Locating that grave would place him within the area he desired if he could just find that one marker.

He stooped down momentarily and picked a handful of beautiful wildflowers. They would hardly bridge the gap in time from his last visit until now, but it was the best he could do. He clutched the stems tight within his fist.

Suddenly, the large polished black ball came into view over the tops of all the other gravestones. As he walked nearer, his heart began to beat faster and faster, and the palms of his hands began to sweat. Like a flash, vivid pictures of that day began to shoot through his mind as if it had happened just the day before.

The same sorrow, pain, and remorse had returned to him. He became short of breath and seriously doubted if he could continue, but his legs continued to move as if to defy his mind's commands to halt and retreat to the waiting car.

What good could come of it? Kimber couldn't be brought back from the dead, nor could this foolish visitation make it any easier to accept. He was happily married, had two beautiful children, and lived a life many could only dream of living.

Why would what happened over twenty years ago cause so much turmoil in his life? He persistently tried to convince himself not to continue as he walked closer to the white marble cross. Wiping a tear from his eye, he hesitated to look beyond the cross but did.

Tears immediately flowed from his eyes and down his flushed cheeks as he gained a glimpse of the hallowed ground. As he bent down to the headstone, he placed the flowers just under her name and bathed them with his tears. For only a brief moment, he saw her beautiful face in his mind's eye.

"Oh, God, why?" he cried into the stillness of the early morning. Clinching his fists, he pressed them against the cold polished marble. "God, why did you take her from me? Why did she have to die?" The moment was nearly unbearable. As he cried, the memory of those last moments flashed vividly through his mind.

It was mid-July. Kimber straddled the gearshift to sit as close to Cade as possible as he drove them from Lorenz up the two-lane highway to Deep Canyon State Park. In less than an hour and a half, Cade and Kimber would climb nearly a thousand feet in elevation on a well-beaten mountain trail lined with sheer granite cliffs on one side and the Popo Agie River on the other.

The sun-faded pickup truck headed up the canyon,

passed the various campsites, and crossed the lodge pole pine bridge.

Cade put his hand between Kimber's legs, grabbed the gearshift, and began shifting down to a complete stop in the parking lot located at the trailhead. A large cloud of dust engulfed the vehicle for a moment as the two of them waited for it to pass with the gentle breeze.

"Well, we're here," Cade said as he opened his side of the truck. "You've been a little quiet on the ride up here, Kimber. Is there a problem?"

She looked at him with those vivid green eyes. They were eyes that could melt a young boy, and Cade found himself enslaved to their beauty. She didn't reply.

"Hey, once you take a look at Mirror Falls, it'll bring a smile to your face. It always has in the past," Cade said. He grabbed her hand as she slid under the steering wheel and exited out the driver's side door with him.

"I've been thinking about some things, you know, about us," Kimber said. "Now that we've graduated from high school, where do we go from here?"

"What do you mean? We're both going to college."

"But different colleges," she said.

"You worry too much. College isn't going to affect our relationship. It's not like we're moving away. There's Thanksgiving break, Christmas vacation, and even Spring break, and we can get back together." Cade traced a heart in the dust that covered the side panel of the truck.

"I do worry. I just don't want to lose you, that's all. I don't buy into that 'distance makes the heart grow fonder.'"

Cade could tell something was really bothering Kimber. He could see it in her eyes, but things would be fine once he got her up to Mirror Falls. He had planned this moment since graduation.

It was a gorgeous, slightly overcast day with hardly a breeze. They saw only one other person on the trail, and he was heading back down with his dog, sniffing all the rocks and wildflowers as it trotted closely behind him.

"Mirror Falls are spectacular," the man commented as he passed by them with his walking staff. "Unusually high water for this time of year, though. Even the other side has water."

"Hey, that's great," Cade said. "You pass any other people on the trail?"

"Nope, you're the only ones I've seen since this morning. Actually, it's better that way. I make this hike once a week in the summer to escape people, but since words gotten out, I have seen a lot more tourists."

"It is a beautiful hike," Kimber said. "You can't fault people for wanting to come."

"That's true, I guess, but I moved to this town thirty years ago because I liked the serenity. I just don't want to lose that." The man nodded his head and continued past them but quickly turned to them and said, "Be careful, kids. The water's really coming over the rocks."

Kimber turned back and smiled, and when she turned back around to continue up the trail, Cade leaned over and kissed her.

"What was that for," Kimber said.

"Just because I wanted to."

He grabbed her hand, and they continued up the trail past huge rock formations and sheer cliffs with various shades of red, orange, and brown swirling along the face. The sun was high in the sky, and a breeze started to stir the leaves as they rolled down the canyon.

Finally, it was in view. It was the last steep surge up the trail before reaching Mirror Falls. The sites along the way were a mere pittance compared to what was offered just over the next ridge. Nature had been cruel, though. It didn't give even a single glimpse, rumble, or spray of mist until crossing over the final ridge. To see Mirror Falls, you had to earn it.

Kimber was the first to cross over the ridge. Cool mist caused every exposed part of her body to tingle. They stood with both arms stretched wide and their eyes closed to experience the feel of it. Then, they opened their eyes. The experience was beautifully breathtaking, and for a split second, she had completely forgotten the painful secret she had been concealing for the last three months from almost everyone, including Cade.

Holding tightly to each other's hands, they continued to climb near the top. Small off-shoots of water tumbled over their fingers and feet as they felt for the next hold.

She's the one, Cade confirmed to himself as he helped Kimber to the next level of rocks. I'm going to ask her to marry me. Not that the wedding will be tomorrow, but after a year or two of college, we'll tie the knot if we can wait that long. He got goosebumps just thinking about it. He'd known the girl next door all his life, and today, in a matter of minutes, he'd ask her to marry him. He just knew she'd say yes. Was he worried about losing her once they took off to college? Not if she wore his ring on her finger.

The anticipation was killing him. Being helplessly drawn in by her temptress's eyes, he nearly blurted the question when they stopped to rest, but he caught himself. The question would be asked when they were at the top of Mirror Falls, not only at the top but in their spot. It was a spot just between the two waterfalls they had been to numerous times before. It was the spot where the two of them first kissed over four years ago.

"That old guy was right," Kimber said just as they reached the top. "There's water coming over the second shoot."

"But it's not much. We can cross it." Cade jumped to the next rock. He turned and stretched out his hand, waiting for Kimber to cross. She was hesitant to move toward him.

"I don't think this is a good idea. The rocks are slick."

"Come on, Kimber. You can do it. It's a cinch. You saw me do it without any problem, didn't you? Just grab my hand."

Kimber looked at the tumbling water smashing against the rocks on its downward journey to the turbulent pool below. She licked her lips, looked up at Cade, and smiled faintly. There wasn't anything she wouldn't do for him. Easing forward and then back a few times as if in a cadence, she finally leaped toward Cade's open hand. He grabbed her hand tightly mid-flight and pulled her to the rock.

"See, Kimber, you can trust me. This next rock's easier. "It's no problem. Just jump like you did the last time." With that last remark, he jumped to the next rock with ease.

Kimber seemed to be more at ease this time but was worried about how she would fare getting back over once Cade revealed his little surprise. "Just tell me what it is. We're close enough."

"Just one more rock, and we're there. Come on, Kimber, it's important to me."

Again, she looked down through the mist. She bit her bottom lip and looked back up at him, pleading with her eyes not to cross. She could sense the importance of what Cade was trying to do, but at the same time, the secret she was keeping weighed heavy on her mind. "Cade, there's something I have to tell you. It's important that you know."

"What's that?" Cade said. "You need to jump over here so I can hear you." Kimber faked a smile.

Standing at the edge of the rock, she swung her arms forward and jumped. Cade stretched his hand out to grab her, but as he reached out, his front foot slipped. He grasped her hand tightly but stood precariously, trying to regain his balance. Kimber was able to plant one foot on the rock, but her other foot got swallowed up in the fast-moving water.

"Cade, I'm slipping!" The water beat against her foot and spun her around. She slid off the rock and dangled from his grasp.

"Hold on, Kimber! Hold on!" He lunged toward her and grabbed for her other hand. "Give me your other hand. Please, Kimber, give me your other hand."

Kimber's face was hammered by the strong passing current. She tried desperately to breathe. Reaching frantically through the strong current into the air, she swiped her hand back and forth, hoping Cade would grab it. He caught a glimpse as it passed and plunged his hand into the water.

"Oh, God, no! God, no!" Cade screamed into the thick mist as he felt his grip begin to loosen. "Kimber, hold on to my hand! Oh, God, don't let this happen! Don't let this happen!" Cade screamed over and over as he plunged his hand into the cold water to help secure his grip when suddenly he felt her hand slip from his. She fell helplessly, crashing against the rocks below. Cade immediately stood up and leaped from rock to rock until he reached the turbulent pool below.

He combed the shoreline, hoping she'd survived the fall, and made it to the bank, but there was no Kimber. He stood there for several minutes pleading with God to stop time and rewind it to where Kimber was safe. Rewind time to when he nearly asked her to marry him, and she'd have said yes. His pain was so deeply felt that he pleaded with God to continue to rewind time so that he'd never been born.

Cade came out of his sudden trance, soaked in his own tears. His cheek was against the polished face of the headstone, and his hands grasped the upper corners. He was weak. It was an experience that he had never fully accepted and never fully healed.

Within weeks of Kimber's death, Cade and his mother moved away. The loss of her husband the previous year had literally devastated them, and with the loss of Kimber, it was much more than the two of them could bear. To this day, she has never returned to her husband's grave or to the home where she had nurtured her only child. Cade, at this excruciating moment, wished he could say the same.

"Goodbye, Kimber," he mumbled as he bid her farewell for the last time. He kissed his fingers and pressed them to her name. He rose to his feet and took in a deep breath. Before flying back to Chicago, he had one more grave to visit that morning.

A lot had happened to him since his father died. He had become a successful doctor and married a lovely, caring woman who had given him two wonderful children. The reuniting of a father and a son was long overdue.

The Winds

He looked around for the other marker that would point him in the direction of his father's grave. A feeling of peace came over him. He could feel his father's presence. For once in his life, he felt free from his inner pain and turmoil, but if this was truly just the tip of the iceberg, he questioned how long this feeling would last.

Chapter 11

It wasn't his intent, but Cade had spent the better part of the morning visiting both Kimber's and his father's graves and knew that if he didn't hurry, he and the kids would miss their flight. Returning to the motel, he found Brit and Zac waiting for him in the lobby with their suitcases on the floor next to them.

"Where have you been, Dad? We were starting to worry," Brit said. She ran over and gave him a big hug.

"The room's all cleaned out. We brought all of the suitcases down, so all you need to do is check out," Zac said. "I would have done that, too, but the man says you have to be the one to sign." Cade rushed over to the counter. The man behind the counter hit a button, and the charges for the room started to print.

"Thanks for getting things packed up, kids. It took a lot longer than I thought. I, uh, well, I had some things I had to do this morning."

The man tore off several pages and slipped them to Cade across the counter. "I assume you want to keep it on your American Express," the man said. Cade nodded as he scribbled his name on the bottom line.

The Winds

"What kind of things, Daddy?" Brit asked. "How come you didn't wake us up so we could come with you?"

Cade glanced down at her momentarily and then looked back up at the man behind the counter. "Thanks, it was a great stay. Maybe we'll come back here next year." The old man smiled. "Sorry, Brit, I can't answer you right now. We really need to hurry."

The three of them grabbed the suitcases and rushed out the door. Cade pushed the button to open the trunk.

"I figure we can still make our flight if we hurry." They threw the luggage into the trunk and slammed the lid tight. "Remember, seat belts save lives," Cade said, as he always did whenever they got into a car, then pulled out on Main Street and headed out of town. They crossed the bridge, drove up the big hill, and quickly veered into the turning lane to make a left just as the turn arrow changed from yellow to red. The rental car came to a screeching halt.

"Damn it!" Cade said as he hit the top of the steering wheel with the palm of his hand. Realizing what he'd done, he looked over at Zac, who was sitting next to him in the front seat.

"Dad, you OK?" Zac said. Cade looked away from him and then focused in on the rearview mirror and saw his daughter, who was sitting in the back seat looking back at him.

"I'm sorry, kids, this morning was very emotional for me," he said. "There's a lot I've been dealing with, and you two are just too young to understand. Right now, the most important thing is that we get on the plane."

After several flow changes in traffic, the green arrow illuminated. Cade made the turn and accelerated to 63 miles per hour on the state highway, which was posted at 55. No State Trooper in his right mind would pull a guy over for only eight miles over the speed limit. This was Wyoming. Towns were few and far between and you could see for miles.

Starting the gradual descent into Hunter, Cade suddenly realized he should've started to slow down from the top of the hill. Just as he began to apply the brake, he noticed a white police car parked behind an old pile of wood just as they passed.

"Damn," Cade mumbled again.

"Geez, Dad," Brit said from the back. "You have a potty mouth today."

Cade ignored his daughter's attempt to lighten the mood and continued to look into his rearview mirror.

The Winds

"Don't pull out, don't pull out," he said.

"What's wrong, Dad?" Brit said.

"Crap! He's pulling out," Cade said. Zac looked back and could see the red and blue flashing lights.

"Dad's busted," he said in a confirming tone. Cade glared in his direction.

"This isn't the time, Zac."

"But if we miss this flight, we can always catch the next one."

Cade continued to glare at his son and then looked into the rearview mirror as the police car approached closer.

"There are no other flights. This isn't O'Hare; we're leaving out of Redding Community Airport." Cade let out a burst of air in his frustration. "And it couldn't have come at a worse time either. We have ten minutes with this cop, or we'll miss our flight." Applying the brake, Cade pulled to the side of the road. The police car pulled behind him and turned the siren off but left the lights flashing.

Cade noticed the car wasn't a State Trooper or a Lorenz Police car. The large green lettering on the side of the car indicated it belonged to the Fremont County Sheriff's Department. The officer got out of his car, put on his black cowboy hat and mirrored aviator sunglasses, and proceeded to walk toward the car. Cade watched his every move in the rearview mirror while Zac fished around in the glove compartment for the car's registration. Cade rolled down the window.

"Good morning, Sir," the officer said.

"Good morning, Officer," Cade replied, then purposely glanced at his watch.

"May I see your driver's license and registration for the vehicle, please?" Looking up at him briefly, Cade put his driver's license and whatever papers Zac gave to him in the Officer's hand.

"Officer, if you don't mind, could you please just do whatever you have to do? We're in a hurry.

"Ya, I could tell," the officer said.

"Really," Cade shot back without hesitation, "We need to catch a flight."

"Oh, so you're on your way out, huh? This will only take a few minutes." Cade just looked at him. The officer walked back to his car.

"Dad, he's got muscles in his cheeks," Zac said very seriously.

The Winds

"He looks like a superhero," Brit chimed in. Cade managed to smile with Brit's humor.

"It's tough being a cop in Lorenz," Cade replied. "It helps if you have superpowers."

"Yeah, right, Dad," Zac said. "I'm sure it's ten times worse than Chicago." After less than two minutes, the officer returned.

"Is everything in order, Officer?" Cade said with anticipation. "Can we go now?"

"Sir, I need you to get out of the car and follow me."

"What for?"

"Just come with me," the officer said.

"I'm from out of town, Chicago, actually. Hey, eight miles over the speed limit. Please, if you're going to give me a ticket, just give it to me, and I'll pay for it through the mail. I told you we're in a hurry."

"I'm sorry, Mr. Hobbs, but this doesn't have anything to do with you speeding. If you could please follow me to my car, I'll try to get this taken care of in short order."

Cade let out a big sigh, unbuckled his seat belt, and got out of the car.

"Kids, I'll be back in a minute. This kind officer has something he needs to talk to me about."

Cade and the officer walked back to the car and got in. The officer then spoke. "So, how did you like our nice little community? Probably a lot different than Chicago."

"I like it well enough," Cade said. "But in all seriousness, I don't have much time to chat. It's the last flight out today." Cade thumped his fingers nervously on the top of the dash.

"I just want to ask you a few questions." The officer turned down the dispatch radio. "Would you mind telling me why you're here?"

"I don't know what you mean. Are you asking me why I'm here sitting with you in a police car chatting when my kids and I are late for our flight, or is it a physiological question of why I'm here on this Earth? Look, I don't have the time to read your mind. We're late for our flight."

"I'm referring to Lorenz. Why did you come back here?"

Cade suddenly became suspicious. *Back here,* he thought to himself. He studied the man's face.

"Do I know you?" Cade said. The officer removed his

sunglasses.

"So how you been, Cade? It's been a long time, what, twenty years now?"

Cade turned and looked straight out the front windshield. "Denton Bauer, you're the last person I thought I would see in this God-forsaken town. So they have you carrying a gun now? That's a scary thought."

"It's good to see you, too, Cade. So, are you going to answer my question?" Cade glared over at him.

"I came to show my kids where I grew up. They got a law against that?"

Denton smiled. "No, just a coincidence; we had our twentieth high school reunion this weekend, and guess who didn't show up."

"Yeah, well, something better came up," Cade replied. "Like a root canal."

Denton reached down and flipped the switch to turn off the flashing lights. "It was fun. You should've been there."

"Well, I wasn't, and I'm over it."

"What was your excuse this time? Couldn't find the new Trapper's Lodge?"

"You know, Denton, it's really none of your business."

"I heard you're a doctor now."

"That's right, I head up an ER."

"You may be some hotshot doc back in Chicago, but you ain't squat here." Reaching down, Denton grabbed his book of tickets, separated the top white copy from the pink, and ripped it out. "I'm sure we could reminisce about old times for hours, but you have a plane to catch, remember? This is just a little memento I'd like you to have. You know, something to remember me by." Cade grabbed it from him and started to look it over. "I expect that ticket to be paid in full in less than thirty days."

"I wasn't going eighty miles an hour!" Cade said.

"I say you were. If you don't like it, you can always come back and fight it in court."

"And see your sorry ass again? I think not." Cade lifted the handle to the door to open it.

"I really am sorry you missed the reunion," Denton said. "It was great, lots of hot chicks."

"And all ready to talk on your bone phone, right? You haven't changed a bit, have you, Denton? Shooter told me you were even a bigger asshole than before."

"How's my buddy Shooter doing now that his wife left him?"

"You're a real jerk, you know that? I think this conversation's over." Cade started to get out of the car.

"So, really, what's the real reason you came back?" Denton was silent for a minute and then – just not quite ready to let Cade go – started to grin. "You know, as a policeman, I've been through some intense psychological profile training." Cade gave him the who-gives-a-shit look and started to walk toward his car. Denton stuck his head out the window. "I learned that eventually, almost without exception, a murderer returns to visit the scene of the crime. You ever read that in some of those college books?"

Cade abruptly stopped, turned to face Denton, and clinched the thin paper ticket into a fist. "What the hell is that supposed to mean?" Cade returned and leaned on the open passenger side door.

"Just wondering if you've been back up to Mirror Falls, that's all."

"You son of a bitch!" Cade skirted around the open door, lunged across the console, and took a swing at Denton's face. Denton grabbed his wrist, brought it down to the side, and held it securely on the console.

"You better watch yourself, Cade. I could throw you in jail for attempted assault on an officer."

Cade withdrew and settled back into the passenger's seat. "You know Kimber's death was an accident. I didn't kill anybody. I loved her."

"Well, you have a strange way of showing it. How can you live with yourself?" Cade was infuriated with that comment. His first thought was to ignore it and leave. Denton wasn't worth the effort, but he couldn't help himself. He had to say it. He had lived with the secret for twenty years without telling a soul.

"I know what you did, Denton. There's no denying it."

"I don't know what you're talking about."

"You raped her. You took her home from that party and forced yourself on her."

"Bullshit! I didn't do anything like that."

"She told me everything. I was traveling with the basketball team, and she needed a ride home and you gave her one. She trusted you, and you raped her."

"It wasn't like that. She wanted me real bad. Hell, we were both drunk. She practically begged me."

"That's bullshit, and you know it. Is that why she kicked you in the face? How about the scratch marks down your chest? I suppose that was some love-making ritual as well?"

"I don't know, Cade, you tell me. I'm sure you slept with her more times than I did; at least you would have if you hadn't killed her."

"You better watch what you say!"

"What are you going to do? Twenty years, and you can't prove anything. Hell, your key witness is dead!"

"I can't believe you're a cop. I guess they'll let any asshole wear a badge these days." Cade pushed the door open, climbed out, and slammed the door shut. Denton pushed the button, and the passenger side window started to open slowly.

"Hey, Cade, you may have killed Kimber, but I've got the next best thing."

Cade tried to ignore him. As far as he was concerned, the conversation was over. He continued to walk toward his car, looking ahead steadfastly.

Denton started the car, shot out into the road, and slowed to match Cade's pace. "And don't even think about coming back. You ain't wanted here."

Cade continued walking through the tall, dried weeds to his car, swearing under his breath as Denton made a quick U-turn, squealing the tires and speeding off in the opposite direction toward town.

***

Brit was the first one out the large revolving doors outside the baggage claim area at Chicago's O'Hare Airport and the first to see her mother standing next to the car, looking at her watch. Turns out, they easily made their flight back thanks to a very agile stray dog refusing to leave the runway.

"Mom!" she yelled. Several ladies within earshot turned to look in Brit's direction, but only one of them yelled back.

"Hey, Brit!" Angie began to walk across the street, which was packed with double-parked cars. She dodged to miss an oncoming taxi and then ducked to miss some idiot trying to maneuver a long package from the back of his truck. "Oh, Brit, come and give me a hug." She walked toward her with her arms opened wide. "I missed you so much. I hope you had fun."

"We did, Mom. It was awesome. Daddy got punched in the nose by a real live Indian and got a ticket from a Deputy Sheriff with a big cowboy hat." Angie immediately set Brit back down on the ground and approached Cade as he was

The Winds

trying to manipulate both his and Brit's luggage.

"What's this about getting a ticket and getting punched in the nose?" she said.

"Hey, don't I even get a hug before you start interrogating me?" Angie just stood there waiting for an answer. "It wasn't a big deal. It was just a speeding ticket."

"And what about getting punched in the nose?"

"That was a totally separate event. The guy who punched me was a good friend. It was just a little misunderstanding. Now give your poor son a hug, and I'll load up the suitcases. We can fill in all the blanks on the way home."

The ride home was nonstop talking. Zac and Brit went on and on from the back seat about the things they saw and did. The kids were animated in their descriptions about the real live Indian they met and the swimming pool at the motel.

"And we ate at the Dairy King and then went to the Tasty Craze for dessert. Dad says they make the best chocolate shakes in the world," Brit said.

"I didn't say 'in the world'; I said they make really good shakes."

"Well, to me, they were the best in the world, Dad."

"And we fed these huge fish with balls of bread and saw a river disappear into the side of a mountain," Zac said. "It was real awesome, Mom. Dad says that when we go back next year, he's going to take us down inside the cave when the water's not very deep." Zac looked up to his dad. "You've been down there in that cave, huh, Dad? Dad said it's so dark you can't see your hand in front of your face, and there's one spot where you have to lay on your belly and shimmy between two huge rocks." Zac struggled to take a quick breath. "And then we're going to hike up into the Winds, Mom. Maybe you can come with us."

"I don't know about that," she said. "I'm not much of the outdoor type. I have to have a real bed to sleep on and a shower every day." The children laughed. "Anyway, what are the Winds?"

"Oh, Mom, they're the most jagged mountains you've ever seen. They have hundreds of lakes with lots of fish in them," Zac said.

"Dad's arm almost fell off once while he was up there from fishing so much," Brit said. Cade looked back at her through the rear-view mirror. "Well, it did."

"It sounds like your Dad is just full of stories," Angie said. "What other things did he tell you?"

"Did you know Dad was a football star?" Zac said.

The Winds

"Yeah, he told us that he..." The stories continued nonstop for the duration of the trip back home, into the house, and on into the night.

Cade and Angie finally got the two kids settled down in their beds, and they, too, had retired for the night. It was late, but Angie still had a lot of questions she needed to ask.

"So, Cade," she said. "You never asked me what I did while you guys were at the OK Corral. Aren't you just dying to find out?" She dimmed the lamp and snuggled next to him with her head on his chest and hand across his other shoulder. She kissed him tenderly on his neck.

"You said you were going to use the time alone to catch up on your reading and maybe go out to dinner with some friends. I just assumed that's what you did," Cade said. He ran his finger over the back of her shoulder and in the crease of her smooth back. "So, is that what you did?"

"That's pretty much it. There's not a whole lot to talk about. I finished my novel and got a good start on my next one. It scared the, well, let's just say it was really scary reading when I'm the only one in this big house."

"You could have called a few of your friends for a sleepover." Cade kissed the crown of her head and gave her a quick squeeze on the shoulder.

"Like who, Tall, Dark, and Handsome?" Angie said as she started to tickle him.

"No need, I'm home now."

"Ok, I'm satisfied," she said, settling back into his warm body.

"Satisfied about what?"

"Satisfied that you wanted to know what I did while you guys were gone. Now I want to hear more about your trip. I mean the details, Cade. I want to hear about the things you were hesitant to talk about in front of the kids."

"Ok, where do you want me to start?"

"Let's start with your so-called Indian friend punching you in the nose. What's up with that? I mean, what kind of friend would do that?"

"First, you have to understand this guy; his name's Shooter. He was always the type of guy who would run on impulse; if it felt good, he'd do it without thinking about it. He was a blast in high school. We did a lot together."

"So why did he punch you in the nose if you two were such good friends?"

"Something about not sending him a postcard."

"So why didn't you?"

Cade continued to caress her bare shoulder as he thought about his reply. "I guess I was too busy. I didn't have much time to write letters through medical school."

"So why do you call him Shooter? That can't be his real name, right? I mean, he's an Indian. Why not Running Deer, Leaping Lizard, or Jumping Jellyfish, something a little more exciting than Shooter?"

"Jumping Jellyfish? Please. The truth be known, his first name's Joseph."

"That's pretty common."

"And his last name's Roaring Bull."

"You grew up with a guy named Joseph Roaring Bull?"

"Yeah, but everyone knew him as Shooter. He was really good at playing basketball."

"I get it." She thought for a moment, and then a smile emerged on her face. "Any cheerleaders in your graduating class nicknamed Hummer?"

"Very funny, Angie."

"So, tell me more about your trip."

Cade thought for a moment. He knew where the conversation was heading, and he didn't like it. There were parts of the trip that he didn't want to tell anyone, not even his wife.

"That's about it. I think the kids had a really good time. I even showed them Twilight hole, you know, the place I used to go skinny dipping with my friends?"

"You never told me about that."

"Oh, I didn't; well, it's not that big a deal. Just kids being kids."

"So what about the ticket?" she asked as she brought her head up near his.

"It was only a speeding ticket. You know how Brit likes to be the news lady. Her last name should be Revere, you know, Paul's sister?" Angie glared at him. "OK, on our way out of town, I got pulled over by a cop. We were in a hurry to catch our plane."

"Brit said that you knew the guy."

"Yeah, I did. His name's Denton Bauer. I went to high school with him. He was a jerk in high school, and now he's a jerk cop. What else did Brit tell you?"

"She said he made you go back with him in the police

car to talk. Then Zac told me you guys were arguing or something."

"I don't like getting pulled over, OK? I told him that I wasn't speeding and that if we continued to argue, we'd miss our flight. He finally settled down, gave me the ticket, and let me go. That was it. I'm telling you, it wasn't a big deal."

"So you went to high school together, and he wasn't happy to see you? You two must have really hated each other. Usually, twenty years is enough time to mend any fence."

"There's no fence between us, more like the Great Wall of China. He's the last guy I wanted to see."

They lay almost motionless between the sheets. Angie pulled the comforter up tight around her neck and continued to rest her head on Cade's chest. He was exhausted from the trip, physically but mostly mentally. It had taxed his every emotion to the extreme. He had become reacquainted with a good friend, confronted his dreaded past by visiting the grave of the girl he truly loved and planned on spending the rest of his life with, and lastly, came face to face with an evil enemy disguised as an officer of the law.

He hadn't been completely honest with her. There was much more he could have told her. She had a right to know; she was his wife, but maybe what she didn't know wouldn't hurt her. As he leaned over to kiss her goodnight, he could hear her long, subtle breaths. He was sure she was sound asleep. Maybe, just maybe, her not knowing all of the details was for the best.

Chapter 12

A week had passed since Cade, and the kids returned from Lorenz. Life was back to normal; that is, if normal meant soccer for Zac, games on Monday and Thursday and practice on Wednesdays, and piano lessons once a week for Brit, followed by softball practice and games a couple nights a week. Angie had her book club once a week, and she and Cade tried to do something together every Friday night without the kids. Throw in the fact that Cade's work schedule would fluctuate depending on how busy it was at the ER, putting him home sometimes past 8 or 9 in the evening, and you had a typical Hobbs' family schedule.

Cade slipped the psychiatrist's business card in a small crack in the dashboard of his car with the phone number highlighted to remind him to give him a call, but a week had passed, and it just wasn't convenient. He hadn't experienced any anxiety attacks since returning; in fact, he hadn't slept better in years. Maybe the tip of the iceberg theory was inaccurate. Maybe the visit he'd made to see the two graves that stressful morning was the emotional breakdown necessary to melt the iceberg altogether – another victim of global warming. Cade could always give the psychiatrist a call if the anxiety attacks reemerged, but for now, he had plans to enjoy the day.

This day just happened to be Brit's eighth birthday.

Cade recognized it by wishing her a happy birthday and giving her a gentle kiss on the forehead while she lay sleeping before he left for the hospital, realizing the best was yet to come. The Hobbs family took their birthdays seriously. They planned birthday parties at least a month before the big event. Angie showed Cade all the presents she had gotten Brittney and hidden under their bed. Since Cade didn't have any time to do any shopping himself, she made him wrap most of the presents before going to bed the night before.

Cade called Angie late in the afternoon when he found a few spare minutes. She informed him that the decorations were up, the cake was on the table, and Brit's favorite kind of ice cream, Tin Roof Sundae with almonds, was in the freezer. She had taken Zac to get some new shoes, and then they were going to pick up Brit from her piano lessons. That was always an event because the teacher was considered one of the best in Chicago and practically lived on the other side of the city.

"So, what time do you think you'll be home tonight?" Angie asked as she talked into her cell phone.

"Things have really slowed down this afternoon. I guess people aren't in the mood for stabbing each other. I think I should be home by six or six-thirty," Cade said.

"Well, I'll believe it when I see it. We'll be home before

six, so I'll plan on having the pizza delivered by seven."

"That'll be fine. Don't tell Brit, but earlier this afternoon, I took a minute to write her a poem. It'll be my little surprise."

"Cade, that's not like you. That's so sweet."

"I didn't say it was good."

"I'm sure she'll love it. We'll all love it."

"Hey, I can reveal my sensitive side now and then." Cade heard some commotion out in the ER lobby. "Well, I knew it was too good to be true. Looks like we just got a gunshot victim. I'll do my best to get out of here; see you soon."

Cade walked into his office and sat down on his chair behind the desk. He was exhausted. Two more stabbing victims, a young kid with a laceration to his face as a result of climbing a metal fence, a small child who had spent a minute or two at the bottom of a pool, and a young man who had apparently overdosed by sniffing gasoline was rushed to the ER since he had talked to his wife less than two hours prior. He picked up the phone and dialed their landline, thinking they would be home by now. He let it ring several times, and then the familiar answering machine came on. He waited patiently and left a short message telling them that it looked like he'd be home in less than thirty minutes and not to start the party without him. He made smooching noises into the phone and ended with saying, "I love you guys," and hung up. He left his office and breezed past the admittance desk, waving his hand rapidly as he passed the attendant.

"See you tomorrow, Doctor Hobbs," she said.

He nodded his head, pushed the metal pad on the wall, and the automatic double doors opened wide. He slipped through them without losing any speed out to his car. Since he was the head of the ER, he had certain preferential benefits, something to help compensate him for all those horrendous years of school and internships. One of those benefits was a designated parking spot closest to the doors. Tonight, he valued that benefit more than ever since he was leaving at a later time than he had hoped.

He threw open the door to his BMW and slid behind the wheel. *That's another benefit of being a doctor,* he thought, *a fast car.* He buckled his seatbelt, shoved it in gear, and sped out of the parking lot toward home, nearly 25 minutes away – 20 if the roads were clear. *This time of night, the roads shouldn't be too bad*, he thought as he merged onto the interstate. Setting the cruise on 85, he put in a CD – the Best of Queen – put his tired head back on the headrest, and sailed homeward.

Fifteen minutes into the drive, his cell phone rang. He

fished through his suit coat pocket from the passenger seat. *Why didn't I turn that thing off?* He questioned himself. All he needed was for something to go wrong back at the hospital.

"Hello, this is Doctor Hobbs," he said as Bohemian Rhapsody blared in the background.

"Yes, Doctor Hobbs, this is Tina at admittance. Doctor Spencer asked me to call you; he said it was an emergency."

Cade could hear yelling and screaming in the background as she spoke. "Just a second, Tina, let me turn down my music. I can barely hear you." He reached down and turned the dial. "Ok, that's better. What were you saying?" He signaled and pulled over to the side of the road.

"Here's Doctor Spencer."

"Doctor Hobbs, sorry to bother you, but there's been a terrible accident on Interstate 290 just west of Central Avenue. Have you heard anything on the radio?"

"I haven't been listening to the radio, Spence. How bad is it?"

"Seven car pile-up, including an eighteen-wheeler, and we're the closest hospital to the accident. The first wave just came in, and our beds are nearly full. It's bad, Cade. It's been a while since I've seen anything this bad. We've got stretchers lined up in the halls. We need your help, and I'm calling in more doctors and nurses."

"I'll be there as soon as I can, and Spence, it'll be all right; you're doing fine." He threw his cell phone into the passenger seat and squealed back onto the freeway.

"That's one more benefit," he said under his breath. "Missing your daughter's birthday party to help others in need." He let out a big breath of air and concentrated on preparing himself mentally for another late night. He took the next exit to return back to the hospital. He hit the speed dial for his home number on his cell phone to let Angie and the kids know that it didn't look like he was going to be able to make it to the party. It was a phone call that he'd made countless times before on special occasions. His family, even though they didn't like it, was getting used to it. He let it ring until the machine picked up again.

"This is the Hobbs residence," Angie's prerecorded voice announced. "We're not at home right now. Come to think of it, we're usually never home. We're probably at soccer, dance, piano, martial arts, or if you're trying to reach mom, she's at the nut hut." Zac and Brit were heard giggling in the background. "You know what to do at the beep." Cade smiled as he waited for the beep to end and then began to talk.

The Winds

"Honey, this is Cade. I was almost home and just got called back to the hospital. There's been a bad accident on the freeway, and we're the closest ER. Sorry, Brit, but it looks like I won't be at your birthday party. I know how much it means to you, but they need me to help. I'm sure all of you understand. I'll make it up to you guys. And Angie, don't worry about me; I'll grab a sandwich when I get a minute. I love you guys more than you know. See you when I get home, but don't wait up." He paused for a moment. "Brit, in case I don't get home until really late, Happy Birthday, and remember, I love you more than you'll ever know."

Cade was back at the hospital in less than ten minutes and pulled into his designated spot. There were seven or eight ambulances with their lights flashing, and another one was entering with its siren blaring. Cade ran through the side door and into the ER.

"Doctor Hobbs, over here," the voice yelled. "We need you over here."

Cade ran into the long hall that was lined with gurneys parked closely to one side. People were moaning, screaming, and crying as they lay bleeding in pain.

"My God," Cade mumbled as one of the nurses held the light green jacket taut in front of him. He slipped his arms through the holes, and she tied them. He slipped on a pair of white rubber gloves and began assessing the injuries. He went from one gurney to the next, shouting directions to the nurses on where one gurney should go and then another. Approaching the next gurney, he saw that the sheets were soaked red with blood, and there was no movement from the small body underneath.

"I'm afraid it's too late for that one," the nurse said as she approached Cade. "It's a small girl. She was DOA. I think this is the worst we've ever had in this hospital."

"I'm sure it is," Cade replied as he rushed to the next gurney.

"Doctor, we need you in number six, STAT!" one of the nurses yelled as she came around the corner. "A young boy, he's fighting for his life!"

Cade immediately turned and ran through the hall to room number six. As he entered, he saw three nurses and one doctor working together to save the young boy's life. The monitor was flat-lined with that hauntingly steady audible tone.

"Doctor Hobbs, we're losing him!" the doctor shouted across the room as he applied pressure to the young boy's chest. The boy was bleeding profusely from severe internal injuries and had several deep lacerations to his face and chest. Cade ran over to the table and began to apply pressure as well and started to bark out orders as the nurses responded with skill and instinct.

Between orders, Cade looked down at the boy's face. "Oh my God!" Cade shouted. "It's Zac. It's my son!" He literally started to shake and stepped back from the table. Peering up to the ceiling, he put his bloody hands to his face. "Oh my God, no! No, don't take my son!" Cade's face flushed white as he stepped back up to the table. Another minute passed as Cade tried desperately to save his son's life.

"Doctor, he's gone. He didn't make it. There's nothing more we can do," the other doctor said as he tried to restrain Cade.

"I've got to save him," Cade said. "Don't you understand? He's my only son!" Cade let out a cry that pierced the entire ER.

Suddenly panicked, Cade ran out of the room and down the hall toward the blood-soaked sheet and threw the top corner up, exposing the little girl's battered, bloody face. Bending down, he clutched the little mangled body in his arms, hugging her tight to his chest and weeping violently. "Oh, Brit, my sweet Brittney!" He rocked her in his arms as he wept. "Oh, God, Angie!" Gently laying Brittney's head back down on the gurney, he ran back into the ER. "Angie, I've got to find my wife. I've got to find her!" His voice was tattered. He ran from one room to another until he saw a team of doctors and nurses huddled around one of the beds. Forcing his way in, he saw that it was his wife.

She was battered and cut on her face to the point that she was barely recognizable. Bleeding and going in and out of consciousness, he could barely hear her mumble his name. He grabbed her hand and pressed it against his face.

"I'm here, Angie. It's Cade. I'm here for you, sweetheart." Her eyes opened to tiny slits, she smiled faintly, then her eyes closed again. The tears rolled down his cheeks as he attempted to speak. "I love you, Angie. I love you with all of my heart. We'll make it through this; you just wait and see. Be strong, Angie." He kissed her bloody hand.

She opened her eyes again. He could tell that she was trying to focus on his face. He bent over even closer than before to where he was nearly touching her face with his tear-drenched cheeks.

"The children?" she said, just louder than a whisper. "Where are the children?" Cade reached across and grabbed her other hand, and held them both in his. His throat was constricted almost to the point of not being able to reply.

"They're fine, honey. They'll be OK."

Her cheeks and eyebrows elevated slightly to show her

acknowledgment. One eye opened wider than the other as she looked deeply into Cade's eyes. She struggled to form the next words.

"Take good care of them and tell them I love them." She wet her lips lightly and closed her eyes momentarily then opened them again. Focusing in on Cade's face and with all the strength she had left, she forced a barely visible smile and said, "I love you, Cade. I want you to be happy." Those few words were the last she uttered. She squeezed his hand, and then her body went limp. The room was filled with doctors and nurses, but it was deathly quiet. Cade kissed her forehead and hugged her for the last time on this Earth.

Chapter 13

Unshaven and unmotivated, Cade turned over in his lonely bed and grabbed the clock off the nightstand. It was 1:45 in the afternoon, one week and five days since the deaths of Angie, Zac, and Brit. Cade had lost his entire family in one gut-wrenching event out on a busy freeway as a result of a businessman caring more about his future client than the rest of the people driving beside him. He sealed a deal of a lifetime over his cell phone and, during his celebration, lost control of his vehicle, resulting in an 18-wheeler jackknifing and causing a seven-car pile up in a narrow stretch of freeway with concrete barricades on both sides.

In the end, six people died, and over twice that number were seriously injured. These were the numbers published in the next day's Chicago Times as they touted it as "Chicago's Worst Highway Fatality" in two years, but those were only numbers, statistics, people without a face, to those that read the newspaper that next morning. To Cade, however, it was his life, everything he'd worked for, everything he had loved.

He turned back over in his bed and looked blankly across the room. What would he do today? Would he continue to go in and out of sleep in his darkened room like he had so many days past? Would he muster the strength to maybe shave and clean himself up? He hadn't been back to work since that fatal day. In fact, he hadn't left his home since the funerals. He just stayed in his room surrounded by painful reminders of his family.

Suddenly, the phone rang. Cade looked at it as it sat on the nightstand and bellowed its annoying tones. "Nobody cares!" he shouted to it, but it kept ringing. Finally, the ringing stopped, but the answering machine came on from the kitchen. Painfully, Cade listened to every word as his wife explained the reasons why they weren't home – because they went to soccer, dance, or piano. Cade thought for a minute as he wallowed in his misery, *"You can add heaven to the list."* Tears filled his eyes. The annoying beep stopped.

"Cade, this is Doctor Morrison, Robert Morrison. I need to meet with you at your convenience; the sooner, the better." There was a slight pause. "Cade, if you're there, I want you to listen closely. We can get through this. We can, do you hear me? YOU can get through this and I can help. Please give me a call."

"Sorry, Dr. Morrison," Cade mumbled, the sound muffled by the pillow. "You'll have to help chip away at someone else's iceberg." He shut his eyes and went back to sleep.

An hour later, the phone rang again. Cade opened his bloodshot eyes and listened as before. "Cade, this is Doctor

Beck. We're all worried about you down here at the ER. We haven't seen you since, well, um, you know." There was a short pause, and then the man attempted to clear his throat, clearly having a difficult time putting into words what he needed to say. "I know that Doctor Spencer and others have tried to contact you and were unsuccessful. Please, Cade, if you're there listening, pick up the phone. I need to talk to you. Really, Cade, the sooner you get back to doing the things you used to do, the better you'll recover from all this. Give me a call. Hope to see you soon."

"The sooner I get back to doing the things I used to do?" Cade mocked as he arose from his bed and walked into the kitchen. "Are you fuckin' kidding me? That's the issue here; all of the things I used to do, I can't do anymore. All of the things I used to do were with my wife, my son, and my daughter, damn it! How can I get back to doing the things I used to do?" Cade's voice rose, and the veins stuck out in his neck. He grabbed the first thing he saw and threw it at the answering machine, hitting it squarely. It fell off the counter and hit the floor with a crash.

"Honey, this is Cade," the answering machine blurted out at its highest volume. "I just got called back to the hospital. There's been a bad accident on the freeway, and they're all being brought to the ER. Sorry, Brit, but it looks like I won't be–"

The Winds

"Shut the hell up!" Cade yelled as he put his hands over his ears. He grabbed the answering machine, jerked the cord out of the wall, and threw it against the refrigerator as hard as his tired arm could throw it. It hit the top freezer door, sending pictures of his children, appointments, shopping lists, and other notes that were held by colorful magnets sailing to the floor.

"Why did you let this happen to me?" he yelled as he fell to his knees on the cold tile floor, looking upwards toward the ceiling. "Why, Lord, why me?" He collapsed to the floor in a heap and bawled and slept intermittently throughout the afternoon.

It was nearly 7 o'clock that evening when Cade woke up with a slight chill from the tile floor. He got up and went to the bathroom to take a hot shower, the first one in nearly a week. As he stood in the hot spray of water, he contemplated his life. Where should he go from here? What should he do? Was working at the ER, a place where death, trauma, and tragedy were a constant awful reminder, a place he could work the rest of his life, or was life really an option? How could he continue to live when all that he had loved was dead? He grabbed the soap and began stroking his shoulders, chest, and arms. Even a shower had lost its appeal. He realized that he was at a crossroads in his fragile life.

Stepping out of the shower onto the rug, he reached for

his towel. Was it the right or the left one? He could never remember. He picked up the towel on the right and closed the shower door. He brought it up to his face and savored the distinct scent. It was *her* towel. He had picked the wrong towel like he always did. Of course, she would put her towel closest to the door – always looking after herself. A glimpse of a smile came to his stone-hard face as he thought about Angie. It was a brief, refreshing intermission from the pure hell he had been living.

Cade finished drying off, brushed his teeth, and combed his hair. After he dressed, he walked over to the nightstand and opened the small drawer. Clear to the back in a small cup-like container, he pulled out Angie's wedding ring and put it in his pocket, following it with his keys and wallet, then put on his baseball cap and left out the front door.

It was near dusk in Chicago. The bright lights were beginning to illuminate, signaling the next stage of this enormous city. The nightlife downtown was amazing. There were people everywhere; taxis, buses, and limos clogged the streets as throngs of people tried to cross at every intersection. He was well accustomed to the nightlife of the city but always had Angie on his arm. They were regulars at the opera, symphony, and all of the off-Broadway productions. It was a painful drive for Cade as he made his way to the pier.

The Winds

Cade pulled into the parking stall and looked out into the darkness of the enormous Lake Michigan – an almost endless sea of blackness. He took a deep breath, got out of his car, and started to walk. It was a beautiful evening. There was a slight breeze, but it felt good compared to the stale air he'd been breathing the past week. He passed a young couple, obviously in love, sitting on a bench, her legs over the top of his, embracing and laughing. *Young puppy love,* he thought. The two of them didn't really know what real love was, but still, it was too much for Cade to witness.

He continued to walk along the concrete walk until he reached the start of the long pier at the edge of the lake. The waves crashed against the huge crushed boulders below, splashing water over the top of the walkway, which transitioned to the large wooden structure that stretched out high above the water. He continued to walk through the darkness between each light pole until he reached the end of the pier. He leaned against the rail and gazed out into the expanse. Darkness was what he felt. It was an awful darkness. The only thing he could see was the large whitecaps below as they crashed against the huge wooden columns supporting the pier. They mesmerized him as he watched each series of waves come in with perfect rhythm.

The feelings of anxiety suddenly returned to him for the first time since his trip back to Wyoming. He began to take quick, short breaths. He felt as if he was experiencing a heart attack as he reached up and put pressure on the middle of his chest.

"I can't go on," he mumbled to himself. "I can't survive without my wife and children. They were my life. Everything I've done, every breath I've taken, has been for them."

He struggled to climb the rail. He planted his feet firmly on the top of the middle rail and leaned out over the edge. He could jump, and nobody would know. His pitiful body would be washed up on shore, and everyone would understand why he did it. Surely, his closest friends would understand. They would all do the same if it had happened to them. He didn't have a choice. Somehow, he would have to be free from his pain, and the only way that could happen was if he removed himself from the living.

Stretching out his arms, Cade looked up to the sky as if beckoning his God for his return. His feet began to lose their grip on the rail below. He felt himself going forward.

Suddenly, he had a quick glimpse into the future. He envisioned his body being thrust about by the fierce waves, ravaged and mutilated against the rocks. A young boy would find him while innocently searching the shore for snail shells. It was a horrible sight. The boy screamed for his mother. She came running toward him and fainted immediately upon discovering the mangled body.

The Winds

Slowly, Cade came out of his daze, readjusted his position on the handrail, and stepped down. He stood there momentarily, shamefully contemplating his next move. He was a doctor; surely, he could think of a more humane way of taking his own life. He was determined to leave this world quietly and peacefully.

He slipped his hand in his front pocket and pulled out Angie's wedding ring. It felt like a hot glowing ember. He gazed down at it, momentarily savoring what it used to represent. It was a continuous circle. There was no end to their love. He had given it to her, thinking they would be together forever. But now, he was faced with the awful, unbearable reality that she was gone. Clutching the ring tightly in his fist, he brought it up to his lips and kissed it as tears fell off his cheeks. He stood in complete silence and then threw it as hard as he could into the endless abyss.

Before returning home, Cade made a quick detour to the hospital. He successfully avoided detection by entering through the back entrance and snuck into the pharmacy. There were a few items he needed to get before returning home for the night. As he left the hospital parking lot, he was thoroughly convinced he could never work there again. He arrived home, finding that the awful pain he felt on the pier had not subsided. "Where there's no hope? There is no life," he mumbled. He had hit rock bottom and couldn't see his way out of it. Convinced that whatever came after death would be better than the personal mortal hell he was living, he walked dejectedly from his car up the long path to his home and opened the large wooden door.

It was an elegant home, a reward for the countless late hours he spent studying to become a doctor, and a testimony of the many years his wife stood by him through the toughest of times. He desired more than anything money could buy to be with her again, to be with her and his two children. This once-happy home would soon become his sanctuary, his way out, his tomb.

Less than an hour later, Cade sat up in his bed dressed in a white shirt, red tie, and double-breasted suit. His wing-tipped shoes were polished, and he had a single red rose pinned on his lapel. His hair was combed, and he was clean-shaven. His wife and children didn't have a choice of when they would leave this Earth, but he did. He wanted to make sure that when he made his exit, he looked his best. Someone he knew and trusted would find his body. There would be no bloodstains to wash off the sides of the bathtub and into the drain or brain matter to be scraped off of the walls and floor. His death would be in a private and professional manner, minimizing the burden it placed on others.

Candles were lit and distributed around the room. The flickering glow set the stage. Cade had two small glass vials that he had taken from the hospital before returning home

The Winds

from the pier. The larger of the two had a common sedative to help him relax. The other had a lethal dose of potassium chloride. He measured each liquid substance into separate syringes and tapped the edge to disperse the air bubbles, then depressed the plunger slightly, emitting a thin, steady stream into the air. He set the syringes side by side on the nightstand, grabbed the telephone receiver, and dialed the hospital ER.

"Hello, Cook County Hospital Emergency Room. Can I help you?" the lady said.

Cade placed his hand over the receiver to muffle his voice. He recognized the voice on the other end, and he didn't want her to do the same. "Yes, Doctor Spencer, please."

"Hold, please."

A few moments later, there was a voice on the other end. "Hello, this is Doctor Spencer."

"Hey, Spence," Cade said.

"Doctor Hobbs? Hey, how are you. I've been trying to get a hold of you for days now. Where are you?"

"I'm just here at home, Spence. Hey, I've got a favor to ask of you, if you don't mind?"

"Not at all, Cade, anything. What can I do for you?"

"Your shift's over in about an hour, right? I was just wondering if you could drop by for a few minutes. I don't know; there are just a lot of things I need to talk to you about. Can you do that for me?"

"Sure, no problem. In fact, I'll probably get out of here a little early tonight. You'll find it hard to believe, but things are a little quiet around here. I should be at your home sometime around midnight."

"That would be fine. I really appreciate it. You've always been a good friend. I'll see you then."

"Great, see you in about an hour."

An hour would be ample time to carry out his deed. In fact, once the contents of the second syringe entered his bloodstream, it was a matter of seconds.

Cade kicked his legs to the side of the bed and walked to the mirror above the chest of drawers. Straightening his tie and buttoning his suit coat, he actually smiled at himself. *Soon, I will be free, free from this pain,* he thought to himself. He climbed back on the bed and scooted to the center. He sat up straight and doubled up the pillows around him to prevent him from toppling out of the bed once he was dead. He reached out and grabbed the first syringe off the table, stuck it into his arm, and slowly depressed the plunger. This would soon put him into a calm, relaxed state of slumber.

Cade looked around the room one last time as he felt the tingling sensation, signaling that the chemical was successfully being transported throughout his body. He looked at the family picture they had taken and framed over six months ago. It hung nicely above the fireplace mantel. Angie loved that picture. He focused on the numerous, smaller pictures of Zac and Brit. Soccer, dance, piano, and ... he started to fade in and out of coherency as he continued to look at the remnants of his life. His vision started to become blurred. It was time.

He reached over and grabbed the final syringe and plunged it into his arm.

This is it, he thought to himself, fully aware of his surroundings and situation, but he knew it wouldn't be for long.

He positioned his thumb on the plunger and started to apply pressure when, suddenly, he saw a glistening object on the mantel. He squinted in an attempt to focus as it reflected the flickering orange and yellow flames of the candles. It was the feather, the eagle feather Shooter had given them, the one that had supposedly been dipped in the pure gold of the Winds.

So much for hope, he thought as he recalled what Shooter had told them the feather represented. If it was so powerful, why did he keep it in a clay pot? The questions continued to fill Cade's troubled mind as he felt more and more the effects of the sedative he'd shot into his arm a few minutes prior. Could it be that he'd lost hope? Could it be that he'd never fully recovered from the loss of his family and had never been at peace since?

It was difficult for him to focus and to move his arms and fingers. He desperately tried to get his hand to obey his commands to depress the plunger on the syringe to release the deadly dose of the chemical. His eyes suddenly became mercilessly heavy and then closed. He had asked too many questions and allowed himself to reach the point of no return. The full syringe of the deadly potassium chloride dangled precariously from his arm as he fell peacefully to sleep.

Chapter 14

Cade fell short of taking his own life with only a few inches of deadly chemicals left in a syringe he'd stuck in his arm the night before. He awoke the next morning to a montage of voices – nurses, doctors, and such – many of whom he knew, looking down at him as he lay on the hospital bed. He was hooked up to a series of monitoring devices to track his vital signs throughout the night. After an intense evaluation from Doctor Morrison, he was released a week later. Doctor Morrison's findings were very conclusive. Cade Hobbs did not, in his professional opinion, continue to display suicidal tendencies and was not a threat to himself or the community in which he lived.

The truth be known, Cade had experienced, almost within a twinkling of an eye, a drastic change in himself and the way he looked at the world around him. He was no longer concerned about taking his own life; in fact, he was no longer concerned about anything anymore – himself or anyone else, for that matter. He had become callused, uncaring, and withdrawn.

It took him nearly three weeks to get his affairs in order, not in preparation to die, as before, but to move. He sold nearly everything he owned, including the home. The home, being located in a very influential neighborhood, had an offer on it within hours of being introduced on the market.

Cade stood in the empty, spacious entryway and looked back with little emotion at the empty hallways and the upper balcony with the decorative spindle railing and even the elegant chandelier before shutting and locking the door to what used to be his life. He walked down the long, winding front walk and stepped into his new extended cab truck. He was able to pack all of his present worldly possessions in the long bed with a matching shell to protect the contents from the weather. The next few days would be spent almost entirely on a freeway that connected Chicago and what was to be his new home.

As he adjusted the seat back and set the cruise at 75, he had plenty of time to contemplate his life. As he passed through Iowa and Nebraska, it was all he could do to keep his eyes open to the road. One enormous field of corn after another, and then grain, and then more corn. He sat and reasoned through the decision he had made. Sure, everyone at the hospital – all of his friends and associates – were sympathetic toward him losing his entire family but appalled when they heard how close he'd come to taking his own life. How could a doctor of medicine be trusted, especially in Dr. Hobbs capacity, head of the ER at a major hospital in the city of Chicago, in making life or death decisions on behalf of another person when he, himself, failed to place any value on his own? It took a lot of personal soul-searching before Cade finally reconciled within himself, and as a result of that reconciliation, he found himself driving on the high,

The Winds

unforgiving desert plains of Wyoming, heading west on Interstate 80 to a town that he thought he'd never see again.

He'd traveled several hours since crossing the Wyoming border, and Rawlins was just a few miles ahead. The town could be easily seen from the freeway. After two long days of driving, he had only two and a half hours left of his trip.

He exited I-80 and took Highway 287, heading north. The sun was setting behind Red Butte as he approached Lorenz from the South. It was beautiful, but Cade failed to see the beauty. He continued down the hill, across the Popo Agie Bridge through the entire town. High school-age kids were driving up and down Main Street, honking their horns and waving to those passing by as the only form of entertainment on a cool summer night, but Cade paid them no mind.

He continued past the Tasty Craze, the Dusty Saddle Inn where he, Zac, and Brit had stayed less than two months prior, and curved past the long, orange rock wall that stretched in front of the high school. He continued to the Indian reservation, down a long, narrow, dusty road, and parked.

The once shiny red truck was now a dingy tan with the words "Wash Me" on the tailgate left as a prank when he stopped for lunch at a local diner the day before. He had driven straight through since Omaha and was stiff and tired.

The front door to the house swung open and Shooter walked out on the old wooden porch. A black cat with a single white paw immediately jumped up on the porch and started to rub on the outside of his leg. He walked down the stairs and crossed the patchy grass. *What do you say to an old friend who has just lost his wife and kids?* Shooter thought to himself. He continued to walk closer, hoping the words would magically come to his mind.

Cade got out of the truck and looked in his direction. "Hey, Shooter," he said. "I don't ever want to drive that again."

"Don't blame you. Driving to Casper for the livestock auction twice a summer 'bout kills me, and that's only three hours." He put his hand on the top of the dusty truck. "Nice truck, is it new?"

"Yeah, it's new. I needed something to haul my stuff."

"What, can't put a hitch on the BMW?" Cade just looked at him. "Well, with that scraggly beard, you look better in a truck than you do in a BMW. I guess you can finally grow one, huh?"

"I could always grow one, just never did. Not professional."

"So why now?"

The Winds

"Cause I've stopped practicing medicine."

"So, you're going to take some time off, right, try to deal with the accident?" Shooter could sense Cade was not himself. Of course, he wasn't himself; he'd just lost his family, but Cade seemed to be short with him with everything he said. The accident was tragic; there was no denying it, but to treat his best friend this way was troubling. Shooter made an attempt to penetrate Cade's seemingly protective shell. "I'm so sorry," he said. He reached out and grabbed his shoulder. "I know it's tough, but you need to hang in there." Cade just nodded his head. "Hey, come on the porch and have a seat. I'll go in and get us both a cold beer. Do you feel like a beer?"

Cade didn't reply; he just started walking toward the porch.

Minutes later, they both sat in their chairs and drank beer together. Cade was on his third and began to loosen up a little.

"So, how have things been?" Cade said.

"Ok, I guess?" Shooter sat back in his chair and looked out over the star-filled sky.

"Something's wrong, isn't it?" Cade said. "Tell me what's wrong."

Shooter sat up in his chair. "It's my father. He never came back from the Winds, and I don't think he ever will. He was supposed to be back two days after you and the kids left."

"Why didn't you tell me this sooner? Why didn't you tell me on the phone?"

"You're dealing with your own tragedy – don't want to make things worse. I know how bad you wanted to see him again."

"You're right; I did want to see him. He was a good man. How can you be sure that something's happened to him? Maybe he just needed to spend more time up there now that your mother's a part of the trip. You said so yourself that she was another reason for him to go up there this time."

"I'm sure, Cade." He pointed out to the pasture. "You see that spotted horse out there standing by himself? That's my father's horse. He showed up three weeks ago at the trailhead. He still had his saddle and harness on."

"Maybe he just ran off, and your father has to walk out on his own. Maybe his leg's broke."

"Can't happen. His horse is his best friend. If he was hurt, the horse would have stayed by his side until they both died. But just in case I was wrong, I spent nearly two weeks up there searching for him. Nothing – no tracks, no feathers, no nothing. I'm sure he's dead."

"What about the authorities?"

"The reservation authorities already had their hands full investigating the disappearance of one of their rangers. Of course, when my Dad came up missing, they looked for him; hey, he's the chief, but they only looked on the reservation side. When I contacted the Sheriff's office, they came out and asked me a few questions, but they basically said there wasn't anything they could do. Well, I should say Denton said there wasn't anything they could do. He said that it sounded more like a reservation issue to him. The county and the reservation have been involved in a turf war ever since I can remember. They're very reluctant to help each other out."

"That's ridiculous."

"There are three thousand lakes and over eight hundred miles of streams connecting them. I don't think we'll ever find him."

"But they don't have to search them all, only the area he was last seen."

"That's just it; he was last seen here loading up the horse. I don't know where he went. I don't think anyone knew where he was going. I looked for two weeks. I've resigned myself to the fact that he's happily beside my mother."

"I'm really sorry. I wish there was something I could do."

"There's nothing anyone can do. It's just something I'll have to get used to. It's going to get pretty lonely around this place without him, but at least you're here for a while. We can support each other and get through this crazy shit together."

Cade was quiet and didn't reply. He took another drink of his beer and looked over at Shooter.

"Don't tell me you're having second thoughts about coming here," Shooter said. "Hey, I know it's not a forever thing. You just came here to help clear your head, maybe get away from the pressures of your life, and escape a few memories. I just thought that since you were here, we could help each other out a bit. You can leave whenever you're ready."

"No, it's not that, Shooter. I haven't told you the real purpose for coming back."

"What's there to tell? I mean, I can see coming back here for a while, but I know you can't stay here forever."

Shooter took another drink, wiped his mouth with the back of his hand, and looked back up at the stars. "You've spent the better part of your life in the city. What do you hope to gain by coming back here besides a little temporary sanity? You can't escape from your problems; you need to deal with them. That's something that I haven't been able to do very well, but maybe this time will be different."

"Shooter, you've always been a good friend. Even separated by all those years, I could feel you there. Good friends remain good friends no matter how far apart they are and for how long, but you just don't get it, do you? I should've never come back for the reunion. It's caused me nothing but trouble."

"How can you say that?"

"Don't get me wrong; I'm not saying that coming here last month had anything to do with my wife and kids being killed. Nobody could have done anything about that. They were just in the wrong place at the wrong time."

"So what are you saying?"

"I didn't tell you this when I called last week, but after my family was killed, I had a very difficult time coping. Let's just say I didn't cope at all. I couldn't go back to work, I didn't leave the house, I didn't call any friends. Hell, I haven't even talked to my mother since the funerals. She's tried to contact me, but I haven't returned her calls."

"You can't go on living like that."

"That's exactly what I realized; I couldn't go on like that. I mean, I couldn't go on, period."

"Don't tell me. You didn't…"

"I did," Cade said. "I tried to kill myself." He lowered his head and peered down at the splintered deck. "I hit the bottom, Shooter, and I mean rock-hard bottom. There wasn't anything left – no hope, no expectations, no nothing. My days were filled with unbearable emptiness. The only thing I felt I could do was to take myself out of the pain."

"So what happened? Apparently, you didn't … well, you're still here."

"Yeah, I'm still here. Because of that damn feather, I'm still here, you son of a bitch!" Cade became irritated. "I was within seconds of putting an end to it all when I saw that feather up on the mantle." He paused and looked out into the pasture at the group of horses illuminated by the large yard light at the top of the barn. "This feather will give you hope, happiness, and wisdom, or whatever the hell you said that night. No offense, but I think it's bullshit about that Great Spirit and being watched through the eye of an eagle, but when I saw the reflection of the gold tip, it just made me realize something."

"That there's hope? That no matter how far you fall, you can still pick yourself up?"

"Hell no! I still think that's bullshit! It made me realize that I can't kill myself. I just can't do it. It's just not right. I realized that if I die," Cade continued as he glanced over to Shooter. "It's going to have to be through other means."

Shooter shook his head. "You can't ask that of me. I won't do it!"

"Relax, Shooter, I'd never ask you to do that. What I have resolved within myself is that I can't kill myself, and I can't cope with life and be happy, so I'll remove myself from civilization and live the rest of my life alone."

"So what are you saying?"

"I'm saying that I came here for a totally different motive than you thought I did. I don't intend on staying here for a while until I feel I can reenter the rat race of life, and I'm not settling down in Lorenz and living happily ever after. I'm saying that those Winds up there will be my new home for the rest of my life for however long that ends up being."

"That's ridiculous, Cade. How will you survive? What will you eat? Where will you sleep? The winters are deadly.

Nobody goes in the Winds during the winter months. It's unforgiving. You won't last a day out there in a tent."

"Who said anything about a tent?" Cade said confidently as he popped open another can of beer. "Have you noticed, Shooter, I'm one can up on you now."

***

The next morning, Cade woke up to the annoying shrill of a rooster. He untangled himself from the bundle of blankets, got up from the living room couch, and walked toward the bright sunlight coming from the front window. He split the curtains and peered outside. Shooter was near the small barn feeding the horses. Cade slipped on his pants and walked out to join him. Shooter heard the squeak of the door and turned toward the sound.

"It's about time, city boy," Shooter said. "I got half my chores done, and you're just getting up for breakfast."

Cade pushed his tangled hair back from his eyes and cleared his throat. "Don't feed me that, Shooter. I'm a doctor, remember? I'm at the hospital before the sun rises and back home after it's set." Cade stopped for a moment and thought about what he had just said. "Well, not that I'm a doctor anymore." He continued to walk in his bare feet across the grass.

"You're not going to be much help without any shoes. You might as well go back in the house and put an apron on and start cooking breakfast and dusting the furniture."

"Are you always this ornery in the morning?" Cade tiptoed through the tall weeds, jumped the small irrigation ditch, and stood on a clear patch of dirt. "This time tomorrow, I want to be at the trailhead. I thought about it all night. I just need to get up there. I can't explain how I feel, but I just need to get up there and get started. I'm counting on you to get everything I need pulled together."

"It'll be tough. You're welcome to stay here as long as you want, you know that, right?"

"I know, but this isn't a social visit. As far as I'm concerned, I'm dead. I'd be dead right now if I had the courage to do it, but I don't, and I realize that. This emptiness I feel will never go away."

"That's what you say now, but time has a way of healing. Kimber's death wasn't your fault. I've told you that before. Accidents happen. That's just a part of life."

"Yeah, accidents happen, alright. My Dad just happened to get blown to bits, my high school girlfriend just happened to slip and plunge eighty feet to her death, and seven cars and a semi just happened to collide and kill my wife and kids. My life's been full of accidents. I'm not going up to the

Winds to escape my life; I'm going up there to protect yours and anyone else's that might know me. I just need to be left alone. I don't want to meet anyone, see anyone, or talk to anyone. Bad things happen to people I care about. I've never been a quitter, but there comes a time when you need to throw in the towel." Cade looked over at Shooter. "So, are you going to help me or not?"

"Of course, I'll help you, but don't expect me to understand you." He stuck the pitchfork into the hay bail. "Come on, we got a lot of shopping to do."

***

Later that afternoon, they returned from their shopping excursion. They went to Redding to pick up all of Cade's supplies. It was nearly an hour out of their way since they had to go roundabout through the middle of the reservation. Lorenz was less than 20 minutes away, but Cade was adamant about going to Redding because he didn't want to risk running into someone he knew. Shooter tried to convince him that with nearly three weeks of growth on his face and twenty years' time under his belt, nobody would recognize him anyway, but Cade held steadfast. He didn't want anyone to know he was in town or what his plans were in the Winds.

"Wow," Shooter said as he started to spread all of the essentials on the front yard grass. "I've never been shopping like that before. You peeled off hundred dollar bills like you wipe your ass with 'em."

"It's only money. I don't need it up in the Winds; that's why I've put your name on the account. I just hope I spelled Roaring Bull right. It's two words, right?"

"What are you saying?"

"I'm saying that as long as I'm in the Winds, you're going to look over my money."

"What about your mother? What part does she play in all this?"

"She's set up financially. That's all I care about. What she does with her money is her business. I can't be bothered with her."

"But what if she calls and asks about you?"

Cade shook his head. "Tell me, how many times has my mother called you in the last twenty years? If she does happen to call you, tell her you don't know where I am. As far as you know, I'm on some extended vacation to help deal with the shitty hand I've been dealt in my life."

"But I don't know how to manage this kind of money. What if I just go crazy and spend it all at once? I bet that would get you to come down off the mountain."

Cade showed no emotion. "I've got it all set up at a bank in Chicago. You get five thousand dollars each month, and you get to use my truck."

"I can't accept that kind of money for nothing."

Cade stopped him from saying another word. "You haven't heard me out. I'm not giving you the money for anything. There are things you need to do. To begin with, you need to pack in all this stuff for me."

"That's not a problem. I have eight horses. It'll take one trip, max. What else?"

"You need to refresh my supplies one more time before winter this year and then again each spring and winter that I'm still alive. Sound simple enough?"

"Yeah, but how do I know if you're still alive? I mean, well, I know it sounds terrible, but I have to know. How do I know when to stop packing in supplies?"

"That's easy; I don't show up, simple enough?"

"Simple, yes, morbid, yes, but is it worth it to you to pay me four thousand dollars a month to do it?"

"Let me put it this way: you're the only person who knows my plan and the only person I can trust to do this. Whether I'm paying you too much or not enough, your salary is not negotiable. Let's talk about the truck. The truck is yours to drive and do with what you please. Take good care of it because the next truck comes out of your five thousand a month. I've allowed for five thousand dollars twice a year for supplies. It shouldn't cost more than that. If it does, then I'll be pissed at you because that means I'll have to come down to authorize more. Do you understand? I trust you with this. The sooner you realize that this is the beginning of your future and the end of mine, the easier it will be to manage the finances. Do you understand what I'm saying?"

Shooter nodded his head.

Chapter 15

Cade and Shooter were up by 5 and at the trailhead by 6:30. It was a beautiful morning, with hardly any wind, which was quite common for the Winds, but generally, the wind would pick up in the early afternoon. Within an hour, they had the horses out of the trailer, saddled, harnessed, and loaded down. Shooter had performed these rituals countless times before.

The trail became more and more familiar to Cade as he rode the horse through every twist and bend through the trees. Some parts of the trail were switch-backs to accommodate the steep terrain. The horses managed the rocky trail with ease. They were well trained for traversing the high mountain country, and like an enthusiastic cattle dog riding in the back of a truck with his tongue hanging out heading to his first cattle drive of the summer, they, too, were visibly excited to have their bags loaded and on the trail again and not standing idle confined to a fenced pasture.

They passed through the last patch of trees over the ridge and ascended above the timberline. All that was visible were a variety of colorful wildflowers sprouting up along the edge of the trail nestled protectively in the dark crevices of the large rocks. Cade remembered hiking with his father and taking the time to admire each variety of wildflowers and actually counting the number of varieties as they walked. He remembered counting 53 different varieties along a 12-mile stretch of trail. It was times like these that he missed being with his father.

As he and Shooter rode within a few hundred feet from the top of the next ridge, Cade pulled back on the reins, and the horse came to a halt.

"What's the problem, Cade?" Shooter brought his horse to a stop as well. Cade just sat there and looked ahead to where the mountain met the sky. He removed his hat and set it in his lap. The cool, crisp air blew through his hair. He shut his eyes momentarily and could hear the sounds of the wind blowing across the grass and through the scattered rocks. This was the place; the place that first made him fall in love with the Winds.

"Isn't it great?" Cade said. "It's just how I remembered it when I was a kid. In college, like during a big final or something, or at the hospital, when I was faced with a trauma victim who wasn't going to make it to the next minute, I would occasionally find myself drifting to this very place. Visually, I could picture it in my mind. I could taste the clean air and smell the wildflowers. To me, there is no finer spot in the world. It's so peaceful, beautiful, and yet so mysterious. Isn't it ironic that I would be destined to spend the rest of my earthly life in such a paradise?"

"Very poetic, Cade; now visualize picking ice crystals

out of your ass this winter." Cade really wanted to laugh but just couldn't. What he said was corny but heartfelt. He truly loved the Winds!

"Get off your horse and walk with me," Cade said. Shooter didn't really understand but could sense the importance to Cade, so he got off his horse and waited for the next instruction. Cade tied the reins to a small bush and beckoned Shooter to do the same. Together, they walked to the top of the ridge. As they neared, Cade closed his eyes and walked the last few steps. When he could feel the intense, crisp breeze hit his cheeks, he slowly opened his eyes and looked out across the wide expanse. It was as if the entire world had been cracked open for him to see inside. It was breathtaking. Snow-capped peaks reached forcibly to the cloud-filled sky as far as the eye could see. Tumbling streams connected countless splotches of dark blue lakes nestled at the base of each canyon. The treeless Wind River Peak stood proudly in the far distance with its sheer, vertical granite faces reflecting the colors of midday.

The steep, dark canyons near the top held large white glaciers within their permanent grasps. They were present year-round, slowly melting and shedding their life-giving water to the lakes and streams below throughout the short, cool summer, only to be completely replenished again through the long, frigid, unforgiving winter. Lush, grassy meadows of various shades of green could be seen at the

The Winds

edges of the trees fed by natural mountain springs from the sides of the cliffs. Huge boulders intricately cut out from the faces of the cliffs hung vicariously, waiting for the slightest shift in the Earth's crust to send them tumbling with fury to the valleys below.

"It's just like I'd remembered it," Cade said, competing with the sounds of the wind. The air was noticeably thin. He slowly took in several deep breaths. "I haven't been here for over twenty years, and it's as if I'd never left."

"That's the neat thing about this place," Shooter said. "It never changes. This is one place on Earth that man hasn't completely screwed up."

After Cade spent nearly an hour admiring the beauty of the Winds, most of it in silence, walking from one high point to the next, they continued down to the bottom of the valley back into the thick pine trees. They continued to travel mile after mile over the rugged terrain with Cade insisting on frequent stops to admire the beauty and to drink from the various cold mountain springs. After several hours of riding since walking over the first ridge, Cade pulled the reins back and shouted for his horse to halt when they reached a small clearing.

"So now what, Cade, the first verse of Kumbaya?" Shooter smiled and brought his horse to a stop. The caravan of horses behind him stopped as well. "Wherever the hell we're going, we'll never get there if you keep making all of us stop to smell the roses."

"Are you mocking me?" Shooter started to grin. Cade became very serious. "You think all of this is a joke, don't you? You think I'm crazy?" Cade got off his horse and approached Shooter. "Right here, this is as far as you need to go. I don't need you anymore."

"Hey, I didn't mean anything by it."

"You aren't listening to me. We're here. Unload the stuff."

"Right here, smack dab middle of the trail? No water within a quarter mile or even a smooth place to set up camp. Out of all the Winds, *this* is where you're going to stay?"

"Yeah, as far as you're concerned, this is the place."

"That's nuts. I have eight horses that can deliver the goods to your doorstep, but you don't want to tell me where that is. I don't get it. What's the big deal? I won't tell anyone."

"Maybe not, but I'm not willing to take that chance right now. I have to make sure that nobody knows where I am. Look at it like a prison sentence. I'm spending the rest of my life out here without any chance of parole, only my cell doesn't have metal bars, a stainless steel toilet, and a roommate named Bubba who has questionable sexual tendencies."

"I still think this is a dumb idea. Trust me, come January, you'll wish you had Bubba to help keep you from freezing to death."

"Yeah, well, it's got to be this way." Cade was serious for a moment, and then a slight smile emerged on his face. "I'll be fine, Shooter. It's just something I have to do. Please try to understand." With that, Shooter got off his horse, and the two of them spent the next hour or two sorting through the supplies and stashing them in the large cavities of rocks and under trees. Cade would spend the next few days retrieving and packing them to his new home.

Cade hiked for nearly three hours with his backpack fully loaded. His farewell to Shooter was bittersweet. A part of him, a very small part, wanted to return down the mountain with him, but the greater part of him was committed and motivated to start his new life in the Winds. Who would have thought that the successful doctor from Chicago would end up a mountain man in an untamed, uncivilized area of the world to fend for himself, only with occasional replenishment of supplies from a hired friend? This question would echo through Cade's mind continually for the next several weeks as he prepared himself for the long, unmerciful winter ahead.

His final destination was a small lake. He had discovered it during one of the detours that he would commonly take when he was up in the Winds with his father and friends. Cade was always convinced that he would eventually find a fishing spot that would be the envy of all who dared to venture into the Winds. It would be a place that only he would know about, and when he had had his fill of fishing it, he would tell only his closest friends. This small lake, he eventually realized, was not such a place.

The lake had no official name and couldn't be found on any of the published maps. It was fed exclusively by a series of slow-melting glaciers whose small trickle would not sufficiently oxygenate the water and was too cold to provide any kind of plant life. With the absence of these two key ingredients, this lake would not sustain fish, but now he felt it would help sustain him. With his secret secure, Cade felt he had a good chance of never being found.

Not only did he discover the lake but also a small cabin nestled deep within the trees at the far corner at the base of a narrow canyon. Now, it seemed a bit smaller than he'd remembered it when he was a sophomore in high school, but it was a pleasant surprise to him that it was still standing. It could have been an early trapper, an Indian, or even the forest service that built it. For being abandoned and apparently unnoticed and uncared for so many years, it was in remarkable condition.

He spent the next several days transporting the remaining balance of his supplies to his newly found and soon-renovated home. Much of the daylight hours were spent patching gaping holes in the roof and walls of the one-room cabin and chopping wood to eventually burn for warmth throughout the winter. The fireplace had remained in good condition. It was made of stones held together by mortar. It had a good draw as he tested it with a large, wet fire. The location of the cabin was exceptional to fit his needs. It could not be seen from any location on the lake's edge or even from the tops of the peaks above. The smoke as it bellowed out of the top of the chimney was literally filtered as it passed through the large pine branches and eventually dispersed out the steep canyon walls above undetectable.

With the holes patched, the walls shored up and sturdy, the windows filled in and sealed to keep out the future frigid winds, and the outhouse rebuilt and sealed with a tight-fitting door, Cade figured that he was ready for the winter ahead. It was exhausting work, but something that had to be done before he could do the thing he loved to do more than anything in this world – fishing.

Chapter 16

She's a beauty, Cade said to himself as he removed the hook from the small vice. He had just tied one of the most irresistible flies for the native trout teeming in most high mountain lakes. Having to hike to neighboring lakes to fish was a hassle, but choosing to reside at a lake with absolutely no fish served him well in preserving his anonymity.

That morning, he had hiked to a small lake over the ridge. A large flat rock at the lake's edge formed his chair as he sat and re-perfected his skill. The fly had a completely black body with gray and black hackles the entire length of the hook's shank. It wasn't anything fancy, but it worked and worked consistently well. His father had taught him how to tie flies when he was very young. They rarely bait fished, if ever – wet flies were the method of choice.

Cade placed the fly in the case next to about a dozen of the exact same style he had tied since the night before. He only used three flies: Mosquito, Black Wooly, and the Mickey Fin. All worked equally well, depending on the weather and the time of day. The Mickey Fin, with its long, thick cow hair dyed red on one half and yellow on the other,

The Winds

tied at the head extending well past the end of the hook with its metallic silver body, was his father's favorite, and his enthusiasm rubbed off on young Cade. This particular fly had an uncanny resemblance to a small minnow when wet and was used just after dark, usually in either the inlet or the outlet of the lake since that's where the larger trout patrolled for an easy meal.

Cade clamped another hook into his portable vice and began to dress the shank with the black thread. Suddenly, he heard something from across the small lake. It was the sound of laughter. He looked up and glanced in the direction of the sound. There were three people on the other side: a man and two boys. The boys were walking several steps behind the dad as they ventured around the water's edge.

Cade had exiled himself to the Winds to be alone and wished it could be that easy, but he realized that it wasn't. He would have to occasionally come in contact with people. He figured it was better than the alternative, which was hiding out the rest of his days. He looked back down and continued to tie his fly as if he hadn't noticed they were there.

The sounds became louder as they worked their way

around the edge of the lake in his direction. He didn't care if they were there. It was uncomfortable for him, but he realized that they had as much right as he did to be there, but he didn't feel much like talking.

"Hello there!" the man yelled. He waved at Cade and continued to walk closer to where he was sitting. "Catch any fish?" Cade continued to wrap the shank of his hook with the black thread and didn't look up or acknowledge the man. "I said, hello there. I was wondering if you've had any luck today."

Cade looked up briefly. "You always catch fish in the Winds," he replied while readjusting the vice. "Today's no exception."

"This is our first time in the Wind Rivers. We just set up camp over there at Spear Lake."

Then why don't you fish over there? Cade thought to himself. "Well, you had three hundred lakes to choose from, hope you like it there."

The man looked back at his two boys. He was a little uncomfortable with the tone of the conversation. So far, Cade hadn't presented himself as the friendliest person he'd

The Winds

ever met, but he continued to talk. "We can't complain about the camp spot, but this high altitude is a killer. I'm not used to it." The two boys unhooked their spinner from the bottom-most eyelet and cast into the water. "We're using spinners right now. A guy back home said they really work during the day." Cade just nodded his head. "In the evenings, I'll use my fly rod. My kids don't know how to fly fish yet. Where we're from, we don't have much of an opportunity to fly fish, but I learned when I was a young boy." Cade just sat there tying his fly, not even tempted by the bait the guy was dangling in front of him.

I'm not asking you where you're from 'cause the truth is, I don't give a damn where you're from.

"Dad said we can't use a fly rod until we're at least twelve," the smaller of the two replied as he tried to untangle his line from a bush near the shore.

"He said we'd snag our ear," the larger boy said.

The dad started to laugh. "Kids," he said. "They're referring to the story I told them when I was a kid about their age. My Dad came home from work, and I was in the backyard practicing my cast with his fly rod. He was amazed that I was using an actual hook at the end. He told me that when he was a kid, he did the same thing and set the hook right in the back of his ear."

It was all Cade could do to sit and listen to this man go on and on about his childhood. Surely, this man could find someone who had the least bit of interest in his story other than Cade.

"I just laughed at my Dad as he went back into the house. I continued to snap the hook back and forth, and within two minutes, I'm serious. Two minutes, I went running into the house with a hook in the back of my ear. See, there's still a scar." The man pinched his earlobe and stretched it tight over his thumb. "See?" Cade didn't look up; he continued putting the finishing touches on his fly. "You're probably wondering how I got it out of my ear," the man continued.

I really couldn't give a shit, but I'm sure you'll tell me anyway, Cade thought to himself.

"I cut the barb off and then pulled it out the other end." The man looked over at his boys. The youngest one was still trying to get his line untangled. He stood back up and looked

The Winds

across the lake to the cliffs on the other side. "I did some reading about the Wind River Mountain Range before we came. I learned that there are all kinds of varieties of fish in these lakes. Let's see if I can remember all the names."

Oh shit, Cade thought to himself. *This guy never quits.*

"There's Brook, Rainbow," the guy paused for a moment to think.

"Cut Throat," the older son yelled out.

"Ah, right, Cut Throat and Brown Trout. I remember reading something about a California Golden Trout, but I don't have my heart set on catching one of those. They said they're really hard to catch."

Cade really wanted to inform the imbecile that he'd caught two really nice ones earlier that morning but didn't.

"And there's one more that escapes me. It's like a cross between a Mackinaw and a Blue Gill or something. I think they call it a Mackingill or, uh, Bluekinaw."

I need to shoot this guy and put me out of my misery, Cade thought. "It's a cross between a Mackinaw and a Brook

Trout. We call it a Brookinaw," Cade replied.

"Yeah! I knew it was something like that. Anyway, there's a lot of variety for the kids to catch."

"If they could ever get their lines in the water," Cade mumbled under his breath.

"I'm sorry, what did you say?" the man asked.

"Nothing, it wasn't important."

"So, you from around here?"

Cade removed the fly from the small vice and gave it a quick inspection before sticking it into the small patch of wool with the other flies just above the top pocket in his vest. He then slipped the vice into one of the lower side pockets. "Nope."

"So where you from?"

"Not from around here," Cade replied candidly.

"So you got a wife, maybe some kids?"

"Nope."

The Winds

"That's too bad. I'd pictured you with a couple of kids. I waited until I was thirty-two to get married, and it took me a few years for my wife to convince me that we needed a couple of kids. Looking back, that was the best decision I've ever made. They're expensive, but they're worth it. I wouldn't trade this experience for anything in the world. You should consider it. It's never too late to have kids as long as you get a young enough wife." The man came a little closer. "Speaking of young ladies, have you met the forest ranger yet?"

Cade shook his head.

"Let's just put it this way: she's the prettiest forest ranger I've ever seen. I thought the State of Texas bred beautiful women, but that was before I came to Wyoming. She's real pleasant to talk to, and she looks real good in khaki green, if you know what I mean. We met her yesterday morning. She's patrolling the area. You don't have anything to worry about. All she wanted from me was to see my fishing license."

Cade's patience had worn thin. He hadn't invited this guy over to his side of the lake. He did everything he could to discourage carrying on a conversation with him. It was time for him to take the action he should have taken when he first noticed them. He stood up, grabbed his fishing pole, and walked away. As he trudged through the trees, he began to reconsider the subject of people. He'd forgotten to consider the consequences of not possessing a fishing license, and now that it had been brought to his attention that a forest ranger was making the rounds in the area, where he sensed there were people, avoidance was unquestionably the best course of action for him to take from this time forward.

Chapter 17

The thin mountain air was crisp and cold, and at this elevation, it meant one thing: winter was just around the corner. Small snowflakes started to fall to the ground as Cade hiked to a predetermined location. He kept a daily calendar so he would know when to meet Shooter for supplies. His supplies were nearly exhausted, so when he saw Shooter's horses approaching from over the rocky slope, it was a welcome sight.

Cade stood silent and still behind a large rock as Shooter led his horses slowly toward him on the trail. The trail was one that was less traveled. It was rocky and wasn't maintained by the forest service, which made it perfect for the two of them to meet in secret. Cade stood silent and watched Shooter's every move to ensure that he had come alone. Shooter sensed he was being watched and brought his horse to a stop.

"Come out, come out, wherever you are!" he yelled into the tall pines. He stepped down off his horse and continued to look around. He studied the rocks and trees and made note of the direction of the cool breeze, but he mainly studied the stillness, listening for the slightest sound. He focused in on one of the larger rocks to the left of him.

"You've had your fun, Cade. Now come on out."

Cade appeared from behind the rock. "I never could sneak up on a damn Indian."

"Old Indian powers," Shooter said as he wiggled his fingers freely in front of Cade's face. Cade was not amused.

"How you holding out?"

"Still holding," he said as he walked toward the lead horse and started to open one of the packs. "Where's the chocolate?" Cade continued to untie the flaps and fish through the leather pouches.

"Good to see you too, Cade," Shooter said with a little sarcasm. "Other side, top pouch. Now answer my question."

"I'm fine. I built me a nice place – safe, secure, and secluded."

"Sounds like you got it all figured out, but what about these little snowflakes? Any thought to what you're going to do when they get bigger and there's lots more of 'em?"

The Winds

"You just can't let it be, can you? Yeah, I've given it some thought. In fact, I've given it a lot of thought." Cade continued to search through the side bags.

"And bears?"

"What about 'em?" Cade said, rather annoyed. "Damn it, Shooter, where's the chocolate?"

Shooter reached over and started to dig to the bottom of one of the bags. "They're here, you know."

"Black bears?" Cade replied. "You get close enough. You can pet those."

"What about the grizzlies?" Shooter said. Cade started to laugh.

"There ain't no grizzlies in the Winds. Too far south."

"Eighty miles really isn't that far to roam in twenty years, Cade. They're here." Cade stopped searching through the pack for a second. "What are you going to do if one of them decides to make you his roommate over winter?" Shooter pulled out a bag that contained several varieties of candy bars.

"How come you didn't tell me there were grizzlies up here?" Cade grabbed the bag and pulled out the first candy bar he could get his hands on. He quickly opened it and took a big bite.

"Would it have changed your mind?"

Cade thought for a moment as he continued to chew. "No, but I'd a come in here better prepared."

Shooter walked over to the second horse and slipped a high-caliber pistol out of a leather holster. "Like this?" Shooter held the pistol in his hands.

Cade took it from him, looked it over carefully, pointed it in the opposite direction toward the pile of rocks, and looked down the narrow sights. "It's perfect, a stainless steel Smith and Wesson Model 4006, a ten-round clip plus one in the chamber."

"I had no idea you knew so much about firearms."

"There are a lot of things you don't know about me. I got a couple of friends in Chicago on the Force. I used to target shoot with them out at the range. This pistol's standard issue for them." Cade shifted the gun from one hand to the

The Winds

other. "It feels great. It's got the white dot front sight and the straight back strap grip. You know, I even got to the point where I was shooting with either hand and pretty good. This was an excellent idea, Shooter, thanks."

"No, thank the supply account. I talked to my buddy in Redding. He's a policeman. They use them as well, as does Fremont County and all of the Wyoming State Parks. I'm not sure if the reservation's the same or not. They usually do their own thing, sometimes just to spite the white man." Shooter paused for a moment as he thought. "Cade, do you even know what a grizzly bear track looks like? I mean, can you tell the difference between an ordinary black bear and a grizzly bear track?"

"No, I don't think I could, but what difference does it make? I'd just shoot whatever moved."

"Grizzly's stalk their prey. Knowing their tracks might give you a heads up if a grizzly's in the area. You could be standing on the edge of the lake fishing and not even know what hit you. It would carry you a mile or two deep into the woods and cover you with pine needles until you're ripe and ready to eat."

"Ok, I get the point. So what's the difference?"

"Besides the grizzly being twice the size, there's a lot of difference. The reason I know is because my Dad taught me when I was a kid. He even showed me how to make 'em in the dirt. It only takes one or two prints to convince someone a grizzly's been around because when they see it, they don't hang around to ask questions. I'm thinking that after the second or third heavy snow, you won't have to worry the rest of the winter."

"Hibernation?"

"Actually, no; they go into a shut-down mode where they pretty much stay in one place, like in a cave or under a big tree. They sleep most of the winter and live off the fat they put on in the summer. They're extremely light sleepers, though, so don't go yelling if you happen upon one."

"Ok, you convinced me. Show me the difference in the tracks."

Shooter got down on his hands and knees and began to press the palm of his hand into the soft dirt. He did this repeatedly, overlapping the previous until he made a long oval shape that was wider at the top. Then, with his thumb, he pressed five distinct ovals in a line that followed the wider top of the pad. "Now, the next thing I do is what really sets the grizzly track apart from the black bear." With a small, sharp stick, he made the claws protruding out from the top of the five smaller ovals. Each claw was roughly twice as long as the ovals were wide, and they each veered toward the center claw. "The black bear's claws are half this long and go straight out."

"Are you serious? A grizzly's claws are that long?"

"And as sharp as razor blades." Shooter threw down the small stick and stood back up on his feet. "Are you sure you still want to stay up here?"

Without hesitation, Cade started digging through the saddlebags again. "So, what other surprises did you bring me?"

"I'll take that as a yes." Suddenly, he put his fingers in his mouth and let out a piercing whistle. Over the small ridge came running a large yellow lab. It jumped up on Cade with his paws against his chest and licked him in the face.

"It's your new friend. Do you like him?" Cade grabbed the dog by the neck and pulled him down to the ground and began to wrestle with him. "I just thought if you got into some trouble this winter, you could use a friend. You know, Lassie could understand complete sentences."

"So what's his name?" Cade asked as he rubbed the dog under the chin.

"He didn't have one the first week of his life. I couldn't for the life of me come up with a good name until he got a little too close to one of the cats and got torn up."

"So his name's Dumb Ass?"

"No, Stitch. That's what it took to stop the bleeding in his ear. The vet put in one lousy stitch and charged me sixty bucks."

"Oh, so *you're* the dumb ass." Cade laughed as he grabbed the dog by both sides of his jowls, making him look him in the eye.

"Stitch! I like it," Cade said.

"Just take me to your place. I can pack this stuff straight to your front door. You do have a front door, right?"

Cade shook his head. "I can't. It's still too risky. I hope

The Winds

you understand. It's important that nobody knows. I don't need anyone's sympathy, and I surely don't need anyone's help." Shooter looked at him sternly. "Ok, besides you. You're the only one I need help from. You wouldn't have happened to bring me a forged fishing license? I guess there are forest rangers patrolling the lakes now. Things have sure changed since I was last up here. Nobody's ever asked to see my fishing license."

"So what are you going to do if a ranger approaches you?"

Cade thought for a moment. "Well, now that I have a pistol…"

"That's not even funny. Really, what would you do?"

"I just can't be seen," Cade replied quite candidly."

"We're close to the reservation. You know that, right? They catch you fishing, and they'll throw your ass in jail. They've adopted a no-tolerance approach to poachers, especially white poachers."

"Poachers hunt animals. I'm fishing."

"To the rez-rangers, there's no difference. They treat you the same. If they catch you, they take your equipment, rough you up a bit, and escort you to jail. There are a couple of assholes assigned to this area, so be careful. They got major attitude since one of their own turned up missing earlier this summer."

"I really hadn't planned on crossing over, but as long as I'm illegal, I might as well be illegal where the fishing's the best. I'm not afraid of the rangers, Indian or white; to me, they're just another person on my list to avoid."

"Suit yourself, but I'm telling you, the rez plays by different rules. The white man has kicked them around for so long that I'm not sure what they'd do to you if they caught you without a permit. If I were you, I'd stay off."

"Well, you're not me, and don't try to tell me what I can and can't do. Frankly, I don't care if they decide to take a couple of shots at me. But keep this in mind: I won't go down without a fight. One thing that hasn't been affected by all the shit that's happened to me in my life is my will to fight. Maybe I have a huge chip on my shoulder, but I know I'll eventually die up here; it's now my destiny, but I'm not just going to roll over and let it happen. Whether it be at the claws

The Winds

of a bear or at the hands of a man, I will never be taken from the Winds."

Shooter couldn't believe what he was hearing. First, Cade self-imposed a sentence to quietly spend the rest of his natural life in the Winds, and now he was spouting off about killing and being killed. In a very short period of time, he had witnessed a not-so-subtle change in his friend. He couldn't even imagine the type of person he'd be next spring – that is, if he survived the winter. Only time would tell.

"So, we stash the supplies like we did before?" Shooter said. He started to loosen all of the straps of the various saddlebags.

Cade nodded and then pointed over toward a large pile of boulders. "I've already cut off a lot of pine branches and put them over there in a pile. All the non-food stuff we'll stack over there in the cavity of that rock and then put the pine branches over it to hide it. I'll start packing the food on the first trip, and the food I can't take, I'll tie up in a tree away from the animals. So it'll take me a few days; trust me, time is not something I'm running short on."

"Suit yourself, but I could take it all for you in one trip."

"Where I'm going, you don't want to take a horse."

Cade and Shooter started to unpack all of the saddlebags and stack the contents in the cavity behind the large rock. Cade continued to place food in his pack until it couldn't hold anymore. Just before Shooter said goodbye for the long winter, he had to let Cade know about what had happened. He struggled to find the right way to approach him.

"Cade, I got a couple of things to tell you." He cleared his throat. "The first thing is good news, but I'm not sure if I should tell you or not. I mean, I'm not sure if you'd appreciate–"

"Just tell me. It's my life that's screwed up, not yours. If you have something good you want to tell me, then say it. What, you got a new girlfriend or something?" Cade continued to place smaller items in the pockets of his pack.

"Well, actually, I do have someone I'm quite fond of, but–"

Cade cut him off before he could finish his sentence. "You didn't tell her about me, did you? All I need is for her to get you drunk, and you go shooting off your mouth."

"You're a pric, Cade. I told you I've been off the hard stuff for over six years now. All I wanted to tell you was that I'm seeing a girl from back in high school."

The Winds

Cade realized what he had done and gave Shooter his full attention. "Ok, who is she? Do I know her?"

"You did. Do you remember Marybeth from high school? She was in our graduating class."

Cade thought for a moment. "I think I'm starting to remember her. She wasn't the one with the big–"

"Careful, Cade, I'm dating her, ok? Yes, she's the one we all used to call Bubbles. She's really nice. I met up with her at the reunion, and we talked for a couple of hours after dinner the second night, and then we went to the picnic together the next day. Everyone else had their kids running around, so we pretty much just sat and talked. I didn't realize I had feelings for her until just a few weeks ago, or I would have told you about meeting up with her at the reunion sooner."

"So, what changed your mind about her?"

"I stepped on an old rusty nail when I was out fixing a fence last month and could barely walk the next day, so I decided to go to the Emergency Room. She's the head nurse there and I'm telling you, I'm not sure why, but those new colorful nurses uniforms are sexy. I enjoyed every minute of my examination, except they had to have put those stethoscope things in the freezer. They're cold."

"First of all, hospitals are kept cold for a reason; bacteria don't like the cold. Second of all, I agree about the nurse's uniform thing. Why do you think I became a doctor?" There was a short silence. "Well, don't go and screw it up, Shooter, and you can thank me later."

"Thank you for what?"

"It's the truck. You don't think you would have had a chance with her without it, do you? I wish you could tell her hi for me, but–"

"Don't worry about it. Your secret's safe with me, even when I'm in the heat of passion."

"So, what else were you going to tell me? You said you had a couple of things."

Shooter thought for a moment and then remembered. "Oh, I got pulled over a couple of weeks ago."

"So, what's the problem?" Cade asked, and then it suddenly dawned on him. "The registration! It's in my name. So, was there a problem?"

"There wouldn't have been, except the cop was Denton. He's still pissed about you and his little encounter on your way out of town. He asked for my license and registration, and, well, I realized that the registration was in your name, so I tried to talk my way out of it, you know, one good friend to another. He knows who I am. Why does he need to see my registration? He got acting real tough, like he used to in high school. Remember that one vein would stick out in the middle of his forehead when he got really mad? It was sticking out, and I thought he was going to pull out his gun, so I handed over the registration. He read it, and a big smile came to his face."

"So he smiled; what's the big deal?"

"Because he told me he told you he'd throw your ass in jail if you came back to Lorenz."

"Yeah, he said something like that, but it was an empty threat. He can't just throw people in jail without a valid reason." Cade thought for a minute. "I forgot to pay that speeding ticket. Whatever, he's just trying to scare you."

"Well, he did a good job of it. My court date is scheduled for a week from Tuesday."

"What? That's ridiculous. What for?"

"Grand theft auto. He claims I stole the car."

"That's bullshit! He can't do that. He knows we're

friends."

"Well, he can because I can't give him any proof that you've given me permission to use your truck. You don't have a phone number, mailing address, or place of employment. Without any one of those, I'm as good as in jail."

"So you're saying I need to go to town?"

"Well, I talked to my buddy, who's a policeman in Redding. Without giving him any details, I told him you were on an extended vacation and didn't want to be bothered. Anyway, he told me that if you drafted a letter with your signature stating that you gave me permission to use your car during your absence, the charges would have to be dropped." Shooter reached into his pocket and pulled out an unsealed envelope. He removed the single piece of paper and unfolded it. "Can I get your signature, please?"

Cade signed the letter and then put a small note to the judge near the bottom of the page. It said, *"And tell Deputy Bauer to stay the hell out of my business!"*

Chapter 18

Cade made several trips to and from the stockpile of food and supplies over the course of the next few days. He was quite frustrated as he approached the last of the supplies to find that they had nearly been destroyed. He assumed the perpetrators to be martens – small, furry varmints similar to ferrets that live in burrows under the pine needles formed between the rocks.

Cade salvaged what he could, which wasn't much. Several bags of flour, sugar, and rice were destroyed, as well as the majority of his spices. Cade sat down on a nearby rock and rested his chin on his hands. "It's going to be a long winter," he said into the stillness. He reached down and patted the pistol Shooter had presented to him a few days prior. "Next time, I'll be ready for you." He stood up and began to gather what he could and stuffed it away in his backpack.

Later that day, just as the sun was beginning to set behind the cliffs near his cabin, Cade was just finishing putting everything away. He was extremely frustrated from the amount of food he lost as a result of the martens and was exhausted from the four-hour hike to bring back what remained of his supplies. He was relieved that it was the last trip he had to make before winter. As he exited the cabin, he saw Stitch chewing on a leather strap of one of the bags.

"Bad dog, Stitch!" Cade yelled. He grabbed the tether out of his mouth and struck him across the back of the legs as he attempted to run away. "You can't be chewing up my shit! All these animals are driving me nuts." As Cade yelled out of frustration into the canyon walls, he saw a distinct movement along the base of the cliff. It was a rock chuck – a portly, furry animal with small ears and a short tail about the size of a cottontail rabbit. They were a common sight in the Winds as they scurried amongst the course of crushed rocks.

Cade looked at it closely and studied its every move until it became still atop a small rock, its tiny paws clutching a small leaf as it nibbled away. He reached down and pulled the pistol out of the holster, and brought it up until it was in line with the sights.

Now's as good a time as any to see if this thing can shoot straight, he thought to himself. He gently squeezed the trigger, and almost instantaneously, the grayish-brown blob disappeared, leaving a bright red splatter against the flat rocks behind. Stitch quickly cowered down behind the woodpile as a result of the deafening sound of the gun.

"Damn, I'm good," Cade said to himself. "I haven't lost my touch." He rubbed the gun down with the front of

The Winds

his shirt and slid it back into the holster.

Just over the next ridge-making camp was the lady forest ranger. She heard the piercing shot echo off the various canyon walls, stopped pounding the tent stake into the ground momentarily, and looked in the direction of the sound. She had been assigned to the area at the beginning of the summer and was on her way back to the trailhead, completing her last trip into the Winds for the season.

That's strange, she thought. *I thought everyone was out by now.* She checked the trip permit printout before she left, and to the best of her knowledge, the last registered party left the day before. Unless someone had decided to stay a little longer, she was under the impression that she was the only one in the area. She finished setting up the tent, readying her horse for the night, and making a fire. By the time she was finished, it had become too dark to go out and investigate. She would have to wait until morning to meet the person responsible for firing the shot.

***

The next morning, Cade arose from his cot to the sound of barking outside the cabin. He quickly put on his pants from the day before, strapped his holster around his waist, and rushed out to see what all the commotion was about.

"What is it, boy?" Cade asked, not expecting an answer. He removed the chain, and Stitch ran through the trees in the direction of the lake. "Wait up, boy!" Cade went back into the cabin and finished getting dressed. He ran down toward the lake but stopped at the edge of the trees and looked over to the opposite ridge. Roughly three-quarters of a mile away, he saw a person riding a horse, descending over the crushed granite rocks toward the lake. It appeared to be a ranger – the lady ranger he'd heard about. "Damn!" Cade said. "I'm not ready for this."

Stitch continued to stand in the clearing, barking even louder than before. Cade realized he had little time to think. He couldn't let anyone know of the cabin. If they did, they would be certain to tell someone, which would result in him having to abolish his plan. A person could only stay in the Winds a maximum of 30 days before being required to either renew their permit or leave entirely. Cade wasn't willing to do either.

"Stitch!" he shouted. "Come here, boy!" Stitch stopped barking and looked back to his master. Cade bent down and began slapping his thighs. "Come on, boy, come here. I got a treat for you." Stitch let out a final bark, turned, and ran back into the trees. "Good boy." Cade rubbed Stitch behind the ears. He grabbed his collar and

The Winds

quickly led him to the cabin. "Ok, Stitch, you have to be quiet now. Don't be barking." Cade led him into the cabin, fluffed his pillow bed, and threw a variety of treats near him on the floor. "Now you stay here and be quiet. No barking, you hear?" Cade exited the cabin, shut the door behind him, and made his way back to the edge of the trees.

"She's coming," he said under his breath. "She must have heard Stitch." Cade stood very impatiently, not really knowing what to do. He tried to formulate a plan just in case she saw him and wondered what he was doing. What if she found the cabin? How could he lie his way out of that one?

Cade started to run through the trees just at the edge to avoid being seen. The strategy was to put some distance between him and the cabin. His heart pounded in his chest, not from running but from the anticipation of what would happen next. He stood there, stealthy silent, watching and waiting.

The horse continued to walk steadily down the loose, crushed rock toward the lake. The ranger thought she'd heard something down around the lake but wasn't sure. The wind was howling at the top of the ridge at the time, which made it very difficult to hear much of anything. She continued toward the lake anyway, even though the shoreline appeared to be abandoned. She suspected as much since she, as well as the other rangers, knew the lake didn't have any fish in it.

She continued to ride following the shoreline, dodging occasional small brush, boulders, and trees, things that normally wouldn't be an issue if following a trail, but there wasn't a trail around this lake for obvious reasons. Nearing the back of the lake, she stopped and got off her horse. Still holding the reins, she bent over to examine something on the ground.

Dog shit, Cade thought to himself. He was within 20 feet of her, well hidden in the trees, watching her every move. His foot was nearly asleep, but he couldn't move it for fear of making a noise.

Tara stood back up and looked around. First, she looked back over to where she came from, then panned across the lake and then ahead toward the cliffs, canyon, and, heaven forbid, the cabin. Cade slowly took in a deep breath, hoping that Stitch wouldn't start to bark.

The horse put its head down and began to munch on the meager portions of grass and green stubble on the rock-laden ground. Tara dropped the reins and began to walk toward the cliffs. Cade watched with much anticipation. Just briefly, he reached down and felt the cold stainless steel of his pistol held securely in the holster.

What am I thinking? he asked himself. He couldn't believe that, even for a nanosecond, he'd consider killing this woman just to avoid being discovered, but then again, this was his life sentence. There was no backup plan as far as he was concerned. If he was found out, he would be forced to either find another set of mountains or embrace society as he knew it. At the present, neither was an option; drastic measures require drastic means. If killing another human being was necessary to preserve his way of life, then it would have to be that way. If you're not a member of society, what is the motivation for being a good citizen? Somehow, the solitude and the lack of communication, association, and habitation with human beings other than Shooter began to take its toll on Cade's ability to distinguish right from wrong. At that very moment, when his fingers touched the cold steel fastened to his hip, Cade Hobbs vowed that he'd kill before being taken out of the Winds. Remaining in the Winds wasn't an option; it was a necessity.

Cade swallowed quietly as he watched her walk to the edge of the lake, stoop down, dip a handful of frigid water, and bring it to her mouth. His view of her was so vivid he could almost taste the water with her as she dipped a second time.

She put the water to her face and then dribbled the remains down the opening of her button-down shirt. She was shapely and beautiful, even more desirable in the standard-issue khaki green uniform. Cade was sure this was the lady ranger that annoying Texan was talking about.

She turned to face the cool breeze. Her auburn hair was thick and full of body with a slightly natural curl. It waved in the breeze as she wet her forehead and cheeks with her hand. Cade hesitated to blink even once in fear he'd miss something. He hadn't been with a woman since Angie died, and the thought of being with someone other than her hadn't crossed his mind.

He looked away momentarily and literally cursed harshly within himself for momentarily thinking, desiring, and lusting like an ordinary man. He wasn't an ordinary man by any rights. He had voluntarily removed himself from society, the very thing that had made him so painfully miserable. He looked back over to her with a completely different set of eyes, the eyes of an animal bent on survival. In his warped mind, she, as well as all other pillars of authority, became the enemy.

Cade didn't fear them; he despised them for who they were and for what they represented. They symbolized civilization, society, and authority – everything that he

The Winds

had come into the Winds to escape. Cade had adapted to a sense of lawlessness. He was under the firm impression and belief that since he was not a part of society, laws that were on the books to control or limit what members of society could and couldn't do were of no use or had zero relevance to him.

Laws that set the limit to the number and size of fish you could catch or the type of animal and time of year it could be killed were two laws he vowed to completely ignore. As far as he was concerned, the Winds were his home now. Whatever he had to do to sustain his own life was of no consequence to anyone else.

However, as he stood camouflaged behind the tree branches, motionless and curious, he could not deny the obvious fact that this lady ranger was strikingly desirable. If he truly viewed himself as an animal, then why should he hesitate to reveal himself and take her as he pleased? When he was finished with her, she could easily be discarded. He pondered the question as he continued to stare intently at the woman as she cooled herself, completely unaware of the stocking, animalistic eyes behind her.

Suddenly, there was a loud snap of a dry twig under Cade's boot. He quickly retreated deeper into the dense cover of the trees. The woman stood up and looked back toward the direction of the sound.

"Hello?" she said hesitantly with a slightly raised voice. She started to walk toward the edge of the trees. Cade watched her every move. "Is somebody there?" She continued to walk across the rocky surface until she reached the edge of the trees and peered within its dense canopy. Her heart began to race as she looked down to the ground just past the first row of branches. A partial boot track accompanied by a freshly turned rock was left in a small dirt patch at the edge of the fallen pine needles. She grabbed a low-lying branch and moved it downward to expose her view deeper within the trees.

"Excuse me, can I help you find something?" Cade asked.

She jumped back from the trees at the sound of the deep voice and quickly turned around to see a tall man with a thick beard and mustache, wearing worn clothes, a hat, and mirrored sunglasses. His face was nearly expressionless, void of a smile or a frown.

"You startled me," she replied as she tried to catch her breath. "Where did you come from?"

Cade looked toward the front of the lake. "From over there. I saw your horse and came to see who was here. So, why are you here?"

The Winds

"My name's Tara Samuels, and I'm the forest ranger assigned to the Beaver Tail trailhead, which includes this and many of the neighboring lakes."

"I guess that explains the green outfit."

"I heard a shot last night and thought I'd come over and investigate this morning." She looked down at the holstered pistol secured around Cade's waist.

"I didn't fire the shot. I only use this for protection." She questioned him with her eyes. "You don't believe me?"

"Why should I?" Tara said. "Are you here alone or with family?"

"Well, I don't have a family."

"Then you're here with friends."

Cade shook his head. "I just came up here by myself for a few days to get away from the city. I'm heading back out tomorrow."

"I'm on my way out today. The last trip in for me this year. Snow could fall any day now. That's funny, though. I don't recall seeing your registration. As far as I could tell, the last party in my area left two days ago."

"Simple, I didn't register. I was coming in by myself and only up here for a couple of days."

"Didn't you see the registration box at the trailhead? It's right in the middle of the trail with a big sign and everything. The fee is used to maintain the trails and stuff, and if you get into trouble, we know you're here and can come with help."

"I don't much care for trails, so to speak. I like to feel like I'm a part of the wild. Trails give me a sense of human intervention, and when I come up here, I want to leave that behind me. And I don't plan on needing anyone's help while I'm here."

"So, I don't suppose you have a fishing license either."

"Sorry, left it in my other pants."

"I'm sensing a little attitude. You don't much care for what I do, do you?"

"That depends. Do you have other things you do besides harass people who are trying to enjoy nature?"

Tara shook her head. "I don't know how we got off to a bad start, but I'm here because I thought someone might be in trouble. I didn't come here to harass you. If I

The Winds

really wanted to make your life miserable, I'd write you a citation and make you leave today. You didn't register, no license, and you're being rude. Before I leave you to the wild, I would appreciate it if you would let me see your gun." She reached out her hand, waiting for Cade to hand over his pistol, which he did without hesitation.

"Smith and Wesson 4006," Tara confirmed. She took out the clip and started to eject the bullets one by one, counting them as they fell into her hand.

"Ten, right?" Cade said with a touch of arrogance.

She looked into the chamber, and it was empty. She then looked down the inside of the barrel and it was clean. She handed the pistol, clip, and loose bullets back to Cade.

"How do you know so much about guns?" Cade asked, slightly impressed. Tara smiled smugly.

"My father was a collector and used to take me and my older sister out shooting at the range when we were growing up. I've been around guns all my life."

"You didn't answer my question. Why do you know so much about this particular pistol?" Cade asked as he continued to reload the clip with the bullets.

"It's standard issue for law enforcement around here. Both the Lorenz and Redding Police use them and the Fremont County Sheriff's Department."

"And?"

"My boyfriend's a Deputy Sheriff. His name's, well, I take you're not from around here, so you probably wouldn't know him anyway, so why bother?"

"You're right; I'm not from around here, and as far as your boyfriend, he probably couldn't care less about me either."

"So where you from?" Tara asked.

"Not here."

Tara looked at him and shook her head. She turned and started to walk toward her horse, then stopped and turned around. "I didn't get your name. I suppose you left your ID in your other pants as well?" A slight smile emerged on Cade's face.

"My name's John."

"Do you have a last name, John?"

"Deere, my name is John Deere."

The Winds

Tara shook her head in disgust. She was tired of his seemingly arrogant attitude, disregard for authority, and this pointless conversation. As she climbed up on her horse to leave, she didn't want to provoke him further but decided to give him just one more shred of advice. "So you're leaving tomorrow?" Cade nodded his head. "Make sure you do. It could snow any day now, and this is one place you don't want to get caught in a storm." She made a clicking sound, and the horse started to walk. "Oh, one more thing, next time you decide to come in the Winds, register."

"Whatever," Cade mumbled to himself.

Chapter 19

During the night, several days after the time Cade deceivingly told the ranger he'd be heading out of the mountains, the wind howled, causing the branches near the cabin to thrash and scratch violently across the walls and roof.

Cade arose, shivering several times during the night to stoke the fire. On one occasion, skiffs of snow had penetrated from under the small gap between the door and the floor. He brushed the snow to the side, rolled up a towel, and shoved it into the void.

That morning, Cade woke up to the first visual evidence that the season had officially changed from fall to winter. As he opened the door to let Stitch out, he saw firsthand what he had anticipated. During the course of the night, four inches of snow had accumulated on the ground, with drifts over two feet in height in some areas from the forceful winds. The lake's edge was laden with a frozen fringe of ice half an inch thick, tapering to paper-thin, extending several feet out to the open water.

The feeling was incredible. There was something about being in the wilderness alone with incredibly white, unspoiled snow covering the ground that could not be conveyed without actually being there. With the presence of snow capping the tops of the branches and drifting on the backsides of the rocks, the same lake took on a whole different feel and appearance. It was a peaceful feeling at present but an eerie feeling for the bleak and excruciatingly cold winter Cade knew to be ahead.

Now that it was apparent how devastating the combination of wind and snow could be, Cade spent the rest of the week painstakingly mending the holes and open slits in the cabin walls, roof and door. If he was to survive the frigid winter, his cabin had to be nearly perfectly sealed from the relentless elements outside. More wood was cut to length, chopped, and stacked neatly and uniformly against both sides of the cabin as well as the back.

The clothesline was removed from between the two trees outside and stretched taut inside from the front to the back of the cabin, a few feet in front of the fireplace and a foot higher than the top of his head. Food was packed into every available vacant space, including under his cot. The balance of the supplies was stored in a small outbuilding twenty feet from the side of the cabin Cade had constructed just for that purpose.

It was constructed with six-inch diameter, or better, logs with a heavy door that could be locked by pounding a large wooden wedge into a metal ring. He considered it to be bear-proof, but since he hadn't seen anything that even remotely resembled a bear, he didn't have any substantial data to support his claim.

The days quickly became shorter. Each day, the sun would set behind the canyon walls noticeably earlier, and the nights consequently became longer and colder. The lake was entirely covered with a continuous sheet of thick ice, two feet or more in most areas. As a result, Cade was forced to melt snow for his daily water usage, which wasn't much.

The majority of his clothes would have to go unwashed, except for his underwear and an occasional pair of socks since they were easy to wash in a small pot and hang dry on the line stretched in front of the fireplace.

Every day brought a new layer of freshly fallen snow. The landscape changed with each successive layer. The trees were nearly covered, and the branches were burdened to the point of snapping under the intense weight. The bushes and even most of the larger rocks were completely covered, giving the false impression that the land was smooth and easy to traverse, but Cade knew better.

He never ventured far from the cabin. He lacked the motivation to do much of anything outside the cabin. It was challenging to walk through the drifted snow, and to this point, there wasn't much of a reason to go anywhere but to get wood from the stack or food from the outbuilding. Of course, a daily trip to the outhouse was necessary, so Cade managed to keep the path well-shoveled.

Each lonely day seemed to run anonymously into the next. There was nothing in his day that would distinguish one from the other, but he kept an accurate count of each day by marking it off the calendar that hung from the cabin wall each time he laid down to sleep at night.

It's not that he cared what day it was because the day of the week didn't matter since he had no obligations to anyone, no bowling night, dates to attend the opera, or even to see the dentist, but it was the day of the month that was important to him.

On May first, Cade was scheduled to meet Shooter for a new batch of supplies to get him through the summer. He had circled that momentous day with a bold red marker.

Most of the daylight hours were spent battling his mind. When he was awake, he was thinking. When he was thinking, he was depressed. When he was depressed, he fell asleep. It was a vicious cycle, but one that Cade had difficulty breaking.

He continued to tie flies to use in the spring and tried to read a little, but he spent most of his time nursing the fire to keep it burning. A burning fire was the breath of life. Flames had to be flickering, or at least a number of red, hot coals had to be simmering in order to keep the temperature of the cabin bearable.

He constantly battled his thoughts and his mind as he sat in the same chair in front of the small fireplace day after day. Stitch no longer barked at the wind or anything for that matter. He would just lie on the same blanket, occasionally scratching and sniffing in his slumber.

As the winter progressed, Cade found it more and more difficult to keep up with the added snowfall and continuous movement of the dry powder from the nightly winds.

He could barely open the door to his cabin a few times, which caused him to think about what he would do if the door was completely sealed with snow. How would he get out? How long could he survive without a trip to the outbuilding for food?

Even more alarming, how uncomfortable would he get before knocking the door down to get to the outhouse? This caused him to rethink the cabin's design and install a small door in the lower center of the existing door, but with hinges that would allow the door to be opened with the swing to the inside. It was similar to a doggy door, but he made it large enough for him to crawl through. At least with this arrangement, he could open the small door and dig his way out if need be.

It was late November; actually, it was Thursday, a day of Thanksgiving to the majority of the country but not for Cade. As far as he was concerned, he had nothing to be thankful for, and that included his own life.

To him, living had become an awesome burden, an unwanted entity, yet he was powerless to do anything about it. In his mind, God was the only one with the power to intervene, and during many of those miserable days, he wished that God would find it in His heart to intervene soon.

It hadn't snowed for nearly two weeks. Temperatures plunging well below zero made it impossible for it to snow. It just seemed to get colder and colder. Cade remembered experiencing cold inversions in Lorenz, where the valley naturally kept the frigid air captive and wouldn't allow it to escape for several weeks at a time.

The temperatures would drop and sustain twenty degrees below zero. He remembered his mother dressing him for grade school, kissing him goodbye, and raising the scarf an inch or two to cover the last exposed part of his body besides his eyes. Exposed skin at those extreme temperatures would experience irreparable frostbite within a matter of a few minutes.

The air was surprisingly dry, and Cade's lungs burned as he dug his way around the opposite side of the cabin for more firewood. He had exhausted the supply on the other side the week prior. It took nearly all of his strength to throw a small shovel full of snow to the top of the pile, which was as high as the eves of the cabin. Stitch followed him out as he always did, barking and running around in circles since there was no place else for him to run.

Suddenly, the stillness was interrupted by what started as a low rumble at first and then progressed to a deafening, crashing sound of tumbling boulders and breaking trees. The canyon walls erupted with sound as the huge wall of turbulent snow flowed down the large canyon on the lake's opposite side, decimating everything in its destructive path. Cade scuttled to the top of the snow bank and stepped onto the roof of the cabin to get a quick glimpse of the tremendous event.

He could only see the large cloud of snow overhead through the dense trees in the aftermath. He continued looking toward the lake but couldn't see anything. Immediately, he was thrown off the roof by the sudden force of the violent accumulation of snow that had fallen nearly four hundred feet below, destroying everything in its path, crashing on the thick ice and ricocheting across the lake toward him.

He landed on a large pile of snow and slid to ground level to the side of the cabin. Stitch had already cowered into the safety of the cabin through the small door. Cade, slightly dazed by his experience, stood up and started to brush himself off. He was covered from head to toe with a fine coating of powdered snow that not only stuck to his clothes but his face as well.

Cade could distinctly hear the sound of waves, something he hadn't heard since the lake had frozen over. The conglomeration of trees, branches, rocks, and other debris fell to the frozen lake below, penetrating and pulverizing a large portion of the thick, undisturbed ice canopy.

Waves protruded over the ice and flowed toward the shore, crashing against the edges. There was a single large wave followed by several successive waves, and then it became silent again, almost deadly silent.

Cade stopped brushing himself off momentarily and listened intently. He could faintly hear another low rumble, this time coming from the canyon directly above him.

"Not another one!" he yelled as he rushed into the cabin. He feared the worst and braced for the inevitable. Within seconds, the low rumble transformed into identical crashing and tumbling sounds. The previous avalanche had triggered another one, this time in the canyon directly above the cabin.

Cade held Stitch tightly as he tucked into a tight ball in one of the front corners of the cabin and instinctively closed his eyes while bracing himself for the furious wall of rushing snow.

The snow and debris hit the cabin with such force that it buckled several of the logs on the backside and tore off a portion of the roof, dumping large amounts of snow inside and successfully dowsing the fire and remaining coals.

Within moments, it was over. The avalanche was minuscule in comparison to the one that preceded it from across the canyon, but the damage to the cabin was disheartening. Cade released the tight grasp he had on Stitch.

They were both covered in snow. Stitch immediately began to shake the snow off his back and head. Cade took a deep breath and just sat there in awe as he looked upward through the gaping hole to the white sky above.

The Winds

Cade quickly secured a tarp over the hole in the roof and shoveled the snow from inside the cabin. There wasn't any damage to the fireplace, which was fortunate because Cade knew that the inability to make a fire meant a certain slow death. He had no qualms about dying; it's just that when he was to leave this miserable world, he had hoped it would be quickly.

Upon further assessment of the damage, he found that the cabin was mainly spared as the result of three humungous pine trees situated directly behind the cabin. They had grown there, slowly each year, year after year, for the last hundred years, and he hadn't paid them any attention until now.

The combination of the three trees directed the path of the destructive snow and debris literally around the cabin and into the lake below. They sacrificed the majority of their low-lying branches, but their main trunks held firm and unwavering. The downside was that the path was diverted directly to the outbuilding that housed all the supplies to sustain Cade and Stitch through winter.

Within less than two weeks, the food stowed within the cabin walls had been consumed entirely, except for a variety of spices and a few cups of flour. Cade knew that he and Stitch would have to dig if they were going to have their next meal.

They left the cabin and began to dig through the snow toward where the outbuilding once stood. Upon reaching the location, Cade's worst fears were confirmed. The entire building had been completely destroyed and distributed downward toward the lake by the passing sea of snow.

He decided to try to get to the lake's edge and start digging up toward the cabin. Assuming that there were food items that did not plunge into the lake with the other timber and debris, he figured this approach would yield the highest rewards.

The hours upon hours of digging were excruciatingly difficult, especially on a stomach that hadn't seen much of anything in the last two days. Stitch was also far less active, preferring to stay in the cabin while Cade dug through the seemingly endless mounds of snow.

Suddenly, he struck something hard. He immediately dropped the shovel and started to dig with his hands. As he cleared the final few handfuls of snow away, he exposed a can with a yellow and green label. It was a large can of creamed corn.

He really didn't care much for creamed corn and even remembered chastising Shooter for consuming the energy to pack it in, but at this moment, that mushy, bland-yellow excuse for food was worth more to him than season tickets to the Bulls.

He quickly retired into the cabin to heat it up. Tomorrow, he would venture out into the cold again with renewed hope and anticipation that there would be more food items hidden in the snowy tomb.

Early the next morning, still feeling the pains of hunger and weakness, he continued to dig from where he had stopped the day before. He dug through the light of day and into the darkness with only the full moon's glow to assist him.

The previous day yielded him a single can of corn. However, today, nearly nine hours into it, still digging with no intentions of stopping, he had recovered three cans of fruit, five cans of vegetables—creamed corn accounting for two of the five—and a single package of spaghetti noodles. His hopes were high but fading with every shovel full of the evil white powder. He was nearly a quarter way to where the outbuilding once stood, and at this dismal rate, his wares wouldn't sustain him for another week.

Christmas had come and gone nearly as fast as it took Cade to mark it off the calendar with his black pen. Of course, in his previous life, he had viewed that special day as one of the year's most enjoyable yet expensive days. Still, this year, he just looked at it as another day closer to that all-important day in May, the day Shooter was to replenish his now nearly consumed supplies. That was his only focus.

As a result of his digging after the avalanche fiasco, he managed to recover a portion of the original supplies, but not near enough to sustain both he and Stitch until the end of April, even following the strictest of rations. According to his calculations, it was only a matter of a few weeks, and Stitch would no longer be a beloved member of the family but an entrée.

As Cade struggled to pass the time, on occasion, a pleasant memory of his wife and two children would flash into his mind, but he was becoming an expert in ridding his mind's stage of such worthless frivolity. It was not his concern or his desire to remember anything of his past life.

As the memories appeared, he would curse and damn the very God that gave him his first breath on this Earth. If that didn't work, he would resort to self-mutilation – a slit on his finger, a cut on his arm, or even a small patch of hair on his head pulled out at the roots to refocus his thoughts and bring separation between him and his past. On several occasions, for some of the tougher memories,

The Winds

after all the other methods proved unsuccessful, he would slam his head into the rock fireplace, knocking himself unconscious, sometimes for several minutes at a time.

Doctor Cade Hobbs was well-educated in some of the finest schools in the country. He was a successful surgeon and father, but the loneliness, hunger, and depression were taking their toll on him. He found it more and more difficult to distinguish reality from fantasy.

On occasion, during the highest point of the sun's arc in the sky, he'd look out the cabin door into the sea of white and occasionally see personages of beautiful women donning vivid colors of red, purple, and orange levitating above the surface of the snow. Their long, wavy hair would glisten in the sun.

They would move about, occasionally looking over at him and smiling brightly. He would call out to them, and they would beckon him to come. He would sometimes strip down to his underwear and run after them, only to find that the extreme cold would quickly jolt him out of his hallucination. He would cower back to the confines of the warm cabin, embarrassed and ashamed.

There was no food. Everything contained in the cabin that was edible had been eaten, and the wood that he'd meticulously cut and stacked the previous fall was nearly gone. The time was near; Cade could sense it in his weak bones and in his vacant belly.

Stitch was of no use to him now. He'd considered killing and eating him weeks prior but couldn't find the strength or audacity to bury the knife in his lean flesh. As a result, Stitch remained alive to see another miserable day, and now he was too skinny to benefit either of them.

As Cade sat in silence, watching the last of the small orange flames flicker around the charred log, he heard a sound. He raised his head and looked toward the door. Stitch was there on his belly, scratching at the door with one paw. Stitch looked back at Cade with as much excitement as he could muster and then attempted to bark.

"What is it, boy?" Cade said just above a whisper. He got up from his chair and agonizingly stepped toward the door. Stitch rose to his feet and slowly wagged his tail. Upon opening the door, Cade heard a scuffle of some sort followed by another. A brown patch passed in front of him, leaped into the snow, and disappeared.

"It's a deer," Cade whispered. He reached across the chair and snatched the pistol off the small table. He stepped outside and looked around. In front of him were five deer, three doe, and two considerably larger bucks; all were standing perfectly still and looking straight over at him.

The Winds

For the first time in weeks, Cade felt his heart race within his chest, and the pain within his limbs subsided. He knew he didn't have much time before they'd leap through the snow and out of sight. He quickly raised the gun and put the large buck in the sights.

Taking a deep breath, he slowly squeezed the trigger until the gun ignited with both sound and smoke. He watched frantically as the larger of the two bucks quickly leaped into the snow, followed by the other three doe.

I missed him, he thought as he tried to trudge through the deep snow toward them to hopefully get another shot, but then a sudden movement caught his eye. In front of him was the smaller of the two bucks. He was wounded trying to pull himself through the snow.

Cade, without hesitation, brought the gun back up and, from twenty yards, put a bullet in its head. The legs immediately buckled, and the deer collapsed to the blood-ridden snow.

Cade wanted to celebrate, but all he could do was stretch his hands above his head and look toward the sky. "Yes," he said. "Yes, yes, yes." He brought his hands down to his face, buried them in his eyes, and fell to his knees. "I'm going to see spring."

But before he could let his excitement sink in too

deeply, he painfully realized that his reward for entering spring was also next year's ticket for another agonizing winter soon to follow.

Chapter 20

Cade became obsessed with the thrill and necessity of the kill. Each day brought a new source of motivation and desire to hunt for his subsistence. With several full carcasses dressed and hanging from the trees near the cabin he still continued to venture out to hunt.

It became a challenge, a way to focus on something other than his past and the miserable present. At times, he would take Stitch but found that taking him was more of an annoyance than a benefit. Stitch struggled to lunge through the deep drifts and scared the prey as he sometimes barked sporadically into the chilled air.

On this occasion, Cade consented to take Stitch along. It was late February, considered the coldest month of the Wind River winter. As they trudged through the snow, large clouds of their own breath preceded them. Cade was in search of a deer, and today, he would not be denied.

He had made several failed attempts to bring home an animal in the last few weeks. His bitter recent memory of being on the verge of death served as his motivation to continue to hunt and not settle for the three deer hanging back at the cabin. Two hundred pounds of fresh venison was not enough. He had to have more, a lot more.

They struggled around the edge of the ice-covered lake and began their ascent up the canyon wall. Cade had become aware of a small natural hot spring just over the ridge. He hadn't noticed it before the cold of winter set in, but once the air became frigid, the hot springs were marked by a shallow, ominous cloud of vapor hovering over the tops of the trees.

The deer occupied the trees surrounding the area. Since the temperature of the water was above freezing, the surface was clear of ice, and the deer would visit the pool during the hours of daylight to drink.

They reached the top of the ridge, gasping for their next breath, and fell into the deep snow to rest. Cade was so hot he was tempted to remove a few articles of clothing but knew that the heat generated from the strenuous hike up the face of the ridge was momentary and exposure to the elements could be tragic.

He sat in the snow, looking around and listening. The dense trees surrounding the spring were within site, less than a quarter mile away. Cade could see the luminous cloud of vapor tickling the tops of the trees.

"Come on, boy," he said as he struggled to get to his feet. Stitch just sat there and looked at him. He was visibly exhausted and unwilling to continue the trek.

"Come on, Stitch. You wanted to come, now come on."

The Winds

Cade walked over to him and tried to assist him up to his feet, but Stitch just rolled over in the snow and exposed his now fat belly. "Ah, forget it," he said, throwing a handful of snow in Stitch's face. "You can find your own way back. I'm not hiking that ridge again today." Cade grabbed his stuff and began trudging through the snow. "Don't wait up, this may take a while." Stitch sat content watching his master walk farther and farther away into the white canvassed background.

Cade reached the trees nearly an hour after he and Stitch separated. He stopped momentarily to rest and get a drink. He stood there and pondered what he needed to do to get close enough for a shot, because this hunting trip, he only brought his pistol. The rifle proved to be too heavy and cumbersome to carry through the snow.

As he stood there, his thoughts occupied by the hunt, he noticed a deep trench-like marking across the snow across the far horizon leading into the other side of the trees. Assuming it was the accumulation of the many deer that wandered the area, he thought nothing of it and continued into the trees.

Once inside the trees, with the absence of birds and other small tree-dwelling varmints, the area was deathly silent. Cade continued to walk carefully amongst the trees and snow-covered rocks until he could smell the distinct scent of sulfur. The center pool, Cade figured, was around one hundred degrees, with the surrounding smaller pools cooling off proportionate to the distance away from the main spring.

Cade stood at the edge of the trees and peered into the clearing. There was dense fog from the warm water vapor condensing from the surface of the pool, but he could see well enough to make out several distinct dark shapes.

There they are, he thought to himself. Again, his heart pounded wildly within his chest as he removed his pistol and brought it up in front of his face. He zeroed in on the larger of the shapes and pulled the trigger. Immediately, the shape fell to the ground. Cade rushed into the clearing and continued to fire one round after another until he had shot all eleven rounds. Within a matter of seconds, he was responsible for ending the lives of three deer.

He stood proudly over the largest deer. It was a mature buck, and Cade could only imagine the size of the rack before it was shed last Fall. It was the largest he'd ever shot, including when he used to hunt with his father when he was a kid. He wished his father could see him now; he'd undoubtedly be proud.

Cade placed the pistol back into the holster and removed one of his gloves. He knelt down beside the animal and began to stroke the tan, coarse hair. He bowed his head,

The Winds

almost in humility, for what he had done.

He felt an awkward sense of compassion toward the animal that had just given its life to help preserve his own, but he also felt a compelling sense of dominance and power over the warm carcass that lay before him.

Since killing the first deer over a month and a half ago, Cade had seriously pondered an old Shoshone Indian tradition that he had learned from Shooter back in high school. The Indian ritual was of a deep spiritual nature, supposed to make the Indian warrior become one with the deer, inheriting its cunningness, speed, and agility and making him more elusive to his enemies.

Upon killing the deer, the Indian warrior would respectfully approach the animal and, with precision, remove the heart and lift it to the endless sky for the Great Spirit to witness. He would then slowly bring it to his mouth and partake of the warm flesh with a single bite. It was so bizarre at the time that Cade had never forgotten it, even after all these years.

Slightly hesitant, Cade reached down into his front pocket and pulled out a large knife with a serrated back edge. He held the blade up high above his head as he looked into the sky above, then brought it down and carefully made a six-inch incision just below the rib cage. He then set the knife down on the soft neck of the deer and removed the other glove, rolled up the sleeve of his coat, and stuck his hand deep into the opening until his entire arm was submerged within the warm flesh up to his elbow. He carefully twisted and maneuvered until he could feel the heart of the animal. Grasping it tightly and pulling it as close to the large incision as possible, he grabbed the knife with his other hand, carefully inserting it into the cavity, and cut the heart free. He removed it and held it in the frigid air. Steam emerged from the surface of the large reddish-blue mass as Cade held it securely in his hand.

Squeamish but determined to invoke the blessings of the Great Spirit, he brought it up to his mouth and took a bite, tearing off a generous portion. A smidgeon of bright red blood trickled from the corner of his mouth, which he immediately wiped away with his finger. He chewed slowly as he fought back the sudden urge to gag.

I can't believe I'm doing this, he thought, and then suddenly, an overwhelming sense of calmness overcame him. As if being swept away in an ambiance of a spiritual high, he savored the warm flesh. After swallowing, he gently placed the heart back into the cavity, wiped the blood from his hands on his coat, and reached over to grab the knife again.

He skillfully began the process of removing the internal organs, readying the carcass to be dragged back to the cabin.

The Winds

It would require several trips, but it was going to be worth it. With only a month and a week left before he was scheduled to rendezvous with Shooter, he figured he had plenty of meat to sustain him.

Cade was too involved with dressing the second of the three deer he'd slain earlier to notice the heavy snorting behind him. Suddenly, the snorts turned into a deafening growl. Cade jumped to his feet and quickly turned around to face the largest, fiercest animal he'd ever seen in the wild.

It stood over eight feet tall from the ground to the top of its head. The thick brown coat rippled as the Grizzly stood on its back legs and thrashed his arms wildly. The bear's nose and mouth flattened and quivered as it expelled its noise of terror. Cade scrambled toward the pool, tripping over the carcass as he ran. He landed face down in the snow, dropping the knife as he hit.

The bear lunged forward and swatted his sharp claws at the moving target, slashing Cade on the back of the leg. Cade was absence of feeling. He didn't realize that he'd been cut until he tried desperately to regain his footing. His leg wouldn't respond, and he was bleeding profusely out of the gaping hole in his snow pants.

The surrounding snow turned bright red as Cade struggled to escape the grasp of the bear. Realizing that running from the Grizzly was not an option, he quickly turned over and grabbed the pistol from his side holster. He pointed the gun at the bear's face and squeezed the trigger.

As if someone had suddenly turned the volume off around him, the only sound Cade heard as it echoed through his mind was that of a single click. There was no other sound, no smoke, and no shot, just the innocent clicking sound when one small cold piece of metal hit against another.

It was a shocking, humbling reality. The pistol was empty. Cade had never reloaded since shooting the flurry of bullets at the escaping deer. He dropped the pistol and tried with all his might to swim through the deep snow away from the angry bear.

One swift swat and the bear struck Cade in the stomach, throwing him against a tree. Cade tried to scramble behind the tree and tuck himself into a small crevice formed by several large rocks, but the Grizzly grabbed him again, turning him over and exposing his face and chest.

Cade's life quickly passed before his eyes as he covered his face. The bear continued to thrash angrily as Cade tried to thwart the blows. The several layers of clothing that Cade wore to help protect him from the bitter cold became his only ally as each swat with the sharp claws tore closer and closer to his flesh.

Suddenly, the bear stood up on his back legs and looked

down at Cade. With its arms down at his sides, he looked over at the larger of the downed deer, turned and returned to all fours, and walked toward the bloody carcass.

Cade remained still as he carefully watched the Grizzly's every move. The bear opened its large mouth and exposed its long, sharp teeth just before it clamped onto the neck of the carcass. With one continuous motion, the bear lifted the carcass, swung it over to the side, and carried it through the deep snow, disappearing into the thick trees.

Cade continued to remain silent. He refused even to move his hand up to clear the blood, which had accumulated in the corners of his eyes and had successfully impeded his vision. He contemplated what he had just experienced and couldn't believe he was still alive.

After several long, agonizing minutes anticipating a second return of the bear, Cade decided to try to sit up and assess his wounds. He could now feel the intense pain from the vicious slashes from the razor-sharp claws, whereas before, he was totally numb with adrenaline. Other parts of his body were exposed to the intense freezing temperatures where the claws had thrashed his clothes to nothing more than thinly shredded strips of cloth.

He sat up and looked around. The snow was red from his blood and packed down solid around him. Every member of his body ached and throbbed. He felt light-headed from the loss of blood as he rubbed his fingers over the warm, sticky wounds on his right leg. Completely exhausted from the ordeal he laid back down into the snow and shut his eyes. Just before he lost consciousness, he could hear a very faint sound in the distance—a dog barking.

Cade regained consciousness when he felt a warm sensation on his face.

"Stitch?" Cade said. Stitch continued to lick his face until Cade was able to push him away with his bloody hand. "I feel like I've been through a meat grinder." Cade attempted to sit up but didn't have the strength.

He could tell by the large, crusted red splotches on his legs and chest that he'd lost a lot of blood. Unbeknownst to him, lying in the snow had undoubtedly helped speed up the clotting process.

Stitch started to nibble on his ears as Cade continued to go in and out of consciousness. Cade realized that the red snow would become his final resting place if he didn't get back to the cabin soon. He pushed himself up and began to pull himself through the snow. Stitch started to bark as he sensed each movement of Cade's limbs.

"That's it, boy, we can do this together," Cade said. Stitch continued to break through the crusted snow just ahead of him. Progress was agonizingly slow, but with every

The Winds

thrust forward was another foot toward home.

Nearly two hours passed when Cade reached the rim and could look down and see the ice-covered lake. It was a very promising site, but he was still several hundred yards from the cabin. Cade made a slight lunge forward and felt his fists break through the crusted snow.

The snow beneath him cracked through, and he tumbled down the steep incline, landing on the snow-capped rocks below. A large pile of snow-covered him, and he was completely buried and out of sight.

Cade struggled for his next breath. His limbs were held firmly in the grasp of the fallen snow, and he couldn't move even a finger.

"Not today," he said as he formed the words with his cracked lips. "I will not die today." He tried to fire off signals to every muscle possible, but nothing responded. He was encased in a snowy tomb and there wasn't anything on Earth that could save him.

Suddenly, he could hear scratching noises from above. It was Stitch. Stitch continued to dig into the snow. He dug until his frozen feet started to bleed.

You can do it, Cade thought as he cast a silent vote of confidence for his best friend. Cade could see the darkness turn to light one paw-swipe at a time. He opened his eyes and could nearly see through the thin layer of snow separating him and his next breath. Suddenly, the thin layer was removed, and Cade felt a sharp pain in his eye.

"Damn it, Stitch!" Cade yelled. Cade sat up in the snow, put one hand over his injured eye, and seriously contemplated slapping Stitch across the head with the other.

The cabin was still fairly warm, with evidence of hot coals lying deep within the fireplace. Cade placed a few small pieces of wood over them, and soon, the orange light from the flames began to flicker throughout the room.

Cade began the painstaking task of removing his outer garments to reveal his injuries. He knew they were serious but didn't know how serious, as he started to feel the pain as the numbness of his body faded away. He began melting away the layers of dried blood with a jar of warm water and a cloth rag. His leg was badly thrashed in two places, with one of the open wounds revealing a small portion of bone.

"Holy shit," Cade said. He knew what he had to do but had never had to do it to himself. He'd mended drug lords and junkies, businessmen and housewives, school children and even little babies, but never had he thought he would have to mend himself.

He thoroughly cleansed each wound with alcohol. Each

The Winds

swipe of the soaked sponge against the severed and exposed nerves was as if someone had thrust a dagger into his side. Never before had he experienced such raw pain, but this was only the start—next would come the needle.

Cade had thought of everything when he bought supplies in case of an emergency, except for local anesthetic. With each prick of the needle through his sensitive flesh, he bit into one of Stitch's rawhide bones Shooter brought for him. As he stitched, one after another, he trimmed away the dead flesh and compensated by stretching the living flesh to meet together.

It wasn't his best work, but it was the best that he could do under the circumstances. The wounds on his legs and chest required nearly one hundred individual stitches—his eyelid, only two, but they were the most critical. One slight error with the needle and Cade could easily have lost his sight in that eye.

Exhausted, Cade pulled the surgical thread taught, tied it off, and cut it to length before easing back into his cot. It had been an extremely long day for both he and Stitch. Earlier that morning, Cade left to go out to hunt but soon found that he was the one being hunted.

Chapter 21

It was the middle of May, and there were few signs of spring. It took longer for the sun to venture across the sky, but that was about the extent of it. The tops of the rocks were mostly exposed, but the snow surrounding them was just as deep but wetter.

The hike to meet Shooter was exhausting. Cade struggled as he walked through the deep snow with the aid of his makeshift crutch. He could still see his breath as he walked, but the frigid air didn't burn his lungs as in the months previous. He could see into the clearing below as he peeked over the crest of the rocky hill. The surface of the snow was blindingly white and free of disturbance or tracks.

Where's Shooter? He asked himself as he slowly and painfully made the descent to the clearing below. *I pay him good money. Where the hell is he?*

Each step felt like it would be his last. The winter had taken its toll on him. At times weak from near starvation and shortly after the bear attack, suffering from hypothermia, Cade was a bitter, callused man. You could see it in his eyes and face. His cheeks were hollow and his limbs weak, but his spirit was enraged.

Society was the enemy, and vengeance was the fuel for

The Winds

the sputtering flame that burned within him. The vengeance he felt toward the civilized world was enhanced by the miserable experiences he faced through the torturous winter and entrenched deeply within his soul. When he finally reached the clearing, he brushed the snow off a flat rock at the edge of the trees, sat, and waited.

The minutes turned into hours as the sun reached its peak in the Southern sky and made its descent to the mountain peaks to the West. The air became more frigid as it started to set. Cade sat motionless on the rock, except for a constant shiver – the hood of his coat cinched tightly over his head.

Suddenly he heard the sound of horses coming up from behind the small ridge. Cade raised his head and peered into the murky distance. It was Shooter on top of his horse, followed by several other packhorses. They struggled through the knee-deep snow as they neared the clearing. Cade slowly rose to his feet.

"You're late!" he shouted with little or no emotion. It had taken Shooter nearly five hours longer than he'd anticipated due to the excessive snow over portions of the trail. He'd never ventured into the Winds this far, this early in the year.

In most areas of the world, the month of May would bring spring flowers and sunny days, but in the Winds, it was an extension of winter. The nights were still long and cold, and the days were just as cold.

"I'm sorry, Cade. By the way, it's really good to see you, too," Shooter replied, smiling but with a hint of sarcasm.

He approached Cade and offered his hand, but Cade's hands remained in the deep, warm pockets of his coat. "You look like you've been to hell and back, but you survived. At least, I'll give you that."

"Why are you late? Is it too much to ask for you to be here on time?"

Shooter looked at him and shook his head. "Sit back down a minute until I can set up camp and get a fire going. I'll get some hot coffee down you and then we can talk."

Forty minutes later, Cade was sitting in a comfortable folding chair next to a roaring fire with a wool Indian blanket over him, sipping a cup of hot coffee and eating a fresh pastry. Shooter continued to set up camp by removing the packs from the horses and pitching the large canvas wall tent. Few, if any, words were spoken the entire time.

Cade suddenly broke the silence. "I'm sorry," he said as he stared into the red-orange flickering flames. "I didn't mean to jump all over you."

The Winds

Shooter unfolded a chair and placed it across the fire from him. He then poured himself a cup of coffee, cupped it with both of his hands, sipped it, and sat down.

"Did you ever stop to think about how your decision to live up here has affected my life? While I'm down there driving your truck, spending your money, keeping our little dark secret to myself, you're up here just trying to survive another day. I don't know from one hour to the next if you're alive or dead. You could be up here bleeding to death, and I can't do anything about it.

I know the Winds like the back of my hand, but yet I don't know where you are or where to look if you get into trouble. Do you know what a helpless feeling it is to watch my friend literally waste away before my eyes? I mean, look at yourself, Cade, you look like shit without the smell, and because of what, your inability to cope with society? How long do you intend on playing this game?"

"My hell," Cade said, "I just said I was sorry. I didn't expect to get a thirty-minute lecture." Cade took another sip. "This game? Is that what you think this is? Just a game? If I make it through the winter, I don't get what's behind door number three or get a free spin of the wheel, and I don't win an all-expense paid trip to Maui.

This is not a game, Shooter; it's my life, and as long as I still have a single breath in my body, this is how I choose to live it. If you choose to continue to spend your monthly paycheck and drive my truck, you will be here on the date and time agreed to. Do you understand?" Cade looked at him sharply, waiting for a reply.

"Tomorrow is the fifteenth of May. I came a day early to ensure I had everything set up and comfortable for you when you arrived tomorrow. I knew there was a good chance you'd be hungry, cold, and possibly injured. From the looks of it, I was right on all three counts."

"You're lying. Today's the fifteenth. I have it marked on my calendar."

"I'm telling you the truth. We were scheduled to meet up tomorrow, and if I hadn't come today, you would have sat here and been frozen to death by morning. I'm more than an employee. I'm a friend. I don't agree with you, but I'll do whatever you need me to do." Cade looked over at him, clearly embarrassed. "So what happened to you? What's with the crutch?"

"Let's just say I had an encounter with something that was many times my size."

"You're kidding, a bear?"

Cade nodded his head.

The Winds

"So where's Stitch? He's still alive, isn't he?"

"Oh yeah, he's still alive. I'm still alive because of that mangy mutt. See this scar?" Cade pointed to his eye. He partially closed it and continued to speak. "That stupid dog about took my eyelid off. I had to crawl through the snow. I just wanted to lie there and die, but Stitch wouldn't let me. He kept digging me out and licking my face to wake me up. His claws are sharp as hell."

"I can see why you're in the ER and not a plastic surgeon by the looks of things."

"Very funny, Shooter. I didn't have a mirror, OK? It's a little tough to perform major surgery on yourself without any anesthetic and using the reflection off a piece of tin foil. I bit into the rawhide chew bone you brought Stitch last fall every time I shoved the needle into my skin. One stitch was so painful I bit through the rawhide and broke my back tooth. Did I care that the stitches were perfectly straight? No, after the bear was done with me, I was just trying to keep my guts from falling out in the snow."

"I'm sorry I asked. I had no idea."

"Hell, no, you have no idea. He was a Grizzly. He attacked me while I was dressing out a deer. I didn't even hear him coming. You said that they bed down in the winter. Damn it, Shooter, the Grizzly attacked me in March."

"You're very lucky to be alive. Grizzlies usually don't take any prisoners."

"Tell me about it." Shooter reached up and grabbed Cade's shoulder.

"I'm sorry, Cade. Is there anything I can do for you?" Cade just shook his head and took another sip of his coffee. "So where's Stitch?"

"I left him. I didn't think he was up for the hike. He's been pretty sick lately."

"I'm sure he'll be fine. Wait 'til he sees what I brought him." Shooter got up from his chair and walked toward the tent. He reached into one of the saddlebags and pulled out a large bag. "We're talking five pounds of jerky, my friend, all for my buddy Stitch." Shooter didn't know that all the two of them had to eat for the last three months was venison.

"Yeah, he'll be really excited to see that." Cade took another sip of his coffee. "This is really good coffee. I'm really happy to see you. So how did that situation between you and Denton work out with the judge?"

"About as good as it could have, I guess. I sat on one side of the courtroom, and he sat on the other as the judge read the letter. When he read the part about you wanting Denton to stay the hell out of your business, Denton got up and stormed out of the room, mumbling something about killing that bastard.

I've only seen him a few times since. He doesn't come out on the reservation. There's too many of us that want to kick his ass. There's one thing about being an Indian. If someone wants to kick your ass, they'll have to be willing to take on the whole tribe."

Cade forced a smile and then painfully rose from his chair, walked over to the saddlebags, and started digging through each of them. "So what did you bring me this time? I hope you brought me something good. Do you realize I haven't had a good strong drink for over seven months?"

"Look in that pouch over there."

Cade lifted up the leather flap and revealed a bottle of Jack Daniels. "Bless you, Shooter. He screwed off the cap and took a long gulp. "Damn, that's painful but good." He limped back toward the fire and offered Shooter the bottle. Shooter shook his head. Cade took another drink, sat back in his chair, and rested his tired feet on a rock near the flames.

"I spent more time drunk than sober the entire year after my wife left me," Shooter said. "I finally realized that my problems were just as bad when I reached the bottom of the bottle. I haven't touched the hard stuff since."

"I appreciate that story. It just leaves more for me." Cade smiled as he took another drink.

"You really do look like hell, you know. I don't see how you made it. You're probably the first one in this century to do it. Mountain men did it, but that was back when, well, there were mountain men. It was a way of life then, trapping beaver, tanning hides and trading with the Indians, but we have heated homes now. We can get what we need at the grocery store, we can go out and see a movie, and if we don't feel like leaving the house, we can pop popcorn in the microwave and watch a good movie on HBO."

Cade brought the bottle down away from his lips. "So what are you implying?"

"I think what you're doing is nuts. I mean, look at you. You probably lost thirty pounds, you could have lost a few fingers and toes, or worse, you could have lost your life. I just think what you're doing is asinine."

"So you think I'm an ass?" Cade looked down at the

The Winds

bottle of whiskey and screwed the cap back on. He slipped the bottle into the front pocket of his coat and rubbed his face with his hand.

"No, Cade, I don't think you're an ass. I don't know what to think of you. Your hair's down past your shoulders. Your mustache has grown over your mouth. No wonder you're so skinny, you can't find where to stick the fork." Cade continued to stare at the fire.

Shooter bent down to try to make eye contact. "I just don't understand what you're trying to do up here. Ok, you lost your family. Life's dealt you a bad hand, but you can't keep living like this. This is no way to live. You're a doctor. You should be helping people get over a cold or putting Band-Aids on little girl's cuts. You're not a mountain man, and you'll never be one. You're out of your element, Cade. Go back to Chicago where you belong, where your friends are, where you left a good life."

Cade grabbed the bottle from his pocket, unscrewed the cap, and took another hit. He stood up and motioned toward the tent. "I've heard this all before. I'm calling it a night. I want to make sure I have a good night's sleep before I start packing this shit back in the morning."

Shooter stood up and grabbed Cade by the arm. Cade grimaced slightly. "Haven't you heard anything I've said?"

Cade became visibly angry. "I don't give a shit what you think of me or anything else for that matter. Our relationship is strictly business, Shooter. I don't pay you to state your opinions. I pay you to bring me food. If that's too hard for you, then maybe I need to find someone else to drive my truck."

"Strictly business? We've been friends for a long time. I'm not doing this for the money or your damn truck. That was your idea, remember? I don't recall applying for this job. It seems to me you just showed up on my front porch."

"But you accepted the terms."

"What terms, Cade? You basically told me what you wanted me to do and I've done them just like you wanted. Do you think for one moment that I didn't lay awake at night thinking about my best friend up here in the dead of winter and that you could have died up here like my father?

I've driven up to the trailhead several times over the past few months against my better judgment, just in case you decided to come down. Every time I approached the parking lot, I was afraid I would find you frozen dead in the snow. I wouldn't have shown up at all if this was strictly a business relationship. The money doesn't mean that much to me. As long as I have a beer in my hand, a little food in my belly, and enough seed to plant next year's crop, I'm happy."

"You don't understand the private war I'm fighting. I look back at my life and have realized that I've lost the people who mattered the most. I can't go through that pain again. If I go back down there, I'm just setting myself up for another disappointment. Yeah, it's tough up here, and it's not a lot of fun, but it's better than taking a chance down there. I don't expect you to understand, and I don't expect you to approve of what I'm doing."

"I'm not sure how you expect me to do this without getting emotionally involved. I'm sorry, Cade, but each time I come up here, you're going to hear what I have to say. Those are *my* terms now. If you don't like them, then you can get some uncaring, black-hearted asshole to bring your supplies. If you want, I'll give Denton a call when I get back down the mountain. I'm sure he would be a good candidate for the truck and overseeing all of your money. What do you think, Cade? Or should I give his girlfriend a call? It would help supplement her meager government salary. She has to come up here anyway."

"What does Denton's girlfriend have to do with anything?"

At that moment Shooter wished he hadn't mentioned anything about Denton's girlfriend. Questions would lead to answers, and answers would lead to problems.

"I only said that because she's a forest ranger. She knows the Winds and could possibly bring you your supplies. But I was just upset, that's all. I realize I'm the only one who can bring you your supplies and make this work out how you want it to. I was upset and said things I didn't mean. Forget I even said anything."

"What does she look like?"

"Who?"

"Denton's girlfriend, the forest ranger. I've only seen four people since last fall, and one of them was a lady forest ranger. I remember she had auburn hair and the deepest green eyes you've ever seen." Shooter became silent. "You can't be serious? That's her?" Shooter nodded his head. "That's Denton's girlfriend? How did he get her?"

Shooter gathered his thoughts and hesitated in telling him further details. "I told you, I was upset. I didn't mean anything by it, but she just happened to pop into my mind at the time." Shooter looked over at Cade and gently put his hand on his shoulder. "Hey, I'm sorry about what I said. I got upset. You know me, when I get upset, I say things I don't mean. It's the same as back in high school."

"At least back in high school, you'd start shouting your Shoshone gibberish, and none of us could understand you." Cade started to smile.

Shooter smiled back, but his expression turned serious. "I think you need to know something else about Denton's girlfriend." He motioned for the two of them to sit back down in the chairs next to the fire.

"So what's the big deal? So Denton has a girlfriend. Why should that matter to me?"

"His girlfriend's name is Tara Samuels, but Samuels is her married name. She was married once before and now's divorced."

"So, lots of women our age are divorced."

"Hear me out on this, please? She's not our age. She's about six years younger. She was in seventh grade when we graduated." Cade hung on every word. "You would know her as Tara Judd."

Cade's face became flushed. "I don't believe it. That

explains her eyes. That's why they looked so familiar. I can see it now. They were identical to Kimber's."

"I noticed the same thing when I saw her. She bears a striking resemblance."

"Why would Denton be dating Kimber's little sister?"

"That's really what all of us were wondering at the reunion."

Cade was silent for a moment. "At the reunion? You knew Denton was dating Kimber's little sister clear back last summer and you didn't tell me? Don't you think that maybe I would like to have known?" He stood up and started to walk around. "All those discussions about Kimber's death, and me coming to grips with myself, and you urging me to visit the cemetery, and not one mention of Kimber's little sister dating Denton? What were you thinking, Shooter?"

Shooter stood up and walked toward him. "I didn't tell you because I was trying to protect you."

"Trying to protect me from what?"

"From you jumping to conclusions, thinking you had to get involved, starting something up with Denton. He's

The Winds

unpredictable, Cade. I don't know what he's capable of doing, but I really don't want to find out, either. The best thing to do is to just leave him alone. You need to calm yourself down, take a deep breath, and think about it for a moment.

When you came back to Lorenz, it wasn't because you wanted to. It was because you had no choice. Remember the anxiety? When you told me about what the psychiatrist thought, I didn't think it was a good idea to tell you about Tara. I didn't want to upset you more."

Cade walked back to his chair and sat back down. "So why is he, of all people, dating her?"

"Other than the obvious fact that she's drop-dead gorgeous, some think he's trying to live his fantasy life with Kimber through her little sister. That's bordering on psychological bullshit, I realize, but there might be some truth to it."

Cade thought for a moment and shook his head. "I'm sorry, but this is almost too much for me." A flood of memories passed through his mind. It was like a movie trailer played in fast motion, quickly revealing the important highlights of Cade and Kimber's relationship.

"So, is there anything more you'd like me to do for you?" Shooter said. Cade didn't respond to his question.

He then glanced over at him with endless hollow eyes. "I never should have told you. I'm sorry."

Cade blinked slowly. "No, really, that's fine. What Denton does is his business. Believe me, I'm not the least bit interested in her. I'm done with relationships."

Cade flashed back to the day he saw Tara at the edge of the lake, her green eyes, the wind beneath her thick hair, and her smooth, supple skin. In an instant, his view of her had changed.

She wasn't his enemy. How could she be? She was Kimber's sister. "I just feel sorry for her. You and me both know what a jerk Denton Bauer is."

Chapter 22

Shooter felt responsible for the way he and Cade parted up in the Winds. He wondered if things would have turned out differently had he been more honest with Cade about Denton dating Kimber's younger sister from the start. It didn't seem like an issue the previous summer since Shooter hadn't seen Cade for over twenty years and really didn't know if he would see him again once he left Lorenz, but it still troubled him.

It troubled him enough that he decided to make a trip into town and pay a visit to the Lorenz Bar. This was something he had become accustomed to the year his wife left him and took the kids with her. It was too much for him to deal with without the help of the bottle.

It was an excruciating year, one that he had tried to forget. Just being back inside the rustic bar brought back a flood of bad memories, but after a few stiff drinks—out of a glass bottle, not a can—nothing seemed to matter, and that was why he had returned.

He sat alone in the darkened room at one of the smaller tables located in the corner near the small dance floor. On occasion, a live band would perform, mainly on the weekends when there were more people, but this was on a Tuesday night, and there were only seven other people in the bar, not counting the bartender and barmaid.

Rock and Roll of the eighties echoed throughout the darkly paneled walls as Shooter raised his empty glass to signal for another round.

"What'll it be this time, another JD?" the barmaid asked as she grabbed his empty glass.

"Please," Shooter replied with a slur. His eyes were bloodshot and droopy, his shirt was wrinkled, and his long black hair was messed up but mostly covered with his cowboy hat and the long, braided ponytail hanging down his back. He had been there for nearly two hours and hadn't talked to anyone. He raised his head and looked around as he sang along with the song.

"Keep on loving you, 'cause it's the only thing I wanna do. I don't wanna sleep." He thumped his fingers along the top of the table with the beat as he sang. "I just wanna keep on lovin' you."

Suddenly, the entrance double door swung open, and a rather large man darkened the opening. Shooter immediately grabbed the rim of his cowboy hat, pulled it down nearly over his eyes, and crouched in his seat. The man looked around the bar, and everyone looked back at him except Shooter.

The Winds

The man let go of the door, and it slammed shut behind him. He walked through the center aisle of the bar, tipped his hat politely at the ladies as he passed several tables, and sat down across from Shooter at the small table.

"Hey, Shooter, haven't seen you around lately. What gives?" he said. He reached over and gave Shooter a quick, hard nudge.

Shooter jerked and sat up in his chair. "Got other things going on, Denton, why?"

"No reason. Just miss those weekly drunken binges, that's all." Denton started to laugh loudly. The other patrons turned to see what was going on. "Relax, people, just talking to my friend, Shooter, here." Denton turned back around and looked at him. "So how's the truck? I saw it parked in the alley out back. Is it getting good gas mileage?"

"What's it to you, Dent? It's just a truck."

Denton smiled and looked around a little. "No, it's not just a truck. It's Cade's truck, remember? So where is he?" Denton reached over and grabbed Shooter by the wrist.

Shooter jerked his arm free. "It's none of your

business where he is."

"It's my business if he's in Lorenz. I've got an outstanding warrant for his arrest."

"What? He didn't do anything." Denton reached into his pocket, pulled out a white piece of paper, and snapped it between his hands. "Yeah, he mentioned something about the ticket. He thinks it's a bunch of crap."

"He didn't pay it, and it's almost been a year. Next time you see him, you need to tell him to pay it, including penalties, or he'll do some jail time."

"Yeah, I'll tell him when I send him my next smoke signal. He's out of the country on an extended vacation."

"Right, and what country is he in this time?"

"Just like he said in the note, it's none of your damn business." Shooter got up, fished through his wallet, and placed several bills on the top of the table. "Good seeing you again," he said. He staggered out the front entrance and onto the sidewalk.

The sun had since gone down behind the hills, and the streetlights were illuminated. He paused a moment and looked up Main Street. Then, he turned and started to walk toward the small side street that led to the alley at the back of the bar. Shooter would always park in the alley back in his drinking days. That way, if he was legally too drunk to drive, nobody would see him get behind the wheel.

He pulled a bundle of keys out from his pocket and brought them close to his face to pick the correct key to unlock the truck. As he shuffled one key to the next, he dropped them into the gravel alleyway.

"Shit!" he mumbled under his breath. As he bent down to pick them up, he heard the gravel scuff in the darkness. He hesitated momentarily and looked toward the origin of the sound. From around the back end of the truck, he saw movement.

He swiped his hand across the gravel, hoping to locate his keys, when he felt something stiff strike him across the face. The force threw him into the side of the car parked next to him and onto the ground.

With a mixture of pain and confusion, he could feel blood trickling from the corner of his mouth. Shooter looked up from the ground, and from the dim glow of the streetlight near the alley entrance, he could make out the familiar face.

"What did you do that for, Denton? I didn't do anything to you." Shooter attempted to get up from the ground, but Denton kicked him again, this time in the stomach.

"Just like back in high school, eh, Shooter?" Denton said. "End of the month. You Indians get your little government paycheck, drive into town in your ugly Camaro's, and blow it on booze all in one night."

Shooter just gave him a blank stare.

"Come on," Denton said. "You know damn well what I'm talking about. We'd wait out here for them to come out, then beat the shit out of 'em. I'm sure I rolled your Dad a few times. What was his name again, Chief Running Bear? From what I saw of him on Saturday nights, they should have called him Chief Drunken Bastard."

Shooter glared at him. "Don't you be talking about my father like that! He's a good man, and he's done a lot for the Shoshone Indians during his lifetime." He struggled to get up again; this time, Denton let him. As he staggered to his feet, he stuck his finger on Denton's face. "And he's not here to defend himself."

"It's too bad he's not. You could use the help about now." Denton punched him in the stomach and then kicked the legs out from under him. Shooter fell to the ground, landing on his hip. He moaned in pain as he

The Winds

struggled to get up again. "Now I'm going to ask you one more time, where's Cade?"

"I'm telling you, I don't know. He just left me his truck while he's gone. That's it. That's not against the law."

"This isn't about the law. This is personal. He killed the girl I loved."

"The girl you loved? You had a fine way of showing it. You were like some control freak. Cade's the best thing that ever happened to her. When they started dating, the smile came back on her face."

"Yeah, I wonder if she smiled as Cade pushed her off the edge of Mirror Falls."

"Don't even go there. It was an accident, and you know it."

"Well, from what I hear, he got what he deserved. I heard he lost his wife and kids."

"How did you know?"

"Ben told me. You remember Ben? He was a grade younger than us. He's on the force and tells me all about Cade. Has for several years now. Both their Moms have been writing to each other since they moved away. I know all about that bastard, how he became a big successful doctor, drives fancy cars, and lives in Chicago."

"He's worked hard for what he's got."

"Whatever. Last letter she got from his Mom said that she hadn't heard from him for nearly a year. That seems a little suspicious to me."

"He's been having a hard time dealing with it. Maybe he doesn't want to burden anybody with his problems."

"Yeah, well, maybe he just decided to come back here and spend a little time in the Winds clearing his head."

Immediately, Shooter felt as if a javelin had pierced his heart. How did Denton know? Had Shooter unknowingly said something to someone? It couldn't have been. He hadn't fallen down drunk for years now. "I know that's where I'd go if my family was killed," Shooter replied sarcastically. "I'd give up all the modern conveniences of life, squat over a rock when I had to take a shit, and then wipe my bare ass with a dried twig. Did you come up with that stupid idea yourself?"

"No, it was something I overheard Tara happened to tell one of her friends last night while she was talking on the phone. They were talking about their jobs and the shit they have to put up with. I heard her say something about a strange, pistol-carrying, ignorant bastard she ran into late last summer at one of the lakes. He wasn't registered to be there and didn't have a fishing license, and she said he was arrogant and rude.

I don't know why she didn't tell me. I'd a rode up there and shot him. You can't treat my girlfriend like that and expect to get away with it. She doesn't know I was listening, so don't go flapping your mouth."

"Well, that doesn't sound like Cade to me."

"You don't know the Cade I know. Nobody in this town knows him like I do. If I were a betting man, I'd say he's up there and up to no good."

"You're full of shit, Denton. Cade's a good man, and everyone in this town knows it. He came to the reunion excited to see everyone again, but he couldn't stand the thought of meeting up with the likes of you. You were such a jerk to him in high school, and for what reason, Kimber? You just couldn't accept the fact that she loved Cade and not you."

Denton bent down and grabbed Shooter by the back of the collar and was about to punch him in the face. "You're not worth it," he said as he let go of his shirt. "If I find him in this town, he's going to jail. If he thinks he can come back here to start a new life, he needs to think again. You tell him that next time you see him." Denton kicked the gravel, hitting Shooter in the face with the small rocks. "Now get up off the ground before you disgrace your tribe." Denton turned and walked back toward the lighted street with sinister laughter. Shooter glared at him as he walked away.

Denton stopped and slowly turned around. "And, Shooter, I wouldn't say anything to anybody about this. This is between you, Cade, and me. Last I checked, driving while under the influence would be a strict violation of your parole." He laughed as he turned back around, walked to the sidewalk, and disappeared around the corner of the building.

Shooter grabbed his jaw and then spit some blood on the gravel beneath him. "I'm going to kill you, Deputy Bauer. I'll kill you if it's the last thing I do," he mumbled under his alcohol-saturated breath.

Chapter 23

There were still large patches of snow under the trees and to the North side of the larger rocks, but the lakes were mostly clear of ice. The fishing was excellent. After a long, hard winter, the fish were tempted to strike at almost anything that flashed.

The air was cool and crisp, but Cade retired his heavy down coat and commissioned a lighter jacket to keep him comfortable in the early morning and late evening hours. The afternoons were sunny and in the mid-fifties.

Over the winter months, to overcome the long silent hours, he had tied nearly four hundred flies, mainly the black wooly, mosquito, and Mickey fin. Still, since Shooter had thought to bring some necks of feathers of various kinds and colors, Cade was able to add a few more styles to his collection, including the "Dirty Rotten Deal," a fly that his father had taught him to tie when he was a kid. It surprised him how he was able to tie it perfectly after the first attempt.

With Stitch leading the way, Cade hiked nearly three miles to one of the neighboring lakes. It was one of the larger lakes in the basin, and he thought that maybe it had a different variety of fish like Splake or California Golden Trout. His leg was healing much quicker than expected, and he was feeling much better. The cut above his eye had nearly disappeared.

Stitch was filled out again and was just as chipper as Cade remembered him when they first met over eight months ago. His golden coat was shiny and healthy, and his teeth were polished white thanks to a few large rawhide chew bones Shooter had brought him.

Cade looked a lot more presentable. Shooter had agreed to give him a trim before he left. Even though he didn't plan on entertaining anyone anytime soon, it made him feel better to trim his beard and mustache so he wouldn't have to open his mouth so wide when he took a bite of food.

He stood nearly waist-deep in the cold, clear water near the outlet of the lake, casting time and time again with his fly rod. The chest waders Shooter brought would enable him to get out to the bigger fish. Many of the lakes were shallow in the places where he had adequate room to back-cast, while sheer cliffs and trees usually surrounded the edges that dropped off rapidly. The sun glistened off the water, making it nearly impossible for him to see the fish. Today, he had to go strictly by feel, which made it more challenging.

Suddenly, Cade felt a quick tug on the line, so he snapped his rod back to set the hook. The fish broke the calm surface of the water and became airborne as it flashed its shiny red scales into the sun. Cade let out a piercing shrill like he always did when he hooked a fish. The sound echoed clearly through the glacier-cut basin.

"You're mine, baby!" he yelled, drawing his line in by the handfuls. "Come to Papa." Cade continued to play the fish as though it was the last one in the lake.

He loved to fish and wondered how long this single enjoyment in his life would continue. He reached down and followed the line to the mouth of the fish, cupped his hand over the head, and snagged it under the gills with his fingers. He carefully removed the hook, brought it up to his lips, and kissed it.

"A little too emotionally attached, don't you think," came a voice from behind him.

Startled, Cade quickly turned around and nearly slipped on the mossy rocks below his feet. He struggled momentarily to regain his balance and inadvertently dropped the large fish back into the water. With a quick flap of the tail, it was gone to the dark depths below. He looked toward shore and saw a lady on top of a horse near the water's edge.

It's Tara, he thought. He figured the snow was still too deep for anyone to be coming in on the trail and wasn't at all prepared for this moment. He hoped she wouldn't recognize him now that his hair, beard, and mustache were neatly trimmed.

"Look what you made me do," he shouted. "That was the biggest beauty I've caught yet." He started to walk back in toward the shore. The water flowed from the crevices of his waders as he approached.

"So, how long have you been at it?" she asked.

"What?" he replied.

"Fishing. You said that it's the biggest one you've caught yet. How long have you been up here?" She climbed down from her horse and wrapped the reins around a branch of a small willow tree.

Cade attempted to gather his thoughts as he continued to walk toward her. "I've been here a few days now. The fishing's been pretty good, but they're small." As he approached closer, there was no question that it was her. Her eyes, how could he forget those deep green eyes? And that uncanny resemblance to her older sister, Kimber, how could he not have noticed last fall?

"So which way did you come up?" she asked as she bent down, brushed off her forest green pants, and tied her boot. Cade couldn't help but look as she bent down.

The Winds

Her green work shirt was partially unbuttoned, and he had a partial peek of her left breast. She stood up, tucked her shirt into the front of her pants, and adjusted her belt. "Sorry, I get all rearranged after a long ride," she said, almost embarrassed.

"That's quite alright. I know how you feel." He reached back and removed the "wedgie" from his butt. "The water pressure makes things hike up back there, if you know what I mean." They both started to laugh.

There was a moment of silence, and then she spoke. "So you didn't answer my question," she said. "Which way did you come up, the Lorenz side, Pinedale side, or..." she waited for his response.

"Lorenz side. You'd have to be crazy to come in from the Pinedale side this early in the year. You'd have to cross over Washita pass."

She nodded her head and looked over to the cliffs on the other side of the lake. The snow was melting from the steep crevices. The icy water was flowing over the large rocks and into the lake. "You're right, but the funny thing is..." She looked at Cade directly.

Cade became a little nervous. He tried to anticipate what she was going to say next. In his mind, there wasn't any room for error. "What's that?"

"I just rode in this morning from the trailhead and didn't see any new registrations. In fact, I didn't see any tracks, horses, or humans. Which trail did you come in on?" she continued to pry.

Cade looked over at the horse and approached it cautiously. He flattened his hand and began to stroke the side of its neck, anything to buy him a little time to think of his response. He had been in the Winds numerous times throughout his childhood, but that was a long time ago. He had trouble remembering the various trails that could get him to where he and Tara were presently standing.

"Same one you took, but I walk really, really lightly," he said with a smile. "Anyway, why the twenty questions? Why do you care how I got here?"

She walked closer to him and stuck out her hand. "I'm Tara Samuels. I work for the National Forest Service. I have the authority to throw your ass in jail, that's why."

Cade reached out his hand, and they shook. "It's nice to meet you and a pleasure to know you, I think." He paused, looked down at the ground, and then back up at her. "Uh, maybe we got off on the wrong foot. Honestly, I didn't know we needed to register before we entered the Winds. It's been a while since I've been up here."

The Winds

"Really," she said. Stitch came up to her and started to sniff at her leg. "Nice dog. What's his name?" she bent over and started to scratch behind his ears. Stitch immediately fell to the ground and exposed his belly.

"Stitch. I named him that because he had to have one single stitch in his ear after being mauled by a cat."

"He can't be more than a year old. If you live right, you could be together for a long time. He seems like a really nice dog."

"So you patrol this part of the Winds?" Cade said.

"Yeah, I'm at the Ranger Station just down from the trailhead. This is my first trip since last fall. We had a tough winter this year. The snow was as deep as my horse's belly a week ago. I can't believe you made it in here. Most people don't even attempt to come in until late June or early July. You must really like to fish." She continued to scratch Stitch. "Speaking of fish, as a forest ranger, I'm required to ask you to show me your fishing license. Could I please see it?"

Cade unhooked his suspenders and dropped the chest waders down below his waist. He reached into his pocket, pulled out a pink piece of paper, and gave it to her. A bit surprised, she smiled as she unfolded it several times and started to read it.

"So what's this, a tardy note from your teacher?" she read further.

"It's a poem I wrote for my daughter. She turned eight last July."

"That's sweet. What did she think of it?"

"I don't know. She never read it."

"So why didn't you give it to her."

"Her mom and me, well, we're divorced and have been for quite some time. I'm afraid that my daughter doesn't remember who I am. I haven't seen her in over three years."

"That's awful. Why haven't you been able to see her?"

"Well, let's just say it hasn't been very convenient."

"Why is it so inconvenient to see your own daughter? Don't you care about her?"

"It's not a matter of caring. It's a matter of not knowing where she is. Her mother left when I was away on business and took my daughter with her. They've never contacted me, and I don't know where to start to look. Once you get through the entire list of friends and

The Winds

relatives, and all of them deny knowing anything about them, then you've reached a dead end." Cade swallowed hard and looked away. "That's why I'm out here in the middle of the wilderness."

"To look for your daughter?"

"No, to escape reality for a week or two. Being in a place like this makes it easy to forget painful memories. It's easy to lose yourself in nature, you know, be closer to your Creator."

"So did you remarry?"

"That's a little personal, but no, I haven't."

"The ring, you're still wearing your wedding ring."

Cade looked down at his hand and started rubbing it with the end of his thumb. *Of course, my wedding ring, you idiot,* Cade scolded himself. He continued wearing his ring even though it served as a constant, painful reminder of Angie. He tried to remove and discard it but found that he was unable to do so. "I guess I got so used to wearing it, I just never took it off. I haven't remarried. Just haven't been able to find the right one."

"I know how that is. I'm single as well."

"I guess being single helps when you're a forest

ranger," Cade said. "I mean, you said you stayed in the Ranger Station near the trailhead, and I suppose you spend a lot of time up here patrolling the lakes. I'd think that would be hard on a family." Cade bit his lip, assuming that maybe he had said too much.

Tara just smiled. "There's been a lot of people who have wondered why I chose the profession I did. I mean, in high school, I was the head cheerleader and had aspirations of moving to the big city and becoming a model or an executive in advertising, something to get out of Lorenz."

"So why did you become a forest ranger? Not for the money, right?" Cade started to laugh.

Tara returned a courtesy laugh and then answered. "Money is just spent on things that don't mean anything after a certain time. Have you ever known anyone that seemed to have it all, I mean money wise? They have more money than they know what to do with, but when it comes right down to it, they're miserable. They're so miserable that even their money can't buy their way out. I was there once, and it was a suffocating experience." She turned her head with an embarrassed laugh, looking straight at Cade. "Why am I telling you this? I mean, you're a total stranger out in the middle of nowhere, and here I am spilling my guts out like you were my

The Winds

hairdresser." Cade began to smirk.

"Would you like your nails done, as well?" he asked.

"Very funny. I've just been having a little trouble with a guy I've been seeing. He's a Deputy Sheriff. It doesn't matter, but my point is that life isn't about money or what money can buy. Life is about relationships and what you do with those relationships. They are the only things that will last the test of time. A good relationship, I mean one where both parties put their partners before themselves in any situation, those relationships will endure forever."

Cade wet his chapped lips and took a big swallow before replying. "That was beautiful, Miss Samuels. Extremely deep, but beautiful." Cade started to smile. "You know, I really hadn't thought of it that way." He paused for a moment to collect his thoughts. "But what if those relationships end in an abrupt and final way without your control, like my wife leaving with my daughter? How do you deal with that? How do you go on?" he seemed to be deviating from his original plan of saying as little as possible and sending the lady forest ranger on her way to do forest ranger stuff.

"Life's a funny thing. Whenever you feel comfortable in your present situation, something changes, and you have to adapt. That's what makes life interesting and challenging, I guess. It's when you aren't willing to adapt to the changes that you stop living. And if you stop living." She paused and took a deep breath. "You might as well be dead." It was deathly silent. Not even the water falling over the rocks or the calm wind whistling through the lodge pole pine could be heard. Stitch lay silent and motionless on the ground, still with his belly exposed, front paw twitching, patiently waiting for the next gentle rub.

Cade reached up and scratched the side of his cheek. "That's heavy. Either you speak from experience or watch a lot of Oprah." He reached out, and she gave him the piece of paper back. He read through it once, quickly folded it, and put it back in his pocket. He reached down to his knees, grabbed his shoulder strap, and reattached it to the buckle.

"So, in other words, you don't have a fishing license, right?" Tara said.

"I didn't say that. Would you like to see my license?"

Tara thought for a moment and then replied. "That's OK. I trust you, but I don't think the next ranger will. I just happen to be the most trusting out of the bunch."

"And the prettiest, I'm sure," Cade said.

The Winds

"If you only plan on being here for a week or two, I think you'll be fine. I'm the only one that will be coming around. Next month, there will be one more ranger to handle the added people coming into the area." She looked at him curiously. "So why the Winds? I mean, of all the places in the country, why did you choose to come up here?"

"The Winds are my favorite place on Earth. I used to come up here with my Dad when I was young. At times, I think I could literally live up here year round."

"Yeah, right, like you could survive a winter up here." Cade just raised his eyebrows and smiled. "So, where do you call home, I mean, when you're not catching all the fish in the Winds?"

"Well, I used to live back East, but right now, I'm in between moves," he said. "I've been moving a lot the last few years." He reached down and started to pet Stitch. Stitch returned the favor by licking his hand.

"So, where did you set up camp? Is it on this lake?"

"No, I've set up a few miles from here and really don't remember the name of the lake. There's so many in these mountains, it's hard to keep track of them."

"Well, what does it look like?"

Cade looked back at her with his eyebrows lowered slightly. "What, the lake I'm camping at?" He scratched his head. "Well, it has crystal clear blue water surrounded by big rocky cliffs, lots of pine trees, and it's teaming with fish."

"I didn't realize how dumb a question that was until you gave just as dumb of an answer. I'm sorry. I shouldn't pry, but I'm telling you, if I hear of any trouble around here, I'm personally coming out here and hunting you down. Remember the jail thing I told you about earlier?"

"I remember, and I promise, no trouble and not a word to anybody." He pressed his finger vertically to his lips and then smiled.

With that understanding, she flashed those deep green eyes, straightened her shirt, and noticed two of the buttons had come undone. She quickly buttoned them and glared at Cade. He shrugged his shoulders and grinned. She climbed back on her horse, waved back at him, and rode back into the trees.

Cade turned toward the lake and took a big, deep breath. He knew it was only a matter of time before Tara would discover the truth, but it would be on his terms. He couldn't deny it; with his newly acquired knowledge of who she really was, coupled with the pleasant last few minutes he had spent with her, he was starting to develop

The Winds

feelings, something he had vowed never to do again.

Chapter 24

Later that day, Tara had just returned back to the station from her first trip of many into the Winds for the summer. She was back in the stable brushing down her horse when she heard a car pull into the parking lot.

"Just a second, boy," she said to her horse as she walked toward the wooden plank gate. "Let's see who that is." She stepped outside into the bright sunlight and shielded her eyes with her hand as she looked toward the station. Moments later, a man appeared from the front.

"Hey, Denton, over here," Tara yelled as she waved to him from a distance.

Denton saw her, smiled, and started to walk toward the stable. "Welcome home," he said. "Did you have a good trip?" He picked her up from around the waist and spun her around, then kissed her.

"It was great, except the snow up there was a lot deeper than usual." She grabbed his hand and led him into the stable, where she could finish brushing down her horse.

Denton looked around a little, grabbed an item off the shelf, and began inspecting it. "So, did you see anyone

The Winds

up there?"

Tara continued to brush. "Only one person."

"Someone was up there alone this early in the year?" He put the item down and grabbed another.

"Yeah, I found it a little strange, but he seemed like he was having a good time fishing."

"So what's his name? Do I know him?"

Tara stopped brushing for a moment and thought. "You know, I never did get his name."

"Well, it had to be on his fishing license, right?"

She was a little embarrassed to admit to Denton that she never saw his license. "Yeah, but I guess I was content just seeing his license at the time."

"So he didn't look familiar?"

Tara stopped brushing again and looked over at Denton. "No, I told you I just met him. He told me he came to get away for a while, something about his wife leaving him and taking the kids. It was a sad story. He had me read a poem he wrote to his daughter but never sent it to her."

"Wow, how much time did you spend with this guy?"

"Only a few minutes. He was anxious to fish, and I was anxious to get back to you. Why, you jealous?" She dropped the brush, walked over to him, and slipped her hands into his back pockets, "So, did you miss me?"

Denton put his arms around her and kissed her. "What do you think?" They kissed some more, and then Denton suddenly stopped and took a step back. "Tara," he said, with all seriousness. "I got something for you."

Tara nodded her head. "Ok, what is it? And don't tell me it's between your legs again." Denton chuckled.

"That's for later, babe," he said. "No, I mean I got something special, something to take our relationship to the next level, you know." Tara witnessed Denton a little out of his comfort zone for the first time since they'd been dating.

"I told you I'm NOT moving in with you," she said.

He reached into his front pocket and pulled out a small blue velvet box. Tara looked down at it and quickly backed away. "That's not what I think it is, is it?"

"That depends. What do you think it is?" he smiled as he went to open the lid.

The Winds

"Don't open it!" she said. She turned around and started to walk away to the back of the stable, then quickly turned around.

"If that's a ring, then there's something you need to know about me first."

"Gotta tell you, Tara, this is not quite how I envisioned it would go." Tara walked over to a couple of bales of hay, sat down, and motioned Denton to do the same.

With a smile, Denton said, "Do you want my pants on or off?" Emotionless, she looked at him and then looked down. Denton now realized that she was serious. He walked over and sat down beside her, bracing himself for whatever she had to say next.

She reached over and grabbed his hand, set it in her lap, and started rubbing his fingers. When she looked back up, her eyes were moist with tears. "There's a lot about my past that you don't know," she said. "I mean, after I graduated from Lorenz High, I left and went back East for college."

"Yeah, I know. You told me you went back there to school."

"But I haven't told you everything I did back there."

Denton was silent and listened while caressing her hand. "After graduating in Business I landed a great job and was happy. New York is a wonderful place, full of countless opportunities."

"You were on Broadway!" Tara tried to smile, but her eyes were still teary. "Hey, it was a joke," he said. "OK, I'll be serious. Keep going."

"I met someone, someone I thought I loved, and he loved me. I was young and stupid, but he was nice to me. He treated me well and bought me lots of expensive gifts. I grew up with practically nothing. I guess I can't say that, but I grew up in a humble home. We didn't have much excess, but we always had enough to eat, and Mom worked part-time to buy us kids extra things for school and stuff. But this guy gave me diamonds and jewelry. He took me to expensive restaurants and the opera. I was living a small-town girl's dream."

"I can do that. I can buy you anything you want," Denton said.

"But then it happened." Tears started to roll down her cheeks. "We dated for a year, lived together for three, and then he asked me to marry him." Denton was quick to interrupt.

"Hey, you lived with him. Why not me?" Tara just

shook her head.

"Denton, are you going to take me seriously or not? I'm trying to tell you something that I think's important for you to know."

"Ok, I'm sorry," he said. "It was just a joke. Keep talking." Tara tried to gather her thoughts again.

"I was so happy. Finally, I could hold my head up and no longer lie to my parents about what I was doing or where I was living. The lies would stop."

"So things were looking up."

"I thought so at the time. It was a wonderful wedding. He agreed to my request to marry in the cathedral and even paid for my parents to come out to be there with me. It was the first time they'd been to the East. It had a fairy tale beginning, but unlike most fairy tales, this one didn't have a happy ending."

Denton reached up and gently swept the tears away. "Hey, just marry me, damn it. I don't need to know this shit."

"But I want to tell you—no, I need to tell you. No secrets. It's not fair to you or me."

"Ok, I'm listening."

"We'd been married less than a year, and the abuse started. He started staying late after work and drinking with his buddies. Many nights, he would come home and yell at me for no reason. He wouldn't touch me. He would just yell at me. He would call me the most awful things, but deep inside, I knew he didn't mean it. He was under a lot of pressure at work."

"That son of a bitch! That's no reason to take it out on you."

"About three years into the marriage, he hit me for the first time. He slapped me across the face. At the time, I couldn't feel anything. I was in shock, but the next morning, I woke up with a black eye. I was so ashamed I didn't leave our estate for a week. We had to cancel several dinner engagements and everything. He just told them I wasn't feeling well, and nobody knew any different. The beatings became more frequent and violent. I wanted to leave but felt trapped. I didn't have anywhere to go. Then I found out I was pregnant."

She looked up and shut her eyes for the longest time. "I was nearly six months along and thought that maybe since we were going to have a baby, it would change the way he treated me. I thought he would appreciate that I was carrying his child. But it didn't change him, at least not for good. He treated me decent up until that time, and

The Winds

then he came home drunk and out of his head and started throwing me around. I pleaded with him to stop, if not for me, for his child. He just looked at me. He was very angry, and he pushed me across the kitchen. I hit the counter and fell to the floor." She looked up at Denton and began to cry uncontrollably.

"I lost the baby. I couldn't forgive him. I left him that very day I was released from the hospital and haven't seen him since."

"And that's when you came back to Lorenz," Denton said. He held her in his arms, and they rocked steadily for a few moments. "So where do we go from here, Tara? I'm not like that guy." He smiled and kissed her on the forehead.

Tara tenderly kissed him on the lips and then put her head on his shoulder. "You were going to give me something." She looked up and smiled. "Do you still want to?" Her eyes were nearly dry now from the previous tears.

"Hell, yea!" Denton reached into his front pocket and again pulled out the small box, opening the lid.

"It's beautiful," Tara said. Denton reached in and slipped it on her finger. She stuck her hand out and admired it as it sparkled.

"Thank you, Denton, and yes, I will marry you." She grabbed him and hugged him tight. They sat back on the fresh straw and began to kiss. Denton reached around her back and started to undo her bra. As he began to caress her firm breasts from underneath her shirt, visions of Kimber came into his mind as they always did each time he and Tara made love over the past year.

Suddenly, she pushed him away and sat up in the straw. "Denton, what if somebody comes?"

Denton grabbed her by the shoulder and gently pushed her back into the soft straw. "Relax," he said. "And I'll make sure we both do."

Chapter 25

Cade rolled over and grabbed his watch. 3:05 in the morning. There wasn't any wind to speak of, maybe a breeze with an occasional swat from a low-lying branch against the cabin wall, but nothing that would keep him from sleeping. Stitch was snuggled in a tight ball, sleeping quietly at his feet.

It was more out of habit than anything to look at his watch in the middle of the night. He didn't really care what time it was. He had no firm commitments the next day and if he felt he needed to sleep into the late morning, that was his prerogative. But glancing at his watch periodically reinforced the fact that he was troubled and couldn't get to sleep.

Those eyes, he thought, *those beautiful green eyes.* He couldn't get them out of his mind. He tried to think of something else but was unsuccessful. He couldn't deny it; contrary to every reason he'd ventured up to the Winds, he had developed feelings for this lady forest ranger who had unexpectedly entered his life. How could it ever work? She was the younger sister to a girl he had loved with all of his youthful heart and witnessed fall to her death. How could he look into those beautiful, endless green eyes without being painfully reminded of her older sister?

The small insignificant seed was planted late last fall when she heard the innocent snap of a twig in the trees. The seed remained in virtually unfertile soil, lying dormant and uncultivated through the winter as he mourned the death of his wife and children and would have undoubtedly shriveled entirely and died had it not been for the unsuspected reunion with her earlier that week.

"It's Kimber's sister," he mumbled out loud. Stitch's ears twitched at the sound and then settled back down.

How could it happen? The intent of secluding himself in the mountains was to avoid coming in contact with people, but even more so, coming in contact with people from his past. When you meet people, there's a good chance a relationship will soon follow.

Whether it be a friendly, adversarial, or, God forbid, romantic relationship, it was a relationship nonetheless.

Thoughts of Angie entered his mind and faded the deep green eyes of another that had been burned into his subconscious. Angie had beautiful blue eyes in contrast to her light reddish-brown hair. She would have looked stunning in that forest green ranger's uniform.

He could envision Angie in Tara's clothes, those loose-fitting pants with the numerous zippered pockets

The Winds

and the short-sleeved shirt, the embroidered forest service logo stitched to the pocket, with the top two buttons undone. He began to undress her in his mind as he began to fantasize.

It was a perfect evening in the Winds. Cade and Angie, the two of them madly in love, standing on a large flat rock overlooking the secluded, still lake. The sun was just setting over the glacier-cut cliffs, casting a shadow over the patch of trees just at the base. The water was a bright orange from the rays of the setting sun. It sparkled with every gentle wave.

Cade reached out, grabbed her soft hand, and pulled her close. He slowly unbuckled her belt and undid the top snap of her pants and zipper. Starting at the small of her back, he reached into her pants and untucked the shirt, working his way to the front. All that stood between him and ecstasy were a few buttons on her collared shirt.

Reaching up slowly, without losing eye contact with her sea blue eyes, he unbuttoned the remaining four buttons, exposing her supple breasts. He embraced her tenderly as she started to slowly undress him. It was the perfect vision of him and his wife, making passionate love on a warm summer's night in the most beautiful, gentle place on Earth.

Cade was caught up in this vision and felt his heart begin to race. He suddenly became too hot and threw open his blanket to expose him to the cool night air. He loved Angie with all of his heart and strength and longed to be with her again.

The vision began to fade as he felt the tears roll off his cheek and onto his blanket. Stitch shifted positions at the edge of his bed, and suddenly, Cade found himself back in his lonely world. He again looked at his watch; the bright blue light cast dim shadows on the far wall of the cabin. 3:11, barely six minutes since he last looked. He shook his head in grave disappointment, realizing that those six minutes of pure bliss would be minuscule to the rest of his long, lonely life.

It was nearly eight o'clock and Stitch began licking Cade's face as he always did that time of morning. It was time for him to relieve himself, and since the small door was locked through the night, his master was the only one who could open it. Stitch continued to lick his face until Cade opened his eyes and looked around.

"Ok, Stitch, I'm awake." Stitch ran around in circles, anticipating the open door. Cade walked over and swung the door open. "You happy now, dog?" He stepped out to the cool breeze.

He looked past the trees and over the lake. It was a

The Winds

gorgeous day, but not for him. The last time he could remember looking at his watch; 6:35 a.m. He figured he had actually slept less than two hours throughout the night. He still battled with the conflicting thoughts he'd had of both his wife and Tara.

As he relieved himself on a large tree several paces from the front of his cabin, he began to cry. He nearly pissed on his hand as he tried to control the unsteady stream. "Oh, God, how can I continue to live!" he cried out into the calm. The echo returned almost immediately as it bounced off the cliffs in front of him.

He stood there for a moment and listened to his own voice over and over again. "Oh, God, how can I continue to live, live, live…"

Suddenly, the answer came to him like a flash across his mind. It was so simple. One thing that he was certain of was that he couldn't willfully take his own life. That was a fact, the end of the story. But he had been a fierce competitor all his life, both on the playing field and off.

How could he have made all-state in football? How could he have gotten such good marks in medical school? How could he have had the courage to approach Angie the way he did and succeed in winning her heart when all others had previously failed?

It was his competitive nature to succeed. It was his ability to focus on a goal and achieve it. Since his family's tragic death, he had been living a lie, living completely opposite of what his life had portrayed. He had rolled over, not without a fight, since he made a serious attempt to commit suicide but had failed to recognize the alternative solution.

Cade's muscles in his face suddenly began to tighten and his teeth clinched in his jaw. He knew what he had to do. It was an all-or-nothing proposition. Either way, he would come out the winner. He quickly turned back toward the cabin and ran inside. He dressed himself in his loose-fitting blue jeans, tee shirt, socks, and hiking boots and pulled his ball cap snug to his head.

That should do it, he thought to himself. He then remembered something very important. He grabbed a pen and paper and began to write a note. It began:

Dear Shooter, my good friend,

If you're reading this, then...

When he finished writing the note, he taped it to the fireplace where he was sure Shooter would find it when he came up looking for him. He strapped his fanny pack to his waist. Slipping in two full bottles of water and grabbing a large strip of jerky, he headed out of the cabin

The Winds

toward the cliffs at the back edge of the lake.

"Come on, Stitch!" he yelled as he continued to step over the rocks and small bushes. "Come on, Boy!"

Stitch dropped the rawhide bone he'd been gnawing on over the past few days, running toward Cade with his tail straight up in the air. He jumped toward him, and Cade grabbed him on both sides of his neck with both of his hands and wrestled with him for several minutes.

"Stitch, you've been a good friend. I love you, Boy. I hope after today, we can still be friends. He let loose of his grip, and Stitch darted out in front of him, leading the way to the base of the cliffs.

Cade stepped over the loose, crushed rock and nearly stumbled to his knees as he looked up along the smooth, vertical face into the blue sky above. Both Cade and Stitch had been on the very top of the cliff over one hundred and fifty feet above and tossed large boulders over the edge to witness them disintegrate upon impact but had gotten there by an easier means.

On the other side of the cliffs was a much more gentle slope with stair-like rocks, making it easy to get to the top, but getting to the cliff this morning was secondary to Cade. How he got there was the most vital element.

It was an all-or-nothing proposition as far as he was concerned. The rules of the game were simple: *Make it to the top and live your life like there's no tomorrow, no regrets, and no holding back. Make a mistake, and you fall to the jagged rocks below to your sudden death, the end, see if there really is life after death.*

Cade had no choice. He couldn't go on living with the constant reminder of his family's death, nor could he continue living without the anticipation or hope that things would eventually get better. One thing he knew for sure: He couldn't survive another winter in the Winds.

Rock climbing wasn't a stranger to him. He had done some back in high school but none since then. He was pretty good and was successful in climbing nearly all of the cliffs on the North side of Deep Canyon. They had various ratings of difficulty, from 5.2 to 5.10.

The toughest he had ever attempted climbing without the security of a rope was a 4.8. He estimated this cliff to be a 5.3, several magnitudes more difficult than anything he had attempted in high school without a rope.

He was much stronger and limber back then, but he basically had his entire life in front of him and had everything to lose. Now, in his mind, he had nothing to lose. As far as he was concerned, either outcome was acceptable.

The Winds

Surprisingly, he was neither afraid nor doubtful of his daunting objective. He spit in each hand and rubbed them vigorously together. Stitch stood at his feet, looking up and wagging his tail.

"Nope, Stitch, you can't come with me today," he said as if it would be the last thing he uttered to his best friend. He reached down, quickly patted him on the top of the head, and started his assent upwards.

The finger holds were deep and spaced closely together at first. He climbed nearly thirty feet in a matter of minutes. He stopped briefly to catch his breath. He wiped the sweat off his free hand on the backside of his jeans.

He reiterated to himself the three-point contact rule with each change in position. He continued to climb, inch by agonizing inch, as his limbs became weaker and more exhausted with every lunge upward. He found it more and more difficult to catch his breath and stopped to rest more frequently. Stitch dangerously distracted him at one point with his loud bark.

"It's OK, Stitch," he said without looking down. "You'll get your turn, I promise." He continued to concentrate on the next small crack or ledge, finding them to be noticeably shallower and farther apart.

On one occasion, he reached for what he thought was a secure hold, and it crumbled under the slightest pressure. Luckily, he was able to recover. His hands and forehead were sweating profusely, and his lungs felt as if they were on fire. His hat became an annoying distraction, and he flicked it off his head, sending it sailing to the rocks below. Stitch picked it up with his teeth and began to growl, tossing it around.

It had been close to an hour, and Cade was nearly two-thirds the way up. He found a ledge just large enough for him to safely shift his weight off his feet and onto his knees. This was a welcome change, but he knew it wouldn't be long until his knees would start to rebel.

He looked toward the top and could see the contrast between the blue sky and the shaded, dark granite. He was suddenly filled with exhilaration but was concerned with what he was now able to see clearly.

The final ten feet sloped slightly outward, and he knew that the only way he would be able to reach the top successfully was to hug the face and, at some point, violate the three-point contact rule, not by choice, but by necessity. Up to this stage in the game, he really hadn't given much thought to living or dying, just accepting the enormous challenge.

As he shifted his weight from his knees to his feet,

The Winds

he continued climbing again. He took quick, short breaths and slow, fluid motions from one handhold to the next as he progressed up the face. He reached for the next small ledge and began to pull the rest of his body upward. Suddenly, he could feel the ledge starting to give way, and he quickly shifted his weight back down and gripped the previous handhold.

"I can't do it!" he yelled. His voice carried across the lake and back again several audible times. Stitch started to bark. "Why did I ever consider this? This is so stupid. Why did I ever think I could do this?" He stood motionless, his body pressed against the cool wall, and his fingers numb and bleeding. He took a deep breath and continued to think out loud. He took a quick glance downward. "I don't want to die. I want to live."

He thought back to the night of the accident while he was in the ER holding his wife's hand just seconds before she passed away. He replayed the last words she uttered. They were plain and simple. "Cade, I love you. I want you to be happy."

Suddenly, he was struck with dire fear. His fingers became rigid, and the muscles in his arms and legs became tight. "Oh, God, I want to live. Please, God, I want to live," he said in a soft whimper. The tears began to flow down his cheeks.

He ducked his head to wipe the tears away on his shirt and caught another glimpse of the jagged grey rocks below with the dark blue water beating a white foam against its edge nearly a 140 feet below. Stitch looked like a small moving yellow dot.

He quickly looked upward and located another small crevice. He gripped it tightly and inched his way to the next position. Finding himself less than four feet from the top, he realized he had reached the final moment.

The next eighteen-inch surge would determine his success or failure. He had come to convince himself that failure was not an option. It all depended on his next move.

He gripped the crack securely with both of his hands and thrust his body upward. As both of his feet left each toehold, he could feel the added weight on each of his tired fingers. As his foot neared the small ledge, he released one of his hands from the crack to the next crack merely eighteen inches above.

He had only one attempt at making it. If he failed, he would fall to an abrupt death. The sole of his boot gripped the sharp corner of the ledge at precisely the time his fingers penetrated the narrow crack, and he pulled his body upward with all the strength he could muster. He let out a loud groan as he felt the muscles in his back strain and twist.

As he thrust his body upward, his face was so near the top he could have spit over the edge. As he stood there motionless, straining every last muscle in his body, his hands gripping tightly with his waist and his face nearly level with the jagged top of the cliff, he thrust his chin over a sharp ledge, allowing him to transfer just enough weight from one of his hands.

He threw his hand up and over past his head and grasped a small bush hanging over the edge. He could feel one of his footholds give way. He desperately tightened his grip around the small bush and scrambled to find another foothold when, all of a sudden, his other foot lost grip, forcing him to submit to the evil force of gravity. He felt helpless as he hung by the small bush, swinging like a pendulum, for what seemed to be an eternity.

Flailing his legs, trying to get any kind of foothold, he swung out from the face and slammed back into it, hitting his head squarely on a rock. Dazed and exhausted, he continued to hang by one hand, helplessly immobile. Every muscle in his body ached, and he screamed out in pain.

Nearly succumbing to fatigue and hopelessness, he heard the piercing screech of an eagle overhead. He gazed up into the sun filled sky and could see the outstretched wings of a Golden Eagle as it floated effortlessly in the canyon draft. He remembered the Great Spirit that Shooter had talked about so seriously to him and his children the night in front of the fireplace.

"It's true," Cade whispered to himself. "I am being watched over through the eyes of an eagle." With his newly acquired faith, hope, and confidence, he calmed himself by taking short breaths and slowly but precisely worked his way up the last foot and inches of the face, holding tightly to the deep-rooted bush.

After reaching the top, he collapsed, took numerous deep breaths, and started to laugh. He laughed aloud, louder with each large breath. Stitch began to howl from below. Cade stood defiantly close to the edge of the cliff as if to say, "I did it! I did it!"

He stretched both of his arms above his head and shouted to the top of his tired lungs, "I DID IT!" He looked intently at the sky and the eagle, flying effortlessly moments before vanishing.

Chapter 26

Tara halted her horse and looked around to try to detect the source of the sound. She grabbed her binoculars from the closest saddlebag and began panning the horizon. On the far ridge, she could see a person standing on the very top with his arms stretched high to the sky. She sat on her horse and watched him through her binoculars for nearly a minute as he jumped up and down, dancing on the top of the ridge.

That guy's nuts, she thought. She bent over, put the binoculars back in the saddlebag, and secured the leather strap; then, by making a distinct clicking noise with her mouth, the horse started to trot in the direction of the ridge nearly a quarter mile away. Anxiety increased with every step. The memory of her last encounter with a man at the base of those cliffs the previous summer was not a pleasant one.

Cade felt like a new man. He had challenged himself and won a savoring victory. He had earned himself a renewed sense of spirit and life by risking everything and conquering the seemingly insurmountable ridge. Nearly leaping down the stair-like rocks on the far side, he couldn't wait to clutch Stitch in his arms.

He realized that Stitch hadn't the least bit of

appreciation nor comprehension for what he had just accomplished, but he knew he would be at the base of the cliff, tail wagging, tongue flapping, and thrilled to see him again.

Cade literally skipped over the rocks and brushed to the cabin with a wide smile on his face. He stopped just before entering and looked back through the trees to the lake. It had a new meaning. The canyon walls of gray granite were no longer his tomb for an old life but a symbol of hope and strength for his new one.

There was so much he wanted to do, and so much he wanted to see now that he could see it for its true beauty and wonder. He entered the cabin and walked to the far side past his cot. He opened a small box and reached inside for the first time since he came the summer before. He held the eagle's feather close to his lips, gave it a kiss, and graciously thanked the Great Spirit for watching over him that morning.

Suddenly, Cade heard a faint noise outside near the lake's edge. It was the sound of a horse approaching. Cade hurried, threw the feather back in the box, and shut the lid tight. He stood next to his cot, motionless and silent. Stitch began to bark outside as if he'd seen another bear.

"Stitch, don't start barking." He could hear the

clomping of horse hooves against the rocky ground. Cade opened the door ajar and looked toward the lake but couldn't see anyone there. He called for Stitch to come into the cabin, which he did. "It's OK, boy, just be quiet for now," Cade said as he held his mouth shut.

Suddenly, the horse let out a loud snort. Tara got off and looked around. The surroundings were eerie and silent, and the surface of the lake was unusually calm, totally void of even a ripple. She led her horse down to the edge of the lake for a drink.

As the horse drank, she turned and looked into the dense trees near the base of the cliffs. Something strange caught her eye. As she walked closer the reflection from the sun became more intense. She bent over and picked it up. It was a spent brass shell casing.

She examined it carefully and then put it in her pocket. She looked into the trees and decided to investigate further. As she walked through the dense cover, the small cabin came into view.

Shivers ran down her spine as she could feel herself being watched, and by the looks of the cabin, by the same man she met up with late last summer; the same arrogant ass, she was now convinced, owned the spent brass in her pocket.

She vividly remembered his gun strapped to his side and the shot that was fired the night before that he denied taking. She unsnapped the holster, drew out her pistol, and grasped it with both hands as she pointed it at the cabin. She continued to walk closer, keeping her eyes peeled for any sudden movement.

Pieces of uniformly chopped wood were stacked neatly on one side of the cabin with a long, white rope stretched taut between two trees on the other side with various articles of clothing hanging and fluttering in the calm breeze.

A dog chain was wrapped around the base of a tree with a worn semi-circular area underneath the shady canopy. A large deer pelt was stretched and nailed to the side of the cabin with the antlers mounted above the doorway. The cabin door squeaked as it started to open.

"Hold it right there!" Tara shouted. "I'm armed and will shoot." The door continued to open. Cade appeared with his hands held high above his head. Tara lowered the pistol and positioned the white dot of her front sight directly in the middle of his chest.

"I can explain, Tara," Cade said. He proceeded to walk out of the cabin. He turned momentarily and made it a point to shut the door. "Bugs, once they get in, it's nearly impossible to get them to come out."

The Winds

"Spare me the bullshit, John. The first time we met, you were an arrogant, lying son of a bitch, and then just a few days ago, you nearly charmed me off my feet. I can't believe you're the same person. Everything you've told me is a lie. Who are you really?" she continued to point the gun at his chest with her finger on the trigger.

"I've had some personal issues to sort out, you know, come to grips with some things. I'm a new man, Tara. I'm not the same person you met a year ago."

"Save it for the judge, John. I'm not interested in hearing it. I'm taking you in."

"Taking me in for what? I haven't done anything. Being an asshole isn't against the law."

"I don't find you the least bit amusing. I'm the one holding the gun, and I'm not in the mood to listen to your wisecracks. For starters, fishing and hunting without a license is against the law. Coming into the Winds without the proper registration is against the law and who knows what else you've done. The Shoshone Indian Chief and a reservation ranger have been missing since the middle of last summer. For all I know, you may have had something to do with that."

"Oh, come on, I didn't kill anyone. You honestly believe that I had something to do with that? Hey, I admit

I was a little messed up, but I'm certainly not a murderer." He slowly put his hands back down to his sides. "There are a lot of things I know about you and a lot of things you don't know about me. Just give me a chance to figure everything out, eventually I'll tell you the entire truth about me, and my past. I'm just not ready yet. I need some time to clear my head."

"What you really mean to say is you need some time to disappear. Put your hands back up over your head. Your sweet talking isn't going to work this time. You're coming with me," she said with a wave of anger in her tone.

Cade looked at her seriously for a moment and made no attempt to raise his hands above his head. He shook his head, turned, and grabbed the door handle.

"Just where do you think you're going?" she didn't appreciate his blatant disrespect for her or her authority.

"The cabin." He opened the door and walked in.

"Hold it right there, John!" she ran to the cabin with her gun leading the way. She cautiously entered through the door and lost momentary sight of him as her eyes adjusted to the sudden darkness.

Cade ignored her as he started packing his pack with

things he felt he needed.

Tara watched impatiently as he placed items of food, clothing, and a few sticks of jerky into the pack. "It's not that far out on horseback," she said. "You don't need to take all this stuff."

He stopped momentarily to look at her. "I'm not packing for the trip out. I told you I need some time to clear my head. I'm not ready to leave the Winds just yet, and now that the cabin's been discovered, I can't stay here."

Frustrated, Tara quickly backed out of the cabin and pointed the gun at his chest again. "I'm not joking!" she screamed. "Like it or not, ready or not, you're coming with me."

She took a step forward and stood in the cabin doorway about four feet from where Cade was standing near his cot and slowly raised the gun to where it was pointed directly at his head.

Cade stopped what he was doing, turned, and looked directly into her eyes for an extended moment without blinking once. He then looked back down, secured the straps to his pack, and started to walk toward the door.

"Oh, I almost forgot," he said. He bent down,

retrieved his holster from under the cot, strapped it around his waist, and grabbed his pack again.

Tara started to tremble as she continued to hold the gun out in front of her. She took a few slow steps back into the middle of the trail leading down to the lake as Cade walked to the front of the cabin and out the door toward her.

He bent down and scratched Stitch behind the ears. "Boy, you need to stay here with this nice lady. I've decided that I can't take you to where I'm going."

He undid the chain to Stitch's collar, then stood up and looked over at Tara. He reached into his pack, grabbed the sticks of jerky he'd packed for Stitch, and threw them at her feet.

"You can either take him with you or leave him here on his chain. It's up to you, but I'm not sure when I'll be back. Now, if you'll please excuse me, I've got a lot of hiking to do before the day ends." He took several steps toward her and then stopped.

She was blocking his way down the trail. He reached out and nudged the barrel of the pistol away from his chest with his index finger and walked past her without hesitation.

The Winds

She drew her pistol back up and pointed it at his back as he walked toward the lake. "This is your final warning. You take another step, and I'll pull the trigger."

Cade stopped and turned around. "You can carry a gun, but unless you have the guts to use it, it won't do you any good." He grabbed the long knife sticking in the side of a tree next to him and continued walking toward the lake's edge.

Tara followed from behind. He stopped a second time and turned around. He could clearly see the look of desperation on her face as the gun nearly shook out of her hands. "If you still feel you need to take me in, then I guess you can find me here in a few days. Goodbye, Tara."

Tara slowly lowered the gun. "Wait, so where are you going?" He continued to walk away. "At least tell me why somebody would want to spend a winter in the Winds?"

He stopped and turned back around. "I'm really not prepared to tell you yet. One thing's for certain: I'm not a killer. Soon, I'll tell you everything about me, and I hope you will understand." He turned and walked around the trees and out of sight.

Chapter 27

Ever since Cade was a young boy, he was intrigued with the reservation side of the Winds. Even though it was only a small, narrow strip and represented less than five percent of the total area encompassed within the Winds' boundaries, it held a certain mystique, character, and even forbiddance.

A special permit was required to enter legally, a cost that exceeded anything that Cade's father was willing to pay at the time. As a result, Cade could only dream of crossing over. Members of the tribe could fish the lakes and streams at any time during the year, but only a few took the initiative. The area was virtually untouched by human hands other than by those who were employed by the reservation to patrol it.

Cade decided that there was one more vital thing he needed to do before his long journey to find himself came to a positive end; he had to venture over to the reservation side of the Winds. However, it was extremely risky and against explicit counsel from Shooter during their last meeting.

Shooter described the reservation rangers as aggressive and threatening, but deep down within himself, Cade knew he had to go.

The Winds

The anticipation was great, but the anxiety was greater. Cade stopped for a moment to rest and dip his cup into a cold spring. As he drank, he seriously questioned what he was doing and why he was doing it. For all he knew, Tara could be on her way out to seek help to find him and take him out by force, but his sixth sense told him that wasn't the case. She was intrigued. He could feel it.

Four hours later, he crossed over what he believed to be the ridge signifying the boundary into the reservation. His father had pointed it out to him numerous times when he was a young boy. It wasn't as obvious as a wide black dotted line like that found on the map, but at the crest of the ridge were strategically placed piles of rock evenly spaced across the ridge.

Two larger columns were placed on either side of the trail. Cade hesitated slightly before entering for no particular reason, only that he'd always known it was forbidden to him.

He walked between the two columns of rocks and looked over the broad expanse. There were large snow-packed mountain peaks, sheer canyons, and grassy meadows dotted with splashes of blue lakes and flowing streams just like anywhere else in the Winds, but it wasn't what he could see.

It was a sense of spiritual awakening for him. He closed his eyes, reached out his hands, felt the cold breeze across his face, and started his descent through the trees to the valleys and lakes below.

Hiking on the sparse, unmaintained trail, he occasionally stopped to admire a colorful wildflower or to get a glimpse of a deer or other animals that dwelled in the area. It was a peaceful feeling, a feeling that he could take with him to start his new life.

Suddenly, there was a snap of a twig followed by a second. He froze momentarily, listening to every sound. Then, he heard the distinct sound of a hammer being pulled back on a pistol. He stood up and turned around to see the end of a gun pointed straight at his chest. There were two rather large men of Indian descent standing together. One was holding a pistol, and the other had both hands on his hips.

"What are you doing?" the man with the pistol asked. The other man separated and started to walk around the other side as if to minimize Cade's options for escape.

Cade instinctively stretched his hands out in front of him as if to signify he was unarmed, but with the pistol strapped to his waist, it was not very convincing.

"Hand it over," the same man demanded.

"I don't want to hurt anybody. This pistol's for my protection only. I heard there's bears in the area," Cade said.

"You heard right and lots of them, but why are you here, and where's your permit?"

"This is my first trip into the Winds. I didn't realize I'd crossed into the reservation."

"So you're here illegally?" the other man asked.

Cade thought for a moment as he recalled what Shooter had told him. They could confiscate all of his gear, tents, sleeping bags, fishing poles, and even his pistol. "I'm not looking for trouble. I just wanted to fish and enjoy nature. I climbed to the top of that ridge, saw this lake, and decided to hike down here and see if there were any fish in it."

"There's fish in all these lakes on the reservation," the man holding the gun replied.

"But I didn't realize I was on the reservation. There are no signs, markers, nothing. How's a guy to know?"

"Don't give me that shit. What about the piles of rocks up on the trail?"

"There are piles of rocks all over. How am I

supposed to know that one pile means one thing and another pile means another? I just came to fish. Now, if you two would excuse me, I'd like to hike the hell out of here." Cade turned and took a step down the trail.

The other man pulled his pistol out and shoved the barrel into his chest. "Give me a good reason to pull the trigger," he said.

Cade looked at him without even a glimmer of fear. "I told you, I'm leaving the reservation. What you do from this point on is your decision." Cade nudged the barrel from his chest and began to walk down the trail.

Suddenly, one of the rangers jumped him from behind and wrestled him to the ground. The ranger held his face to the ground with one of his arms wedged behind his back as the other kicked him in the side.

"You're not very smart, are you?" the one doing the kicking asked. "You have a difficult time recognizing authority. Up here in the Winds, we make the rules. We don't like strangers snooping around, especially the white ones."

"I told you, I don't want any trouble. Just let me up, and I'll leave."

"No, you don't understand. You've come to a place

The Winds

you're not supposed to be."

Cade struggled to breathe through the pine needles.

"Let him up," a voice said. A large man appeared from the edge of the trees. The ranger let loose his grip around Cade's arm and allowed him to get up from the ground. Cade slowly arose and looked at the man as he approached him.

"I had a hunch I'd find you up here. Good to see you again, Cade."

Cade couldn't believe his eyes. "Denton? What are you doing here?"

Denton started to laugh. "That's funny. That's the same question I'm going to ask you, and you better give me a straight answer."

"Like I told these guys, I didn't realize I was on the reservation."

"Complete unadulterated bull shit, Cade. You've been up here more than I have growing up. You know the Winds better than your own balls. You're up here for a reason, and I don't like it. Why have you been hiding up here for the last year?"

"Personal issues. Anyway, I don't have to tell you

anything. Your jurisdiction stops at those piles of rocks. If these two are going to arrest me, then fine, arrest me. If not, then I'll be on my way."

"It's Tara, isn't it? You want to steal her from me like you did, Kimber. Well, it ain't gonna work this time. We're already engaged."

"Engaged?" This revelation hit Cade with full force. Tara was his main motivation for climbing the cliff and releasing himself from his personal bondage.

"Yep, imagine that, me married to Kimber's little sister. She's not a virgin, but then again, neither was Kimber."

"Yeah, you, of all people, should know that, you rapist son of a bitch."

"I told you I didn't rape her. She wanted me."

"And I suppose she wanted your child, too."

Denton took a step back. "What are you talking about?"

"You raped her and got her pregnant. She was carrying your child when she died."

"You don't know that for sure. How could you know

that?"

"Her parents told me. It was discovered during the autopsy. They were upset and wanted me to know, but I didn't tell them that it wasn't my child. I haven't told anyone, but the child she was carrying was yours."

"You know that's not true. You were dating her at the time."

"The timing's there, the party, you taking her home that night, it all added up. You raped her, and you know it."

Denton was enraged. He knew that he could be ruined in the community if this became public. With modern technology, Kimber's body could be exhumed, and the fetus could be positively linked to him through his DNA. He walked closer to Cade, spit a long string of brown chewing tobacco to the ground, and reached out his hand.

"The gun, Cade, give it to me."

Cade reached down and put his hand over the pistol. "Look, I told you I didn't know I was on the reservation, and I'm hiking back out. This is my gun, used for my protection, and I'm not handing it over to anyone, especially a psychopath like you. Now, if you would excuse me, gentlemen, I have a lot of hiking to do." Cade started to turn around when one of the men suddenly hit him in the face.

Cade stumbled and tried to regain his balance, but the weight of his pack forced him to his knees. Denton then stepped up and kicked him in the stomach. Cade looked up at him with blood oozing from his nose.

"The pistol, Cade. We can do it the easy way or the hard way. It's your choice," Denton said.

Cade reached down and slipped the pistol out of the holster. "So you're going to arrest me?" Denton nodded his head. "On what charge?"

"Being on the reservation without the proper permit and fishing without a license. Now get up." Cade slipped the heavy pack from his shoulders and stood up.

"But I just hiked in this morning. I had no intentions of fishing," Cade said.

"Nobody hikes into the Winds to count the wildflowers. I find it hard to believe you didn't come here to fish." Cade just shook his head and handed the pistol to Denton. "Thank you. You have the right to remain silent. Anything you say can and will be used against you in the court of law."

The Winds

"You're reading me my rights?"

"No, I'm not reading you anything. I have them memorized," Denton said sarcastically.

"Don't you think you're being a little zealous?"

Denton looked at him and laughed. "Maybe, but there's an outstanding warrant for your arrest—something to do with a speeding ticket last year that you forgot to pay."

"That's garbage, Denton. The only reason I forgot to pay it is because my entire family happened to get killed on the highway. Don't you think paying a stupid ticket was low on my priority list at the time?" The two reservation rangers smiled and laughed at the comment. Denton glared at them, and their smiles immediately left their faces.

"Ok, there's one other charge," Denton said. "Make that two other charges."

"And what would they be?" Cade said.

"Two counts of homicide."

Cade shot forward and made an attempt to swing at Denton's face, but the rangers restrained him. "Hey, I didn't have anything to do with Shooter's father or that ranger last summer. I wasn't even here!"

"Those aren't the two I'm talking about," Denton said. Without the slightest hesitation, Denton pointed Cade's gun at the chest of one of the rangers and pulled the trigger. The ranger stumbled backward to the ground. Blood immediately covered his chest.

He then turned and pointed it in the direction of the other ranger. With a look of horror, the ranger immediately turned and started to run for the trees. Denton pulled the trigger and shot him in the back and then fired a second time, hitting him in the back of the head. The ranger fell lifeless and bloody to the ground.

Cade stood frozen in his tracks. He spent a few seconds analyzing the events to see if they actually happened or if he was just imagining them.

Denton looked at him with hate in his eyes. "That will get you life in prison."

While Denton put Cade's gun in his other hand and then reached for his own gun, Cade seized the opportunity to turn and run. He ran toward the trees. A shot was fired, hitting a rock to the side of him, followed by another shot that grazed his shoulder.

Running on pure adrenaline, Cade didn't even realize

that he'd been hit. Several hundred feet up the canyon, he found himself too exhausted to continue. He settled between two large rocks to catch his breath. He looked back but didn't see any movement. Suddenly, he heard a loud, angry voice from the trees.

"Run if you want, Cade, but I'll find you. I'll hunt you down like a rabid dog. First-degree murder, the state of Wyoming doesn't take kindly to murderers, and neither do the Shoshone. With any luck, they'll catch up to you first, and there won't have to be a trial."

Chapter 28

After catching his breath, Cade continued to climb upward. There wasn't a trail or an easy way out from the canyon walls, but he managed to traverse the ledges and cliffs without being noticed. He found refuge in a natural cavern between the rocks in the middle of a vast area of large boulders as a result of a massive rockslide that cut the trail off between Spear and Priest Lakes over 30 years ago.

He assessed his injury and removed one of his boots, ripped off the sock, and cinched it securely around his arm, covering the wound to curtail the bleeding. Due to the loss of blood and the miles of walking, Cade was completely exhausted and laid down on the cool rocks and fell asleep.

He slept for several hours. The sun had set completely, causing the shadows to disappear and darkness to fall across the field of boulders. Cade was awoken by the sounds of a coyote in the distance. He sat up and looked across the darkened horizon. As he pondered the day's events, he realized that in his attempt to remove himself from the grips of society, he'd become a wanted man.

He was being framed for killing another human

being, and the impact of that realization hit him with severe force. As he sat quietly in the cavern, he was left with nothing but the hollow whistle of the wind through the rocks and his own desperate thoughts.

After nearly an hour of just sitting, contemplating, and agonizing over his fate, Cade decided he needed to act. He needed to return to the cabin and get enough supplies to sustain him for the next few days to buy him some time to figure out what to do long-term.

Hiding for the rest of his life in the Winds, though plausible, was not an option. He had beaten the challenge of "the cliff" and, therefore, committed himself to relationships, peace, and hopefully a life of happiness.

He reached into one of the many zippered pockets of his jacket and pulled out a small flashlight he'd normally use while fishing at night. He panned the small cavern and found it went farther back than he first observed. Even though the thought of a bear crossed his mind, he immediately dismissed it and crawled further into the darkness. The temperature dropped considerably. It was like being in a refrigerator.

The beam was small but bright, carving a hole in the darkness as he crawled further into the cave. He flashed the beam across the sharp rocks and thought he saw something but didn't quite know what it was. Curious,

David J. Bunnell

Cade continued to crawl deeper into the cave.

Scanning the depths of darkness with his tiny flashlight, he was a little uneasy about what he might find and considered turning back as he started to feel goosebumps emerge on his neck and arms.

As the light slowly moved its way ahead of him, he stopped abruptly. There in the circle of light was a body, a man's body laid upon the rocks, face up. Startled, Cade jumped back and hit his elbow on a sharp rock as he turned to escape. The flashlight flew from his hands and onto the rocky floor, wedging itself between two rocks. The small tunnel of light focused directly on the profile of the dead man.

After making a conscience effort to calm himself by taking several deep breaths, he grabbed the flashlight and crawled further toward the body for a closer look. The man appeared to be of Indian descent. He was wearing a ranger uniform like the two men he had encountered earlier in the day.

Cade reached over and felt the hollow cheeks on the Indian's face. The skin was as hard as leather and amazingly well preserved, but the man's face was unrecognizable. The eyes were sunk into the skull and the mouth was drawn tight around the teeth and slightly open. There was no stench, signs of animal activity, or even

The Winds

flies, nothing to advertise the body's existence.

Searching for some sort of identification, Cade dug deep into the man's pockets only to find nothing except what he thought was course sand. He pondered a moment and thrust his hand back into the same pocket. He pinched a few of the flakes and brought them out and, with the help of the flashlight, got a closer look.

He sorted through the flakes, pinched one of the larger ones between his fingers, and rotated it in the light. It glistened brightly. He brought it to his mouth and bit into it. It was a metal, but it was soft.

It's gold, pure gold, he thought to himself. He emptied the man's pocket entirely of its contents into the palm of his hand. There was about a teaspoon full of gold flakes, which he put into a pocket in his vest. As he resumed inspecting the rest of the body, he made a grisly discovery.

There was a piece of a splintered arrow protruding nearly three inches lodged deep in the side of the man's neck. Dried blood encircled the wound and apparently ran down the man's shoulder and partway down his sleeve.

Cade continued to try to put the pieces of the puzzle together. *Who would want to kill a ranger, and why would an arrow be their choice of weapon? And why did he have a pocket full of gold?* As he leaned back to ponder the situation he aimed the beam of light further past the body.

Another reflection caught his attention. He crawled over the body to get a closer look. Crawling nearer, he focused the light between the rocks and found it to be a feather. He picked it up and examined it closely. It appeared identical to the one Shooter had given him and the kids the previous summer, an eagle feather dipped in pure gold, but this one was attached to a necklace of sorts.

He raised the light and shined it a few feet further in front of him. Lying among the rocks was yet another body, this one dressed in complete Indian attire, from the thick beaded choker around his neck to the leather moccasins on his feet.

Cade could clearly see the remains of dried blood on the man's face, apparently originating from the top of his head following the hairline to the back of his neck. He reached across and lifted the blood-crusted hair from off the forehead and discovered a small hole, a single gunshot wound to the head.

Suddenly, events from the previous summer flashed across his mind as he began to process the information in front of him. There were two bodies, both of Indian descent; one was wearing tribunal Indian attire, while the other was an Indian reservation ranger. Both men came up missing in the Winds at approximately the same time frame.

"It can't be," he mumbled to himself. "But it is, it's Shooter's father."

Cade could barely hold back his emotions. He thought of Shooter's anxiety, the many days of searching this vast wilderness for his father, who had met his doom several days before and made this dark, frigid cavern his tomb. The foul play never once entered his mind. As far as Shooter was concerned, his father died a peaceful death in a place set aside above all others and was reunited with his wife for eternity.

Cade was confused. It was apparent that Shooter's father had killed this man with an arrow, but who killed Shooter's father, and how did the two of them end up in the cave? There had to be another person. Something had to have gone wrong. Cade was certain that whatever happened had something to do with the gold he had found in the man's pocket.

Cade hiked back to the cabin in the complete darkness of night. He was grateful he had his small flashlight because he received little help from the slender slit of the moon above. Denton and his men would be hitting the trail early the next morning to pursue him; of that, he was confident. He had to be ready. He had to act.

He entered the cabin and started to pack a few essential items into his backpack. During his long walk in the dark, he figured out exactly what he was going to do, what he needed to bring with him, and where he was going to go next. He figured he needed just enough supplies to last him long enough to find the gold.

Shooter was telling the truth about the legend of the gold. How much was truth and how much was legend was up to Cade to determine. He wondered if Shooter knew the real reason for his father's annual trip into the Winds. Cade was confident he had solved the riddle.

Shooter's father was the appointed chief of the Shoshone Tribe. His annual trip was two-fold: Commune with the Great Spirit and bring back pure gold to help finance the tribe for the coming year. How else could each member be given an eagle's feather dipped in pure gold?

But how many members of the tribe knew of the gold and its location? Why didn't the Indian leaders push harder to get outside help in searching for their chief? The answer lay hidden in the gold. The way Cade saw it, gold was more precious to them than an old chief. If they had pushed for intervention from the white man, chances were that the white man would have found the gold. This would have been disastrous to the Shoshone Tribe.

Cade's pack was filled to capacity and then some. He

The Winds

even packed some of the pertinent medical supplies he'd been stockpiling in case he needed them. He tidied up the inside of the cabin to make it appear as though he hadn't returned. He was certain that Denton would inform Tara of him and engage her involvement since she was the only person who knew of the cabin at the shores of the unknown lake.

Of course, this would be after an intensive, brutal interrogation with Shooter. Cade just hoped that Shooter would be convincing enough that Denton would believe him when he said he didn't know where he was staying.

Cade was counting on the cabin as being their first stop of the morning. Their complete search of the cabin would give him the necessary time to carry out his plan to buy him time to locate the waterfall, the same waterfall that Shooter revealed to them that night beside the fireplace in his home, the waterfall that was swallowed up by the mountain.

"The map!" he turned around, grabbed it off his cot, and walked out the cabin door. As he walked past the trees and along the lake's edge, he felt like he'd forgotten something else that was important to him. He stopped momentarily to think.

There's something else, he thought. *I just know I'm forgetting something.* He started to walk, and then suddenly, he heard a coyote chattering and howling from the top of the ridge across the lake. *It's Stitch! I've forgotten Stitch.* He motioned to turn around and head back to the cabin, then remembered he'd left Stitch in good hands. *I'm sure Tara's taking good care of him,* he thought to himself. He looked up at the new moon and then continued to walk into the darkness.

Chapter 29

Denton and three of his men each sat on top of their horses and formed a large circle with the horse's heads facing toward the center. It was still very early in the morning; the sun hadn't even peaked from the dark horizon. Tara was with them to show them the way to the cabin. She had her own horse and stood outside of the circle, but she could hear every word out of Denton's mouth.

"Men," Denton said. "I've asked Tara to come with us to help ferret out this mountain man, Cade Hobbs. For those of you who don't know, he used to be a friend of mine, but not anymore. I don't make friends with cold-blooded killers."

Suddenly, from around the trees, Shooter came riding his horse. He approached the circle of law enforcement. He then looked at Tara as he made his way to the circle. "Cade's no killer, Denton." Shooter's face was swollen and battered, and his right eye was black.

"What do you think you're doing?" Denton asked. "I don't remember inviting you to the party."

Shooter continued to approach closer. He was expressionless, but on the inside, he was furious. "Party?

Looks more to me like a lynching," Shooter said with a sarcastic remark as he stopped his horse across the circle from Denton. "If you think I'm going to let you ride up there and shoot my friend in cold blood, you got another thing coming."

"Cold blood? Not hardly. He shot those two Rangers yesterday. I got his gun. Same one that shot 'em. I just want to arrest him and throw his ass in jail, not kill him." Denton leaned over and spit a long string of tobacco. "But if he tries to run away like yesterday, we have no choice but to take him down."

"He didn't kill them, and you know it!" Shooter shot back with his split, bloody lip. "He just wanted to get away from people like you." Shooter knew without a doubt that Cade didn't kill those Rangers and was determined to help his friend to the bitter end, including death if need be.

His hatred toward Denton reached an all-time climax after the severe beating he'd received late the night before. Denton was sure that Cade would return to the place he'd settled in for the winter to dress his wounds and lay low until he felt the heat was off.

Denton was also sure Shooter could provide him with the location. It took him twenty minutes and just as many or more punches before he realized Shooter didn't know

The Winds

anything.

"Yeah, we know you're good buds with him, Shooter. I think that truck has blurred your understanding of what's right and what's wrong." Denton started to laugh. "And Tara here, she's going to take us to Cade's infamous cabin." Denton glanced across a couple of the other Officers. "I hope it has a hot tub." The men started to laugh.

Denton made it a number one priority to reveal the true identity of the mysterious mountain man to Tara upon his return from the Winds the night before and made it even more of a priority to paint that man as a cold-blooded killer, a man who should be feared and not trusted. Denton had lost his first love at the hands of that same man, and he'd be damned if he'd let that happen again with his second!

"We don't have a lot of time," Denton said. "Let's ride!" With that said, he motioned with his hand, and all of them turned and headed up the road toward the trailhead.

After several hours of riding, the men secured the horses a few hundred yards from where Tara told them the cabin was located and started making their journey further on foot. They moved under the cover of darkness in and out of the trees, around boulders and bushes with their weapons drawn.

With great anticipation and a nod of Denton's head, one of the other officers kicked the door in. Denton quickly entered, pointing his pistol forward and yelling at the top of his lungs. The other two officers followed closely behind. They were all sorely disappointed. The cabin was tidy and clean but completely unoccupied.

"Damn it!" Denton yelled. "We're too late." He shoved his pistol back into his holster and exited the cabin with a scowl on his face. "He's not here," he yelled over to Tara and Shooter, who were waiting by the other horses.

"He's not stupid," Shooter mumbled so only Tara could hear.

Tara continued to look straight ahead. She was still battling the notion that Cade had lied to her about everything. What was he trying to hide? Was he really a cold-blooded killer? And what about Shooter? Did she really know him, or could he and Cade be involved in something together?

Things just didn't make any sense. What would be so important that people would have to be killed? She continued to ponder similar questions as Denton and the other men returned to the horses. She wondered what

The Winds

Denton's role, if any, pertaining to the series of events was. His apparent hatred for Cade was astounding. Was the hatred mutual between them?

"Well, it looks like we have an outright manhunt on our hands," Denton said as he untied his horse. "Put a set of handcuffs on Shooter's wrist and secure the other end to the saddle horn." Shooter peered at him and shook his head in disgust. "Sorry, Shooter, it's a necessary precaution. This man's wanted for murder, and frankly, I can't trust you." Shooter climbed on his horse, and one of the officers cuffed his wrist to the saddle horn as instructed.

After they had all mounted their horse, Denton followed with further instructions. "I'm afraid Cade is a little more cunning than I'd given him credit. One of you will have to ride back to the trailhead and get the bloodhounds. That's the only way to catch a fox. Meet us on the other side of the ridge near Priest Lake. That's the last place we saw him. If I was a betting man, I'd say he's hiking deep into reservation territory."

Denton spit a long string of chewing tobacco-laden saliva and then looked over at Tara. "Oh, and take Tara with you. We don't need her anymore." Denton grinned with a few grains of chew between his front two teeth.

"You and your men didn't help search for my Father.

You said it was a reservation issue," Shooter said. "Why the sudden change?"

Denton looked over at him with his eyes without turning his head. "Because now it's personal, my friend."

Several hours later, they were met with the dogs near the mouth of Priest Lake as arranged. He brought three bloodhounds with him, each secured on a long leash. Denton pulled out one of Cade's shirts that he'd grabbed from the cabin and stuck it in the face of each of the dogs.

"Now go find him," he yelled. The dogs were released, and they bolted out ahead, howling and sniffing across the rocks and bushes toward the other side of the lake. They followed the dogs closely on horseback. It wasn't more than fifteen minutes later when one of the dogs caught the scent and took off into the heavy trees. The other two dogs followed and eventually caught the scent as well.

"Well, boys, it's show time," Denton said as they all veered into the trees.

The dogs suddenly stopped and began to whimper. They double-backed, walking away from the small clearing and toward the horses.

"What's wrong, boys?" one of the deputies asked the

dogs, recognizing that something wasn't right. As they approached the clearing, they came upon a gruesome discovery. Before them was a blood-soaked shirt, a ripped-up hat, and what was left of a shredded pair of pants. There were scratch marks on a few trees and splashes of blood on several rocks.

"What the hell?" Denton said. They got off their horses and began to look around.

"What happened here?" one of the other officers said. He picked up a small piece of one of the bloody garments and found it to still be moist and sticky. He wiped his fingers on his pants. Denton combed the area for movement. There was none. He reached down, picked up the bloody shirt, and squeezed it in his hands.

"Same shirt he was wearing last night." He continued to look around the area. "Something just isn't right. A bear attack, but no tracks?" He looked at the others.

Shooter was still on his horse, secured to the saddle horn by the handcuffs. "Denton, let me loose," Shooter demanded. Denton motioned with his head, and one of the officers walked over to Shooter and unlocked the cuffs.

Shooter got off the horse and began to look around the area. He analyzed several of the scratch marks on the trees and then combed the small areas of soft dirt for any signs of bear prints. He crouched down and pressed his finger into the freshly stirred dirt.

"Over here," he said. Denton and the others quickly approached him to see what he had found. They looked down at his finger and saw the print. It was a partial print, half of which fell on a flat rock. "Grizzly."

"Let me see," Denton said. He shoved Shooter out of the way and crouched down next to the print. He put his finger in the indentation and worked his way to the claw marks. There were five claw marks, each nearly twice as long as the toe pads were wide and converged to the center. Denton also questioned a smaller print.

"It's the dew claw," Shooter said. "Sometimes it shows up in the print, but not always. Apparently, this is a very large Grizzly bear."

"I'll be damned," Denton said. He threw the bloody shirt at one of the officers and instructed him to stuff it in the saddlebag. "I just want to make sure it's a match."

"How could you be so callused?" Shooter said. "My God, Denton, show the man some respect." He turned from him and walked toward his horse. Denton glared at him as he watched him walk the other way.

"So what do we do from here?" one of the officers asked.

Denton turned to him and thought for a moment. "The search is on hold until we get the results back. No use wasting time chasing a ghost. If it matches, as far as I'm concerned, case closed, and as far as that Grizzly's concerned, dinner is served!"

"And if it doesn't?" the officer asked. Denton looked over at Shooter.

"Then I'd hate to be Cade."

Chapter 30

As Cade sat hidden in the rocks high above the activity, watching and waiting, he assumed his bear attack decoy had worked as he watched the posse turn and ride back out, but he wasn't sure for how long. He had to make every minute count as he combed the rugged slopes for the mysterious waterfall.

Previous to Cade finding the gold in the pocket of the dead ranger, he thought of the waterfall as purely legend, someone's vivid imagination, but now, he knew it existed; he just didn't know where. He continued to consult the topographical map for ideas as to where to look next.

He searched all of the lakes in the general area of the rock slide, and where he'd found the two bodies, figuring that at the time Shooter's father was killed, he was probably either at the waterfall or nearby.

His detailed search of the East Fork Lakes, Heart, Spear, and Priest Lakes was in vain. The outlets didn't have any sizable waterfalls or anything that resembled a mountain swallowing up the water. He continued his trek Northeast along the Washita Trail past Sage Lake in pursuit of Hatchet Lake. The topographical map showed a lake nestled along a sheer canyon wall similar to the

The Winds

lake he shared in his cabin.

The hike was several miles. He couldn't help but think that maybe this journey would be in vain as before. He stopped occasionally to check the horizon with his binoculars for any signs of Denton and his men.

Even if he came across some hikers or fishermen, he couldn't take the chance of them seeing him. For all he knew, his picture could be plastered on every store window from Lorenz to Redding and, possibly, throughout the State.

The trail followed a small stream, which Cade determined to be the outlet to Hatchet Lake. It was mid-afternoon, and the wind had picked up just as it had this time of day every day since the beginning of summer. Cade removed his heavy pack and propped it against a rock while he walked over to the stream to get a drink.

As he stood there drinking from his tin cup, he noticed something quite odd. It appeared that the small stream had the potential of being a rather large river. As he walked further, he noticed an off-shoot of the stream that at present was dry but undoubtedly held water at some point during the year, namely in the spring when most of the thawing occurred in the high valleys and filled the lower lakes beyond capacity.

He followed the dry bed of polished rocks, broken twigs, and tattered logs until he reached a cliff. As he peered over the edge, he could see an area of flat crushed rock below surrounded by dense tree growth. At the very base of the mountain, he could see the same evidence of a once free-flowing steam, but there was no evidence of the stream between the bed of crushed rock and the valley below.

A waterfall that is swallowed up by the mountain, he thought. Could this be the place? Could this be the waterfall that Shooter had revealed to them in the form of a legend? Cade didn't take much time to ponder the thought as he immediately started to search for the easiest way down the cliff.

He found a side shoot that wasn't much trouble and reached the crushed bed of rock within minutes. He stood there trying to imagine water flowing over the flat rocks above, disguising the small cavern just steps in front of him.

This is it, he thought. *This has got to be the place. It's just as Shooter described it.*

He walked toward the cavern and stepped inside. A thick vein of pure gold, nearly four inches thick, surfaced on the side of the cavern. It showed obvious signs of digging and scraping almost in an organized fashion, working from the front of the vein with occasional chips and gouges toward the back.

"Amazing." He reached out and pressed his fingers into the deep scars in the gold vein. He thought of all the Indian chiefs previously who had come to this very spot to reap the blessings of the Great Spirit. The thought was tantalizing.

Suddenly, the look of amazement and astonishment left Cade's face. His thoughts focused on Shooter's father as he thought of him standing behind this very waterfall early last summer. *How did it happen? Was there a struggle?* He turned to look outside the cavern into the brightness of the afternoon day.

He looked into the trees and noted that anyone could have been hiding in the rocks and trees. Anyone could have sat waiting silently, calculating their next move. It was an eerie feeling to knowingly be in the middle of the vast wilderness but had the impression that you weren't alone.

Was he not alone? Had someone followed him to this very place? He immediately discarded the thought and walked out of the cavern. As he did, a flash in the bed of crushed rock caused him to raise his hand to shield his eyes.

He slowly approached the object. He bent over, removed a few small rocks from around the flash, and exposed a large knife with a bone handle. He inspected it in detail. It was apparently handmade. There wasn't an engraved brand name or manufacturer.

The bone was curiously fashioned smooth, fitting every curve of Cade's hand. The blade was nearly razor sharp and had a slightly gold sheen the last few inches or so of the sharpened tip. Cade took his fingernail and scraped the edge of the knife. Small, thin flakes of gold collected on the edge of his fingernail.

In his hand was the very knife used to scrape gold out of the cavern, but to what chief did it belong? After numerous years and chiefs coming to this very spot, it was difficult for Cade to imagine that the knife hadn't been found until now. Maybe the water was muddy, making it difficult to see the knife, but the only thing that made sense was that the knife hadn't been there very long.

The blade was still sharp, free of chips and cracks, and the bone handle was still intact and didn't show any signs of wear. Cade was convinced that the knife he was holding belonged to Shooter's father. Cade tried to imagine what had transpired just over a year ago at this very spot. Within these canyon walls held the secret of Chief Running Bear's tragic murder and the identity of

The Winds

the perpetrator. If only the walls could talk.

It was late. The sky was clear, revealing the billions of stars above, but the moon was just a dim sliver on the horizon. Tara sat comfortably in her soft chair near the fireplace while Stitch lay at her side on a colorful Indian blanket, sleeping with his head on his paws. His ears twitched slightly from the crackling of the small, homey fire.

Tara was emotionally spent. She tried to relax by reading a good book but found it difficult to concentrate, so she had to reread several of the last pages. She became frustrated, slipped the marker in between the pages, shut the book, and set it on the small table. She looked down at Stitch and smiled as she scratched lightly behind his ears.

The events over the last few days were taxing on her mind and spirit. The victim could have easily been her up there. She had confronted the man who was now wanted for murder and wondered what might have been had she had the courage to pull the trigger when she had him in her sights.

The loss of the two reservation rangers weighed heavy on her mind as she thought of them losing their lives in the call of duty. She blamed herself because she could have prevented it.

Suddenly, Stitch lifted both of his ears, raised his head, and opened his bloodshot eyes. He began to growl.

"Hey, Stitch, what's wrong?" she reached down and stroked the top of his head. He looked up at her and then started to growl again, this time coming to his feet and approaching the window. He then started to bark.

"What is it, Stitch?" She jumped out of the chair and over to the chest of drawers, opened the top drawer, and brought out her pistol. She quickly returned to the small table and turned off the lamp. The light from the parking lot showed dimly through the thin curtains into her room. She ducked behind the chair and watched the window.

Stitch became frantic. He ran from the window to the door and then back to the window, barking every leap and bound. Tara reached out, grabbed him by the collar, and pulled him in close to her to quiet him down.

She could feel her pulse increase with every eerie second that passed in the stillness of the night as she stood crouched behind the chair, pistol pointed directly at the window.

There was a soft scuff of gravel and then another, followed by the shadow of a man standing outside of the window. She heard several pebbles hit the windowpane, and then the man came closer, cupped his hands on the window, and pressed his face into the glass pane. Tara pulled the hammer back. The end of the barrel was shaking as her finger pressed lightly on the trigger.

I can do this, she told herself. *Just be calm.* She pressed with a little more force and felt the trigger indent the flesh of her index finger.

"Tara, are you in there?" the voice said. He backed away from the window, and his silhouette became fuzzy. It disappeared momentarily and then reappeared. Tara could hear more tapping noises on the glass. "I know you're in there. I saw the light turn off. It's me, Cade," he said a little louder. "I'm sure you know who I am by now. Tara, I didn't kill those two rangers. I didn't kill anyone. You've got to believe me."

Tara stood up from behind the chair and approached the window. Pointing the pistol to the window, she parted the thin curtains with the barrel and looked through the slit to the outside.

Cade was standing in full view. "Please, can I come in? I don't know how long I can stand out here."

"Go away! I'm calling the Sheriff."

"No, don't call the police! I'm begging you. I'll tell you everything, I promise. I didn't kill anyone. I can prove it."

"Everything you've told me has been a lie. Why do you think I'll believe anything you say now? I'm calling the Sheriff. You move, and I swear I'll shoot this time." She reached up, pulled the curtains open, and pointed the barrel at Cade's chest. She quickly grabbed her cell phone and dialed 9-1-1.

"Please, you're the only one that can help me right now. I didn't kill anyone. You have to believe me. I had to fake my death in order to give me some time to think of a way out of this mess."

Suddenly, the Police dispatch came on the line. "Operator, what is your emergency?" the lady responded. Tara held the receiver tight to her ear as she looked at Cade's sudden desperation. "Operator, what is your emergency?" the lady said again.

Tara hesitated to answer and pulled the phone from her ear. She glared at Cade standing outside her window, shook her head, and quickly put it back to her ear again. "This is Tara Samuels at the Bears Ears Ranger Station. There's a disturbance outside my window."

"What type of disturbance?"

"I don't know for sure. It's dark, but I have a gun."

The Winds

"Don't panic. I'll dispatch the nearest officer. He should be there in twenty minutes."

"Twenty minutes?"

"I'm sorry, Miss Samuels, that is the best we can do. The nearest officer is just outside Fort Washita."

"OK, but tell him to hurry."

"I'm sure he will, but in the meantime, make sure all the doors are locked and stay away from the windows."

"I'll do that, thank you." Tara hit the off button to disconnect the call. She set the phone back down on the table, walked closer to the window, and slid it open a few inches, still pointing the pistol at Cade's chest.

"Don't make me kill you. I didn't pull the trigger last time, and it cost two men their lives."

Cade stood in front of the window with his hands partially above his head. "You've got to believe me. I didn't kill them."

"Then who did?"

"I'll tell you everything, but you need to let me come in."

Tara took a deep breath and then tightened the grip on the handle of her pistol. "No way, you're a liar. Tell me who killed those rangers from where you stand. You move even a muscle besides your mouth. I swear I'll blow your head off."

"Can I at least put my hands down?"

"Tell me who killed those men, and then I'll decide if you can put your hands down."

Cade took a hard swallow. "Denton did it. He killed 'em in cold blood. I saw it with my own two eyes."

"But it was your gun."

"Denton was with the rangers when they approached me on the reservation. In an attempt to arrest me, he confiscated my gun and then turned it on the two rangers. It happened so fast. He shot the first one in the chest, and then when the other started to run, he shot him in the back of the head. It was horrible, Tara. It took me a moment to realize what was happening. I took off running into the trees, and he shot at me several times. One of them hit me in the shoulder."

"So why come here? Why not the police?"

"Because everyone thinks I killed them, and I'm supposed to be dead. What chance do I have of them

The Winds

believing my story without proof? They'll never believe that the killer is one of their own." Cade looked away for a moment and then looked back at Tara. "Can I put my arms down now?"

Tara loosened her grip on the pistol and lowered it to her side. She nodded her head.

"Now, can I come in? I'm tired, and I'd really like to see my dog."

Tara nodded her head and motioned for him to go around to the front door. *I can't believe I'm doing this*, she thought to herself. When she came to the front door, Cade was already waiting for her.

"I still don't know if I can trust you. Denton's my fiancé. I know him better than most people in this town. He has his faults, but murder isn't one of them."

"You just have to trust that I'm telling you the truth this time. I have a lot I need to tell you with very little time. You're the only one that can help me. The only friend I have is Shooter, and I don't have a way to contact him. Please, open the door."

She hesitantly unlocked the door and opened it. Cade walked in, and she shut it, and locked it behind him. "Stitch, come here, buddy," he said as he kneeled down. Stitch jumped to him and started licking his face. "It's been a while. Sorry I left you at the cabin, but it was for your own good. It looks like Tara has taken good care of you, boy." Cade looked up at Tara and smiled. She was expressionless and still holding the pistol at her side. He stood up.

"A bear or coyote would have gotten him. I figured I had no choice," she said.

"I don't expect you to forgive me for the awful way I treated you."

Tara turned and started to walk down the hallway to her room. She motioned with the pistol for Cade to walk ahead of her. They entered her room. She sat on the bed and motioned for him to sit on the fireplace hearth where she could keep an eye on him.

"I don't blame you for being cautious, but I'm not going to try anything stupid."

"So why did you leave me up there? You had a pistol pointed at your chest. How did you know I wouldn't pull the trigger?"

"Actually, I didn't, but it wasn't time for me to leave the Winds quite yet. I went in the Winds on my own terms and was determined to leave them the same way. At least if I was carried out strapped to the back of a horse, dead, it was my decision. After I left you, I hiked to the reservation side. I was compelled to do it.

When the rangers approached me, they got very physical with me when I wouldn't give them a good reason for being there. Then, they went ballistic when they found out I didn't have a permit. One of them had me pinned on the ground. That's when I heard Denton's voice.

He told them to let me up and then started yelling at me. The next thing I knew, he asked me for my pistol and then shot those two rangers and then turned the barrel on me. I ran for my life into the trees. I didn't realize I'd been hit until I stopped to rest about half a mile up the canyon." Cade unbuttoned his shirt and exposed his shoulder. It had a blood-soaked bandage that needed to be changed.

"So why would Denton even be up there? He doesn't have any jurisdiction on the reservation."

Cade reached into his pocket and pulled out a small bag. He opened it, reached over, and poured some of the contents into Tara's hand.

"What is it?"

"It's pure gold from the Winds. I found it. That's why I had to fake my death. When I was hiding from Denton, I found two bodies hidden deep in a cave. One was Shooter's father, and the other was a reservation ranger. Remember, both of them came up missing around the same time last summer? I found gold flakes in the ranger's pocket and realized they were the motive behind the killings. The Shoshone have known about the gold for centuries, and all of us have heard the legend, but apparently, Denton found out about it last summer, and it cost Shooter's father his life."

"Shooter's father? What does he have to do with this?"

"Shooter's father went to the Winds every summer. He was the chief of the Shoshone Tribe, and I'm sure he went up there every year to get gold to help fund the tribe."

"Can you prove it? Can you prove Denton killed him?"

Cade thought for a moment. "Right now, I can't, but in time, and with the help of my friends, I'll be able to. I need your help. I've got to get to Shooter's."

"I can't believe this is happening. I thought I knew Denton. How did I not see it?"

"He's the master of disguise. He's done it his whole life. He can portray someone he's not better than anyone I know. You stop ten people on the street and ask them what they think of Officer Denton, and they'll all tell you he's a great guy, but if you ask Shooter, myself, and a few other classmates, you'll get a far different answer. We've all seen

The Winds

the evil side of Denton, the side that's extremely difficult to recognize. But once you've seen it, you know it's always there." There was momentary silence. "So will you help me?"

She hesitated for a moment, then nodded her head. She placed the pistol on the small table. "I'll help get you to Shooter's, but not tonight. It's too late. You can stay the night here, and we'll go first thing in the morning. But you can't sleep until you tell me everything." She thought for a moment. "First of all, why did you lie to me?"

"It's a complicated story, but I guess I have all night if you do."

Suddenly, headlights appeared in the window. Tara jumped up, went to the window, and peeked between the curtains. She said. "It's Denton!"

The Sheriff's vehicle pulled into the parking lot and came to a screeching halt in front of the station. Denton quickly got out and ran up the stairs to the front door. "Tara! Tara, are you in there? Open the door." He continued to bang on the door. Stitch ran down the hall and started to bark.

"What do I do?" Tara said.

"Calm down. Everything will be fine. I'll just slip under the bed out of sight. It'll be OK. Just give me the pistol in case there's trouble." Tara handed over the gun. "I'm trusting you on this just like you have to trust me. You can't tell Denton I'm here. I will get the proof, Tara. I just need time." Cade quickly dove under the bed and out of sight.

She walked down the hall and opened the front door. "Denton, thanks for coming so quickly."

"Are you alright?" He grabbed her by the shoulders.

"It turns out it was nothing. I was reading my novel, and I guess I got scared and started hearing things. It's a way scary book. You can read it when I'm done."

"You were reading a book?" Denton looked around the front office and then peered outside into the parking lot. "You're sure it's nothing? That's not like you to get spooked."

"I know. I don't know what got in me. It was just a strange noise, and it startled me."

"Well, if you're sure."

"I'm sure."

Denton quickly looked at his watch and then grinned as he thought. He walked past her and into the hallway.

Tara quickly followed him into the bedroom. "Denton,

The Winds

what are you doing?"

Denton turned around smiling and began to unbutton his shirt. "Hey, as long as I'm here, I might as well make it worth your while."

"Denton, please, not tonight. It's late, I'm tired, and you're on duty. I don't think it's right."

"Sex is always right, baby." He sat down at the edge of the bed and started to remove his pants.

Cade lay quietly under the bed as he felt the force of the mattress press against the side of his face. He had the pistol drawn near his side. One of Denton's shoes tumbled under the bed near him.

"Come on, Tara, just a quicky. I'm not asking for much. It'll only take a minute. It'll make me feel better about coming all the way out here for nothing."

Cade took the end of the pistol and slowly pushed the shoe back to the outer edge of the bed.

"Is that what you think? You came out here for nothing? Tell me, if I was really in trouble, would you still insist on having sex before you left?"

"Now you're being unrealistic. Of course, I wouldn't, but you're not in trouble, and I thought that since–"

"You thought that since you were here, I would just lay down and happily spread my legs for you?"

"Well, when you say it–"

"How insensitive can a man get? I seriously thought I was in trouble. You showed up, and I appreciate that, but now I want you to leave."

"But, I didn't mean–"

"I'm tired, and I want to go to bed…alone."

Denton, slightly embarrassed, stood up and put his shirt and pants back on. Then, he reached for his shoes and slipped them back on. While he was still trying to tuck his shirt in, she led him down the hall and to the front door. He walked out on the porch, took his cowboy hat off, and held it in his hand. "Do I at least get a kiss good night?"

Tara glared at him. "Good night, Denton. Don't call me tomorrow. I have a lot to do."

Denton stepped down and onto the gravel. He stopped momentarily and looked back at her seriously. "For what it's worth, I just got the test results back from the bear attack. It's confirmed. The blood on the clothes is a match. As far as I'm concerned, case closed. I'm not spending the taxpayer's money looking for a pile of bones. The only thing

The Winds

I have left to do is take a few trophies out of the case at the high school."

"You lost me there, Denton. What are you talking about?"

He smiled. "Nobody wants to remember a murderer." He opened the car door. "OK, so I'll call you the day after tomorrow. That should give you enough time to forgive me, right? I love it when we make up after a good fight!" He grinned as he got into his car and sped off in a cloud of dust.

Tara leaned over the porch and watched until she could no longer see the taillights of the car. She backed toward the door and felt a sudden touch on her shoulder. She quickly turned around. "Cade, don't do that! You startled me."

"That was a close one. I appreciate what you did, Tara. You did really good."

"Did I really have a choice? If Denton's capable of killing those other men, he's certainly capable of killing me or you."

"At least for now he and everyone else think I'm dead. That'll give me time to sort things out and get the evidence I need before I go to the police. Nobody can know I'm alive except for Shooter."

"I'll take you to Shooter's first thing tomorrow morning, but I want you to tell me everything right now. Why did you hide up in the Winds and lie to me like you did? I also want to know everything about you and Kimber. I was too young to understand when she died. I want to know everything."

Cade nodded his head. He led her back to the bedroom where they could talk comfortably.

"First, about me. I'm sure you heard about my wife and two children, right?"

Tara nodded her head. "Yes, that is so tragic. I don't know how anyone could cope with that."

"That's just the point. I didn't cope. I tried to kill myself and failed. I sold everything I had, bought a truck, and came out here to live the rest of my life in the Winds. This whole time, Shooter's been the only one who knew about it. He brought me supplies and drove my truck."

"That explains the stolen truck Denton told me about. He told me you were out of the country or something."

"That's what I wanted him to think. I wanted everyone to think that. Going into the Winds was my way of dealing with the loss of my family. I didn't want to risk entering into another relationship and then losing it again like, well, first Kimber and then my wife, Angie."

The Winds

"So tell me about your relationship with Kimber. You loved her, right?"

"I loved your sister very much. The day she died was the day I was going to ask her to marry me." Tears filled his eyes, and he had trouble speaking. "It was a great day, and I was so excited. We hiked up to Mirror Falls to our spot, the spot where we first kissed. I know that sounds pretty stupid, but it was important to me. I made her cross the waterfall. Halfway across, she slipped. I tried to hold onto her hand, but the force of the water was too strong. All I can remember is her screaming my name just before her hand slipped from mine. It was horrible. I spent the next hour looking for her at the bottom, but I knew in my heart that she was gone and out of my life forever."

Tara clenched onto her pillow as he spoke. Tears rolled down her cheeks as she listened.

"Moving was the best thing that could have happened. I couldn't stay in Lorenz. The memories were too painful. Once I left, I never wanted to return. I let a lot of people down, but I just hoped they would eventually understand."

"So why did you return after twenty years?"

"Anxiety attacks. I couldn't live a normal life harboring the memories. It was starting to affect my family. I had to return to confront my past, but when I got to the door I couldn't go through with it. I sat in the parking lot and watched my classmates go in and out of the reunion dinner, imagining the conversations about me behind those closed doors."

"About you? What do you mean?"

"I'm sure everyone was talking about me and Kimber's death."

"That's not true. I was there, and the only conversations I heard were very positive. They all spoke highly of you and wished that you had come. I was uncomfortable at first going to the reunion with Denton, knowing a little of the history between you and him and because I was Kimber's sister, but I found out so much more about my sister than ever before. They loved her. She touched so many lives while she was alive, and for that, I am forever grateful I went."

"So, what have you heard about me and Denton?"

She hesitated for a moment. "You two were real competitive in high school, both on and off the playing field. You both dated Kimber and from what I heard, Denton was pretty upset that you and Kimber ended up together during your senior year."

"Yeah, what else have you heard? What about after Kimber's death, did your parents tell you anything?"

The Winds

"I'm not sure what you mean."

"Did they tell you about Kimber being pregnant at the time?"

Tara nodded her head. "Several years later, they told me she was pregnant. I can only imagine what it felt like to lose a child, Cade. I'm so sorry."

Cade turned away from her and wet his lips slightly before he spoke. "At the time, I could only imagine as well."

"What do you mean?"

Cade looked her in the eyes. "It wasn't my child."

Tara quickly put her hand to her mouth. "What are you saying?"

"Kimber was pregnant, but it wasn't my child."

"If you weren't the father, then who was?"

"Denton. I was gone playing a basketball game. He gave her a ride home from a party, and he raped her, only she told me he *tried* to rape her. I guess she was too scared to tell me the truth. I confronted him when he tried to arrest me on the reservation. That's when he snapped."

"I don't believe this. I hate that man," she said.

Cade grabbed her by the shoulders. "I hope you realize how deep you are in all of this, Tara. Denton is a dangerous man and will stop at nothing to get his way."

Chapter 31

News of the accusation against Cade Hobbs for the killing of the two reservation rangers ravaged the small town like a wild forest fire. It became the subject of every conversation that next morning.

"How could a successful doctor commit such a heinous crime," one would ask as he sipped his coffee at the coffee shop before work.

"I remember him as being such a nice young man when he lived here. It's the death of that young girl. It made him crazy," another was heard saying.

It was even more of a shock when, after it was confirmed by Denton representing the Sheriff's department at a small news conference, the front page of the Lorenz Journal informed the community of Cade's death. Most people believed it to be true, while others thought there must have been some grave mistake.

There wasn't any doubt that Cade Hobbs was dead; that was not the issue. The blood samples were an identical match, but there hadn't ever been a legitimate Grizzly bear attack in the Winds. Livestock had been killed near Togwotee Pass recently by Grizzlies, and one had been seen near the small town of Dubois, but that was nearly sixty miles away. It was just difficult for the old timers to accept that the Grizzly was again a part of the Winds.

For the few hours left of the night, Cade slept on the chair by Tara's bedside, and woke up starving.

He hadn't had anything to eat for nearly a day and had hiked fifteen rigorous miles to the trailhead earlier that night. After a quick bite, he and Tara drove to see Shooter at his home. Tara drove while Cade hid himself in the back seat of her car. The entire town of Lorenz thought Cade was dead, and he wanted to keep it that way, at least for now, but soon, the entire truth would be revealed.

Tara drove down the dusty dirt road leading up to Shooter's home. They just assumed he'd be there. Cade's truck was parked diagonally in the driveway. There was nothing out of the ordinary. The horses stood at the edge of the fence as they watched the car approaching in a large plume of dust.

"So, does it look like he's home?" Cade asked from behind the front seat.

"There's a few vehicles in the driveway."

"There should only be two."

"No, there's three."

"What kind are they?" Tara looked closely at the vehicles.

"One's your truck. It's a red Dodge, right? There's an old sports car, bright red with a spoiler on the back."

"Yeah, he's had that since high school. It's a 1977 Chevy Camaro Z28. What else?"

"A Ford Escort. It's dark green and sporty." Cade thought for a moment, then raised his head just enough to see the car over the top of the seat.

"I don't know anything about that car. It's not Shooter's." He looked at the car more closely and read the license plate. It was from County 10, which was Fremont County, so the car was local, but it was a custom plate with the capital letters IMNRN. The letters didn't make any sense to him, but Tara, after hearing Cade repeat out loud what he read on the plates, said, "I got it! It says I am an RN."

"I'd be willing to bet it's Marybeth's car," Cade replied. "She's an RN. Shooter told me they'd been seeing each other."

"So what do you want me to do?" she said. Cade stuck his head above the front seat again.

"Go to the door and first make sure it's Marybeth with

him. If it's not, just tell him you want to express your personal condolences for my death, and then we'll come back later after whoever has gone."

"And if it is Marybeth?"

"Then just tell Shooter I'm out here."

Tara looked into the rearview mirror. "Just tell him you're here? Cade, he thinks you're dead."

"No, he'll just wonder what took me so long." Tara was confused, but did what Cade had instructed her to do. She approached the front porch and was ready to take a step up when the front door opened. It was Shooter.

"Hey, Tara, so where is he? He's with you, right?" Shooter asked as he looked toward her car. Tara couldn't believe what she was hearing.

"So am I the only one here who thought Cade was eaten by a bear?"

"You, Denton, and all of Lorenz. Tell him to quit hiding and come into the house. There's nobody else here." Suddenly, Marybeth came from around the door wearing one of Shooter's shirts. "Well, nobody but Marybeth."

Cade peaked over the top of the seat and Tara motioned him to come into the house, which he did. They all sat in the living room while Shooter went to the kitchen to pour them all a cup of coffee. After he returned, Cade told the detailed story about the bear attack.

"So, how did you know it was a hoax?" Tara said, looking at Shooter.

"I'm an Indian. Indians track things. There were two Grizzly bear tracks, right?" Tara nodded her head. "Cade picked the perfect place to stage the attack because most of the ground was crushed rock, and what dirt was exposed was too hard to realistically leave an imprint, even for something as heavy as a bear."

Tara continued to look at him but started to get confused. "I really don't know where this is heading."

"Because you don't know much about Grizzly bears, and neither does Denton and his men." He turned and looked at Cade. "For just learning how to make the tracks, you did quite well. The proportion of the foot to the toes was good. The claws converged toward the center, but the—"

"Dewclaw was on the wrong side," Cade said. "I had to leave something to tell you I was alive."

"That was pretty risky if you ask me. We both know Denton's a moron, but what if one of the others picked it out?"

"I had to take the chance. I made three assumptions. The first assumption I made was that you would be with them when they came across the scene of the attack. That assumption was correct because, as far as Denton knew, you were the only one who knew I was up there. The second assumption I made was that you would pick up on the dewclaw, but Denton and his men wouldn't. That assumption was also correct."

"OK, so you're two for two. What's the third assumption?" Shooter said.

"That you would come into the Winds to find me." There was a short pause. "But I can see now that you were preoccupied." Cade looked over at Marybeth, and she just grinned.

"But what about the blood?" Shooter said. "They took samples to test."

"Go ahead, Tara, tell him," Cade said.

"Denton paid us a little visit last night at the Ranger Station. While Cade hid under the bed, Denton told me the blood tested positive. Denton's convinced that Cade is dead. There's supposed to be a big write-up in today's Journal."

"So you are telling us that you scattered your own blood at the scene?" Marybeth said.

"Have you guys forgotten? I'm a doctor? I know how to draw my own blood."

There was further conversation about the attack, the investigation, Shooter's interrogation from Denton, and a couple of his men, but then Cade became very somber and sat down by Tara on the couch and invited Shooter to sit down in the chair next to him.

"I've got some disturbing news, Shooter," Cade said. He reached over, grabbed a small duffle bag he'd brought, and pulled out an eagle feather dipped in gold.

Shooter took hold of the feather and examined it closely. "This was my father's. I know because he cut a piece out of it after my mother died. Where did you find it?"

Cade put his hand on Shooter's knee. "I found your father's body in a small cave located in the rock slide between Spear and Priest Lakes when I was hiding from Denton."

Shooter clutched the feather tightly between his fingers. "How did he die?"

"From what I could tell, he took a single gunshot in the head."

Shooter immediately stood up and looked at the ceiling

above. "Oh, God!" Marybeth jumped up and grabbed his arm. "He was murdered?" Cade nodded his head. Tara looked over to Cade. You could see it in her eyes. She knew that there was more to the story.

"That's not all. There was another body in the cave," Cade said. "It was a man. I'm sure it's the body of the reservation ranger that was reported missing about the time your Dad was due back from the Winds. It appeared that your father shot him in the neck with an arrow. The arrow was broken in half, but the tip was still lodged in his neck."

"So there were more involved," Shooter said.

"Whoever killed your father, or knows who killed your father, is out there." It was silent for a few moments, and then Cade reached into the bag again, this time revealing the bone-handled knife.

Shooter immediately recognized it. "That knife belongs to my father. Did you find it on his body?"

Cade shook his head. "I found it at the waterfall, you know, the waterfall with the gold?"

"You found the gold?"

Cade nodded his head.

"What gold," Marybeth said. "What are you guys

The Winds

talking about?" She looked over at Tara. "Do you know anything about the gold?"

"We've all heard about it, but until now, it was just some Indian legend," Cade said.

"Not entirely," Shooter said. "A few years ago, my father told me that the legend was more than a legend. He just didn't tell me where it was."

"So you knew why your father was in the Winds?" Cade said.

Shooter nodded his head.

"Why didn't you tell me?"

Shooter was silent for a moment. "I did, but you didn't listen."

"So, how did you find it?" Marybeth said.

Cade just shrugged his shoulders.

"The Great Spirit's watching over you, Cade," Shooter said. "There hasn't been a white man yet who has found the location of the gold. They only know of the legends."

"I'm afraid that there might be another white man beside me that knows where the gold is."

"Whoever it is probably killed my father?" Shooter sat back down on the chair. "Where did you find the knife?"

"I saw its reflection when I was coming out of the cavern. It was down in between some rocks at the waterfall's base, but the waterfall was dry, with no water at all. I could tell that at some time, there had been a lot, but right now, there isn't any. The stream is really an offshoot of the larger river coming out of Hatchet Lake."

"Hatchet Lake, so that's where the gold is."

"Yes, and I also think the gold is the reason those two reservation rangers were killed."

"Why do you think that?"

"Because I'm confident that the same man that killed your father killed those two rangers."

"You say it like you know who the killer is," Marybeth said.

Cade looked over at Tara and grabbed her hand. "I was there when the rangers were killed. Denton shot them in cold blood, and I'm sure he's responsible for your father's death as well."

"Denton killed my father?" Shooter quickly stood up. "That son of a bitch! I'll kill him!"

The Winds

Cade jumped up and grabbed his arm to help contain and calm him. "You can't do that, Shooter. I saw him shoot the two rangers, but I don't have any proof that he killed your father, but with all of your help, we'll get it."

"So what do we need to do?" Marybeth said.

"For starters, I have to remain dead. Nobody can know I'm alive."

"And then what?" Shooter said.

"This is where Tara and I got stumped late last night. We were hoping that you might have some ideas."

Shooter thought for a moment. "So you said you found my father's knife in the rocks below the falls. They were dry, so you could see the knife."

"That's right."

"But at the time my father was there, I'll bet there was plenty of water coming over the rocks. If that was true, then that's probably why he couldn't find it."

"True, but how did it get in there in the first place?" Tara said.

"What if there was a fight?" Cade stood up and began pacing around the floor before the fireplace. "What if your

Dad was defending himself against his assailant and dropped the knife after he had been shot?"

"That would be the only way he'd let go of the knife," Shooter said.

"What do you mean?" Tara said.

"My father doesn't go anywhere without his knife. He's had it since he was made Chief. If he had dropped it in a twenty-foot snake pit, he would have crawled down and gotten it. I think Cade's right. My father probably dropped the knife after he'd been shot. His murderer probably didn't think to go after it because, in his opinion, it would never be found. But there's one thing that bothers me."

"What's that?" Cade said.

"I can't imagine my father going down without a fight. He must have been surprised."

"But the other body in the cavern, it had an arrow in his neck," Cade said.

"But what happened after he shot that guy? Maybe my father shot that man, and Denton or someone else approached him from behind."

"Your father was shot in the forehead at point blank. For what it's worth, Shooter, it's my opinion that he died

The Winds

instantly." Shooter acknowledged what Cade was trying to say. "The point I'm trying to make is that whoever shot your father didn't sneak up from behind. Your father knew he was there."

"But I can't accept that he went down without a fight. My father was a born warrior. I would like to have seen my father's killer."

"What do you mean?" Cade said.

"I bet he had slash marks from head to toe, even if the jerk brought a gun to a knife fight."

Suddenly, a chill ran down Marybeth's spine. Up to this point, she had been a nearly silent observer. "Shooter, your father was in the Winds during late June, early July of last year, is that correct?"

"That's correct. He left for the Winds around the last week of June for three weeks."

"It may be a complete long shot, but that was about the time Denton came into the emergency room with that awful cut on his chest, like right over his collar bone."

"That's right," Shooter said. "He showed us at the reunion. He said it was from a branch."

"He came back about a week after the reunion

complaining of pain and oozing," Marybeth said. "The doctor looked at it, removed several stitches, and had me clean it out."

"Clear down to the bone?" Cade said.

"Yes, and we took several X-rays because we thought there might be some damage the doctor had missed the first time he treated him."

Cade looked over at Shooter and motioned for him to give him the knife. He looked at it closely again, but this time with different intentions. "Shooter, look at the blade's edge and tell me what you see."

Shooter took the knife back and looked at it closely. He scraped the edge of it with his fingernail, and thin minute flakes peeled off. "It's gold. My father must have used this knife to peel off the gold."

"And to slash Denton's chest," Cade said. "Now, all we have to do is prove it."

Chapter 32

Cade, Shooter, and Marybeth sat in the living room discussing their options. Tara had since left hours earlier to return to the Ranger Station to avoid suspicion. Marybeth reiterated how she took several X-rays of Denton's chest, suspecting that the complications due to infection could have possibly been attributed to a deep injury to the bone.

"Did the X-rays reveal anything?" Cade said.

"The doctor reviewed them and concluded that the damage to the bone was slight at most and probably didn't cause the complications of infection," Marybeth said.

"Of course, at the time you reviewed the film, you had no indication the wound might have been contaminated with tiny, almost undetectable, flakes of gold."

"That's a true statement. At the time, we were looking for contamination in the form of organic material like splinters of wood or dirt left from the branch."

"Marybeth, I need to review the X-rays. Are they still available?"

"I'm sure they are. We normally keep X-rays filed for at least two years. I can probably sneak them out and bring them to you if you want."

Cade thought for a moment. "I think that would be too risky. I think it would be easier to interpret them at the hospital. Remember, the images we're trying to see are very small."

"I'm working graveyard tonight. Maybe I can let you guys in through the back, and you can review the X-rays in the room behind surgery," Marybeth said.

"I think that will work, but remember, I'm dead. Whatever we do, we can't let anyone see me. If word gets out that I'm alive, they'll hunt me down, and without evidence, there isn't a jury in this state that will believe Denton's a murderer."

**

Much later that night, Shooter pulled into the back of the hospital parking lot and settled into the shadows near the back. Cade was riding low in the passenger seat of Shooter's Chevy Camaro.

"Why did we have to bring this old thing?" Cade said.

"What, my Camaro? This baby's a classic and it's still the fastest thing on four wheels in Fremont County. That includes Redding."

The Winds

"Yeah, but don't you think it's a little obvious, bright red with that big spoiler in the back?"

"The only other vehicle I have is your truck, Cade, and I don't feel comfortable driving a truck that belongs to a dead guy."

"Good point." He smiled as he illuminated the face of his watch, looked at it briefly. "12:28, right on schedule. Ok, so you wait here for me. It shouldn't take very long."

Cade slipped out of the car and walked to the back entrance while looking around casually for anything unusual. His hair was neatly trimmed, and he was wearing a baseball cap, tennis shoes, and jeans. The sign above the door said it was for Authorized Personnel Only. As he approached the door, it suddenly swung open.

He ducked into the shadows behind the bushes. Two nurses walked out, one dangling a cigarette between her lips as she brought the lighter up to her face. The end of the cigarette glowed bright orange as she quickly removed it and expelled a large cloud of smoke.

"God," she said to the other nurse. "I thought this night would never end." They continued to walk into the parking lot to their cars. Cade waited there until both of them left. The door suddenly opened again. Cade ducked further into the darkness. Another nurse came out, but this time it was

Marybeth. She held the door open as she looked up and down the sidewalk.

"I'm in here, Marybeth," Cade whispered. The light above the door revealed his face as he eased his way out from the bushes. "That was close."

"I'm sorry, Cade. They had to work later than usual tonight. Things are pretty heated in the ER. Some nights are like that."

"You don't have to convince me. I know all about the ER."

She escorted him down a series of halls and into the surgery wing.

Cade wore his ball cap down on his face slightly. He noticed, like in most hospitals, there were cameras at the end of each of the halls.

"So here we are," Marybeth said as she pushed a small stainless steel table from in front of the light board. She snatched the X-rays from behind one of the cabinets, hung them on the board, and flipped the switch. The board lit up brightly behind the clear sheets, exposing the bones of Denton's face from the nose down and past the collarbone from all angles.

The Winds

Cade moved closer to the board and studied each plastic sheet carefully. He pointed to an area of the cut. "See these small specs?"

Marybeth moved closer to him and looked at the area where Cade was making a small circular motion with his finger. "I see them and remember the doctor commented on them as well. He thought they were just inconsistencies in the film."

"Now look over to this one. See the specs here as well?" Marybeth nodded her head. "Now look at the last one. Do you see the specs?" Marybeth confirmed that she indeed could see them. "If you look really closely, you can count the specs on each of the slides."

"I count the same number," Marybeth said.

"That resolves the inconsistency theory, doesn't it," Cade said. Marybeth seemed to understand.

Cade thought for a moment. I remember you saying that when Denton came in the second time, you suspected infection. First, you took the X-rays, then you reopened the wound and cleaned it out."

"That's correct. Actually, the wound was so badly infected that when the doctor took out the stitches, the wound just opened up on its own. He cleaned it out and stitched it back up.

"Don't think I'm crazy, but I have to ask you. What did you do with the stuff?"

"You mean the gunk the doctor cleaned out of his chest?"

"Yea."

"Well, I remember rinsing the tray with alcohol into the infectious sink. Why?"

"Have you ever panned for gold?"

"No, but something tells me we're about to?"

"Do you remember which sink?"

"Yes, the third bed in the ER."

"Good, now show me to the nearest janitor's closet. I need a plumber's wrench."

"I'm afraid to ask you why?"

"Simple, I'm going to take the sink apart. All sinks have a P-trap. It's that curvy pipe under the drain. Anyway, that curvy part is always full of water to keep the gasses from escaping up through the drain."

"So, you lost me."

Cade started to smile. "Back to my question about panning for gold. When you pan for gold, you use the principle that gold is much more dense or heavier than the sand. When you slowly swirl the pan, the sand is washed out, and the flakes of gold stay in the bottom of the pan."

"And?"

"That P-trap works the same as if you were panning for gold. If you washed that crap down the sink, everything else, basically the organics, has since washed away, but if we're lucky, the gold chips will still be there."

"So you want to take the sink apart and get whatever's in the P-trap to see if there's gold in it?"

"Exactly."

"Tell me one thing. How does a doctor such as yourself know so much about a sink?"

Cade started to smile. "Angie dropped her wedding ring down the drain once. It was a two-carrot rock, and I thought it was history. But when the plumber came to retrieve it, I watched him so I would know what to do the next time she did it."

"That explains it, but how will we know there's gold in

it? A lot of stuff is washed down the sinks in a hospital. I'm not quite sure what you'll find in there. You might even get hepatitis C."

"Hey, it beats going to jail if it works."

"How will we know if the flakes are in there? You plan on using that pan thing?"

"Nope. I think I know someone who can help us. He may be old, but he knows his chemistry."

Chapter 33

Denton turned off the flashing lights, got out of his car and rushed back to the car parked directly behind him in the Emergency driveway of the hospital. A young man, visibly shaken from the drive to the hospital, was at the passenger side assisting his expectant wife out of the car. A nurse came out of the Emergency Room entrance pushing a wheelchair. The woman was screaming and moaning as she continued to breathe heavily, holding her stomach.

"Thank you so much for the escort to the hospital, officer," the young man said. "Sorry for not stopping when you tried to pull us over, but I knew you'd understand once you got up here." Denton helped assist her into the wheelchair, and the nurse wheeled her in through the automatic entrance doors.

"No problem, but I'm telling you, I was a little pissed and was ready to call for backup!" Denton smiled and tipped his hat as the young man quickly turned and ran into the hospital to catch up to his wife.

Denton returned back to his car, got in and twisted the key to start it. He paused momentarily and took the keys back out of the ignition. He got out and walked into the ER, past the admissions desk, and down a long hall. There was a door that had a big red sign hanging from it that read

Security. He twisted the knob and found it to be locked.

"Hey, Gus," Denton yelled into the door as he knocked a few times. "I know you're in there. Let me in." Denton put his ear to the door and could hear shuffling sounds followed by footsteps on the hard linoleum tile.

"Keep your badge on, Denton. Don't you know it's lunchtime for me now?" The door opened, and a rather large man stood in the opening. "Well, what brings you here this time of night?"

Denton smiled, pushed the door the rest of the way open, and walked past the man. "Gus, you haven't changed a bit since you quit the force." Denton looked around the small room filled with TV monitors, computer equipment, and garbage. "Look at this place, it's a pig sty."

Gus scooped some garbage off the main desk and threw it in the garbage can next to it. "I told you, it's lunchtime." Denton picked up a small box that contained a stale donut and dried crumbs from the previous donuts that were once there.

Gus tilted his head. "OK, I haven't had time to clean up from breakfast. Give me a break, would ya? So why are you here?"

"Just in the area and thought I'd drop by," Denton said.

The Winds

Gus stepped back and sat down in his chair. He motioned for Denton to sit in the other chair. Denton refused, approached the series of monitors on the wall, and started scrolling through the pictures as if it were a slide show. "You ever pay any attention to these?"

"Well, yeah, I'm a security guard, and that's why they call those security cameras."

Denton continued to scroll through the various camera angles and views around the entire hospital. "I can't believe you left the force to do this. Don't you ever get bored?"

"Yeah, but zero stress. There's no putting my life on the line for this job."

Denton started to laugh. "In this town? When did you ever put your life on the line, Gus?" Denton thought for a moment. "Oh yeah, the donut skirmish of ninety-eight."

"Very funny. I don't know. I just like sitting in an office rather than driving around in a car. Hey, once you help an old lady change a flat in the middle of the night in the middle of winter, it gets you thinking about your career path."

Denton shook his head, then moved to another screen and scrolled through the views. Most of the halls were empty this late at night with an occasional nurse or janitor, and there was nothing out of the ordinary until he came across a view of one of the back halls. "Hey, Gus, take a look at her ass," Denton said as he hit the zoom button. The camera lens brought the image closer. A lady was standing in the hallway facing an entrance to one of the rooms and appeared to be carrying on a conversation with someone just out of sight.

"Oh, that's Nurse Peterson. She's hot, probably the hottest nurse in this place. And her boobs, watch out, baby. I wouldn't mind spending a little quality time in ICU with her."

"Been there, done that. She stitched me up last year when the branch whipped me across the chest." Denton continued to play around with the camera, trying to get a better, clearer shot of her upper body.

"She did ok. At least you're not any uglier."

"Oh, you're real funny," Denton said as he continued to adjust the knobs. "She's definitely hot."

Suddenly, Marybeth moved farther into the hall. Denton quickly zoomed out to where the entire width of the hall was in view. A man entered the picture wearing a baseball hat. The man looked up and then down the hall, motioned something with his hands and then started walking toward the back entrance, toward the camera.

"Well, who do we have here?" Denton said.

The Winds

Gus moved closer to the screen. "It's not one of the doctors, and it's definitely not Shooter. Hey, you know Marybeth and Shooter are an item. Have been for like a year. Talk is that they're going to get married. Maybe you guys can get married on the same day. You and Tara set a date yet?"

Denton didn't acknowledge his question. He was enthralled with trying to establish the identity of the mystery man. "Who is it?" Denton continued to zoom in on the face. It was difficult to get a clear shot because of the brim of the baseball cap. Denton zoomed out momentarily to get the full body shot. He studied the walk, the way he swung his arms and held his shoulders. Denton couldn't believe it. The mystery man talking to Marybeth in the hallway was Cade Hobbs. But how could it be? Cade was dead. Denton immediately pushed the button, changing to the view of the main lobby.

"Gus, I gotta go, bud. Something's just turned up."

"Where you going?" Gus said.

"I think I just saw a ghost." Denton shot out the door and into the hall. He ran through the ER lobby, out the entrance, and into his car.

I can't believe it; Cade Hobbs is still alive, he thought to himself. *But what's he up to?*

"How long does it take to read an x-ray?" Shooter said as Cade climbed into the car.

"You'll never believe it. Not only do the x-rays show the gold chips, but I got the actual gold chips." Cade showed him a small plastic bag.

"What are you talking about? How can that happen; it's been a year?"

"I know it sounds ridiculous, but it's true, well, I hope it's true. We won't know until we get to Mr. Burk's house."

"Mr. Burk, the old Chemistry teacher? What does he have to do with anything?"

"Look, if there's gold in this handful of crap, then Mr. Burk can find it."

"But it's one thirty in the morning." Cade looked at him sternly. "OK, we'll go to Mr. Burk's." Shooter started the car and drove to the exit of the parking lot.

Denton put the key in the ignition and started the police car. He pulled out from under the covering to the entrance of the Emergency Room and parked alongside the sidewalk near the side entrance, the only exit of the back lot. He sat and waited then within less than a minute a red older model Camaro drove past. Denton recognized it as Shooter's car

The Winds

and gave it time enough to make the first corner before he pulled out into the street to follow them.

Denton realized that with Cade alive, his entire world could come crashing down in an instant. He was the only witness to the murders of the two reservation rangers, but as it stood now, it was Cade's word against his, but with Cade living in the Winds by himself through the winter like some animal, and with the way he treated Tara up at the lake he was sure that a jury would believe him, a valiant officer of the law, with nearly twenty honorable years on the force, over Cade.

Shooter took a right on First Street, which turned into Buena Vista Dr., and ran along the edge of Capitol Hill until they came to the intersection at Highway 287. The lights from the town below showed brightly under the star-filled sky, but they didn't notice. They had a lot more important things on their mind. What Cade had contained in a small plastic bag could be the evidence to clear his name and put Denton away for a long, long time. Cade had been away from Wyoming for so long that he wasn't sure if they had adopted the death penalty or not, but where Denton was involved, he hoped that they had. He deserved it, and for these crimes, death would be the closest thing to justice.

Shooter turned left onto Highway 287, which turned into Main Street closer to town. Denton followed within sight of their taillights as the Camaro went out of sight momentarily as it descended the hill into town. Denton crested the hill just in time to see the Camaro take a quick right onto 2nd Street.

Denton thought to himself, *that's not the way to the reservation.* He made the right hand turn and continued to follow them out to the north of town.

Denton assumed that since it was so late, they'd be going out to the reservation to spend the night at Shooter's house, but apparently, he was wrong unless they were taking the long way to avoid the chance of being seen in town. The road turned into Hillcrest Lane, which made a complete loop back to the opposite side of town. Essentially, they could take a right back onto Highway 287 and continue to the reservation. It was nearly eight miles out of their way but a small price to pay compared to the ramifications for being seen. Convinced that this was their motivation, Denton sat a little easier as he kept their taillights just barely in view.

"What are you doing?" Cade said. Shooter continued to slowly decrease his speed.

"I noticed a set of headlights behind us since we turned on 2nd Street."

"So you think someone's following us?"

The Winds

"Either that or some farmer's coming home awfully late tonight. I'm just going to pull over around this next turn and see what happens." Shooter drove a few more hundred yards until he couldn't see the headlights and pulled over to the side of the road. Within less than a minute the headlights came around the corner and suddenly slowed down almost to a stop.

"Shit!" Denton said to himself. He wasn't quite sure what to do, but knew he couldn't just stop like they had done without creating suspicion. At the same time, he didn't want them to know that he was on their tail. He continued to roll forward and accelerate slightly toward them when the lights of his car swept across Shooter's car. Cade looked back and could see the lights on the top of the car.

"It's the police!" Cade said. "I think they're on to us." Shooter looked in his rearview mirror. He could see the silhouette of a cowboy hat in the police car.

"It's the Sheriff."

"It's Denton, It's gotta be Denton. He knows I'm alive." Cade ducked down further into the seat. "It's this car of yours, Shooter. We might as well be the lead float in a parade."

"Hey, enough about my car! What do you want me to do?" Shooter tapped nervously on the steering wheel. The car continued to approach slowly.

"We can't go to old man Burk's. Just punch it, Shooter. Let's see what this thing can do, and let's lose the bastard." Cade sat up in his seat, and Shooter hit the gas. Gravel sprayed out from behind the rear tires as the car reentered the road, followed by a high-pitched squeal and smoke from the same back tires, only this time against the asphalt.

Denton punched the gas as well, accelerating in an attempt to close the gap. He reached for the radio as he routinely did if confronted with a high-speed chase and put it to his mouth. Suddenly, he realized that he didn't know what Cade was up to or how much he knew or told Shooter or anyone else for that matter. Requesting backup was not appropriate for this chase, he determined. He placed the radio back into its holder, put both hands on the steering wheel, and buried the gas pedal into the floorboard. He would handle this himself. With any luck, both Cade and Shooter would be dead when it was all over.

"We're not going to make it," Shooter said. The sound of his engine was deafening. Cade looked at the speedometer, and it was pegged at 120 miles per hour and the tachometer had penetrated the red. "There's only one way out, and they'll have it blocked." Cade looked over his shoulder.

"No flashing lights, Shooter. I don't think he's called for

backup."

"Why not?"

"Because he doesn't want anyone to know I'm still alive. I think we can lose him once we get on Hillcrest Lane." Shooter looked over at him, questioning his last statement.

"But it goes right back into town."

"Think back to high school. Remember what we used to do?" It suddenly registered with Shooter, and he smiled and gripped the steering wheel.

"Count me in." Shooter slowed to just over 40 miles an hour to make the 90-degree turn onto Hillcrest Lane, cutting as close to the inside as possible while still staying upright on the road. The tires squealed as they gripped the pavement. Denton made the turn at a slightly higher rate of speed, closing the gap between them. Shooter let out an Indian yell and pegged it at 120 again within the first quarter mile, and then the hills started.

"Hold on!" Shooter yelled. They became airborne over the crest of the first hill. The car landed in a nest of orange sparks. Cade looked back, and Denton's car did the same thing.

"He's still on us, Shooter!"

"Don't worry, we'll get our chance in a minute." They reached the bottom and began their ascent on the next, larger hill. The headlights beamed over the crest into the midnight sky.

"Brace yourself, this is a big one," Shooter said as he kept both hands on the steering wheel. "We either make it, or we die." The car crested the hill again, flying through the air, this time veering toward the edge of the road into the gravel. Shooter overcorrected, sending the car into a slight tailspin. Denton's car wasn't as responsive as Shooter's, and he was losing some ground. The distance between them increased with every hill.

"OK, Shooter, do it just as you touch down after this next hill. All lights off! I mean it, you can't even touch the brakes, or he'll be on to us. Do you understand?"

Shooter nodded his head. "I've done it many times before."

"This time's for keeps." They neared the top of the hill. Cade glanced back and Denton hadn't reached the bottom of the last hill yet. If Shooter could keep the car on the road and maintain his speed, he figured they could be over the hill and out of sight. Over the next hill were several farmhouses with several vehicles, farm equipment, and the like. Without the taillights in front of him, Denton might hesitate and assume that they had ducked into one of the gravel side roads to hide.

The Winds

Just that moment of hesitation would provide Cade and Shooter with the few precious seconds it would take to get away.

"This is it, only have one chance. Just like high school. You can do it." Cade stuck his hands out in front of him and braced himself on the dashboard. They crested over the hill and became airborne again, this time hitting the road nearly halfway down the other side. Shooter hit the lights, and everything became dark. He kept a tight grip on the wheel and stared toward the night sky ahead, just as Cade had instructed. As they were nearing the top of the next hill, they could see Denton's car fly over the top and land in a sea of sparks. Cade watched closely as they neared the top of the hill and could see Denton's brake lights illuminate from behind. The headlights seemed to become less bright, and suddenly, they panned a full ninety degrees and started off on one of the dirt roads.

As Cade let out a yell, they crested the last major hill. Midway through the air, Shooter quickly reached down and turned on the lights only to find that he was going to land at the edge of the road.

"Brace yourself!" Shooter yelled as they hit a large patch of weeds, followed by the corner post of a barbed wire fence. Dirt, wood splinters, and other debris flew over the hood and hit the windshield, shattering it in their laps. Pieces of glass flew everywhere, including the back seat. Shooter hit the brakes, corrected several times, and swerved back onto the road. He let out another yell and hit the gas again. "We made it baby!"

Denton continued onto the gravel road, turned on his spotlight, and began to pan both sides of the road with the intense beam. He looked in and around the farm equipment, and at one point, a coyote ran in front of his car.

"Damn," he shouted. "Those sons a bitches." He hit the steering wheel with his hands. Cade and Shooter made it to the highway and quickly turned right toward the reservation only ten miles away. Once on the reservation, they knew they'd be home free.

"Where to now?" Shooter asked as he passed by the Milford store. "My place?"

"No way, Denton could come looking for us. Do you have any other place we can go?" Shooter thought for a moment. "We can stay at the cabin."

"You have a cabin?"

"No, but my friend does. It's just barely on the reservation on the other side of Clear Lake. It's small but cozy. My friend hardly ever goes there, and I know where he keeps the key. The best thing is that nobody knows about it, at least I'm sure Denton doesn't, and that's what counts, right?"

Cade nodded his head. "I don't plan on being there very long. We need to get to Burk's house first thing in the morning. If we find gold in this stuff, then I'm sure we can convince the Sheriff."

"But what if he's waiting for us?"

"What, waiting for us at old man Burk's house? Not a chance. He doesn't know anything about this stuff. He just thinks we took the loop to avoid going into town."

"But why was he at the hospital in the first place?

Cade shrugged his shoulders. "Dumb luck, I guess. But come tomorrow, his luck will have run out."

Chapter 34

Cade and Shooter arose a few minutes past six o'clock that same morning and left the small cabin without having anything to eat. They knew that time was not on their side now that Denton knew Cade was still alive. They drove in the direction of town on Highway 287 as the sun was just sneaking over the horizon and turned left on Hillcrest Lane.

As they drove along the road, they could see the evidence in the form of grooves and scrapes in the asphalt near the crest of each hill, as well as feel the pieces of glass under their feet from the shattered windshield.

Mr. Burk's place hadn't changed since Cade had last seen it over twenty years ago. It was nestled in a small canyon about a quarter mile off the road. Shooter eased up the dirt drive toward the home. As they pulled into the driveway, they could see Mr. Burk in the side yard working in the irrigation ditch.

"Hey, Mr. Burk," Cade said. Mr. Burk stood up and turned toward them.

He raised his sunglasses a bit and squinted his eyes. "It can't be. The Cade Hobbs I knew is dead." He stepped from the middle of the ditch onto the bank and walked closer to them. "I saw you and your kids last year about this time. I

The Winds

heard you were wanted for murder, and then you were killed by a bear. Can somebody please tell me what the hell's going on?"

Shooter stepped forward. "We can explain everything, but we really don't have time for it now."

"You're Shooter, right? Why I haven't seen you two together since you both graduated from high school. What brings you to my house so early in the morning? I thought that you younger generation liked to sleep in 'til noon."

"It'd been nice, but we really need to ask a favor of you," Cade said.

"I'll do anything for you two. All you have to do is ask. But let me ask a favor of you first."

"What's that?"

"Please, call me by my first name." Cade and Shooter looked at each other because neither one of them knew his first name. They'd always called him Mr. Burk.

"Ah, it doesn't matter. Call me Mr. Burk if you want."

"Mr. Burk, we need you to help us find some gold," Shooter said.

Mr. Burk raised his eyebrows. "Help you find some

gold? If I knew where some was, I wouldn't still be living in Lorenz. I'd be somewhere down South like Arizona or, better yet, Texas. I always wanted to live in Texas." He put his shovel over his shoulder and began to walk toward the house.

"You don't understand; we'd like you to find gold in this." Cade took the small plastic bag out of his pocket and held it up for him to see.

Mr. Burk put down his shovel and rested it against his hip, then grabbed the bag, took off his sunglasses, and inspected it closely. "You're right, I don't understand. Where did you get this stuff?"

"From a sink in the hospital. It's a very long story, and we don't have much time. You're the only one we know who might be able to help us."

"You're going to have to give me more to go on than this. Where did the gold come from? Does the gold have anything to do with you being wanted for murder?"

"Last year, I lost my family in an automobile accident. I decided that I couldn't cope with life anymore, so I sold everything I owned and came out here to live in the Wind River Mountains. Shooter kept me with supplies, and I spent the winter up there and almost died on several occasions. Anyway, I met up with some rangers while I was on the

The Winds

reservation side. Denton showed up, and he shot them both in cold blood with my gun. I escaped, but he shot me in the shoulder. While I was hiding out in a cavern, I came across Shooter's father and another ranger."

"I remember reading about your father missing in the Winds. I'm terribly sorry, Shooter. He was a good man."

"He wasn't lost. He was murdered," Cade said. "He was shot in the head, and the ranger was killed by one of Shooter's father's arrows. Remember the legend of gold up in the Winds?"

"I've grown up with the legend but never knew if it was really true or not. It had to do with the gold being hidden behind a waterfall or something."

"That's correct. I had to fake my death in order to buy some time to find the gold. The ranger's body in the cave had flakes of gold in his front pocket, so I knew the legend was true. I just had to find it to prove my theory."

"What theory?" Mr. Burk said.

"Denton Bauer's behind it all," Cade said. "He killed Shooter's father last summer. He's found the gold, and it appears that he'll stop at nothing to see that he gets all of it."

"So how does all this tie into this bag of stuff?"

"Before he died, Shooter's father cut Denton's chest with his knife. I found the knife at the base of the waterfall. The blade had small fragments of gold on the edge, and when I talked to Marybeth–"

"Marybeth, Marybeth who?"

"Marybeth Peterson from our graduating class. She's a registered nurse at the ER. She worked on Denton's chest. The second time was for some serious infection. They took some X-rays, and I reviewed them last night at the hospital. Gold is very dense so even the tiniest of particles show up on the film. It appears that Denton had gold fragments in his collar bone deposited by Shooter's father's knife blade. That's what's in the bag."

"Wait a second. You're telling me that you've found the same gold fragments that were cleaned out of Denton's chest over a year ago?"

"That's where the sink comes in. Marybeth washed the instruments and tray in the sink. If there's gold, it would have stayed in the P-trap."

"You always were a good student. Kid, you've done your homework this time. Let's go inside the house. My lab's in the basement. I think I just might know a way to find that gold."

The Winds

Marybeth slipped the key into the lock and twisted the knob. It was just after eight o'clock, and she had just gotten off her shift and was ready to get some sleep. She picked up the paper from the doormat and walked into the house. She threw her keys on the kitchen table and slipped off her white nursing shoes. "What a day," she said to herself. "Or night, whatever you want to call it."

Working the graveyard shift always left her bewildered. She found it difficult to get a good sleep after her shift because the normal body knew that sleeping in the daylight wasn't natural. She left all the curtains in the entire house drawn to shut out the sun. It had to be completely dark, or she couldn't begin to close her eyes to relax and eventually fall asleep.

"I hate working this shift," she continued to say as she untied the waist of her colorful flowered scrubs and slipped them off on the way down the hall to the bathroom. She entered the bathroom, pulled her matching shirt off over her head, and threw it on the floor, followed by her bra.

She gazed in the mirror, grabbed both her breasts, lifted them slightly, and turned from side to side. She then bent over and started to pluck at her eyelashes and rub her tired eyes. She turned on the cold water and then started adding a little of hot until it was warm to her touch.

She bent over and splashed water in her face a few

times, then stood up and reached for the towel that was usually hanging through the hoop at the side of the sink. With her eyes closed, she made several attempts to snag the towel but was unsuccessful.

Suddenly, she was grabbed from behind. Hands grasped her large breasts and pulled her backward. Startled but amused, she quickly cleared the water from her eyes.

"Shooter?" she said, smiling. There was no answer. She opened her eyes and turned around, expecting to find Shooter standing there, but it wasn't Shooter. She screamed and slapped Denton squarely on the face.

"How dare you!" She grabbed for her robe to cover herself. "You shouldn't be here. How did you get in?" She brushed past him and into her bedroom, trying to shut the door as she entered. Denton quickly put his foot in the door and then pushed it open against her will. "Denton, you're scaring me! Say something!" All Denton could do was look at her with craziness in his eyes. He approached her as she backpedaled, falling onto the bed. "What do you want?" Denton jumped on top of her and slapped her in the face.

"You know what I want. He quickly doubled his fist, but then slapped her with an open hand to get her attention.

"You're hurting me. Stop! I didn't do anything to you."

The Winds

"You knew Cade was alive all along, didn't you?" He managed to secure each of her arms and held them tightly above her head.

"I don't know what you're talking about. Cade's dead. He was eaten by a bear. Everyone knows that."

"So is that why you were with him last night at the hospital…or were you talking to his ghost?"

"How do you know this? How do you know Cade was at the hospital?"

"That's not important, but I saw him and chased him and Shooter in that beater car of his. What are they doing? Why were they at the hospital?" Marybeth turned away and was silent. Denton let go of one of her arms and backhanded her across her face. "Tell me! What was Cade doing at the hospital?"

Marybeth screamed at the top of her lungs and fought back with her free hand. Denton hit her squarely in the face, this time with a closed fist. She became silent, bloody, and still.

"He was looking at something," she finally said. Blood was flowing freely from her nose and oozing from a cut just above her right eye.

"Looking for what?" Marybeth remained silent, eyes closed. Denton became enraged. He reached down, grabbed his pistol, and stuck it under the side of her chin.

"God, no, Denton! Don't kill me!"

"Then don't fuck with me, Marybeth. Tell me everything you know." He pushed the barrel into her neck until it hurt her.

Marybeth closed her eyes momentarily and then spoke. "Your face, Denton. He was looking at X-rays."

Denton let go of her and stood up from the bed. "Why?"

"Because he didn't think that you got cut by a branch. He thinks it was a knife."

"How could an X-ray show the difference?"

"I don't know. He just wanted to look at the X-rays." He shoved the barrel further into her neck. "He thinks there were gold chips from Shooter's father's knife. He dug the stuff out of the drain. It all sounded so bizarre I didn't think much of it." She paused momentarily and looked around the room. Her eyes then settled back toward his. "I don't believe him. I think he's just trying to cover his own ass. He killed those rangers, and he's trying to set you up. I just cooperated with him until I could give you a call. I was going to call you this

The Winds

morning after work, honest." She pleaded with him and then started to cry again.

"Where are they now? What's he going to do with that stuff?"

"I don't know, he didn't tell me. I've told you all I know. Please, Denton, leave me alone." Suddenly, the landline phone rang.

Denton held the gun tight against Marybeth's head. "Don't answer it." The phone continued to ring, and after the fourth ring, the answering machine picked it up. After Marybeth's recorded greeting and a series of beeps, a voice came on the line.

"Marybeth, this is Shooter. Hey, I thought you'd be home from the hospital, but you must have had to work a little late. We didn't make it to Mr. Burk's house last night after we left. We ran into a little trouble. Denton spotted us and chased us around the loop. I'll tell you more about it later, but right now, we're at Mr. Burk's, and he's testing for the gold as we speak. This guy's amazing. He has every kind of chemical imaginable down here. Anyway, I'll let you know what we find. I called Tara and got her out of bed. I told her everything. She said she had a few things she had to do at the station this morning, and then she'd meet up with us later. I'm going to tell you the same thing I told her: Whatever you do, stay away from Denton. He knows Cade's alive, and he's a crazy man. I'm convinced that he'll stop at nothing to see that Cade is dead. We both know what he's capable of, so just stay in your house and keep your doors locked. I'll drop by a little later. Take care and I love you, Marybeth. Bye for now."

Denton lifted the gun from her neck and put it back in the holster. Marybeth watched his every move. He again stood up from the bed and put his hand out to assist her up as well.

She hesitantly grabbed his hand, and he started to pull her up. As she stood up, he reached to the side of his belt and quickly pulled out his knife.

"No, Denton, they didn't tell me anything. I didn't know anything about it. You got to believe me. I told you everything I know." She started to shake as she continued to plead with him. "Please." He raised the knife up to her throat and shifted the blade from side to side against her neck.

She looked at him and attempted to scream, but no words escaped her mouth.

Slipping the knife back into the sheath, he grasped her with both of his hands, one around to the back of her head and the other on her chin, and with a quick, forceful jerk, her body went limp as he eased her to the floor at the foot of her bed.

The Winds

"One down and two, no, make that three, three more to go," he said to himself. He had just found out that his fiancée, Tara, was involved as well.

Chapter 35

Mr. Burk sat at the dimly lit table on a tall stool while Cade and Shooter stood behind him, watching as he separated the contents of the plastic bag by sifting it through a small mesh screen. "You could tell by the X-ray that the gold particles were very tiny, so I'm just interested in testing the small stuff," Mr. Burk said.

Chemistry was his passion. He'd maintained a small lab in a single room of the basement just to occasionally run an experiment or just dabble with a few chemical reactions now and then. The only reason he retired was because of his age. He always enjoyed teaching and cracking the same stale jokes with each new influx of students.

"Do you think it will work?" Cade said.

"If there's gold in here, we'll know it. The two chemicals I'll be using have the ability to detect the presence of both gold and platinum. If you think back to high school, you'll remember that both have nearly the same reactivity. Remember the Periodic Chart?"

"All I can remember about the chart is Na stands for Sodium, and Cl stands for Chlorine. Put 'em together, and you get table salt," Shooter said.

The Winds

Mr. Burk separated the large particles from the small and tapped the smaller particles into a glass concave dish. He passed a magnet over the top to separate the ferrous metal particles from all the others. Several particles clung to the magnet.

"That's a positive," he said. "Gold is much more dense than steel. If the steel particles didn't wash away there's an excellent chance the gold didn't either. We'll see." He reached up and grabbed two small glass bottles, each had a glass stopper. "Ok, gentlemen, it's show time." He held up one of the bottles, removed the glass stopper, and poured a tiny amount into a small glass beaker. "This is Nitric Acid. It's nasty stuff. I'll mix it with a little HCl, which is?" He looked over at Cade.

"Hydrochloric Acid."

Mr. Burk, always teaching, nodded his head as he unscrewed the second bottle and poured a near-equal amount into the same beaker. He mixed it thoroughly. Visibly, nothing much happened. "A little anticlimactic now, but if there's gold in this stuff, we'll know it immediately. This mixture is an aqua regia. It's the only thing that will cause a chemical reaction with gold."

He held the beaker above the small glass dish. The beaker shook as he, in his old age, tried to steady his hand as he poured. He poured the entire contents into the dish, and immediately, it began to bubble and foam. Setting the beaker aside, he began to stir the fluid into the material, causing even more violent bubbles. "Well, gentlemen, there's gold in them there hills."

"I knew it," Cade said. "I was right. Denton killed your father, Shooter. You will see justice."

Mr. Burk set the dish down and looked over to Cade. "I would assume that this is all of the stuff you found in the sink. Is that correct?"

"Yes, but why?" Cade said.

"It looks like I've just become your key witness." He looked down at the glass dish. The bubbles were nearly gone, clearly indicating that the fine gold particles were gone as well. "Aqua regia doesn't know when to quit. All the gold's history."

"So what are you saying?" Shooter said.

"The evidence is gone," Cade said. "The evidence that will put Denton at the scene of the murder has just been eaten up by the acid."

"But I'm a chemist. I saw the reaction. Your theory was correct. The particles in Denton's face were gold. I don't mind testifying. I never liked Denton as a student or a cop.

The Winds

You ask me, he's a pompous ass. Anyway, it'll give me something to do besides irrigate my yard." He stood up and then put his arms around each of them. "I haven't had so much excitement for years. Thank you, gentlemen. It's been a pleasure."

Suddenly, there was a loud knock at the door on the main floor. Footsteps could be heard going across the old wooden floor above. It was Mr. Burk's wife as she made her way from the kitchen. The three of them waited anxiously as they listened to every sound. They could hear a very faint conversation and then a piercing scream followed by a crash on the floor.

"What's going on?" Mr. Burk said. He turned to walk toward the old wooden stairs leading up to the main floor.

"It's Denton!" Cade said. He ran toward the stairs.

Mr. Burk grabbed his arm. "You can't go up there without a weapon."

"But your wife!"

"Denton's a killer," Mr. Burk said. "And he won't hesitate to kill us all. Quick, out the back entrance. There's a short concrete stairway to the backyard. Take it and get the hell out of here."

"But what about you and your wife?" Shooter said.

"There's no time. I can take care of things. Now go, go to the police!"

Cade and Shooter ran across the room and into a short, darkened hallway. They unlocked the old whitewashed door, opened it wide, and shot up the stairs to the backyard.

Mr. Burk stumbled over to a cabinet and grabbed a 12-gauge shotgun. He could hear footsteps coming down the stairs. He pointed the gun and squeezed the trigger. Denton ducked behind a wooden column. The majority of the lead shot hit and pulverized the side of the old wooden beam.

Denton stood up and quickly fired a single round, hitting him in the chest. Mr. Burk immediately fell back against the cabinet and slowly dropped the shotgun to the floor.

Seeing daylight from the back hallway, Denton ran through the hall and up the stairs just in time to see Cade and Shooter speeding away down the dirt road in the red Camaro.

Denton quickly put his gun back in the holster and ran to his car. He started it up, threw it into gear, and just before he punched the accelerator, took his hands off the wheel and began to think. He nodded his head, and a slight grin came to his face.

The Winds

Cade and Shooter returned to the small, secluded cabin to try to think things through. Things had happened so fast that they felt they needed some time to come up with a viable plan. With their only evidence now dissolved in the bottom of a tiny glass dish and their key witness presumably dead, they had to figure out how they could approach the police and convince them that Cade was innocent of the murders and that the true killer was indeed one of their own.

"Why don't we just go to the police and tell them the truth?" Shooter said.

"Because there's no proof. They'd just throw me in jail."

"No proof? I heard the shots fired back at Burk's. You know old man Burk and his wife are dead. Even if they don't believe us at first, you're probably safer in jail than you are out here. Denton has now killed four people. If we don't go to the police, who knows how many other people will die. He's a crazy man, Cade. We have to go to the police."

Cade fell back into his chair and rubbed his forehead. Suddenly, his face flushed white, and he sat up in his chair. "Shooter!" Shooter stood up from behind the refrigerator door. "How did Denton know we were at the Burk's place?"

Shooter looked at him and then slammed the door shut. "Oh my God, Marybeth! The phone message!" He ran toward the front door.

The two of them rushed out of the cabin, down the steps, and into the car. "I swear, if he's hurt her in any way, I'll kill him."

They reached Marybeth's house in less than ten minutes. Shooter was the first out of the car and onto the front porch. Finding the door to be locked, he pounded on it repeatedly. "Marybeth, open the door! Marybeth, it's Shooter, open the door!" He continued to pound.

Cade approached him. "You have a key, don't you?"

Shooter quickly reached into his pocket and fumbled through the keys. He slipped it into the lock, opened the door, and ran in. "Marybeth? Marybeth, are you here?" He immediately crossed through the living room and into the back hall. He attempted to open her bedroom door, but it was locked. "Marybeth!" He rammed his shoulder into the door, breaking it off the hinges. He looked down and saw her body propped up against the side of the bed. "Oh, Marybeth!" He fell to his knees beside her. He began to wail as he grabbed her hand and began to stroke it. Cade followed him into the room. Shooter looked up at him with tear-filled eyes. "I loved her, Cade. She was my life. I can't bear to lose her. What am I going to do?" He continued to stroke her limp, cold hand repeatedly.

The Winds

"I'm convinced. I need to go to the police before anyone else is killed," Cade said. Cade looked around the bedroom, and the red flashing light caught his attention. He walked over to the side of the bed and pushed the button on the answering machine. A long beep was emitted and then Shooter's voice.

"Marybeth, this is Shooter." They both listened intently to the lengthy message and then it said, "Anyway, I'll let you know what we find. I called Tara and got her out of bed. I told her everything. She said she had a few things she had to do at the station this morning, and then she'd meet up with us later. I'm going to tell you the same thing I told her: whatever you do, stay away from Denton."

They were both overcome with horror as they listened to the chilling message reveal that Tara was involved and knew everything about her fiancé. They came to the sudden realization that Tara was in immediate danger.

Cade quickly reached over, picked up the receiver, and dialed the number to the ranger station. It started to ring. On the third ring, she answered.

"Hello, Bears Ears Ranger Station, this is Tara. Can I help you?"

"Tara!" Cade said.

"Cade?"

"You're in danger. You need to leave the station immediately. Denton's on a rampage. He's killed Marybeth, and we're sure he's killed Mr. and Mrs. Burk. He knows you're there. You've got to leave immediately."

"But where should I go?"

"Anywhere, but where you are now. Denton knows you're there and–" The phone suddenly went dead. Tara quickly turned around, and there he was, Denton, with his finger on the button.

"Hello, Sweetheart, who was that on the phone?" He reached out his hand; she gave him the receiver, and he placed it back in the saddle.

"It was nobody important. Just some guy wondering if he could take a motorcycle up into the Winds." Tara was visibly nervous and frightened.

Denton walked over to her and grasped her in his arms. "And so what did you tell him?" She took a big swallow before answering. Denton started to rub his fingers through her hair.

"I told him that motorized vehicles are not allowed in a national forest." Denton nodded his head. Suddenly, he

The Winds

pushed her to the front counter. She slammed against it and fell to the floor. "Liar!" He backhanded her across the face. "Now get up; we've got some riding to do." He bent down, grabbed her under the shoulder, and lifted her to her feet.

"But–"

"Don't but me; you're riding into the Winds with me. I'm going to show you what we could have had together until Cade came into the picture again. I detest that son of a bitch. He's not going to win this time. If I can't have you, nobody will."

"She hung up on me. Right in the middle of a sentence, the phone went dead," Cade said. He quickly dialed the number a second time. He listened as it rang several times.

"Something's wrong," Shooter said. "She'd have answered by now. Do you think Denton's there?"

Cade set the phone back down. "That's got to be it. She wouldn't have just hung up on me like that."

"Cade, we're in this too deep. I think we need to get the police involved."

"I don't have time for that now. Tara could be in serious danger. We need to go to the station. She needs us."

"But we don't have a gun. What good can we do?

Denton will shoot us on the spot."

Cade grabbed Shooter by the shoulders. "We'll have to take that chance. Tara needs us now!"

Chapter 36

They arrived at the Ranger Station as quickly as they could. Their worst nightmare was confirmed when they saw the Fremont County Sheriff's vehicle parked in front. They immediately pulled the car over to the side of the road behind some trees and ran to the log fence surrounding the area.

Shooter grabbed Cade's arm before he went any further. "What if he's still here? We have to have some sort of a plan," he said. "Remember, we're unarmed."

Cade nodded his head and motioned for Shooter to go around the back through the back door. "We don't have time for anything else. We just need to storm the place and maybe surprise him." Shooter acknowledged with a nod, slipped through the fence, and headed around the back.

Cade ran to the front and onto the porch. He carefully pushed open the screen door and walked into the station. He looked around, listened and then proceeded into the back hall toward Tara's room. The door was slightly ajar.

Shooter came from the back door through the kitchen and met Cade in the hall. They remained silent as Cade carefully nudged open the door. It squeaked, so without hesitation, he burst into the room with Shooter on his heels.

"Nothing," Cade said. Shooter continued to look around the room and into the closet. The vivid, awful images of Marybeth kept appearing in his mind as he searched. "She might still be alive."

"But where is she?" Shooter asked.

Cade began to think. "And why is Denton's car still pulled up in front?" He quickly ran out of the room, down the hall, and out the front door.

"Wait for me," Shooter said. They ran around to the far side of the station and looked toward the stable.

"He's taken her up to the Winds," Shooter said.

"How do you know for sure?"

Shooter pointed down to the ground. There were two sets of fresh horseshoe prints in the soft dirt. He followed them with his eyes until they disappeared on the hard gravel road. "I have a hunch those prints lead to the trailhead."

Cade ran to the stable door and quickly went inside. "Hurry, grab a saddle."

Shooter did as Cade had instructed, and within minutes, they both were ready to ride. "I have to tell you, Cade, I have an awful feeling. We aren't prepared for this ride. Denton's a dangerous man. You saw what he did to Marybeth."

The Winds

"Yes, and it will happen to Tara if we don't ride now. There are two of us and only one of him. He just killed the woman you loved, Shooter. Use that anger to fuel the fire. If you ask me, that is more deadly than any weapon he could ever use against us." With that said, both Cade and Shooter tore off with the horses across the gravel parking lot and onto the dirt road toward the trailhead.

Denton led the way up the rocky, steep trail, with Tara following behind. Her horse was tethered to his, and one of her hands was cuffed to the saddle horn. The first few miles were silent. He just faced forward with his cowboy hat pulled down over his forehead.

"So why did you do it?" Tara asked, finally getting the courage to break the silence. Denton didn't reply for several hundred feet up the trail. Just when Tara thought that she'd asked the question in vain, he answered very simply.

"For you."

Tara was taken aback by his response. "For me? You killed all those innocent people for me?"

Denton suddenly tugged on the reins. He tipped his hat up and looked up to the blue sky then turned around in the saddle. "You got it all wrong. They weren't all innocent. The three Rangers were in on it from the start. That's the only way I could find the gold. I had to let them in on my little venture so they would quit giving me shit every time I went into the reservation to look for the gold. I finally found it, but without their help, I never would have."

"You mean, without Shooter's father's help, you never would have."

Denton started to laugh. "You're pretty smart for a redhead. I'd heard the legend about the gold when I was just a kid. We've all grown up with it, but I took it a step further than that. I set out to prove it. When I got wind of Shooter's Dad, the big chief, what was his name, Running Bear? When I heard Shooter bragging about how his Dad goes up in the Winds once a year to commune with the Great Spirit, I knew it was bullshit. He was going up there for the gold. You know Indians, they never take more than what they need. I figured that was the case with the gold as well, so there would be plenty there for me. I tried to figure out when Shooter's Dad went up there, but he never went the same time each year."

"So that's when you got the rangers on the reservation involved."

"Yep. I found out that one of them really didn't like his job. He said it didn't pay enough for what they expected him to do, so when I approached him with an offer, he snatched it up. He recruited the other two, and between the four of us, we were able to follow the old bastard to the gold."

The Winds

"And to show your appreciation, you killed him."

"Yeah, I killed him, but he deserved it. If he had just gone off the mountain, he would be alive today, but he doubled back and ended up putting an arrow in one of the ranger's necks. Once he knew that others knew about the gold, that would be the end of it so–"

"You shot a poor old man, the Chief of the Shoshone Tribe, point blank in the face."

"From the sounds of it, I can see that you don't fully appreciate what I was trying to do for us."

"For us? You started this before you even met me."

"No, I've known you practically all of my life. It's just that you were always too young for me to take a serious interest."

"Ok, before you and I were dating."

"That's true, but my motivation changed. When I started dating you, I realized that it was time for me to settle down, maybe have a family, coach baseball–"

"You're a murderer!"

"They just got in the way, and I dealt with it like I'm going to deal with Cade and Shooter."

"You make me sick, Denton. Everything you told me about us was a lie. You don't love me. You love my sister, Kimber. Besides yourself, she's the only person you've ever really cared about. I don't know how I could be so blind this whole time. People tried to tell me you're a jerk. You treated me good, but deep down inside, it was Kimber you really wanted."

"Well, it really doesn't matter now, does it? I'm going to grab the saddlebags full of gold, wait for Cade and Shooter to come to your rescue, kill 'em, then ride into the sunset out the Pinedale side and disappear forever. That's what I should have done a long time ago, but I stuck around for you. That was a big mistake." He leaned over and spit a long string of brownish liquid out the side of his mouth. "Do me a favor and keep your mouth shut until we get there. I don't feel like talking about this anymore."

At this point, the fear of being killed was insignificant to the fierce anger she felt for Denton. Human nature is such that one tends to occupy their thoughts formulating how to survive rather than dwelling on the likelihood of being killed. Tara was no exception, except not only were her thoughts focused on survival, but taking it to a higher level, she desired to kill her captor. They rode for several more miles and Tara didn't say a word. She just tugged and pulled on the handcuffs, but they were too tight around her wrists.

The Winds

The trail leading from the trailhead was inundated with various horseshoe prints. When Cade and Shooter came to a junction to Heart or Hatchet Lakes, he started to veer toward the Hatchet Lake trail. Shooter was hesitant to follow.

"I'm telling you, that's where they're going," Cade said.

"How do you know for sure? They could be going anywhere."

"Trust me, he's not just looking to escape. He's looking to get the gold before he makes a run for it. He's afraid. For all he knows, we've gone to the police, and they're all mounting to come in and hunt him down. That's why he didn't call for backup. He realized we had too much on him." Shooter agreed, and they took the trail heading to Hatchet Lake.

They continued to ride along the trail. Occasionally, Shooter would fall behind. Thoughts of Marybeth kept surfacing, and he couldn't control them. He loved her with all of his heart and was planning to spend the rest of his life with her. Nothing seemed to matter anymore except revenge. Nothing seemed sweeter to him than to see Denton dead.

Life in prison was too good for him. He needed to pay for his horrid deeds. He would personally see to it that Denton didn't ever have the opportunity to see the inside of a jail cell.

"Come on, Shooter, I need you now more than ever. You got to stay up with me if we're going to have a chance of catching up to them." Shooter buried his heels in the horse's flanks, and it quickened its gait. They rode for several more miles, and then Shooter stopped his horse.

Cade stopped to see what was going on. "What's up? Do you hear something?"

Shooter continued to look toward the next ridge. "I think I know a shortcut to the place you were talking about. I seem to remember when I was a kid, my father and I sat on top of our horses right here in this very spot. Look up there and tell me what you see."

Cade looked up and noticed the rock formations at the top of the ridge. He shook his head. "I don't see anything."

"That's just it, nobody does."

"What are you talking about, Shooter? You're not making any sense."

Shooter pointed toward the center of the sheer cliff. "Do you see the slight discoloration running across the middle of the cliff?"

Cade looked at it closely. "Yeah, so?"

The Winds

"It's a narrow passage up the canyon, not wide enough for a horse, but just wide enough for a human to pass. If I'm correct, that waterfall is just over that ridge. If we ride up to the base of the cliff and then go on foot the rest of the way, we'll stand a good chance of getting there before they do." Shooter looked over at Cade. "You're positive that Denton's returning to the gold, right?"

"I'm positive. He's probably the most selfish, greedy person I know."

"Then let's get there first."

Denton and Tara dropped into Hatchet Lake and continued to ride along its edge to the outlet. They then followed the outlet until they came upon the dry stream. Denton led his horse along the narrow, dry bed and followed it into the trees with Tara still handcuffed and riding the other horse. They meandered through the trees and came out into a clearing just before the steep drop-off, where the water usually made its initial descent to the rocks below.

Denton got off his horse but kept the reins in his hand and walked to the edge of the cliff. Denton stood there momentarily, looking out over the vast expanse of green, gray, and blue. He turned back to face his fiancé.

"Whoever imagined that these mountains would someday make me a very rich man?" He took a big breath of the clear mountain air. "Well, it's time to get you off that horse. We have a lot of work to do before your friends show up."

"And if they show up before we finish?"

"We'll finish the job after I kill them."

"And what about me?"

"I'll let you know after you help me load up the gold." He smiled, then walked over and unlocked the handcuffs. He then made an attempt to help Tara down from the horse. She refused and insisted she dismount on her own.

"You'll never get away with this. By now, the whole department has probably figured out what you've done. You plan on taking them all on?"

"If need be, but let me point out that I have a hostage. If I don't make it out of here alive, you won't either." Tara felt compelled to spit in his face, but successfully fought off the urge. She would have to be patient. She would have to let the right opportunity present itself, and then she would strike him like a venomous snake.

Suddenly, the bushes came alive. Cade rushed toward Denton and hit him at the waist. They both fell to the rocky ground. They fought madly as each tried to get an advantage

The Winds

over the other. Tara bent over and grabbed a large rock. She lifted it above her shoulder, waiting for just the right moment to bury it into Denton's skull.

Cade and Denton rolled around, hitting and kicking. Cade punched Denton a few times in the face, and then Denton returned the punches, knocking Cade backward to the ground. Denton jumped on top of him, grabbed a rock, and thrust it into Cade's face.

Cade blocked most of the blows with his hand but suffered a severe cut across his wrist from the sharp, jagged rock. Blood spurted out across the ground as he and Denton continued to exchange blows.

While Cade rolled over to grab a rock, Denton quickly reached to his side, pulled out his pistol, and pointed it at Cade's face. Cade was on all fours, looking up into the barrel. He tossed the rock aside and put his hand back down on the ground.

"It's over, Cade, you lost this time." He pulled the hammer back, but before he could pull the trigger, Tara launched her rock into the air, hitting Denton in the side of the head. He yelled and grabbed his head with his hand, but when he did, Cade arched, swung his feet around in front of him, and kicked at the gun. The gun flew out of Denton's hand and over the cliff. Denton kicked Cade in the face, sending him back to the ground.

Denton reached to the other side of his belt for his knife but was knocked off balance as Tara hit him from the side. She fought violently, scratching at his eyes and face and kicking with her feet. Denton subdued her before Cade could compose himself and get to his feet.

Denton slipped the knife out of the sheath and lifted Tara up by his side. He grabbed her around the neck and put the knife to her throat. Tara grimaced from the tight grip around her neck and struggled to breathe.

"Give it up, Cade. You won't take me alive. I've got nothing to live for anymore."

Cade stood up and struggled to regain his balance. He was bloody and light-headed. "All of this you brought on yourself. You can't blame anyone else this time. Your whole life has been an excuse. You've never taken responsibility for anything you've done. You raped Kimber, and she conceived your child, and to this day, you won't admit it. You lead Tara on to think that it was her you loved when, in reality, you were in love with a memory of her big sister. You killed Shooter's father, the Burk's, and Marybeth."

"That's not my fault," Denton replied, pointing and shaking the knife at Cade. "They got in my way. I didn't plan on hurting anyone. Marybeth betrayed me. She told me she didn't know anything, and she did. I trusted her."

The Winds

"Shooter loved her. You took her away from him."

Shooter was climbing toward the top of the cliff when he saw the pistol hit a rock close to him and continued tumbling down the series of rocks. He quickly climbed the last thirty feet just in time to hear Denton's last remarks. He stood at the edge of the cliff, waiting for the right moment to pounce.

"If he's so upset, then why isn't he here? If he's been such a good friend, then why didn't he come with you? Shooter's as big a coward as his father was just before I put a bullet in his head. I thought Indians were supposed to fight, not roll over like a whipped dog."

Suddenly, Shooter sprung from over the edge of the cliff. Denton heard him and quickly turned and revealed the knife he held close to Tara's throat. Shooter stopped and Denton motioned with the knife for him to walk over and join Cade on the other side of him.

"That's not true. My father was a true warrior. He fought for his family and the Shoshone Tribe all of his life and sealed it with his own blood, the blood that you shed."

"And it was my pleasure," Denton said.

Shooter became outraged. The veins in his neck popped out and were as tight as piano strings. His dark eyes became mere slits.

"You call yourself an Indian?" Denton said. "You couldn't sneak up on sleep." Denton started to laugh.

Shooter glanced over at Cade and tightened his fists. "Take care of yourself, Cade. You've been a good friend."

Suddenly, Shooter bolted toward Denton as hard and as fast as he could. Tara, sensing the situation, reared back with her head, catching Denton in the jaw, then hit him in the stomach with her elbow.

Denton released his grip from around her neck, and she quickly spun free just as Shooter hit him chest-high, wrapped his arms tightly around his torso, and continued to drive his legs until both of them tumbled over the cliff and landed in the jagged rocks nearly eighty feet below.

In her haste to get away, Tara tripped and stumbled precariously toward the steep drop-off. Cade lunged for her and was able to secure a grip of her hand just as she was falling over the edge. Tara tightened her grip and frantically kicked into the loose rocks for a secure foothold.

All of a sudden, Tara's screams for help were dampened by the screams of her older sister. It was as if Cade was reliving the nightmare of that fateful day. He could feel the cool mist against his face generated by the forceful water

The Winds

crashing on the rocks below. He could feel the awful desperation as he sensed his grip slipping from Kimber's cold, slippery hand.

"Not again!" he shouted into the vastness. "You will not win this time!" Cade returned to the present and could hear Tara pleading for her life. Cade was lying flat with his arm stretched over the edge of the cliff. He could see streaks of his own blood on the jagged rocks from his arm being dragged across the serrated edges while Tara hung, twisting and turning just over the edge.

He let out a huge yell and pulled with all of his strength. Tara found a foothold and was able to push herself upward and grab Cade's other hand. Cade continued to pull until she was over the top.

Cade released his grip and fell back to the ground. Tara immediately fell into his arms. He held her tight as she wept.

***

Two Years Later

Cade rocked slowly in his chair as he sat on the front porch holding his seven-week-old son. Stitch trotted around the grassy yard, sniffing and digging as always, while Tara, brushed one of the horses across the fence.

The evening sky was a vibrant orange and appeared as if it was on fire from the setting sun. The Western horizon, though smooth with the outline of gradual rolling hills, was a deceptive disguise for the rugged high mountain peaks of the mighty Wind Rivers that lie ominously behind.

As the last evidence of the day disappeared behind the foothills, Cade sat up in his chair and gently nudged his infant son. He reluctantly opened his eyes at the sound of his father's voice and began stirring under the soft Indian blanket.

"Hey, Lit'l Shooter, it's time to say goodbye to another wonderful day."

Cade openly admitted that it was the Winds that gave him another chance at life, a life that he could learn to love again and truly be happy. He would never look at a sunset without pondering how things could have ended for him.

To him it was a reminder of his inner personal struggle to make sense out of a world that in his mind hadn't played fairly. He'd been slapped hard with tragedies in his life that no man should have had to endure, but he did.

The winter he'd spent in the Winds, totally dependent on his own skills, courage, and sheer will to survive, taught him a lesson in life that he would always remember and would pass on to future generations, starting with his infant

The Winds

son.

In a few years, he would take his son into the Winds and show him all there was to learn, admire, and ponder of both her spectacular beauty and her undeniable danger. He would explain the delicate balance between man and nature and the ability of man to kindle her fury when he became too controlling or greedy with her resources.

He would teach his son the value of friendship and how it played a vital role in his ultimate survival in the Winds. He would tell him about his lifelong Indian friend, Shooter, for whom he had perfect respect, and instill in him a sense of pride for the privilege to share his name.

He would reveal to him the story of his adopted grandfather, the old Indian Chief, Running Bear, whose courage and ability to fight for what he believed in ultimately cost him his life, but undoubtedly sealed his happiness into the eternities.

The Great Spirit had found favor with Cade and had watched over him through the eyes of an eagle. He had given Cade a gift that lay hidden deep within his soul without him realizing it. It was what the eagle feather, dipped in the pure Wind River gold, represented. That single thing was hope.